Drawing on every bit of willpower at his command, Ty lifted his head, breaking off the kiss. Meg's mouth clung to his with innocent hunger, weakening his determination. He stared down into her flushed face, watching as her lashes slowly came up, revealing the deep blue of her eyes. The look in those eyes was almost his undoing.

Ty swallowed a groan and forced his hands away from her. He should be horsewhipped. This was exactly what he'd sworn wasn't going to happen, what he'd promised himself he could avoid. Well, he'd proved just how good he was at resisting temptation.

And the worst of it was that he wanted nothing so much as to pull her back into his arms and kiss her again.

DALLAS SCHULZE

The Way Home

A DELL BOOK

Published by
Dell Publishing
a division of
Bantam Doubleday Dell Publishing Group, Inc.
1540 Broadway
New York, New York 10036

ISBN: 0-440-21465-3

Printed in the United States of America

Published simultaneously in Canada

January 1995

10 9 8 7 6 5 4 3 2 1

For Art.
Just 'cause.

ACKNOWLEDGMENTS

I'd like to thank several people who made the writing and publication of this book go more smoothly: Robin Kaigh, for believing in the story; Tina Moskow, for taking a chance on something a little unusual; Gretchen Susi, for maintaining order during a somewhat tumultuous time; Barbara Schenck, for taking the time to read the manuscript and correct any "Iowa" mistakes. Any errors remaining are strictly my own. And last, but definitely not least, Barbara Bretton, who told me I wasn't crazy to do this book. Everyone should be blessed with a friend who tells such terrific lies.

Chapter 1

It was going to be a scorcher of a summer. Everyone agreed on that. It seemed as if winter had slipped right into summer with only a passing nod to spring. Regret, Iowa, baked under the big yellow sun hanging still and bright in the clear blue sky. Barely June and already the farmers were looking at the sky and shaking their heads over the possibilities for needed rain.

Tyler McKendrick was fourteen, and he was concerned with more important things than the crops baking in the fields outside town. His grandfather was a farmer, and Ty knew that rain was important for the crops so he dutifully hoped for rain. But he didn't hope for it today.

Especially not today. Today he was going to catch enough catfish for supper. Never mind that he'd taken his fishing pole down to the creek twice this past week and both times he'd come back emptyhanded. Today was going to be different. He just knew it.

There was a feeling about the day. Something special was bound to happen. He'd felt it in his bones as soon as he woke this morning. Lying in bed, staring up at the ceiling, he'd felt an almost shivery excitement. It had to mean he was going to catch that big old catfish who'd been stealing his bait without getting himself hooked. There was just nothing else worth this feeling of anticipation.

Whistling under his breath, he climbed over the fence that edged old man Pettygrove's field. Perched on the top rail, Ty scouted the field with a quick look, making sure no one was in sight. Old man Pettygrove wasn't above peppering a trespasser's behind with a bit of buckshot. As if a body had any right to fence off the best shortcut to the fishing hole, Ty thought indignantly.

Satisfied that the old man wasn't around, he jumped off the fence, landing in the thick grass on the other side. His fishing pole balanced on one shoulder and the paper sack containing his lunch in his hand, he strode boldly across the lush field. He wasn't scared of old man Pettygrove and that blunderbuss of his.

Still, he was just as glad to slip under the fence on the other side. The creek waited a few yards away, and he could just practically feel a big ol' catfish tugging on his line.

Passing the huge weeping willow that nodded over the stream, Ty stopped, cocking his head as a sound caught his attention. For a moment, he thought he might have imagined it but then it came again. Someone was crying. He scowled. He'd come to think of this as his own private spot, a secret place no one knew of but him. And now that privacy had been invaded. Probably by some girl, he thought, disgusted.

He started to walk on but another wrenching sob stopped him. There was something in the sound that tugged at him despite himself. Heartbreak, his sister Louise would call it. Louise was seventeen and the silliest thing he could imagine, always making a drama out of everything. She'd probably be happier than anything to have some unseen presence sobbing at her. Give her a chance to wring her hands and emote all over the place.

But Ty was just annoyed. That was it, he told himself. He was going to check on the source of the sobs just to make it clear that, whoever they were, they could take their crying somewhere else. This was his spot and he didn't need some *girl* crying all over the place, scaring the fish more than likely.

As soon as he ducked through the willow's soft branches, the crying broke off, ending on a startled little gasp. The bright sunlight was muted by the leafy cover, and for a moment Ty couldn't see anything. But as his vision adjusted to the softer light, he saw the source of his annoyance.

A child was crouched on the ground next to the tree's trunk. Tears had left clean streaks on her dirty face, making her eyes look huge. In a town the size of Regret, everybody knew just about everybody else, at least by sight, so Ty had no trouble putting a name to the child.

It was little Meg Harper. Her folks lived on the south side of town. Her older sister, Patsy, was a few years behind him in school. Meg was four or five, he guessed, hardly more than a baby, from the perspective of his own advanced years. She was watching him now with big blue eyes. Her thin frame shook with an occasional half sob but she said not a word.

He tried to scowl to show that he really didn't care what had caused her tears. He couldn't seem to put his heart into it, though. She reminded him of a puppy he'd seen once that didn't have a home—too thin, eyes all sad and hopeless. His mother had refused to let him take that puppy home, saying that it wasn't the sort of dog a McKendrick would have. He'd never quite forgotten the look in the puppy's eyes when he'd walked away and left it. And now, here was Meg Harper looking at him with those same big, sad eyes.

"What're you bawling about?" Ty asked gruffly.

Wordlessly she thrust out her arms. Cradled in them was a doll. It hadn't been a particularly nice doll to start with. Louise had a whole shelfful of dolls in her room, and the cheapest of them was nicer than the one Meg held. But whatever slight charm the doll had once had was gone now. The head had been smashed in, destroying one painted eye completely. Despite a general contempt for "girl things" like dolls, Ty winced at the toy's condition. From the ragged state of the doll's cheap dress, he could guess that it was something Meg had treasured.

"Mary's broke," she told him. The simplicity of the statement tugged at emotions he was half ashamed to admit to having. Telling himself that he just wanted her to go away and if looking at her dumb doll would help accomplish that, he'd look, Ty crossed the short distance that separated them and crouched down next to her.

She allowed him to take the doll from her. Ty examined Mary solemnly as if her total destruction wasn't obvious to even the most casual of glances.

"Can you fix her?" The question was asked without any real hope. Glancing at her, Ty was surprised by the strength of his desire to answer in the affirmative. There was something so hopeless in those wide blue eyes.

"She's too broke to fix," he admitted reluctantly.

Meg nodded, unsurprised by the verdict. She took the doll back from him, stroking a small hand over the ruined head.

"She was my friend," she said simply.

"What happened to her?" he asked, for lack of being able to offer any real comfort.

"Daddy hit her against the wall. He was angry."

She didn't seem to find anything extraordinary in this bit of information, as if this was a normal thing in her life. Ty tried to imagine his own father getting angry enough to break anything and failed. His father rarely even raised his voice.

Looking at the bruises on Meg's arms, it occurred to him that her father might have caused those. The thought sent a shiver through him. Never in his life had either of his parents raised a hand to him in anger.

"What happened to your arms?" he asked, forgetting to sound gruff and indifferent.

Meg's small face closed up in a way that made her look older than her years. She seemed to draw in on herself, hugging the ruined doll against her narrow chest, her eyes slipping away from his. "I fell."

"Oh." He didn't believe her. He knew, as sure as if he'd been there to witness it, that her father had left those bruises on her arms. His safe world was shaken by the idea of a parent capable of committing an act of violence toward his own child. He said nothing simply because he could think of nothing to say.

It was quiet under the willow tree, the outside world

blocked by a wall of gentle green. Meg didn't seem to feel any need to break the silence. She remained crouched against the trunk of the willow, the doll clutched to her as she rocked gently back and forth. Her silent grief chilled him despite the warmth of the day.

"Maybe we should bury her," he said abruptly, needing to break the silence. "You know, have a funeral or something."

Meg stopped rocking and looked at him, her hands tightening over the doll. "Say a prayer?"

"Sure."

She appeared to consider the idea, her grubby face solemn. "Okay," she said at last.

Having made the suggestion, it was Ty's responsibility to find something with which to dig the grave. After some consideration, Meg agreed that the best place to lay Mary to rest was beneath the willow tree. Ty found a sturdy stick and managed to hack a hole of the proper dimensions in the soft earth.

When the time came to lay Mary in her final resting place, Meg did so with solemn care, straightening the doll's worn dress around her, her tiny fingers lingering for a moment before she stood up and clasped her hands behind her back.

Ty filled in the grave, patting the earth carefully into place. He straightened, dusting his fingers on the sides of his pants. Catching Meg's expectant gaze, he remembered his casual promise that they could say a prayer over the doll. *Was God likely to resent him saying a prayer for a doll?* he wondered uneasily. But there was no getting around the fact that he'd promised. And the look in Meg's blue eyes seemed more important than the vague threat of eternal damnation.

A tendency to daydream in the middle of the sermon on Sundays had left him woefully short of prayers, particularly the sort suitable for a solemn occasion such as this. Racking his brain, he could come up with only one that he knew all the way through. He began hesitantly, groping for the words.

"Now I lay me down to sleep. I pray the Lord my soul to keep." Meg's hand stole into his and his fingers closed over hers. "If I should die before I wake, I pray the Lord my soul to take."

His voice seemed to echo in the stillness beneath the willow, giving the familiar prayer a significance he'd never noticed before. When it ended, the silence was absolute for the space of several slow heartbeats.

Drawing a quivery breath, Meg broke the quiet. "That was nice. Mary will be okay now."

Her simple acceptance caused a pain in Ty's chest that he did his best to ignore. It was just a stupid doll, he reminded himself briskly. And Meg was nothing but a silly baby. But he didn't pull his hand from hers.

Drawing her away from the tiny grave, he picked up the fishing pole and lunch sack he'd set down. Ducking out from under the willow's branches, he narrowed his eyes against the bright sunlight. He was surprised to find that so little time had passed. He'd expected to find the day nearly over. But the sun was still high in the sky and the creek still rushed merrily over its rocky bed. It wasn't even lunchtime yet. Aware that someone might be able to see them now, he eased his hand from Meg's.

Glancing down at her, she seemed even smaller and more fragile than he'd thought at first. The tearstains that marked her face had been joined by a fresh streak of dirt. Her feet were bare and twice as dirty as the rest of her. He found himself wondering if she even owned a pair of shoes, an incredible thought.

Her dress was old and worn, a hand-me-down from her sister, he guessed. It was nothing like the frilly dresses he'd seen other little girls wearing. The neckline was too big, sliding down to expose her collarbone. And the sailor collar that had should have been crisp white was grayed and limp. A tear near the hem had been mended with neat stitches.

She looked forlorn, like an orphan in a storybook he'd had when he was little. But she wasn't an orphan, he reminded himself firmly. She had a home and she could just go there. She'd already spoiled enough of his day with her silly doll.

She reached to brush some bits of grass from the hem of her rag-taggle dress and the bruises on her arms caught his eye.

"You want to watch me fish?"

She tilted her head back to look up at him, those wide blue eyes considering, as if she were weighing the sincerity of his offer. Satisfied by what she saw, she smiled at him. The expression transformed her thin little face into something almost pretty.

"Yes, please," she said simply.

Her presence did not spoil his fishing as he'd thought it might. She didn't chatter like his older sister Louise would have. And she didn't look bored, like Jack always did. Jack was his best friend but he didn't like fishing. It was, as far as Ty was concerned, Jack's only real flaw.

Meg sat quietly next to him, sometimes braiding strands of grass together into tiny wreaths, sometimes just watching the water rush by.

In an odd way, her quiet companionship reminded Ty of his older brother. It had been Dickey who'd taught him to fish. He'd been the best fishing pal a boy could hope to have. It had been four years since Dickey was killed in the Great War, fighting in the trenches in France. Ty still missed him. He blinked quickly, ashamed of the tears that stung at the back of his eyes. He pushed aside the memories of the big brother who'd never come home and pulled his line out of the water, checking the hook with fierce concentration.

When his stomach announced that it was time for lunch, Ty propped his fishing pole between a pair of rocks and opened up the sack lunch Daisy had packed for him. Daisy did all the cooking and most of the cleaning in the McKendrick household. She had skin the color of a Hershey bar and made the best apple turnovers in the whole state.

He took out a sandwich wrapped in waxed paper. There was also a fat dill pickle—Daisy's own recipe—and, wrapped in a piece of clean toweling, a big wedge of cheese. Daisy understood just how hungry a boy could get after a morning spent with a fishing pole. The paper crackled as he unwrapped the sandwich—thick slices of bread, piled high with slices of last night's roast beef.

Ty's stomach rumbled hungrily but he hesitated, glancing at Meg. She was looking at the sandwich, but when she felt his eyes on her, she looked away, plucking at a stalk of grass as if the food held no interest for her.

"You hungry?"

Her eyes skittered back to the food and then lifted to his. She nodded slowly.

"Well, you can't eat with a face as dirty as that," he told her. Feeling very adult, he dug a handkerchief out of his pocket, shaking the bits of lint from it. Taking it to the creek, he knelt and dipped it in the cold water. He handed the wet cloth to Meg and she carefully scrubbed her face, washing away the dirt and tearstains. When she lowered the handkerchief, Ty studied her face carefully before nodding.

"You'll do," he said, repeating the phrase his mother always used when pronouncing him ready to sit down for a meal. After draping the wet hanky over a convenient rock, he settled himself next to Meg and handed her half the sandwich. She bit into it hungrily.

He split the contents of the sack with scrupulous honesty, except for the dill pickle, which made Meg wrinkle her nose. Breaking the turnover in half caused him a pang of real regret, but she took her portion from him with the proper reverence. He consoled himself with the thought that at least she appreciated it. Besides, if he'd committed a sin by reading a prayer over her doll, maybe he was making up for it by sharing his lunch.

Meg dozed off after the meal, curled on her side in the soft grass, one hand tucked under her cheek. Since his fishing pole didn't require constant attention, Ty found himself watching her. He didn't have much experience with little girls. His sister was older than he was by almost four years. He tried to imagine Louise, at any age, content to sit quietly and watch someone fish. The image simply wouldn't come clear. Even when she read those dumb tabloids of hers, she shrieked at something on every other page.

The memory made him sneer. All in all, he had to admit that Meg Harper wasn't bad company—for a girl anyway.

The afternoon drifted by. Ty didn't catch a fish but it didn't seem to matter much. He'd forgotten all about the feeling of anticipation that had seemed so strong this morning. It was just another lazy summer afternoon.

Meg was so quiet, it was almost possible to forget she was there at all. When she woke, she played quietly, picking a bouquet of dandelions and arranging them with all the care his mother would have shown for her finest roses. Sometimes she hummed to herself, wordless little tunes.

It was late afternoon when Ty heaved a sigh and lifted his line out of the stream. He looked at the water with regret. He was sure that there was a big old trout just eyein' his line, thinking about biting. But he'd promised his mother he'd be home early. The whole family was going to the picture show. Ty liked picture shows well enough, but it seemed a waste to have to go home just when the fish were sure to start biting.

Still, there was no help for it. He stood up, dusting off the seat of his trousers. Meg stood up too, saying nothing, just watching him with those big blue eyes.

"I got to go," Ty told her. "Can you get home by yourself okay?"

She nodded, her expression solemn as she watched him stuff the crumpled lunch sack in his pocket, where it made a lump.

"Come on, I'll walk you back out to the road."

She hesitated for a moment before falling into step with him. Ty didn't cut across Pettygrove's field this time, not wanting to set a bad example. After all, it was one thing for him to do it. He was a boy and could run pretty fast if old man Pettygrove showed up with his shotgun. But Meg was hardly more than a baby and it wouldn't be right to encourage her to do things she shouldn't.

The feeling of adult responsibility helped to make up for the annoyance of taking twice as long to get back to the road. He scrambled up the bank onto the gravel surface, turning to give Meg a hand up.

From here, their ways separated. Meg's home lay south, on the far side of town. Ty's family lived a little way outside of town on what was known locally as the Hill.

He squinted in the direction she'd go. There were some thunderheads building up to the west of town, promising rain before too long. The breeze held a cool edge to it. "If you want, I could walk you home. You bein' little and all."

She shook her head. "No, thank you."

Ty was relieved by her refusal. A gentleman always had to look out for women and children, his dad said, and he'd have done his duty, but he knew he'd have taken an awful ribbing if anybody saw him walking with a girl, even if she was just a baby.

"Well, then, I guess I'll be on my way. You get on home now. Looks like it's goin' to rain."

She nodded but didn't move. Ty found himself strangely reluctant to leave her. She was so little and there was something fragile about her, as if a strong wind might just blow her over.

"Well, good-bye."

"Good-bye."

He hesitated but she didn't say anything more, only watched him with those solemn blue eyes. Feeling awkward, Ty turned and started down the road toward home. It seemed to him that he could feel her eyes on him every step of the way, but he didn't turn until he reached a bend in the road.

Turning back, he saw his guess had been right. Meg was standing just where he'd left her. Distance had foreshortened her figure, making her look even smaller and more vulnerable. He lifted his hand, waiting until he saw her wave in return before resolutely turning back to the road.

It wasn't his problem if she wanted to stand there until dark. He'd done more than a body had any right to expect.

Meg watched Tyler McKendrick go out of sight before moving from the spot where he'd left her. She hurried down the road, ignoring the sharp bits of gravel that dug into the bottoms of her feet. The only pair of shoes she owned were too small, and they pinched her toes something fierce. Her soles were toughened from walking barefoot.

Leaving the road, she wiggled under the fence that bordered Pettygrove's field and cut across the sweet green grass to the other side. After slipping under the second fence, she ran to where Ty had been fishing.

The handkerchief he'd dampened so she could wash her face still lay draped over the rock where he'd put it to dry. Meg picked it up, her brows coming together. Maybe she should have said something. Maybe he'd want the handkerchief back. Her small fingers tightened over it. Surely he wouldn't miss one handkerchief. Didn't Patsy always say that folks that lived on the Hill was all rich as sin?

Feeling guilty, she folded the square of linen hastily and thrust it into the pocket of her dress. If'n he wanted the handkerchief back, she'd give it to him. But maybe he wouldn't miss it and then she'd have something to keep—a keepsake, Mama would call it, though Meg knew she wouldn't tell her mother about today.

Casting a last glance toward the willow tree where her doll was buried, she ran back to the fence, slipping under it and hurrying across the field. If she didn't get home lickety-split, she might be late for supper and then Daddy'd be mad again.

She was breathless by the time she reached the road but she didn't slow down, her short legs pumping as she ran. She'd lost Mary and that still hurt, but she'd never in all her nearly five years spent such a wonderful day. And if she never saw Tyler McKendrick again, she'd have the hanky to remind her.

Chapter 2

SIX YEARS LATER

Ty caught the white gleam of Jack's smile beneath the visor that protected his eyes. Though they flew almost wingtip to wingtip, the solid roar of the engines made communication possible only via hand signals. Jack pointed down and then lifted his thumb in a good-luck sign. Ty returned the gesture before angling the Curtiss Jenny downward and away from Jack's plane.

Below he could see the fairgoers, hardly bigger than ants at first, gradually increasing in size as he descended toward them. He waited until the last possible moment before rolling the Jenny over and finishing his descent flying upside down. Feeling the blood rush to his head, Ty sent the plane roaring along the edge of the field upside down and barely ten feet off the ground. Seeing the blur of green that marked the edge of the field, he pulled the plane up, skimming the tops of the trees before righting the plane. Though he couldn't see it, he knew Jack would be right behind him, repeating the maneuver like a winged shadow.

Ascending into the pale-blue sky, Ty felt the same rush of exhilaration he did every time he flew. There was no other feeling like it. It was as close to heaven as a man could possibly get. Laughing with the sheer joy of it, he pulled the Jenny's nose up in a loop before heading for the ground again, this time to land in a more decorous fashion.

Standing on the ground, Meg Harper craned her neck to watch the two planes in the air. Everyone around her was doing the same, all eyes glued to the airplanes as they looped above, first one and then the other inscribing a graceful circle against the cloudless blue of the sky. It was only when the first plane started to land that people began talking again.

The crowd drifted toward the field where the planes were now touching down. They looked like big, oddly graceful birds, Meg thought as she allowed herself to be swept forward. She heard some people mentioning Charles Lindbergh. Hadn't he flown over Regret just a few short months ago? Daniel Peterman had painted the town's name on the roof of his barn in big white letters so the famous flyer would know that Regret, Iowa, appreciated what he'd done and welcomed him.

Meg knew what Lindbergh had done, of course. No one had talked about much else for days last spring. She guessed that flying all the way across the Atlantic alone must be a pretty impressive thing to do, judging by the way people talked about it. But at age ten, she found it hard to imagine anything more impressive than what she'd just seen.

She found a spot near a fence post at the edge of the field and watched as Tyler McKendrick got out of the first plane, stepping onto the wing and then jumping to the ground. He reached up to tug off the close-fitting leather helmet and goggles he wore, and the late-summer sun found blue highlights in the thick blackness of his hair.

Meg was hardly aware of Jack Swanson's plane coming to a halt just behind Tyler's. She didn't notice the way the sun turned his hair to polished gold or the warmth of his smile. If Lucky Lindy himself had stepped into sight at that moment, she still wouldn't have taken her eyes off Tyler McKendrick's tall frame.

Helen McKendrick was the first to reach him. Meg wasn't close enough to hear what she was saying, but from the agitated movement of her hands, it wasn't hard to guess that she wasn't happy about her son's demonstration of his flying skills. Meg dismissed her worries as pure foolishness. Anyone could see that Ty had been in perfect control. It just wasn't possible to think he might have crashed.

He'd never be like Icarus, she thought, remembering the story she'd read in a book from the library. He'd be able to soar as high as he wanted and never fall. Meg wrapped one thin arm around the fence post and leaned her cheek against its rough surface, her eyes never leaving Ty's lean figure.

He was, as far as her ten-year-old mind was concerned, the epitome of masculine perfection. When he smiled, she thought that the sun shone suddenly brighter. She sighed unconsciously, her eyes growing a little dreamy. Her sister, Patsy, could sigh over Rudy Vallee and John Barrymore but, as far as Meg could see, neither of them held a candle to Tyler McKendrick.

"Are you coming home now?"

At the sound of his mother's voice, Ty straightened away from the Jenny's fuselage and turned to look at her. She was approaching across the dirt like an oceanliner steaming across the Atlantic. Such was Helen McKendrick's presence that it took a moment for Ty to notice that his father was with her, trailing half a step behind, his expression resigned.

"Mother. I thought you'd already gone home." Ty leaned down to brush a dutiful kiss across her lightly powdered cheek, surprised, as always, by how small she was.

"Your father and I thought you might need a ride home."

Nice of her to include his father, Ty thought, knowing perfectly well that it hadn't been Elliot McKendrick's idea to come back to the fairgrounds.

"Actually, it's going to be awhile before I'm ready to go," Ty told her. "Jack's parents left the Packard for him. He'll give me a ride home later."

"I'd prefer it if you came home now, Tyler." Helen's eyes clashed with her son's and Ty felt his temper rise.

In his entire life, he'd never once seen his mother gracefully accept the possibility that she might not get her way. When he was a boy, he'd had little choice but to accede to her wishes. But he was not a child anymore. He was a man and perfectly capable of deciding when he wanted to go home.

"I'll be home shortly," he said, making a determined effort to keep his voice pleasant.

"You're not going up in that *thing* again?" The words hovered somewhere between order and question.

"I don't know." The truth was, he'd had no intention of taking the Jenny up again. The sun was low in the western sky. He was tired. His shoulders ached from the hours of flying he'd done that day, taking passengers up for a quick taste of flying. His ears still buzzed with the sound of the plane's motor, and he hadn't planned anything more vigorous than going home and having a hot meal, a bath, and a good night's sleep.

But he'd take the plane up and fly all night rather than give in to his mother's iron will.

It had been Jack who'd suggested that they could earn some gas money by working the fairs, providing rides for people who'd never been up in a plane. And he'd been right. In some parts of the country, planes had become such a commonplace that there wasn't much excitement about their arrival. But they were still enough of a novelty around Regret that they'd had all the passengers they could handle. At two dollars a ride, they wouldn't have to worry about gas money for a while.

"I can't believe you actually left college to spend your time in that . . . that *thing*." There was contempt in Helen's voice but there was a genuine bewilderment as well, and that was what softened Ty's anger.

"I want to fly," he said simply.

"But you'll need a degree if you ever want to run for office," she protested. "You could work for your uncle Matthew's firm for a few years. When you're a little older, you could try for your grandfather's old seat in the Senate. People loved your grandfather, and you can never underestimate how far sentiment will take you," she said shrewdly.

"I don't want to be a lawyer, Mother. Or a senator," Ty

said, his voice holding the weariness that came of having said the same words more times than he cared to remember. "I want to fly."

"Nonsense. You can't spend your life flying. How will you earn a living?"

"We didn't do too badly today," Ty pointed out, aware of his pleasantly full pockets. He saw no reason to say anything about the short rations he and Jack had been on the past few weeks.

"Today is one thing, but what about tomorrow? It's not like you have a real job where you can count on a paycheck. Do you plan on spending your life just flying from town to town like some hobo?"

"Actually, Ivan Gates has asked us to join his flying circus. Jack and I are leaving for New York tomorrow." He couldn't keep the pride from his voice. Gates Flying Circus was one of the biggest and best in the country.

"A flying circus! Oh, my heavens." Helen put her hand to her forehead as if she actually felt faint at the thought. Though the gesture was theatrical, the fact that she disarranged her fashionable cloche hat was an indication that she was genuinely upset. "Next thing we know, you'll be marrying some tart in a spangled costume and expecting me to welcome her into the family."

Ty could have pointed out that she had the wrong kind of circus, but he decided it would be a waste of time. He could talk until he was blue in the face and nothing he said would ever reconcile her to his decision to leave college.

"I don't know where we went wrong," Helen said, looking at Ty in bewilderment. "Your father and I have done our best for you, and *this* is how you repay us."

"Now, Helen, don't exaggerate." Elliot spoke for the first time. "Tyler's a grown man and he's got a right to do as he sees fit."

"Even if it means ruining his life?" She pulled an embroidered linen handkerchief from her handbag and dabbed at her eyes.

"I doubt he'll ruin his life, Helen." Elliot threw his son a sympathetic look. "Sometimes a fellow's just got to kick up his heels a bit, that's all. He'll do just fine. Now, why don't you and I head on home? Tyler can follow when he's of a mind to."

"I just don't understand it," Helen said, looking at Ty as if she'd couldn't believe he were really her son. "Dickey would never have acted this way. *He* would have understood the importance of finishing college."

Ty stiffened at the old, familiar lament. His older brother had been dead for almost ten years now, but his shadow still loomed large in the McKendrick family.

"Dickey's gone now," Elliot said firmly. "And the boy had a mind of his own, which you sometimes choose to forget."

"How can you say that?" Her wrath veered toward her husband. "Dickey was an absolutely perfect son. He would never have disappointed me this way."

Ty paled and a muscle began to tick in his tightly held jaw. But he didn't say anything. What could he say? He'd been barely ten when Dickey was killed in France. In his eyes, Richard McKendrick *had* been perfect—or at least as close as it was possible for an older brother to be.

"How can he waste his time in one of those silly airplanes?" Helen asked, shifting the topic back to her remaining son's lamentable lack of perfection. "He could be president someday, if only he'd apply himself to it."

"Now, if everyone who thought that actually applied themselves to becoming president, there wouldn't be anybody left to run the country," Elliot said with chiding humor. "He'll do just fine, Helen. Now let's go home and let the boy alone." He slipped his arm around her shoulders and turned her away, giving Ty another sympathetic look.

Ty watched them walk across the packed dirt of the field. It wasn't until they'd walked down the shallow slope that led to the area where most people had parked their cars that he allowed some of the tension to leave his shoulders. He thrust his fingers through his hair, ruffling it into dark waves, and his mouth twisted with bitter humor. A full day of flying had not been nearly as tiring as five minutes of conversation with his mother.

"I think flying an airplane is much more exciting than being president."

Startled, Ty turned toward the childish voice. A little girl stood on the other side of the wing, the late-afternoon sun catching in her long blond curls.

"You do, huh?" He grinned at her.

"Yes." Her eyes were a beautiful deep blue and surprisingly solemn for one so young.

"How do you figure that?" Ty leaned against the fuselage, feeling the last of the tension draining away.

"Well, anybody could be president, but to fly . . ." Her voice trailed off as if she sought the right words. "It's like the story about Icarus," she finished in a rush.

"Didn't he fly too close to the sun and end up falling into the sea?"

"You'd never do that. You could fly as high as anything, I bet." She flushed, her eyes dropping to the ground, embarrassed by her own enthusiasm.

At twenty, Ty was old enough to recognize a case of childish hero worship when he saw it and still young enough to be flattered. Her blatant admiration went a long way toward soothing the sting of his mother's contempt for his flying.

"Well, I don't think I'm in much danger of getting too close to the sun," he said, smiling at her.

"No." Her voice had dropped to almost a whisper and she couldn't seem to lift her eyes.

"You're Meg Harper, aren't you?" he said, suddenly putting a name to the sweet, childish face. She nodded, flushing as if embarrassed to find herself the focus of his attention. She glanced up at him and Ty felt his chest swell a little at the blatant hero worship in her eyes.

"Have you ever ridden in a plane, Meg?"

"No." She threw a look at the Jenny that was nearly as admiring as the one she'd sent Ty himself. "I never did."

"How'd you like to ride in this one?"

"For real?" She flushed again and then paled, her eyes

big as saucers as she contemplated the incredible possibility he'd just suggested.

"For real," he said, feeling downright beneficent.

Meg slid her hand in the pocket of her skirt, her fingers worrying the two nickels that resided there. Her mother had given her a quarter that morning, cautioning her to spend it wisely because there'd be no more when that was spent.

Since a quarter was the most money of her own Meg had ever possessed, she'd taken her mother's advice to heart and spent carefully. A dime had gone for a hamburger and some ice-cold lemonade for her lunch, and she'd used a nickel to buy a ride on one of the swings. She'd spent most of the afternoon watching Tyler McKendrick and his friend fly, which hadn't cost anything. Still, she only had two nickels left. And even if she hadn't spent any of the money, a quarter fell far short of the two dollars she knew he'd been charging to take people up in the air.

For a moment, she considered the possibility of letting her lower lip quiver a little and allowing her eyes to fill with the tears that hovered close at the thought of not being able to go up in the sleek red airplane. She'd watched her older sister Patsy use those techniques to get her way with Pa since she was little.

If Pa was sober, more often than not, Patsy got whatever it was she was angling for, whether it was money to go to a picture show or a nickel for an ice cream soda. Since Pa had been killed in an automobile accident last winter, Patsy had used the same quivering lip on Mr. Davis, who'd started coming to call on Mama. And it usually worked on him, too. Patsy said that men were suckers for a pretty girl, especially one who knew how to use what the good Lord had given her.

Though Meg couldn't imagine Tyler McKendrick being a sucker, maybe the same kind of persuasion would work on him. She knew Patsy, with the wisdom of her almost sixteen years, would certainly think so.

* * *

Ty watched her, wondering what was causing the quick shift of emotions across her expressive face; wondering if she remembered that summer day by the creek. Probably not. She'd been little more than a baby. He hadn't thought there was any real question about her accepting his offer so he was surprised when she shook her head slowly.

"I don't have two dollars."

Ty opened his mouth to tell her that he hadn't planned on charging her, but something in the proud lift her chin had him swallowing the words. He remembered all he'd heard about the Harpers, or at least about her father. Lazy and good-for-nothing were probably two of the more complimentary descriptions. Along with the denigration of George Harper usually went a sigh for his family. What a pity Ruth Harper and those two girls have to live with a man who was little better than white trash. And generally there'd be a wise nod or two and some comment about the nut not falling far from the tree and blood telling. The fact that her father was dead wasn't likely to change the way people viewed his family.

No doubt Meg Harper knew exactly what people said about her father—about her family. In a town as small as Regret, you couldn't avoid knowing what was being said—about yourself as well as about anyone else. In her eyes, he saw a pride older than her years, the kind of pride that came of knowing you were starting out with two strikes against you and that you had to prove you deserved the same level of respect most people took for granted.

Ty knew that feeling, at least in part. Hadn't he spent half his life trying to show his parents that he was as worthy of their love as his older brother had been? That Dickey might have died in the trenches of France but they still had a son? He doubted that Meg's pride would make anyone forget that she was a Harper, any more than he'd ever been able to make his mother forget that her favorite son had been taken from her. But he couldn't slap at that pride by offering her charity, either.

"Hey, you ready to go home?" Jack's voice preceded

him as he came around the Jenny's nose. "Hello." He gave Meg a friendly grin.

"Hello." Meg was already starting to edge away.

Afterward, Ty couldn't have explained just why he didn't let her go or why he was so determined that she have her ride in an airplane. Maybe it was the wistful glance she threw at the Jenny as she took a step back. Maybe it was the fact that her blatant hero worship had soothed the sting of his mother's attitude. Or it could have been the stubbornness that his mother claimed was his besetting sin. Whatever it was, he was damned if this big-eyed little girl was going to go home without getting a taste of flying.

"Just a minute, Meg. I may need your help." He made sure she'd stopped her retreat before turning to Jack. "I thought I should check the gyroscopic balance of the lower magneto. I'll need a passenger for that, and I was thinking that Meg might be just about the right weight."

Jack's eyebrows rose but to his credit, his mouth didn't even twitch at this string of nonsense. He turned to look at Meg, considering her with the solemnity the question deserved.

Meg held her breath, waiting for his verdict. If she'd be helping Tyler by going up in his airplane, then it wouldn't be the same as taking charity.

"I think she'd be heavy enough," Jack said after a moment, having let the tension stretch until Meg was sure she would explode with it. "And you certainly don't want to let that magneto get out of balance," he added, shaking his head to indicate what a serious problem that could be.

Meg felt her chest swell and her cheeks flush with excitement. Not only was she going to get to ride in an airplane, but she'd be helping Tyler. It just didn't seem possible that two such wonderful things could happen on the same day.

"Would you mind helping me, Meg?" Ty hardly needed the vigorous shake of her head to give him his answer. She was nearly quivering with eagerness. She straightened her shoulders and tugged the bottom of her blue cotton middy into place over her pleated skirt, like a soldier preparing for inspection.

"If you really think I could help," she said, not bothering to hide her enthusiasm.

"Like Jack said, it's important that the magneto be properly balanced, and I have to have a passenger to do that." If it occurred to Meg that Jack could very well have provided the necessary weight, she didn't feel obligated to point it out.

Jack grinned as he watched Ty lift Meg up onto the Jenny's wing. He'd just started to lift her into the seat when they heard someone calling Meg's name.

"It's Patsy." Meg's voice was flat. Ty set her down and she slid off the wing to the ground. He jumped down and stood next to her. "I imagine I've got to go," she said, watching her sister approach. There was no emotion in the words, no indication of the disappointment he knew she felt. He had the feeling there'd been so many disappointments in her young life that she'd come to expect them more often than not.

"I knew I'd find you here." Patsy paused when she saw the two young men. She reached up to pat her hair, bobbed just this summer so that it framed her pretty features like a soft brown cap. Her voice deepened to what she fancied was an alluring huskiness. "Mr. Davis says it's time we went and he sent me to find you. I figured you might still be here watching the flying. It was so exciting, it nearly took my breath away."

She smoothed her hands down her hips, curving her spine just the way she'd seen the models do in the Sears Roebuck catalogs, drawing attention to the sleek lines of her figure.

"We aim to please," Jack said, grinning at her obvious attempt to look seductive, though he couldn't help but notice that she was really a very pretty girl. Too bad she wasn't a little older.

Ty set his hand on Meg's shoulder when she started to move away. She hadn't said anything but he could feel the disappointment radiating from her. He had the feeling there were few enough treats in her life. It didn't seem fair that she should have to miss this one, too.

"Meg was going to help me run a test. Do we have time for a quick flight?"

"I don't know." Her expression softened when she saw the plea in her little sister's eyes. "Course, it might have taken me a good bit longer to find you, I suppose." She hesitated, nibbling her lower lip. Meg's small body was tense under Ty's hand as she waited for the verdict.

"You know, it occurs to me that I ought to check out the balance on my magneto, too," Jack said suddenly. "Can't ever be too careful about those things. Since I'd have to have a passenger to do a proper test, maybe you'd be willing to go up with me?" he asked Patsy.

"I might." She hesitated only a moment longer before tossing her head, making her bobbed hair swing out from her face. She slanted Jack a flirtatious look. "I reckon I can always say that it took me awhile to find Meg."

Ty didn't wait for more. He lifted Meg bodily and set her in the front of the plane. Meg sat docilely while he tugged a leather cap over her hair and buckled it under her chin. She took the goggles he handed her and slid them on, hardly aware of what she was doing, unable to think of anything beyond the fact that she was actually going to go up in an airplane.

She felt no trepidation. Her confidence in Tyler McKendrick was absolute. She gripped the sides of the plane as it lumbered down the field. It felt heavy and clumsy, nothing like she'd imagined. But before disappointment could take hold, the wheels lifted off the ground and they began to angle away from the earth and Meg forgot how to breathe.

It was everything she'd imagined it would be and more. So much more that she didn't even have the words to describe it. The ground fell away beneath them, becoming a patchwork quilt of green fields and trees with crisp edgings of brown where roads cut through. Ty turned the Jenny's nose westward and suddenly Regret lay spread beneath them, the houses like a child's building blocks lined up in neat rows.

Meg tilted her head back to look up at the sky. It was a vast blue arc, the color paler and yet sharper than it was from the ground. It seemed as if she were a part of the sky, as if she

belonged there, as if she'd found a place that could truly be
hers. Up here, earthbound concerns were small and insignifi-
cant. It didn't matter if her dresses were hand-me-downs or
that there might not be enough food for supper. Those were all
distant things that didn't matter up here.

She laughed up at the sky.

Ty felt his heart contract at the sheer joy he saw in Meg's
face. Over the course of the afternoon, he'd seen many reac-
tions, from fear to a distinct greenish tint that indicated a quick
landing to be a wise choice, to a cautious pleasure. Not once
had he seen the elation he saw now.

It made him wish the flight could be longer, that he could
give her more than just a taste of what flying was like. But the
light was starting to fade and he could see Jack's plane already
taxiing to a halt near the edge of the field. He brought the
Jenny around and started down.

He stopped the plane behind Jack's, pulling off his leather
cap and tossing it in the seat as he jumped to the ground and
moved forward to help Meg out. The cap had flattened her pale
hair against her head, crushing all the fat curls, but her eyes
shone bright blue. He'd half expected a spate of words. Most
children couldn't wait to talk about their short freedom from
the bonds of earth. But Meg didn't say anything until he'd set
her on the ground. They could both see her sister and Jack
approaching, Patsy's steps quick and hurried.

"Come on, Meg. We've got to hurry or Mr. Davis'll bust
a gusset," Patsy called from a few yards away.

Meg hesitated a moment longer, looking up at Ty with
those big blue eyes. "Thank you. It's like being right next to
heaven."

She darted off before Ty could think of a reply. Not that
there was much he could have said except that he agreed. Patsy
threw a last look in Jack's direction, her smile pure flirtation,
before she hustled Meg in the direction of the fair.

Ty was still watching the two of them when Jack reached
him.

"You know, when she gets a little older, that girl is going

to be pure dynamite,'' Jack commented, his eyes on the carefully cultivated swing in Patsy Harper's walk.

"I think you're right,'' Ty said, thinking of the fathomless blue of Meg Harper's eyes. "She's going to be a heartbreaker.''

Chapter 3

SEVEN YEARS LATER

Ty had nearly forgotten what summer was like in Regret. Hot and dry or pouring rain—there didn't seem to be any happy medium between the two conditions. He stood on the front porch of the house where he'd grown up and looked down the hill at the tidy streets of Regret, Iowa.

It was, he admitted grudgingly, a pretty view. One he'd even missed occasionally over the last few years. But just because he'd missed it didn't mean that he was looking forward to spending his summer looking at it.

Sighing, he moved down the steps, favoring his left leg. He'd learned the hard way that airplanes and trees were a bad combination. The plane had been repaired inside a week. Unfortunately, his leg was taking a good bit longer than that. Be patient, the doctor had told him. The bones needed time to knit. Plain in the doctor's tone had been the thought that he was lucky it hadn't been his neck that was broken.

Well, he was going to have plenty of time to practice being patient, Ty thought sourly. He leaned over the door to put his fishing pole and the basket that held his lunch in the passenger seat of his car. The car, like the fishing, was another consolation for the weeks of boredom that undoubtedly lay ahead.

His father had presented it to him, saying that he'd need a way to get around. He knew, firsthand, just how hard it was to say no to Helen McKendrick once she had her mind made up. And she'd made up her mind that Ty—*her only remaining son,* she'd said, her voice breaking—would spend the summer recuperating at home. Otherwise she wouldn't be able to rest, wondering if he was taking care of himself. And he'd given in, cursing his weakness even as he heard himself agreeing to stay for the summer.

The opportunity to have Tyler firmly under her thumb had been so enticing that she'd even decided to cancel their trip to Europe. Which was when his father—God bless him—in a rare display of husbandly authority, had put his foot down. They'd planned to go to Europe and he'd already paid for the their crossing. Tyler was recovering from a broken leg, not a broken back. He didn't need full-time nursing.

So it could have been worse, Tyler told himself as he pulled open the driver's door and stepped up on the running board. He could have been facing the next couple of months with his mother hovering over him. As it was, she was safely—and he hoped happily—on her way across the Atlantic, and he was the owner of a snappy little roadster, courtesy of his father.

The car wasn't new but it was a honey. And even if it had been nothing more than a rattletrap, it would still have represented a certain freedom, the illusion that he could leave whenever he wanted, instead of staying out the summer as he knew he would. Not because his leg would take that long to recover, but because he'd promised his mother he would stay.

He drove past the Vanderbilts'—no relation to *the* Vanderbilts, Edwina Vanderbilt liked to say, giving a coy smile to suggest that there *might* be a relation but she wasn't the sort to boast. Edwina and his mother were at once bosom chums and heated competitors in everything from gardening to hairstyles. No doubt Edwina would be keeping a discreet eye on his comings and goings, happy if she could report to his mother that he'd behaved just as he should, even happier if there were a few indiscretions she could pass on.

Ty was just considering the likelihood of finding an indiscretion to commit and coming to the sad conclusion that, in Regret, indiscretions weren't as easy to come by as he might have liked, when he saw the girl.

She was walking down the sidewalk, doing absolutely nothing to draw attention to herself. But with a figure like that, she didn't have to do anything but just breathe, Ty thought. He whistled softly under his breath, taking in the slender waist and gentle curve of her hips. Her dress was navy with white polka dots. The full skirt ended below her knee, exposing only a few discreet inches of slender calves and a pair of shapely ankles. Her hair was shoulder length and softly waved, golden blond and eminently touchable.

Even without seeing her face, Ty was sure he didn't know her. It wasn't possible that he'd have forgotten that figure and that hair.

"Now, if ever I saw a potential indiscretion . . ." Ty muttered, guiding the Chrysler to the side of the road and stopping a few yards in front of her.

He swung open his door and got out, turning to watch her approach across the width of the car. He put on his best, nonthreatening smile, trying to look as harmless as possible. Accosting women on the street was not his usual style, but he simply had to see if the front view was any match for the slim allure of her rear view. And it most definitely was.

Golden blond hair framed a soft oval face. Dark brows arched over large blue eyes that seemed to echo the summer sky above. Her nose was short and straight. Her mouth was a soft rose pink that owed nothing to lipstick, the full lower lip an almost blatant invitation. Her chin held more than a hint of strength, a contrast to the incredible—kissable—softness of her mouth. As he watched, color ran up under her skin, tinting it a delicate pink, making him realize that he'd been staring like a lovesick schoolboy.

"I didn't mean to stare," he said, widening his smile in

what he hoped was a reassuring smile. "It's just that . . . I know this sounds like a pickup line, but don't I know you?"

"Perhaps." She blushed again, lowering her eyes so that the dark crescent of her lashes was visible against her cheeks.

"I'm Tyler McKendrick."

"I know." She looked at him from under her lashes, her mouth curving in a shy smile.

"So we *have* met." He shut the Chrysler's door and walked around the hood, stepping up on the sidewalk to stand in front of her.

"We've met," she admitted.

"I can't believe I'd have forgotten a girl who looks like you," Ty said, thinking that he finally understood how a woman's skin could be compared to a rose petal.

"I was a bit younger the last time we met," she said, still blushing.

"I haven't been home much the last few years," he said, speaking as much to himself as to her. How old was she? Twenty? He glanced up the street behind them, mentally going over the inhabitants, trying to come up with someone who had a daughter the right age.

"Do you live around here?"

"I live in town," she allowed. She sent him another one of those shy smiles, and Ty was shocked by the urge to kiss it from her mouth. *Good grief, I must have been spending too much time indoors.* A fellow just didn't go around kissing strange girls, even ones as pretty as this. Now, if he got to know her a little better. . . .

"Give me a hint," he said.

"Well, last time we met, you took me flying."

"Took you flying?" Ty's brows rose as he considered that. Since just the sight of him with an airplane made his mother's heart go in to palpitations, he hadn't flown home in years. And surely, if he'd taken her flying, he'd have remembered. It wasn't like he took every girl he met up in an airplane. That was more Jack's style.

He stared at her, trying to place her face, his attention coming back to her eyes. It was those eyes he remembered.

They were such a clear blue, smiling now but with something behind them that spoke of loneliness. And he had a sudden image of those big blue eyes looking up at him from under sadly flattened golden curls and a childish voice thanking him for giving her a glimpse of heaven.

"Meg Harper?" The words weren't exactly a question, nor were they quite a statement.

"You've grown up," he added awkwardly. And grown into quite a beauty, he added to himself. But not grown nearly enough. She must be, what? Sixteen? Seventeen? Just a kid.

"Most people do," she said, her smile revealing a dimple in one cheek. Ty blinked, still struggling to shift his thinking, to see her as the kid she was rather than the woman she seemed.

"Can I give you a ride home?" It was the offer he'd planned on making when he stopped, but his original intention had been to suggest a detour for coffee at Rosie's Café or an ice cream soda at Barnett's Drugstore.

"That would be nice." She gave him that shy smile again and Ty felt a twinge of real regret. If only she was a few years older.

Meg felt Ty's hand under her elbow, steadying her as she stepped up onto the running board. She hoped he couldn't tell that her pulse was beating too fast. She'd heard that he was home, of course. Mrs. McKendrick had told Mr. Fenton at the general store and Mrs. Jennings had overheard and mentioned it to Ruth when she brought over a top to be quilted. Meg's mother hadn't been much interested in the news that Tyler McKendrick was going to be spending the summer at home. But Meg had been very interested.

More interested than she had any business being, she admitted to herself as she settled onto the leather seat of the little roadster. Ty might have figured in more than a few of her girlish fantasies but, at seventeen, she was old enough to know just how foolish those fantasies were. Still, she couldn't seem to help the way her heartbeat accelerated when she saw him.

"Are you staying in Regret long?" she asked as he started the car.

"For the summer. I let my mother talk me into looking after the house while she and my father are in Europe. Otherwise, I'd be on my way back to California by now."

"In Hollywood?" Meg's voice held the reverence of one who spent every Saturday afternoon in the movie house watching the flickering celluloid images on the big screen.

"That's the plan." Ty slowed at a corner and glanced both ways before turning left onto Main Street. "Jack's lined up some work in the movies for the two of us. Only then I tried to land on top of a tree so . . ." He shrugged. "I'll head out that way at the end of the summer."

Hollywood *and* flying. Meg wondered if it was possible to come up with anything more perfectly romantic.

"What about you?" Ty asked, glancing at her. "Are you still in school?"

"I graduate in a couple of weeks." She wished she could add something to that, something sophisticated and witty about her future plans. But the truth was, she didn't *have* any plans for the future, at least none that had any hope of coming true. There wasn't any money for her to go on to college and not much chance of her being able to find a job, not with the whole country in the midst of a depression.

"Is Miss Klienman still teaching English?"

"Yes. I think she'll be there forever."

"Does she still carry that ruler to smack your knuckles if she catches you passing notes or being inattentive? For such a small woman, she packed a powerful wallop into that skinny little ruler." Ty's smile was reminiscent, even a little fond.

"She still carries a ruler, but I can't say whether or not she still packs a wallop since she's never hit me with it."

"I bet she hasn't. You're probably one of those students who actually work," he said, throwing her a look of mock disapproval.

"And you were probably one of those 'rowdy young men' who give her such trouble."

"Guilty," he admitted without a trace of remorse.

"I think she secretly likes the students who give her trouble," Meg said. "They're more of a challenge."

"If she liked me, I wish she'd have gone a little easier on my knuckles." Ty left one hand on the wheel and rubbed the fingers of the other over the knuckles as if he could still feel the bruises from Miss Klienman's ruler.

Meg laughed, a soft, light sound, and Ty took his eyes off the road long enough to look at her. The wind blew her hair back from her face, giving him a clear view of her profile.

Damn, but she'd grown into a beauty.

He followed her directions and turned into the long drive that led up to a small house on the edge of town. He'd almost forgotten that her mother had married Harlan Davis. He remembered his mother commenting that it hardly seemed proper, what with George Harper in his grave less than a year. But from what Ty remembered of George Harper, he couldn't imagine that anyone, not even his widow, had spent much time grieving over the man's death.

He stopped in front of the small, almost painfully neat house. Flower beds marched in regimented rows along either side of the short walkway. Harlan Davis owned the small hotel in Regret, and he prided himself on his reputation for keeping a neat establishment. From the perfect symmetry of the house, Ty guessed that pride extended to his home.

He was almost sorry to see the ride end. He'd had two weeks of his own company and that was more than enough. He'd enjoyed these few minutes with Meg Harper. On the other hand, she made him think things he had no business thinking, so perhaps it was just as well that they were parting soon.

Meg felt no such ambivalence. Sitting high up in the roadster, with the sun shining and the wind blowing through her hair and Tyler McKendrick at the wheel was like a dream come true. She only wished they had a lot farther to go. But Ty had already stopped the car in front of her stepfather's house.

Ty got out of the car and came around to open her door,

the first time Meg had ever experienced such a common courtesy. She set her hand in his, letting him help her out of the car. A shiver of awareness ran along her spine as his hand closed around her fingers, and she kept her eyes down, afraid of what he might see in her face.

"Thank you for giving me a ride home." She looked up at him and smiled, wishing she could think of something clever and witty to say to keep him with her for a few more minutes, wishing he'd suggest seeing her again and knowing he wouldn't.

"You're welcome." He smiled at her, his brown eyes warm, and Meg felt her heart thump.

Though she wanted to linger, she gave him what she hoped was a casual smile and then turned away. She didn't want to stand there gaping at him like an infatuated child, even though that was what she felt like.

Meg was conscious of Ty watching her as she moved up the dirt walkway to the front porch. She wished she knew how to swing her hips the way her sister Patsy always did. She wished she were older, more sophisticated, the kind of woman a man like Tyler McKendrick would want to see again.

As she climbed the steps to the porch, she heard him start the roadster's engine, and it took every ounce of her willpower to keep from turning around. But the minute she was safely inside the screen door, she spun around, confident that, even if he looked, he wouldn't see her. And he did look. Before he began backing down the short lane, he looked right at her, or so it seemed. She was too far away to read his expression, but surely the fact that he'd looked meant something. Didn't it?

Meg watched until the roadster reached the main road before turning away from the door, her expression dreamy. Her mother was in the parlor, sitting in front of the quilting frame that hung from hooks in the ceiling. She looked up as Meg entered.

"Did Mrs. Rutledge pay you for the quilt?"

"Five dollars. And she gave me fifty cents for delivering it." Meg pulled five neatly folded bills from her pocket, along with two quarters, and handed it to her mother.

"You keep the money she gave you, sugar. By rights, you ought to have at least half of this, too. You did at least half the quilting."

"I don't mind." She knew as well as her mother that the money Ruth made doing quilting for other women helped make up the difference between what Harlan Davis was willing to give his wife for housekeeping and what it actually cost to feed and clothe the three of them in a manner he thought appropriate.

Meg slipped the quarters back into her pocket and walked around the quilting frame to sit across from her mother. Sliding on a worn silver thimble, she picked up the needle where she'd left it at the end of a row of quilting the day before.

"You'll never guess what happened today, Mama. Tyler McKendrick gave me a ride home," she continued, too impatient to share her news to wait for a guess.

"Helen McKendrick's boy? I'd heard he was home, recovering from crashing that airplane of his. I didn't think he'd be up to driving."

Ruth Davis squinted down at the fabric in the frame, concentrating on sliding the needle in and out along the dimly marked quilting lines.

"He limps a little, but he looks just fine other than that." Meg's tone made it clear that it would take more than a limp to make Tyler McKendrick look anything less than perfect.

Ruth glanced across the frame, taking in her daughter's dreamy expression as she used the thimble to rock the needle in and out of the muslin. Worry deepened the lines beside her mouth.

"The McKendricks live on the Hill," she said, her words a warning against the dreams she saw in Meg's eyes.

"I know." Meg's mouth tightened at having the fragile bubble of her dream pricked by the reminder of the gap that existed between the families on the Hill and everyone else. "He just gave me a ride home, that's all."

They quilted in a silence for a few minutes.

"Don't tell your stepfather," Ruth said abruptly.

"Don't tell him what?" Meg had been thinking about Ty,

wondering if she'd see him again, wondering if he thought she was pretty.

"Don't tell him about Tyler McKendrick giving you a ride home."

"Why not? There was nothing wrong with it."

"Just don't say anything," Ruth repeated. If she felt Meg looking at her, she refused to lift her eyes from her quilting. "Do as I say, Margaret." The use of Meg's given name was deliberate, emphasizing how serious she was.

Meg started to demand an explanation and then shrugged. "It's not likely I'd have said anything anyway," she muttered, dropping her gaze back down to the quilt.

The truth was, she said as little as possible to Harlan Davis. She didn't like him. Though his methods were more subtle, Harlan Davis had managed to complete the process of breaking Ruth's spirit that had been begun by her first husband. Though he wasn't as quick to physical violence as her father had been, he didn't need to lift his hand when he could cut so keenly with his tongue.

Over the past seven years, Meg had grown to hate the sound of his soft-voiced criticisms, the constant dissatisfaction with everything her mother did, everything she was. She'd watched the last spark of life fade from Ruth's eyes, the last traces of Ruth wither away, leaving her an old woman at forty-two.

Meg forced aside the old anger. There was nothing she could do so it was better not to think about it. She'd think of something else instead. Something like Ty McKendrick giving her a ride home in his snappy little roadster.

As she rocked the needle in and out of the fabric, Meg allowed herself to dream a little, imagining Ty being so entranced by her charm and wit that he invited her out to dinner at some highbrow restaurant—never mind that Regret boasted no such place. From there, it was a short hop to picturing the two of them attending a spectacular premiere in Hollywood together. She'd be wearing a swanky fur coat and dripping diamonds. Ty would look devastatingly handsome in his white tie and tails. Women would be swooning with admiration when they realized that he was the dashing pilot in the film. But he wouldn't pay any attention to them. His attention would be all for her.

She sighed quietly, her eyes dreamy, so wrapped up in her small fantasy that she didn't see her mother looking at her across the quilting frame. Or notice the anxiety that deepened the lines around her mouth.

"I'll have a coffee soda," Ty said as he sank onto the stool in front of the counter.

"Comin' up," the white-coated soda jerk said cheerfully. "You're Ty McKendrick, aren't you?"

"Yes." Ty looked at the younger man, trying to put a name to the vaguely familiar face.

"Eddie Dunsmore, Al's kid brother." Eddie grinned, revealing crooked front teeth.

"Sure. How are you?" Ty shook hands with him across the counter.

"Can't complain. I heard you were back in town. Heard you cracked your plane up pretty bad," he added, giving Ty a speculative look as if seeking evidence of injury.

"The plane recovered quicker than I have," Ty admitted, his mouth twisting ruefully. He rubbed his leg, aware of the dull ache that was with him more often than not. "How's Al these days?" He was more than a little tired of explaining his treetop landing.

"He's doing all right. Got married four or five years back, lives in Sioux City these days. Teaching school and figuring to be principal by the time he's forty, I guess. Two kids of his own."

"Seems like a lot of the old gang is married," Ty commented, trying to picture Al Dunsmore as a husband and father. The picture wouldn't come quite clear. His most vivid memory of Al was from grade school when Al had succeeded in gluing Miss Randall's dress to the seat of her chair, which might not have caused much uproar if Miss Randall hadn't been wearing the dress at the time. The entire class had been dismissed for the afternoon, making Al something of a hero, at least until the perpetrator was revealed and punishment descended on his sandy head.

"You in town long?" Eddie asked. He didn't seem in any particular hurry to prepare Ty's coffee soda, but Ty didn't rush him. It wasn't as if he had any pressing appointments.

"For the summer," he said, trying not to think how endlessly the season stretched out in front of him. "My parents are in Europe and they didn't want to leave the house empty."

Eddie's sandy brows rose in silent comment on the idea that anyone would worry about leaving a house empty in a small Iowa town that had so little crime that a teenager taking a joyride in his father's car was likely to be front-page news.

"I guess you can probably use a vacation," Eddie said, looking a little dubious.

"Yeah. Plenty of time for fishing," Ty said, trying to look as if three months of fishing didn't seem like way too much of a good thing.

"Lot of fishing," Eddie commented with unerring accuracy. Before Ty could think of a response, he seemed to remember the coffee soda and turned away from the counter.

Ty pushed one foot against the counter, turning the stool so that he faced the interior of Barnett's Drugstore. When he was a kid, having a soda at Barnett's was practically the high point of his week. It was a sad thought that, twenty years later, nothing had changed. He'd never have believed that three weeks could seem like three months. Or that three months could look like three years.

He was just about to turn back to the counter when he caught a glimpse of sun-colored hair. She was standing in front of the magazines with her back to him, but Ty didn't hesitate to put a name to her. Meg Harper. There couldn't possibly be two girls in Regret with hair that color and a figure like that. He'd left the soda counter and was walking toward her even as he realized who it was.

"Fancy meeting you here."

She turned, those beautiful blue eyes widening a little when she saw who had spoken. Her lashes lowered and a light flush came up in her cheeks. "Hello. How are you?"

"Can't complain," he said, echoing Eddie's earlier greeting. The fact that he *could* complain, loud and long, didn't seem important now. "No school today?" he asked, his thoughts more on the creamy softness of her skin than on what he was saying.

"It's Saturday," Meg said, looking surprised.

"Of course it is." Ty flushed. "I wasn't thinking." *At least not about what day of the week it was.*

"There are days I wouldn't mind forgetting, but Saturday isn't one of them."

"I usually don't forget it, either. It's just that, lately, there hasn't been much difference between one day and the next. It makes it hard to keep track of what week it is, let alone what day."

"I guess it would," she said, though it was obvious she couldn't imagine forgetting a Saturday, no matter what the circumstances.

There was a brief pause and then Meg glanced down at the magazine she was holding. Ty sensed that she was about to make some comment about it having been nice to see him and go on about her day. And he suddenly didn't want her to go.

"Could I buy you a soda?"

Her eyes flew to his face, wide, startled blue pools that a man could practically lose himself in. If he didn't keep in mind that she was a kid, Ty reminded himself sternly.

"I don't know. I've got to pick up a couple of things for my mother."

"Think of how warm it is today. Wouldn't a nice, cold ice cream soda taste good? Besides, you wouldn't make me drink mine alone, would you?" He grinned at her, shamelessly coaxing, not sure why he was so determined to have her company but unwilling to let her go.

"Would that be so terrible?" she asked, but her smile told him she was going to give in.

"Horrible. You know, they've done a study and found that people who eat alone are five times more likely to go bald."

"You don't look in any real danger of that," she said, her eyes going to his hair.

"The effects are cumulative," he said solemnly. "And I've eaten a lot of meals alone lately. I don't know when it'll reach a critical point."

"I guess that makes it practically my civic duty."

"Absolutely."

"Well, in that case, I'd love an ice cream soda."

"I'm indebted to you." Ty stood aside to let Meg pass him, falling in behind her as she walked to the soda fountain. It took a conscious effort to keep his eyes off the soft length of her spine and the inviting curve of her hips.

Meg settled herself on one of the red stools in front of the soda fountain, laying her magazine on the counter. She was wearing a dress of some rose-colored fabric with small white flowers scattered across it, and the softly flared skirt settled gracefully around her calves as she sat down, crossing her legs at the ankles.

"Hiya, Meg." Eddie set Ty's coffee soda on the counter in front of him and gave Meg the full benefit of his smile.

"Hello, Eddie."

"Don't see you in here very often."

"No." She didn't offer any explanation and Ty wondered if she didn't come in often because she couldn't afford it. Her stepfather's business, like most businesses, had to have suffered the last few years.

"What can I get for you?" Eddie asked, leaning a little too close for Ty's taste.

"I'll have a Cherry Chopped Suey Sundae, please."

"Comin' right up." He grinned at her again but Meg didn't seem to notice the invitation in his eyes.

Her lack of response gave Ty more pleasure than he had any business feeling.

"Cherry Chopped Suey Sundae?" The words were a question.

"Cherries, pineapple, and pistachio ice cream." She laughed when he pulled his features into a comical grimace. "It's very good. You should try one."

"I'll stick with coffee, thanks." He absently stirred his straw through his soda, his attention on the girl beside him.

"Kind of dull, isn't it?" she asked, wrinkling her nose teasingly.

"I get enough excitement flying. I like my ice cream sodas to be nice and safe."

"Are you going to miss it very much this summer—flying, I mean?"

"Yeah. I already do. It's like being in a cage. You can see daylight through the bars, you just can't get out into it."

"Does your leg bother you very much?" Meg's question made him realize that he'd been absently rubbing his fingers over his thigh again.

"Not really. Landing in a tree was harder on my pride than anything else." He smiled to lighten the atmosphere, a little surprised that he'd revealed so much of how he felt. She was surprisingly easy to talk to.

"Here you go, Meg. I put extra pineapple and cherries on the bottom."

"Thank you, Eddie." Meg smiled at him as he set the sundae on the marble counter in front of her. He showed signs of lingering but when he caught Ty's gaze, he changed his mind and discovered he had something else to do.

Obnoxious puppy, Ty thought, watching the younger man move away. He looked at Meg as if she were a juicy bone. Not that he could entirely blame him, he admitted reluctantly. He watched Meg dig into the sweet concoction with delicate greed, dipping up a spoonful of ice cream and nuts, careful to get a little of the canned fruit from the bottom of the clear glass dish. She put the spoon in her mouth, her eyes half closing as she savored the taste.

Ty was shocked to feel a quick stab of arousal. *She was just a kid,* he reminded himself sternly. There was nothing wrong with buying her a soda—that was just being friendly— but it wouldn't do to forget that she was strictly off limits.

Ty was just being friendly, Meg told herself as Eddie walked away. She'd be lying to herself if she pretended it was anything more. The idea that Tyler McKendrick might actually be attracted to her was simply ridiculous.

"How's Patsy these days?" Ty asked.

"She's fine." Meg dipped her spoon into her sundae, wondering if Ty was one of the many boys who'd wanted to date her sister. "She got married about five years ago, you know."

"I'd heard that."

And regretted it? But she couldn't ask him that, of course.

"I don't see her much. She lives in Herndale," she said, naming a town about thirty miles away. "She doesn't come home very often."

"You must miss her."

"Yes." At least she missed the sister she'd known when they were growing up. Patsy had changed a lot in the last year or two she'd been home. By the time she'd married Eldin Baker, Meg had felt as if she barely knew her anymore.

"You like the movies?" Ty asked, tapping the copy of *Photoplay* that lay on the counter.

"I go almost every Saturday," she admitted. "You must like them, too. If you were going to work in Hollywood, I mean."

"I like them well enough. But working in Hollywood had more to do with making money than liking movies. There's work doing stunt flying for the studios."

They continued to talk while Meg ate her sundae. She'd never been so sorry to reach the bottom of the dish in her life, and the regret had nothing to do with finishing her treat. Once it was gone, there was no more excuse to linger and who knew if she'd get another chance to talk to Ty McKendrick.

He paid for their sundaes and then waited while she paid for her magazine before walking outside with her. They stood on the sidewalk in front of Barnett's, letting their eyes adjust to the bright sunshine.

"It's a beautiful day," Meg said, falling back on the banal comment as a way to prolong the moment just a little longer.

"Beautiful," Ty agreed. If she'd been looking at him, she'd have seen that his eyes lingered on her as he spoke. But she was looking at the squat brick building that was her stepfather's hotel. It sat kitty-corner across the street from Barnett's, and she suddenly remembered her mother's insistence that Harlan Davis not be told that Ty had given her a ride home.

"Can I give you a lift home?" Ty asked, as if reading her mind.

"No, thank you. I have a few more things to pick up for my mother." She didn't really, but she had a sudden memory of her stepfather's thin face twisted in anger when Patsy came home from the movies with a boy. He was home today and she suddenly didn't want him to see her drive up with Ty. She smiled up at him. "Thank you for the sundae."

"You're welcome. Thank *you* for the company." The warmth of his smile made her heart bump in her chest.

"You're welcome." She hesitated a moment longer, reluctant to leave. But unless she wanted to change her mind and let him drive her home, there was no excuse to linger. "Goodbye, then."

"I'll see you around." Ty was still smiling as she turned away.

Meg held both the smile and the words close to her heart as she stopped at Lewison's General Store and bought a spool of quilting thread for her mother. As she walked home, she replayed every moment of their time together, feeling as if she were walking on air.

She wasn't silly enough to read anything in to him buying her a sundae. She didn't need her mother to remind her of the gap that lay between her and Ty McKendrick.

But didn't it almost seem like fate, the way their lives had touched over the years? the dreamy romantic Meg whispered.

Certainly not, the more practical Meg responded. Living in a small town, it was surprising their paths hadn't crossed more often than they had.

But in the movies, unlikelier romances found happy endings.

The movies had nothing to do with real life. And thinking about things like fate and happy endings was only going to lead to someone's heart getting bruised. And she knew just whose heart it would be.

* * *

But later in the afternoon, when she was waiting to get her ticket for the matinee at the Criterion, she felt someone tap her shoulder. Surprised, she turned and suddenly felt almost dizzy when she saw Ty smiling down at her.

"Looks like we both decided to catch the picture. Must be fate that we'd bump into each other again like this. We'll have to sit together now."

"Yes." She couldn't seem to get out more than that one breathless syllable as she gave a quarter to the woman at the ticket window and took her ticket. She watched as Ty paid for his ticket, feeling her heart beating much too quickly.

Fate, he'd said. Was it possible? Even just the smallest bit possible?

Despite her determined practicality, Meg felt hope flutter delicate, foolish wings inside her.

Chapter 4

Ty glanced sideways at Meg, watching her face in the flickering light from the screen. They'd sat through the newsreel and chapter five of a serial that had ended with the hero's car plunging off a cliff, apparently sentencing him to a fiery death. Since there were at least five more chapters remaining in the thrill-packed series, Ty suspected that the resourceful hero had somehow managed to exit the car before it plummeted into the gorge.

The movie that followed was a melodrama, and by halfway through it, Ty had already decided that the cad of a husband was going to be forced to repent his callous behavior when he discovered that his wife might be dying of some unnamed but fatal illness. He wondered if he was the only one to notice that she showed no symptoms other than a tendency to occasionally place a graceful hand to her forehead and sigh.

Certainly the thinness of the plot didn't seem to bother Meg. She gave the screen her full attention, hardly remembering to dip her hand into the box of popcorn he'd insisted on buying for her. She was completely absorbed, her expression reflecting the emotions being played out on the flickering filmstrip. As far as Ty was concerned, watching her face was far more entertaining than the histrionics on the screen.

* * *

"It was so sad, the way she died." Meg dried her eyes with the handkerchief Ty had thoughtfully provided during the movie's final scene.

"I don't see why she forgave her husband."

"Because she loved him and she didn't want him to feel guilty after she'd died."

"Considering the way he treated her, I think a little guilt would have done him a world of good." His hand cupped Meg's elbow as they walked up the carpeted aisle toward the heavy curtains that separated the theater from the lobby.

"When you love someone, you don't want them to suffer, no matter what they've done."

They followed the other patrons out the door and into the faded sunlight. Without talking about it, they turned left, walking down the sidewalk together.

"Do you really believe that? That loving someone means you want their happiness, no matter what the cost to yourself?"

"Of course." Meg looked up at him, her eyes wide with surprise, as if she couldn't imagine why he'd need to ask such a question. "That's part of loving someone," she said, as if there could be no question about it.

"I know a few people who'd disagree with you," he said cynically, thinking of his mother.

"But isn't a big part of loving someone wanting them to be happy?" They'd stopped in a pool of shadows between two buildings and Meg looked up at him, frowning a little. Ty reached out to take her arm, drawing her a step closer to him to allow room on the sidewalk for an elderly couple to pass.

"I've always thought it should be," he said slowly. Looking down into her eyes, he couldn't help but notice what a deep, clear blue they were, with not a trace of gray to dilute the purity of their color.

He still held her arm and he could feel the warmth of her skin through the soft cotton of her dress. His fingers tightened, drawing her imperceptibly closer. She drew a shallow little breath, her eyes widening. For a moment, Ty half thought that something passed between them—a tingle of awareness he'd never felt before.

Up the street, a car backfired, the sound sharp as a gunshot. Startled, Meg jerked her head toward the noise and the momentary spell was broken. Ty let his hand fall from her arm and the odd tingle disappeared. His imagination was starting to run wild.

"Can I give you a ride home?" he asked. He was relieved when she shook her head, saying that she'd enjoy the walk.

He didn't argue and after Meg had thanked him for the popcorn, they parted company. Walking to where he'd left the roadster, Ty gave himself a mental lecture. Meg Harper was just a kid, still in high school, for crying out loud. The more time he spent with her, the harder it seemed to be to remember how young she was.

Remembering how she'd been able to lose herself completely in the movie had him half smiling as he pulled open the roadster's door and stepped onto the running board. He'd certainly seen much better films, but he couldn't remember the last time he'd enjoyed one as much. Seeing it through Meg's eyes had made it seem a little less stale.

He settled onto the soft leather seat and set his hands on the wheel but didn't immediately start the car. There was no question, a smart man would stick to his original decision and keep a distance between himself and the temptation of those big blue eyes. And he'd always considered himself a very smart man. He sighed as he started the engine.

It might be nice to be a little less smart sometimes.

Smart or not, Ty found himself outside the Criterion the following Saturday afternoon. It was just to give himself something to do, he'd argued as he walked to the theater. But then he saw Meg's smile when she saw him, and he admitted that he'd wanted to see her again.

After all, where was the harm in watching a movie together? And if he bought her a soda at Barnett's afterward, that wasn't a proposition, was it? The fact was, he was tired of reading, tired of listening to the radio, bored with fishing, and most of all, bored with his own company. Meg Harper was good company. Spending an hour or two with her now and then would help to pass the summer, which had begun to stretch endlessly before him.

"I thought I might see you here," he said as Meg stepped away from the ticket office.

"You did?"

"I'll buy you a box of popcorn if you'll let me sit with you," he offered, giving her a smile that had been known to persuade women to agree to much more than a box of popcorn.

"You don't have to buy me popcorn," she protested, looking surprised that he'd think a bribe was necessary.

But he insisted and a few minutes later they settled into their seats. Ty was aware that, for the first time in a week, he didn't have the restless feeling of an animal caught in a cage. There was something ineffably soothing about Meg's quiet presence.

He'd been a conceited fool to decide to avoid her just because she was attractive. No doubt, in her eyes, a man of twenty-eight was practically ancient.

Meg found it hard to concentrate on the flickering images on the screen when she was so vividly aware of Tyler's shoulder only inches away, of his long legs so close to hers. She was glad she'd worn one of her prettiest outfits, the soft blue rayon dress that had belonged to Patsy. She'd left it behind when she moved out five years before. Meg had restyled it only a few months ago, adding a white pique collar and cuffs that made it look practically new.

He probably wouldn't notice that the blue of the dress echoed the blue of her eyes or the way the slim-fitting skirt flared out to swirl gracefully around her calves. But she knew she looked her best, and she couldn't help but be glad Ty was seeing her that way.

Meg was even more glad when he suggested a soda at Barnett's after the movie. She hesitated only a moment before agreeing. But as they walked to the drugstore, she reminded herself not to read too much into the casual invitation. Ty had already commented that most of his old friends were either married or had moved away. If he seemed to be seeking out her company, it was only because his options were limited at the moment. She'd be a fool to think otherwise.

But her stern mental lecture did nothing to still the foolish, fragile flutter of hope inside.

"Gladys Martin mentioned that she saw you and the McKendrick boy together at the motion-picture house on Saturday."

"We happened to meet there," Meg said. She could feel her mother's anxious eyes on her from across the quilting frame, but she refused to lift her gaze from her stitching.

"She said that it wasn't the first time she'd seen you there." Ruth Davis's tone was worried.

"Lots of people go to the movies on Saturday," Meg said, lifting one shoulder in a shrug, knowing it wasn't the answer her mother wanted.

It was hot in the parlor, even with the windows open. She wanted to go outside and curl her bare toes into the sweet green grass. Maybe even walk down to the stream and dangle her feet in the cool water. But her mother had promised Mrs. Morgenson that she'd have her quilt done by the end of the week, and there wouldn't be much time for walking barefoot in the grass or enjoying the cool shadiness along the stream until it was done.

Ordinarily, Meg didn't mind helping her mother with the quilting she took in. She enjoyed the soothing rhythm of her stitches, and there was plenty of time for dreaming, for losing herself in fantasies. The fact that, lately, most of those dreams had involved Tyler McKendrick was no one's business but her own.

"Gladys said she saw the two of you go into Barnett's together," Ruth said, persevering in the face of Meg's silence.

"Mrs. Martin seems to spend a lot of time keeping track of what I'm doing," Meg said tartly.

"She can't help seeing what's in front of her nose."

Especially not when her nose is always poked in someone else's business. But Meg kept the thought to herself.

"Ty bought me an ice cream soda," she said, trying to sound as if this were a matter of so little interest that she couldn't imagine why they were discussing it at all.

"Someone might have seen you," Ruth said worriedly.

"We weren't doing anything wrong," Meg snapped, and then sucked in a quick breath as the needle slid through the soft muslin and pierced her fingertip. She popped the injured finger in her mouth, careful not to let so much as a drop of blood fall onto the soft pastels of the quilt.

"Someone might tell your stepfather." It was a measure of Ruth's distress that she didn't automatically caution Meg about getting blood on the quilt.

"I don't see why he'd care," Meg said. She examined her fingertip and, assured that the small injury had closed, slid it back into place under the quilt.

"He wouldn't like it." Ruth's hands were still, her faded blue eyes fixed on her daughter.

"There's nothing to not like, Mama." Seeing Ruth's worry, Meg softened her voice, trying to reassure her. "We just happened to meet at the movies and he offered to buy me an ice cream soda afterward."

"I suppose that really isn't much," Ruth said after a moment. She began quilting again, rocking her needle smoothly in and out of the quilt, but the anxious frown still lingered.

"Nothing at all." Meg hoped her mother wouldn't hear the regret in her voice. She wished with all her heart that there were something more to her relationship with Ty.

She'd neglected to mention that they'd shared movies and an ice cream soda every Saturday for the past four weeks, but that hardly mattered.

The fact was, he treated her as if she were his kid sister. No matter how she tried, she couldn't read anything into his companionship except that she offered a pleasant change from his own company. There were, as he'd told her, only so many hours a day a man could fish.

Meg didn't care so much about what might happen if her

stepfather found out about her improbable new friendship. The most he was likely to do was shout at her, the way he always did when something upset him. Of greater concern was the knowledge that, at the end of summer, when Ty left Regret, he was going to be taking a piece of her heart with him.

The only real question was just how big a piece it would be. She wanted to believe that she wasn't foolish enough to let herself actually fall in love with him. Just because her whole body tingled with awareness whenever he was near and her pulse beat a little too fast, that didn't mean she was in love with him. Did it?

She supposed that, if she were smarter, she'd ease away from Ty now, try to soften the hurt she knew was to come. It wasn't as if she thought his feelings were going to undergo a sudden change; that he would see her as a woman rather than a child. That wasn't going to happen, and she was going to get hurt. But she'd made up her mind to enjoy whatever time she had as his friend; to savor the laughter and companionship while it lasted. And when summer ended, she wouldn't feel a single regret.

The sky arced overhead in a clear blue bowl, holding the promise of a beautiful summer day. But Meg wouldn't have noticed if dark clouds had been piled up on every horizon. Her steps were quick, her golden hair bouncing on her shoulders as she hurried along the sidewalk.

"Mornin', Meg."

"Good morning, Mr. Guthrie." Meg slowed her pace to smile at the old man. From fall through spring, Amos Guthrie was the janitor at the school. He spent his summers working at odd jobs around town.

"Nice day," he said, leaning on the broom he'd been using to sweep the walk in front of the Luddie's Feed and Seed.

"It's a *beautiful* day," she corrected.

"Girl lookin' as pretty as you ought to be goin' to meet a beau." His teeth shone white against the leathery darkness of his skin.

"You think so?" Her smile had a coquettish tilt.

"I know so."

Meg gave him another smile, refusing to commit herself one way or another about whom she might be hurrying to meet. The rapid tap of her heels on the walk beat a counterpoint to her pulse. Ty was waiting for her.

Her smile widened when she saw him. He was standing beside the Chrysler, wearing a pair of tan slacks and a short-sleeved shirt that left his strong arms bare. The sun picked out the blue highlights in the thick blackness of his hair. Just looking at him made her feel breathless. He was so handsome. She felt her stomach tighten with awareness. Her skin suddenly felt too sensitive and there was a warm, heavy feeling in the pit of her stomach. She was still surprised by her own reaction to him, this strange feeling that was almost a kind of hunger.

As if sensing her presence, he turned. He smiled, his dark-brown eyes welcoming, and Meg felt emotion well up thick and hard in her throat. She couldn't remember anyone in her life ever looking so pleased to see her.

"Am I late?" she asked, hoping he'd attribute her breathlessness to her hurried pace and not to his presence.

"No schedule to keep," he said. "You left those behind a couple of weeks ago when you graduated. And I don't believe in 'em." He gave her a grin that made her heart flutter and then turned to open the passenger door for her.

"Where are we going?" Meg stepped into the roadster and sat down, tilting her head to look up at Ty.

"Somewhere away from the hustle and bustle of the city," Ty said as he shut her door.

"Yes, I can see how the noise and traffic might get to you," Meg agreed as he slid behind the wheel. She looked around, noting the dog sleeping on the walk in front of Rosie's Café, the old men who occupied a bench in the tiny park. It was the middle of the week and the middle of a hot afternoon and Regret lay somnolent under the sun, dozing in the heat, waiting for rain, waiting for better times.

"I'd forgotten just how full of life this place was," Ty commented, following her glance around the sleepy little town.

"It must be quite a shock after the peace and quiet of Los Angeles," Meg commiserated.

"It's a shock all right." He started the engine and pulled out into the street.

Meg felt excitement bubbling up inside her as they drove out of Regret. At first she put one hand on her head, holding her close-fitting hat in place. But they'd barely left the town behind before she gave up and pulled the sleek felt confection off and set it on the seat between them, letting the wind blow through her hair.

Catching Ty's smile, she grinned, feeling free and daring, as if she were one of the dashing women she sometimes saw in the movies. If it wouldn't have been childish, she would have been bouncing in her seat. She'd graduated from high school nearly two weeks before, but the excitement of leaving school behind paled in comparison to the excitement of spending the afternoon with Ty.

She'd assumed that a movie and an ice cream soda on Saturdays was the most she'd ever see of him. When he'd asked her if she'd like to go on a picnic, it had taken all her self-control not to shout her acceptance.

So here she was, sitting in his sleek little roadster, the wind blowing her hair as they zipped along the quiet country road. A picnic wasn't really a date, she reminded herself sternly. He'd probably have asked a favorite niece along on a picnic. But there was a rebellious little spark of hope inside that refused to go out.

Ty turned the car off the main road and into a rutted lane, just visible through the tangle of weeds that had overgrown it. Meg clutched at the top of the door as the roadster bounced over the washboard surface. Just when she was sure that her teeth were going to be permanently loosened, she saw a house up ahead. A few seconds later, the roadster came to a halt in the weed-choked yard in front of it.

She loosened her grip on the door and glanced at Ty, wondering who lived on the neglected property. He seemed to have momentarily forgotten her presence as he stared at the house. From the shocked expression on his face, it was obvious that what he was seeing was not what he'd expected.

Meg followed his gaze to the house. She'd only glanced at it before, but a more careful look made it clear that no one lived here. The clapboards showed traces of having once been white, but the paint was now cracked and peeling, gray with dirt and age. The windows were dirty enough to make curtains irrelevant. The front porch sagged tiredly, looking as if even the lightest of footsteps might cause a complete collapse. One of the posts that supported the porch roof had broken years before, and the cracked end was supported by a ramshackle stack of bricks and old boards that brought it more or less in line with its companions.

Obviously the place had been empty for a long time. The only signs of life were the rambling roses that twined around the posts and then clambered over the sagging porch roof in wild abandon.

"I didn't know it was like this," Ty said slowly.

"Who lived here?"

"My grandparents. My father's parents," he clarified. "Grandma died seven or eight years ago and Grandpa went a year later. I haven't been out here since then."

"It doesn't look like *anyone's* been here since then," Meg commented, gauging the growth of the roses.

"They always took such pride in this place. Grandpa used to boast that there wasn't a weed in the county that could get by Grandma's hoe." Ty rested his forearms on the steering wheel, his eyes scanning the property as if trying to find some trace of the immaculate scene he remembered.

"It must have been nice," Meg said, wishing she could see it as he remembered it.

"When I was a boy, I thought this was just about the best place in all the world." He pushed open his door and got out. As he circled the car to open Meg's door, his shoes crunched on the dried remains of last year's weeds, concealed by the fresh spring crop of grasses.

Meg stepped out, the hem of her skirt catching in the tall grass as she followed Ty up to the porch. Seen up close, the house looked even more neglected. The windows that flanked the front door stared blindly out at them, like an old woman whose eyes were dimmed by age and hopelessness.

"Watch your step." Ty took her arm, guiding her around a splintered board. The door wasn't locked but lack of use had stiffened the hinges, and he had to put his shoulder against it to force it open so that they could step inside.

The dirt on the windows blocked most of the sunlight, keeping the rooms in deep shadow. The house smelled musty and old. Meg followed Ty as he walked through the empty rooms, trying to imagine what it must have looked like with furniture and curtains, the oak floors polished and a fresh coat of paint on the walls.

"It must have been very pretty when your grandmother was alive," she said, using her fingers to brush the dirt off a patch of wall, revealing the floral wallpaper underneath.

"I don't think I ever thought of it one way or another," Ty said. "But it always felt like home."

More so than his mother's house? Meg wondered but didn't ask. ·

"There was never a speck of dirt in this house, unless I'd just tracked it in. But Gram never scolded, even if she'd just mopped. And the kitchen always smelled of bread or cookies."

He turned slowly, looking at the thick layer of dirt on every surface, the rust that marked the huge black wood-burning stove. A rag hung at the window over the sink, the only remains of a pair of crisp white curtains. There was something approaching grief in his eyes as reality replaced memories.

"It wouldn't take much to put it into shape again," Meg said. "It's mostly just dirt. A little elbow grease and it would look shiny as a new penny."

He shook his head slowly. "It doesn't matter. They're gone."

"It must be very hard to lose someone you love," she said quietly. He turned to look at her, his dark eyes unreadable, and she flushed, wondering if he was thinking of the fact that she'd lost her father and should know what it felt like to lose someone she loved.

"Of course, it was terrible when my father died." The words were flat and unemotional, a gesture to convention.

"You were pretty young," Ty said.

"Yes." Meg ran one finger through the dust that coated the Hoosier cupboard that sat against one wall. "I was ten. He was hit by a car."

"Do you miss him?"

It struck her that Ty was the first person to *ask* if she missed George Harper. After he was killed, everyone had murmured their sympathies; commented on what a pity it was— what with him so young and all; said how much his family would miss him even though, when he was alive, the same people had called him a lazy, good-for-nothing bum. Meg had wondered what was wrong with her that she felt none of the regret everyone seemed to think she should; that her father's death had left her with nothing more than a vague feeling of relief. Now, for the first time, someone was asking her how she'd felt rather than telling her. And she didn't know what to say.

Tyler watched the play of emotions across her face, wondering what she was thinking, wondering why he'd asked the question in the first place.

"No." It was hard to say which of them was more surprised by the flat denial. He could see in Meg's eyes that it wasn't what she'd intended to say. "No, I don't miss him at all."

"Maybe that's tougher than missing him a lot," he said slowly, trying to imagine what it must be like to have no real regrets about your father's death.

"The day he was killed, I'd dropped a pitcher and broken it." Her voice was unemotional and her eyes looked past him at something he couldn't see. "When Mama told me he'd been killed, my first thought was that it meant I wouldn't get a whipping that night. It took awhile for it to settle in that I wouldn't get a whipping from him ever again."

"It must have been hard for you," Ty said, feeling as if

the words were hopelessly inadequate but at a loss for anything more profound to say.

"You get used to most anything," she said, shrugging one shoulder.

"But there are some things no one should have to get used to." He had a sudden memory of the bruises on Meg's thin arms that day he'd found her crying under the willow tree, and he was surprised by the depth of anger he felt.

"Maybe. But that's the way life is, I guess." She looked around the dusty kitchen and changed the subject determinedly. "This must have been a wonderful room."

"I always thought so." He accepted her lead, knowing there was nothing he could say that could change what her father had done all those years ago. He shook himself, abruptly aware of the melancholy turn the day had taken.

"Let's go back outside," he said briskly. "I know a good place for a picnic and I don't think it will have changed much."

Twenty minutes later he was spreading a blanket over the ground under the branches of an elderly apple tree. There was a small orchard south of the house where a few trees still clung to life, but the apple tree stood to the west, magnificently apart, still beautiful despite the years of neglect.

Since Ty's culinary repertoire was limited, lunch was thick slices of bread piled high with meat and accompanied by crisp pickles and wedges of the cherry pie that Mrs. Vanderbilt had baked for him, taking pity on his bachelor condition. They ate in companionable silence, enjoying the warmth of the day and the clear sunlight that filtered through the apple's branches.

Ty had never known a woman who was so comfortable with silence. Most of the women he'd met—and a goodly number of the men—became uneasy if more than a few seconds went by without someone talking. But Meg didn't seem to feel any of that uneasiness. On the other hand, he didn't think he'd ever known anyone who was quite so easy to talk to.

"When I was a boy, I thought that being a farmer was the most exciting thing in the world," he said.

"You didn't always want to fly?"

"I wanted to farm. I'd come out here every chance I got and follow Gramps around, 'helping' him." He laughed softly. "I probably set his workday back a couple of hours every time I set foot on the place."

"I doubt if he minded."

"Probably not. It meant a lot to him to think that there'd be someone coming after him, someone who loved the soil as much as he did. But when I told him I wanted to fly, he helped me come up with the money to buy my first plane."

"He sounds like a wonderful man," Meg said quietly.

"He was. It would break his heart to see the way I've let this place fall apart." Ty's eyes drifted past the shabby house to the neglected fields beyond it, bare of any crop but weeds.

"I think you meant more to him than this farm. And I'd guess if you're happy, he's content."

If he was happy. If someone had asked him whether he was happy, Ty wasn't at all sure how he'd answer. At this moment, he was content in a way he'd rarely known.

Meg began packing the remains of their lunch back into the basket and Ty found himself watching her hands, noticing their slender grace. From there, his eyes wandered to her face. She was intent on fitting everything neatly inside the wicker hamper, and a small frown of concentration drew her brows together. He had the urge to reach out and smooth that frown away.

"I ought to get back," she said reluctantly once the hamper was packed. "I promised Mama I'd help her finish up a quilt for a lady in Cedar Rapids."

"Does your mother do a lot of quilting for people?" Ty asked the question as much to extend the peaceful afternoon as anything else.

"As much as she can. The money comes in handy."

"I thought your stepfather's hotel was doing pretty well," he said idly. "Since it's the only one in town, it seems to do a pretty fair business."

"It does all right."

Something in her tone made Ty take a closer look at her

expression. There was a subtle tightness around her mouth and a chill in her eyes that made him think that there wasn't much love lost between her and her stepfather.

As far as he was concerned, he'd have been content to drowse away the warm summer afternoon under the shade of the apple tree. But Meg had other things to do. He more than half envied her. The novelty of being idle had long since worn off.

"Well, I suppose we ought to get going, then." His movements slow, Ty stood up. He glanced around the neglected property regretfully. There were a lot of old dreams here, his grandfather's and his own childish plans to be a farmer. He tilted his head to look at the blue arc of the sky, knowing that flying might hold most of his heart but there was a small part of him that would always love the soil.

"Nobody gets to do everything they'd like." Meg's voice was soft and Ty turned to look down at her, wondering how she could read his thoughts so easily.

"I guess not." He smiled, shaking off the vague melancholy and extended his hand to her. Her hand felt almost fragile in his. As he drew her to her feet, he found himself noticing how small she was, the top of her head barely reaching his chin.

"Is something wrong?" Meg's question made him realize he'd been staring.

"Sorry. I was thinking of something else." He could hardly tell her that he'd been thinking how soft her mouth looked.

"I thought I had dirt on my nose or something." Her fingers brushed away an imaginary smudge, her smile a little self-conscious.

"No. Your nose is perfectly clean. Which reminds me." He snapped his fingers and then grinned down at her. "I almost forgot. I have something for you."

"For me?" He enjoyed the way her eyes widened in surprise as he pulled a small package from his pocket. "A present for me?"

"I don't see any other recent graduates around here," he said teasingly.

"A graduation present? You bought me a graduation present?" The idea seemed to amaze her.

"Well, I couldn't just let it go by without getting you *something* to mark the occasion." He wondered if it was possible that no one else had given her some little token. Surely her mother and stepfather had given her a gift. But the stunned look on her face and the way her fingers trembled as he gave her the package made Ty wonder if he was the only person who'd thought to mark the occasion.

Meg pulled the ribbon from the box and tucked it into her pocket before lifting the lid.

"It's not much," he said, suddenly afraid that she'd be disappointed by the inexpensive compact he'd bought on impulse.

"It's beautiful." There was something approaching awe in Meg's voice as she stared down at the slender black case. She lifted it out, letting the box fall to the blanket at their feet as she snapped open the lid to reveal a compartment that held both rouge and a tiny brass lid that sealed in the loose powder. There was a mirror and two puffs to complete the set.

"I just wanted to get you some little thing," he said, wishing that he'd put more thought into the gift, given her something more personal.

"Oh, Ty. It's so beautiful." She closed her fingers tight around the compact and looked up at him, her eyes bright with tears. "No one's ever given me anything half so pretty."

With another woman, he would have assumed that she was exaggerating to make him feel good. But somehow, he knew that Meg was telling nothing more than the truth; that the little compact that had cost him less than a dollar was the nicest gift she'd ever been given. The knowledge brought an odd spurt of anger. She should have all the pretty things she wanted.

"I'll keep it always," she said. "Thank you so much."

As if mere words couldn't possibly express her feelings, she stood on tiptoe and pressed a kiss to his cheek. Ty's hands came up automatically, settling on her slender waist to steady her. She smelled of powder and sunshine. He felt the gentle swell of breasts brush his chest as she leaned into him, the soft warmth of her mouth on his cheek.

She drew back and looked up at him, her eyes deep blue and shining. Ty was hardly conscious of his hands shifting, his palm flattening against the small of her back, his other hand coming up to let his fingers slide into the sun-colored silk of her hair. Meg's eyes widened as his head bent to hers, endless, deep blue pools that he wanted to lose himself in.

He ignored the voice that warned him he was stepping over the line he himself had drawn. One kiss, he told himself. A simple kiss. What possible harm could it do?

Her mouth was just as soft as he'd imagined it to be, soft and yielding and his. He threaded his fingers deeper into her hair, cupping the back of her head to tilt her face up to his, deepening the pressure of his mouth on hers.

Her hands came up to rest against his chest, the compact clutched in one small fist as she leaned into him, surrendering completely to the moment. To him.

For weeks he'd been trying to pretend that he didn't want her, that he saw her as little more than a child; that he could enjoy her companionship and forget about her femininity. All it took was the feel of her slim body against his for him to know he'd been lying to himself. The hunger he'd been keeping in check slipped loose, making his body tighten with need.

His mouth hardened over hers, his tongue coming out to stroke across her lower lip. He heard her soft gasp of shock and she stiffened against him. It was only for a moment and then she seemed to almost melt against him. But it was enough to make Ty realize what he was doing.

This was not an experienced woman he was kissing. This was a girl who'd plainly never been kissed like this. Hell, she'd probably never been kissed at all.

Drawing on every bit of willpower at his command, Ty lifted his head, breaking off the kiss. Meg's mouth clung to his with innocent hunger, weakening his determination. He stared down into her flushed face, watching as her lashes slowly came up, revealing the deep blue of her eyes. The look in those eyes was almost his undoing.

How was it possible for her to look at once the quintessential woman and as innocent as a child? That she felt the same hunger he did was obvious. She wanted him. But beneath the want lay an uncertainty that said she wasn't even sure just what it was she was asking for.

Ty swallowed a groan and forced his hands away from her. He should be horsewhipped. This was exactly what he'd sworn wasn't going to happen, what he'd promised himself he could avoid. Well, he'd proved just how good he was at resisting temptation.

And the worst of it was that he wanted nothing so much as to pull her back into his arms and kiss her again.

"Ty?"

Meg hardly recognized the sound of her own voice. Her mouth felt as if it didn't quite belong to her anymore. In fact, her whole body felt different—alive in a way she'd never known, as if she'd spent her whole life half asleep, coming completely awake only when Ty kissed her.

"We'd better get going," he said, his eyes shifting away from her.

"Yes." She moved off the blanket, bending down to pick up the box she'd dropped and slipping the compact back into it. She was hardly aware of her movements as she helped Ty fold the blanket, draping it over her arm while he picked up the hamper.

He retraced the path they'd taken back to the car, following the pattern of crushed grass. Meg followed him, thinking how everything could change in such a short time. She'd tried so hard not to let herself dream too much, knowing that her time with Ty was only this summer, only this short space of time. Wanting anything more would only lead to heartache.

But now he'd kissed her. And everything was changed.

Ty opened the door for Meg and put his hand on her elbow to steady her as she stepped onto the running board. He kept his touch strictly impersonal, releasing her the moment she was seated, avoiding her eyes as he shut the car door.

He was just going to have to put some distance between them, he thought as he slid behind the wheel. The last thing he wanted to do was hurt a sweet kid like Meg. She'd had enough hard knocks in her life. He didn't want to add to them.

He'd just keep his distance, that was all. There was no real harm done so far. If he kept his distance, she'd soon forget him and turn those beautiful eyes in another man's direction, someone closer to her age, someone who could fulfill all her dreams, someone who'd be good to her, put a ring on her finger that would sparkle as brightly as the stars in her eyes.

And whoever the lucky guy turned out to be, Ty already hated his guts.

Chapter 5

"That can't happen again," Ty said firmly, breaking into Meg's dreamy silence.

"What can't?" She knew, of course. Certainly she'd thought of nothing else but that kiss. But from the sound of Ty's voice, his thoughts hadn't been as pleasant hers.

"Me kissing you. It can't happen again." He kept his eyes on the road, but she could see the solid set of his jaw.

She'd been staring dreamily at the passing fields, spinning gentle fantasies of what her life would be like if Ty were to fall in love with her. Now those fantasy images started to shimmer like a mirage.

"Why not?" It took every ounce of courage for her to ask the question.

"Why not?" Ty glanced in the side mirror that was perched atop the spare tire and then pulled to the side of the dirt road. He shut off the engine and turned to look at her, resting one arm on the back of the seat.

"Why not?" he repeated.

"That's what I said." She couldn't meet his eyes, keeping her attention focused on her hands, which lay in her lap.

"Because I shouldn't have kissed you at all."

"I didn't mind," she whispered. The words sounded like an invitation, and Meg felt the color come up in her cheeks.

"You're just a kid, Meg."

"I'll be eighteen in a few months."

"And I'm twenty-eight."

"That's not so old," she told him, forcing her eyes up to his.

"It's too old for you," Ty said firmly. "The last thing I want to do is hurt you."

It was too late, she thought bleakly. *Couldn't he hear the sound of her heart cracking?*

"I don't see how a kiss is going to lead to a broken heart," she said, forcing a lightness she didn't feel.

"Maybe not. But it can't happen again," he said flatly. "Even if you were older, I'm still only here for the summer."

"I know."

She'd had plenty of practice at concealing her feelings, at presenting a blank facade—to deflect her father's rage, to make herself invisible to her stepfather, to keep her mother from worrying. Now she called on every bit of that ability and forced a smile.

"It was only a kiss, Ty. I may not be as ancient as you," she said teasingly, "but I'm old enough to know that a kiss doesn't have to mean anything."

Ty looked surprised and then relief crept into his expression. His eyes searched her face and Meg kept her smile firmly in place. After a moment, she sensed some of the tension going out of him.

"Am I acting like a pompous ass?" he asked her.

"Only a teeny bit." But her smile took any sting out of her agreement.

"I should have known you were too sensible to blow things out of proportion."

"Just call me Sensible Meg." The ache in her chest went too deep for tears.

"You're a sweet kid, Meg." Ty's smile was warm with affection.

"Thanks."

She kept her smile pinned firmly in place as he started the roadster and pulled onto the road. Staring out at the fields,

Meg wondered numbly how it was possible to feel her heart bleeding inside and still be able to smile and talk as if nothing were wrong.

It had been stupid to believe that one kiss could change her life; could suddenly make a future with Ty possible. She had his friendship for this summer and that was all she was ever going to have. It was enough.

She'd make it enough.

As unlikely as a friendship between himself and Meg Harper seemed to be, Ty had to admit that, aside from Jack, he'd never known anyone with whom he was so at ease. The summer days that had stretched before him in an endless ribbon of boredom were going by faster than he'd have believed possible.

He saw Meg two or three times a week. They met at the theater every Saturday and went to Barnett's for an ice cream soda afterward. A few times he'd coaxed her into letting him buy lunch at Rosie's, but they were more likely to picnic somewhere outside of town, though never again at his grandparents' farm.

It had nothing to do with the fact that he'd kissed Meg there. They'd put that behind them and he never thought about it, never thought about how good she'd felt in his arms, how nicely her slender body had fit against his; never remembered the softness of her mouth or the innocent eagerness of her response. And if, on rare occasions, the memory did creep up on him, he promptly shoved it to the back of his mind and forgot about it again. Almost.

Meg was a good listener but she was much more than that. She might have spent her life in Regret, Iowa, but she'd read just about everything she could lay her hands on and her view of the world extended well beyond the boundaries of the small town. Ty sometimes found himself challenged to hold up his end of the conversation when it came to the situation in the world at large.

She also knew how to make him laugh, sometimes even at himself.

As the days drifted by, he found himself thinking less about the end of summer than he did about when he was next going to be seeing Meg.

"Where are you off to, Meg?"

At the sound of her mother's voice, Meg hesitated. She looked longingly at the front door, wishing she could pretend she hadn't heard her mother and just leave. Knowing she wouldn't do any such thing. She turned and went into the parlor.

"Hello, Mama."

Ruth straightened away from the quilting frame, her thin face tightening in a brief grimace of pain as her back protested the hours she'd spent hunched over the quilt. Her faded blue eyes skimmed over her daughter, taking in the crisp white crocheted collar and cuffs that Meg had made to update last year's navy print dress, making it look almost like new.

"You're going out?"

"Yes, Mama. I'm going to the fair, remember? I asked you if you'd mind."

"I'd forgotten it was today. You've been going out a lot this summer," she commented. She rubbed absently at the ache in her lower back and Meg was instantly guilt-stricken.

"I'm sorry, Mama. I know I haven't been helping you with your quilting as much as I should have. I'll work on Mrs. Smith's quilt all day tomorrow, I promise." She pressed a kiss against the top of her mother's head.

"A girl your age ought to have some fun," Ruth said, smiling up at her daughter. "You never did make friends easily."

"I always liked books more than people," Meg said lightly, thinking of how lonely she'd felt, watching other little girls playing with their friends. Being George Harper's daughter had set her apart, made the other children look at her with either contempt or pity, reflecting the opinions of their parents.

"You always did have your nose stuck in a book," Ruth said, her smile reminiscent. "It's good to see you having fun." But the smile quickly faded, the lines of tension settling back around her mouth and eyes. "Heaven knows there's little enough when you grow up."

Meg looked at her mother's prematurely gray hair, the worn lines of her face, and tried to imagine her ever having fun. She couldn't remember the last time she'd seen her mother laugh. Even her smiles were tight and close, holding little real joy.

"Why don't you come with us, Mama?" she asked impulsively. "The quilting can wait a few hours. You hardly ever get out of this house."

"Oh, I couldn't, Meg. There's just too much to do, what with the kitchen floor to mop and supper to fix, not to mention Mrs. Smith's quilt needs finishing. But it's sweet of you to ask," she added perfunctorily. She smoothed her hand over the quilt. "Is the McKendrick boy taking you to the fair?"

"Yes." Meg didn't add anything to the flat response, knowing her mother wouldn't approve.

"You know no good can come of it."

"We're friends, Mama. I can't see the harm in that." Meg gave her a coaxing smile but the worried frown didn't ease. "I know you think I'm going to get hurt, but that's just not going to happen."

"Your stepfather's bound to find out," Ruth reminded her. "Someone's bound to tell him. He won't like it."

Meg's spine stiffened as a wave of resentment washed through her. "I don't see that it's any of his concern," she said, her voice sharper than she'd intended. If Harlan Davis hadn't been cordially disliked by most folks, someone would have told him about her friendship with Ty long before this.

"He won't like it," Ruth said again. Her fingers pleated the soft, faded pink cotton of her housedress. "I wish you'd stop seeing the McKendrick boy, Meg. Maybe Harlan wouldn't find out at all then."

"I don't care if he does find out," Meg said impatiently. "I haven't done anything wrong. Ty is a fine, upstanding citizen. His parents are respected in this town. I'd think Harlan would be pleased enough to see me making friends with somebody from the Hill."

"Don't you ever let him hear you call him by his given name, Margaret. It's disrespectful."

"I'm sorry, Mama." Meg had to force the apology out. Before the argument could continue, there was a knock on the door.

"That must be Ty."

Meg had been so absorbed in the conversation with her mother that she hadn't even heard the roadster pull up. Usually she met Ty at Barnett's. On the one or two occasions that he'd insisted on picking her up at home, she'd made it a point to be outside waiting for him. Now she hesitated, caught between answering the door and the need to reassure her mother.

"You'd better go let him in," Ruth said.

The door had been left open in a futile attempt to catch a breeze that might help cool the stuffy little house. As Meg approached the door and saw Ty's tall figure standing on the other side of the screen, she felt her heart give the same little bump it did every time she saw him. He was so tall and handsome and when he smiled, she felt something warm uncurl deep in her stomach.

"Hello, Ty."

"Hello, Meg. You look swell," he said, giving her an admiring but depressingly brotherly once-over as she opened the screen door. "Ready to go?"

"Yes. Just let me get my purse." She hesitated a moment and then stepped back, opening the door wider to invite him into the house. "Would you like to wait inside while I get it?"

"Sure." He stepped inside and the little hallway seemed to shrink with his presence.

Once he'd come in, there was no way to avoid introducing him to her mother, since the parlor opened directly off the hallway and Ruth was plainly visible. Meg made the minimum of introductions and then fled to her room to grab her small clutch bag from the bed. Habit made her pause long enough to make sure that she had a clean handkerchief and a comb as well as her precious compact. And then she hurried back out to the front of the house.

"I'm ready," she announced breathlessly.

"That's fine." Ty had been perched uneasily on the edge of the old horsehair sofa, and he rose, looking grateful to see the end of what had probably been an awkward conversation. "It was a pleasure to meet you, Mrs. Davis. I'll take good care of Meg."

"Yes," Ruth said, her fingers plucking restlessly at her skirt, her eyes as distracted as her voice.

"Good-bye, Mama. Don't work too long on that quilt. I'll help you finish it tomorrow." Meg brushed a quick kiss over her mother's cheek and then turned and hurried out of the room, out of the house before guilt could overwhelm her and make her tell Ty that she couldn't go to the fair, after all.

She felt a strange kind of relief once she was settled in Ty's car and he'd backed the roadster around to head out the drive, rutted by summer rains. She'd work extra hard tomorrow, quilt twice as fast to make up for today. Even as she made the guilty promise to herself, she knew it wasn't the quilting that had her mother so worried.

But she couldn't promise to stop seeing Ty. Not when so little time remained before the end of summer, before he'd be leaving Regret and going to California. Besides, she didn't really care whether Harlan Davis approved of her friendship with Ty or not, she thought resentfully.

As if thinking about the man had conjured him, his car was slowing to turn into the short lane just as Ty steered the Chrysler out onto the road. Meg had a quick glimpse of her stepfather's round face and pale eyes as they passed him.

"Wasn't that your stepfather?" Ty asked.

"Yes." Meg heard the flatness of her response but was helpless to put more life into it.

"You don't sound particularly fond of him," Ty said after a moment.

She wasn't going to say anything, of course. She'd grown up knowing that it was wrong to air dirty linen in public. Family problems stayed in the family, no matter what.

"He's a small man," she said at last, half surprised to hear the words.

"You don't like him because he's short?" Ty threw her an incredulous look.

"No. I mean small in other ways." She stroked her fingers over the smooth surface of her purse, keeping her eyes on the movement, half wishing she hadn't said anything, even as she struggled with the need to put words to the way she felt about her stepfather.

"He's little inside. He pinches pennies, not because times are hard and he *needs* to pinch them but because he *likes* to pinch them. He likes making my mother come to him for every nickel she needs to buy food or clothes. And he likes telling people how good he was to marry George Harper's widow and take on his two orphaned girls." Unconsciously her voice took on a tight, nasal edge that echoed Harlan Davis's tones.

"I think he only married Mama so he could tell people how good he was," she said bitterly.

"I can't say I've ever had much contact with the man," Ty said, obviously groping for words. "The hotel seems to do all right."

"Oh, he's a good businessman." Meg shrugged, wishing she'd just said something noncommittal when Ty asked about her stepfather. "Let's not talk about him anymore. It's too nice a day to waste on talking about Harlan Davis."

Ty didn't argue and Meg determinedly forced all thoughts of her mean-spirited stepfather from her mind. She was going to enjoy today, no matter what.

Ty hadn't been to a fair just to have fun in at least ten years. Usually, when he was at a fair, he was giving earth-bound fairgoers a quick, dizzying trip into the air. He had neither the time nor the desire to wander the fairgrounds, eating hot dogs and drinking sticky, sweet lemonade.

But somehow, with Meg's enthusiasm as an example, it was impossible to do anything less than have a good time. From the moment they parked the car in the field next to the fair, she'd been bubbling over with eagerness. She wanted to see everything, from the two-headed lady to the snake charmer. It didn't matter how obvious the ruse, how old the trick, she drank it in. Just when Ty would think she was actually fooled by something, their eyes would meet and he'd see the laughter in hers. But seeing through the facade to the slightly tawdry reality didn't seem to spoil her enjoyment in the least.

He didn't think he'd ever known anyone who took so much pleasure from life. Little things pleased Meg as much as big; silly things as much as spectacular. She simply enjoyed it all.

They rode the Ferris wheel and Ty enjoyed her delight at the spectacular view from the top. He felt a momentary pang when he thought about how much more spectacular the view was from an airplane. It reminded him of how much he missed flying. But he'd be back to it soon, he reminded himself as the Ferris wheel began to turn again, lowering them toward the ground. It wouldn't be long before his parents's liner docked in New York. They might spend a day or two in the city but then they'd take the train home and he'd be free to leave his hometown, leg in perfect working order again and conscience clear.

He looked at Meg, whose profile was to him as she leaned out of the swaying basket, trying to see everything at once. He was going to miss her, he thought suddenly. If it hadn't been for her companionship, these past weeks would have been nearly intolerable. Instead, when he left, he was going to take more than a few pleasant memories with him.

It really had been like having a little sister for a few weeks, he thought as he helped her step out of the basket. Of course, his thoughts hadn't always been exactly brotherly, he admitted as Meg linked her arm through his and tilted her head to smile up at him. But that was something he tried not to think about too much.

"Oh, look. Kewpie dolls." Meg stopped at the edge of a booth, admiring the row of fat pink cherubs that perched on one of the shelves. "Aren't they sweet?"

"Practically like having an angel in the house, miss." The man behind the counter was short and round, his thin dark hair combed sideways across his scalp and heavily pomaded. "They'll bring you good luck," he added.

"Really?"

"Of course. Why don't you try your hand at knocking over the bottles," he said, offering her three small balls. "Just knock over a few bottles and I'll give you your pick of those little dolls."

"Oh, no." Meg shook her head, smiling ruefully. "Thank you but I could never hit even one of those bottles."

"How about you, mister?" The man promptly turned his attention to Ty. "You gonna let your girl go home without one of those little dolls she's got her heart set on?"

Ty glanced at Meg, seeing the way her cheeks had flushed at hearing herself described as "your girl."

"Of course not," he said, grinning at the huckster. He winked at Meg. "Who could pass up an opportunity to win a little good luck?"

Ten minutes, two dollars, and uncounted missed bottles later, the man behind the counter handed Meg the kewpie doll she'd picked out.

"Isn't she darling?" Meg hugged the doll to her and then smiled up at him, her eyes sparkling. Her pleasure was so real that Ty was half sorry he hadn't won her something more spectacular. "Thank you, Ty."

"You're welcome."

"Seems to me the man deserves a kiss." The older man leaned against the counter, giving the two of them an indulgent smile. "Fella goes to all that work to win something for his girl, he ought to get a reward. Go on, miss. Don't mind me."

Flushing, Meg stood on tiptoe and brushed a kiss across Ty's cheek. He felt the light pressure of the hand she set on his shoulder for balance; caught the warm, clean scent of her hair and suddenly remembered the softness of her mouth under his, the gentle weight of her body against his. As she drew back, their eyes met and he knew she was remembering the same things. Ty felt his hands lift, the idea of pulling her close half formed in his mind.

And then she dropped her hand from his shoulder and

looked down at the doll she held, breaking the tense little moment.

"Thank you for the doll," she said, her tone almost formal.

"I hope she brings you luck," he said.

Maybe it was just as well he was going to be leaving soon, he thought as they walked away from the booth. If he spent much more time with Meg, it might be easy to forget all the reasons she was strictly off limits.

"Meg?" At the sound of her name, Meg turned, relieved to have the awkward moment interrupted. The woman who'd spoken was a little taller than Meg, a little older, a little heavier. Her pale-brown hair was cut in a cap of short curls more practical than fashionable. Her eyes were blue, but a paler shade than Meg's.

"Patsy?" Meg hadn't seen her older sister in more than a year.

"It *is* you, Meggy," Patsy exclaimed, her face creasing in a smile.

"Patsy!" This time Meg's voice held warm affection.

They embraced, a quick hug that reaffirmed the warmth that had always been between them. When they stepped back, Meg's eyes took in the changes in her older sister. She'd seen so little of her since her marriage five years before, a quick visit at Christmas had been about it, and last year, there hadn't even been that much.

Meg had accepted Patsy's withdrawal, the same way she'd accepted everything else in her life that couldn't be changed, from her father's abuse to her feelings for Ty. She'd never seen much use in questioning the reasons for why things happened.

"How are you? I haven't seen you in so long." Patsy kept her hands on Meg's shoulders as if she couldn't bear to let her go.

"I'm fine. How are you? And Eldin?" she added, dutifully asking after the brother-in-law she barely knew.

"We're both fine. Eldin travels a lot, you know—selling farm equipment and all. He's working harder than ever these days, what with things being the way they are. Farmers don't have much money to spare."

"I guess not." Meg searched for something else to say, shocked to find that it was necessary. After all this time, there should have been a hundred things she wanted to ask Patsy or tell her. But the Patsy standing in front of her wasn't the teen-age sister she'd known so well, and she found herself groping for something to say to the woman she'd become.

Meg sensed more than saw Ty shift slightly and turned to him, relieved to have a distraction.

"You remember Tyler McKendrick, don't you, Patsy? Ty, this is my sister, Patsy Baker." She stumbled slightly over the last name, still unfamiliar after five years.

"If you don't remember me, you probably remember my friend, Jack Swanson," Ty said, grinning easily. "He was the one who dunked your pigtail in the inkwell when you were in first grade."

"I remember you," Patsy said, leaving her memory of Jack open to question. "It's good to see you again," she added politely.

"And you. I heard you'd gotten married."

"Yes. Five years ago." The fingers of Patsy's right hand sought out the plain wedding band on her left as if needing to confirm its presence.

"Is Eldin here with you?" Meg asked, glancing behind Patsy for her brother-in-law, wondering if she'd recognize him if she saw him.

"No. I came with friends. They're watching one of the shows. It was dark and stuffy in the tent so I slipped out. You know how I hate being closed in."

"I remember." Meg remembered when George Harper had shut his eldest daughter in the toolshed overnight to "learn her." Remembered, too, how her six-year-old self had climbed through their bedroom window and slipped the latch on the shed door to let Patsy out.

She saw the same memory in Patsy's eyes, and, for a moment, it was as if the last five years had never been and she felt all the old closeness.

"You're welcome to join us until your friends' show ends," Ty told Patsy.

"Thank you, but I imagine it's about over. I should get back." Patsy glanced from Ty to Meg, her gaze speculative. Meg flushed, hoping she wouldn't say anything. "Well, it was nice to see you, Meg."

"It was nice to see you, too." They hugged again, more awkwardly this time. Meg was aware that Patsy hadn't said anything about seeing her again. When Patsy released her, their eyes met and Meg thought she read a plea—for understanding?—in her sister's look. But then Patsy turned away, giving Ty a polite smile.

"Nice to see you again, Ty."

"You, too."

Patsy glanced at Meg again, her expression unreadable, and then turned and walked away. Meg watched her for a moment before turning away, disturbed by the meeting, though she couldn't quite put her finger on the reason. She was aware of Ty's curious look but she didn't want to talk about her sister with him.

"Oh, look. A snake charmer." She pointed to the colorful sign in front of a tent and smiled up at Ty, putting the meeting with Patsy behind her, determined that nothing was going to intrude on this evening. "It says he's a real live Indian, all the way from India."

"Probably from Cleveland," Ty said with good-natured cynicism, but he didn't protest when she headed toward the small tent.

It was well after dark when they left the fair. Meg thought briefly of the fact that her stepfather would surely be home before she was, but since he'd already seen her leaving with Ty, there seemed no reason to rush. If her mother was right and he was going to be upset by her friendship with Ty, then he'd just have to be upset. So when Ty asked her if she needed to be home before dark, Meg shook her head.

She was vividly aware of the fact that summer was ending. Ty would be leaving soon and heaven knew when—or if—

she'd see him again. Oh, he'd come back to Regret to visit his family. But she couldn't fool herself into thinking that she'd be high on his list of people to see. She was darned if she was going to cut short their visit to the fair in hopes that it might placate her stepfather.

At her insistence, Ty didn't come to the door with her. If her stepfather was angry with her, she didn't want Ty there to witness any scene he might create. He waited until she reached the porch and turned to wave before turning the roadster and heading back out to the road. Meg watched until his taillights disappeared, hugging the day's memories to her, along with the kewpie doll he'd won for her.

Surely there had never been a more perfect day, and she was reluctant to spoil it with the scene she suspected awaited her inside. But she could hardly linger on the porch forever. With a last glance in the direction Ty had gone, Meg turned and pulled open the screen door.

"Margaret. Come here." Harlan's nasal voice twanged from the small living room the moment the door shut behind her.

Meg felt her spine stiffen with resentment at the autocratic command. For a brief moment, she considered just going on to her room as if she hadn't heard him. She couldn't quite imagine him coming to get her. But her mother would be the one to suffer for it. Reluctantly she obeyed his order.

"Hello." She conjured up a smile for her mother.

"Meg." Ruth's voice was hardly more than a whisper, and she didn't lift her eyes from her lap, her attention all for the restless movement of her fingers as they pleated and then smoothed the fabric of her skirt.

"Do you know what time it is, miss?" The question forced her to look at her stepfather. It had always seemed to her that his features huddled in the middle of his face, as small and stingy as his personality. His eyes were a blue so pale they seemed colorless, and they peered out at the world with disapproval.

"I'm afraid I don't know what the time is," she said, forcing the dislike from her voice.

"Too busy spreading your legs to look at a clock?" he snapped.

Meg gasped. The crude accusation was so unexpected that she was struck momentarily speechless.

"No." The word was a choked denial.

She looked at her mother's bent head, waiting for her to say something, to tell Harlan how wrong he was, but Ruth kept her head bent over the restless movements of her fingers as if, if only she pleated the worn fabric just so, the unpleasant scene in front of her would go away. Meg knew there'd be no help from her mother.

"You've no right to say that," Meg said, outrage making her throat tight.

"No right?" His voice rose to a shout. "I've every right to say anything I please to you. Who do you think puts the food on the table and provides the money for the clothes on your back? And you repay me by going out whoring."

Her face white, Meg turned to leave, wanting only to escape the rage in her stepfather's eyes, the ugly words he was spewing out. She hadn't taken more than a step when his fingers closed over her arm, digging into the soft flesh with force enough to draw a cry of pain as he spun her around to face him.

"Don't you dare walk away when I'm talking to you." He grabbed her other arm, dragging her close enough that she could smell the slightly sour odor of his breath.

"I'm not a . . . what you said," she protested, frightened by the rage in his face. "We just went to the fair. I didn't do anything wrong."

"You're just like your sister," he snarled. "Whores, both of you."

"I'm not." Meg gasped. "And neither is Patsy. You're a filthy liar."

He moved quickly. The impact of his hand on her face jerked her head to the side and drove the soft inner flesh of her lips back against her teeth. Meg felt the salty, sweet taste of blood fill her mouth. Through the ringing in her ears, she could hear him shouting that she was a whore—just like her sister.

It was the first time since her father died that someone had struck her in anger. She'd have thought all the old responses buried too deep to find, but now she felt the old freezing calm welling up inside her. If she just went far enough away, it wouldn't matter what happened here.

She swallowed the blood in her mouth but didn't lift her hand to check the extent of the damage. She stared at her stepfather but she was looking through him, her eyes focused on nothing at all as she gathered the protective mental blanket around herself. It didn't matter what he did. He couldn't really hurt her. Not inside, not where it counted.

As if watching a picture on a movie screen, she saw him draw back his hand to strike her again, but she didn't feel any fear. She didn't feel anything at all.

"Now, Harlan." Her mother's voice shook with fear as she put her thin hand on her husband's arm. "I'm sure there was no harm done."

For a moment, he didn't seem to hear her. He continued to stare at his stepdaughter, his hand poised to slap her, his eyes holding something small and dark that reached inside the layers of protection Meg was trying to put up, making her shudder with fear.

"Please don't hit her again, Harlan," Ruth begged softly, her faded eyes flicking anxiously from her husband to her daughter.

The plea seemed to reach him and he let his hand drop. "You've raised a pair of whores, Ruth," he said angrily.

"I've done my best, Harlan. They're good girls, really they are."

"They're sluts," he snapped. "Sluts, just like all women." Ruth had no reply for that but only hung her head in apparent acquiescence. "I married you when no one else would have you and your two brats. I took all three of you in. If it wasn't for me, you'd all have starved in a gutter."

"Yes, Harlan," Ruth whispered, not lifting her gaze.

"This is what I get," he said, his eyes flicking from her to where Meg still stood, apparently frozen in the center of the room. "I won't have people talking about this family."

"Of course not, Harlan. I'm sure Meg didn't mean any harm." Meg saw her mother dart a quick look in her direction as if hoping she would agree that she hadn't meant any harm; that she'd help pour oil on the troubled waters. Meg said nothing, feeling as divorced from the scene being played out in front of her as if she'd been in another room.

"I won't have it," Harlan said again, but the worst of the rage seemed to have left him. He lifted one hand and smoothed it over his hair, and Meg noticed that his fingers were shaking. "I've a good name and I won't have it dragged through the mud."

"Of course not, Harlan," Ruth murmured soothingly.

"May I go now?" Meg asked, her voice as dead as she felt inside.

The question seemed to momentarily renew his flickering anger. "Get out. I can't stand to look at you."

Without another word, Meg turned and walked out of the room. She paused in the hall, picking up her purse and the kewpie doll from the table where she'd set them when she came home. She went to her room and closed the door behind her with a quiet little *snick* that seemed to reverberate inside her head.

She began to shiver and her purse hit the floor with a thud. But she held on to the kewpie doll as she crept onto her narrow bed. She lay down, drawing her knees up to her chest and closing her eyes. Her cheek ached and her mouth felt puffy as her torn lip started to swell.

She hugged the plump little doll closer, trying to remember how happy she'd been when Ty gave it to her. But the warmth of that memory wasn't enough to drive away the chill that had settled in her chest.

She'd been completely unprepared for the depth of her stepfather's anger. And no matter how she tried, she couldn't understand his accusations. Deep inside, a memory stirred—of hearing the same words, the same accusations. Only it had been Patsy he'd been calling a whore, and Meg had pulled the covers over her head, trying not to hear the ugly words, the hateful tone.

"Meggy?" Her mother's voice was hardly more than a whisper. She scratched at the door. Meg squeezed her eyes shut, wishing she could simply pretend to be asleep as the door opened and her mother crept into the room.

"Are you all right, sugar?"

How many times had she heard her mother ask that question after one of her father's beatings? She'd creep into the girls' room, nursing her own bruises even as she tried to soothe theirs. And she'd always ask the same question. *Are you all right, sugar?* And always, she got the same answer.

"I'm fine, Mama. He didn't really hurt me."

Meg opened her eyes as her mother sank down on the edge of the bed. So caught up in the past was she that Meg was half surprised not to see any marks on her mother's face, no evidence that the violence had turned in her direction after Meg left.

"I'm sorry, Meg." Ruth reached out to brush a strand of golden hair back from Meg's face. "I tried to tell you how upset he'd be."

"Why? Why should it upset him if I'm friends with Ty? The McKendricks are a good family. Why did he call me those things and get so angry just because I'd gone out with Ty?"

"He's worried about your reputation," Ruth said.

"He's worried about his own," Meg corrected her bitterly. "He said those same things to Patsy, didn't he? I remember hearing him shouting at her and then it would get quiet and after a while she'd come into our room crying. Did he hit her, too? Did he take a strap to her the way Pa used to do?"

"Don't think about what happened between him and your sister. That's all in the past," Ruth told her, her eyes shifting uneasily away from Meg's. "You just think about not riling him. He's not a bad man if you step a bit careful."

"You mean if I do exactly what he says, the way you always do?" Meg asked. The bitterness in her voice made her mother flush and look away.

"He's not a bad man," Ruth repeated, her voice weak.

Meg looked at her a moment longer and then closed her eyes. "I'd like to go to sleep now, Mama."

"Of course, sugar. You get some sleep and everything'll look better in the morning. You'll see."

Meg didn't respond. She heard her mother's quiet footsteps go across the room and then pause.

"Just try not to make him angry again, Meggy," Ruth pleaded softly.

Meg didn't open her eyes until she heard the door close behind her mother. When she lifted her lashes, a single tear slipped from the corner of her eye and was quickly absorbed by the pillow.

Hugging the plump, smiling little doll, she wished with all her heart that she was still child enough to believe her mother's promise.

Chapter 6

T he day after taking Meg to the fair, Ty opened the door to an unexpected visitor.

"Jack!" Ty's voice was warm with pleasure. "When did you get into town?"

"Yesterday. How've you been?" Grinning at each other, they shook hands.

"Pretty good, all things considered. Come on in."

"Is that coffee I smell?" Jack sniffed and gave Ty a hopeful look.

"Your mother still serving tea?" Ty asked, laughing as he held open the door so that Jack could enter the house.

"Yes. She's convinced that the consumption of coffee is the source of half this country's problems. Thinks if we'd all drink something more civilized, like tea, we'd be much better off. Course, things don't look too rosy in England, either, and the British drink gallons of the stuff."

Jack followed Ty into the kitchen as he spoke and watched eagerly as Ty took a cup from the row of hooks under one cupboard. He picked up the sturdy aluminum pot that sat on the back of the stove and filled the cup before handing it to his friend.

"It's hot," he warned as Jack lifted the cup to his mouth.

"It's coffee" was Jack's response as if nothing else mattered. Risking a scalded tongue, he sipped at the dark brew and then sighed with pleasure.

"You're an angel of mercy, Ty."

"I aim to please." Ty topped off his own cup and sat down at the table, gesturing Jack to a seat. "From the look of you, you must have spent the entire summer lying on a beach," he said, giving his friend's tan a look of mock disapproval.

The sun had bleached Jack's hair to a pale blond and the dark-gold tan made his eyes look emerald green in contrast. Jack Swanson had never had any trouble finding female companionship, and the tan gave him the look of an adventurer that surely wouldn't diminish his appeal. Ty was willing to bet that he'd had more than enough company for any trips he cared to make to the beach.

"A fellow can't work all the time," Jack protested, looking hurt.

"True enough. What are you doing in Iowa? I thought I was going to meet you in Los Angeles in a couple of weeks."

"Mother sent me a letter hinting rather loudly that I might want to come home for a visit," Jack said as he sat down. "I caught the train east and figured I could fulfill my filial duty and then drive back to California with you. If I'd known the weather was going to be like this, I might have ignored Mother's hints, no matter how loud they got."

Ty glanced out the window at the drizzling rain and shrugged. "You can't expect palm trees and sunny beaches in Iowa."

"I suppose not. Especially this time of year. I guess I should be grateful it's not snowing."

"It's a little early for snow," Ty said, but his eyes were thoughtful as he looked at the gray sky outside. Summer was over. Odd, he hadn't given it all that much thought lately. Yet, a few weeks ago, that's all he'd wished for.

"So, how was your summer?" Jack asked, almost as if reading his thoughts.

"Fine." *And wasn't it a surprise to be able to say that and mean it?*

"Beryl tells me you've had plenty of company," Jack commented, arching one dark brow in question.

"I thought Beryl was staying with your aunt Marion on Long Island. I wouldn't have dared risk spending the summer at home if she hadn't been gone. Mother would have spent all her time in Europe buying wedding presents," Ty said, smiling.

Beryl was Jack's younger sister, and it was one of Helen McKendrick's fondest fantasies that Beryl and Ty would one day marry. No matter how pointed their disinterest, she refused to give up hope.

"She was but she's home for a few days before going back to Vassar and apparently she has friends who keep her up-to-date on all the local gossip. So what gives?"

"With what?" Ty asked, annoyed to find himself flushing uncomfortably.

"With the gorgeous dame you've been seen around town with," Jack prompted in a creditable tough-guy voice.

"She's not a gorgeous dame," Ty snapped. "I mean, she's gorgeous but she's not a dame."

"Not a dame? Then this must be love," Jack said teasingly, pressing one hand over his heart.

"Lord save me from small towns." Ty stood up and went to the stove, lifting the coffeepot to add coffee to his nearly full cup. "Everyone spends too much time wondering what everyone else is doing. I've spent some time with Meg Harper, that's all."

"Meg Harper. Patsy Harper's little sister?" Jack's voice was sharp, all the teasing humor abruptly gone. Ty turned and looked at him, the coffeepot still in his hand.

"Yes. Do you know her sister?"

"No." It was Ty's turn to raise his brows, and Jack seemed to realize that the flat denial sounded odd. "She was in school with us, I think."

"A few years behind us," Ty said. He topped off his friend's coffee cup and set the pot back on the stove before sitting down again. "You dunked her pigtail in an inkwell, if memory serves me."

"Could be."

"You sounded like you remembered her pretty well," Ty said curiously.

"She was pretty. You know me. I never forget a pretty girl." Jack lifted one shoulder in a half shrug and grinned though the expression didn't quite reach his eyes. But if there was more that could be said about Patsy Harper, Jack didn't seem to have any inclination to say it, and Ty decided not to pursue the question.

"Her sister's more than pretty," Ty said slowly. "She's a real beauty. Just a kid, of course, but beautiful."

"She can't be all that much of a kid," Jack protested. "She's got to be, what? Seventeen? Eighteen?"

"Seventeen."

"Lots of girls are married by that age. Beryl says you've been squiring her about quite a lot."

"Beryl seems to say a great deal," Ty said with some annoyance. "Doesn't she have studying to do or something?"

"Not in the summer, Ty." Whatever shadows might have been in Jack's green eyes were gone, and they shone with laughter. "That's what summer vacation is about—you don't have to study."

"Well, next year maybe she should take a few extra courses. It would give her something to do besides keep tabs on me."

"It wasn't Beryl," Jack protested. "It was actually Louise Draper who told Beryl you and Meg had been seen together a few times."

"We've happened to go the movie at the same time and a couple of times, I bought her a sundae at Barnett's afterward. Not much to tell."

"Well, it's apparently enough to set people talking," Jack said.

"She's just a kid, for crying out loud," Ty snapped angrily. "I'm practically old enough to be her father."

Jack's brows shot up, his eyes widening. "Not unless you were very precocious."

"All right. Her older brother, then," Ty conceded.

"I could point out that you could also have been Anne Masterson's older brother, but there wasn't much brotherliness about your relationship with her," Jack said.

"You know what I mean," Ty said irritably.

He got up again, shoving his chair back so that legs scraped across the black and white linoleum in a way that would have made his mother scold. Restless, he walked to the window and leaned one hip against the deep sink.

He didn't like the idea that people had been linking his name and Meg's, though he realized he should have expected it. He might have been away from home for ten years, but he shouldn't have forgotten how fast gossip could get started in a small town.

"It doesn't matter, really," Jack said, his eyes on Ty's brooding expression. "You'll be leaving soon and any gossip will die down pretty quickly after that."

"Yeah." He heard the flatness in his voice and made an effort to shake off the odd mood that had gripped him for the last few days—ever since he'd realized that his time in Iowa was coming to an end. He straightened away from the sink and turned to meet Jack's curious look. "You're right. Besides, there wasn't anything to gossip about in the first place. It must have been a slow summer for most of the town's old biddies," he said, forcing a grin.

"Probably. That's one of the problems with small towns. People blow things all out of proportion." If there was still a lingering doubt in Jack's eyes, Ty was able to ignore it. He changed the subject.

"So, tell me what you've been doing. How much work are we going to have?"

It seemed to Meg as if the summer were rushing to an end. She wanted to grab hold of it somehow and force the days to slow down. It didn't seem possible that it was already September. But the nights were cool and it wouldn't be long before the grass would crunch underfoot in the mornings, coated by a beautiful crystalline layer of hoarfrost.

In years past, she would have said that autumn was her

favorite season. She'd always loved to see the leaves change, summer's deep green reluctantly giving way to soft golds and reds. And in a few weeks, those, too, were forced to surrender to winter's paler shades.

But this year she wanted to cling to summer, to force it to linger past its allotted time. For when summer was gone, Ty would leave Regret. And take her heart with him.

"I think she was a fool to wait for him," Ty said.

"She loved him. What else could she do?" Meg looked at him as they exited from the theater.

"She could have found someone who wasn't a thief."

"But she loved Blackie."

"He was no good," Ty said critically. "He lied to her. She was arrested for a crime he committed and nearly went to prison."

"But then he realized that he loved her and came forward and confessed," Meg pointed out.

"Too little, too late, as far as I can see. She should have married the lawyer."

"She didn't love him," Meg protested.

"He could have supported her."

"That's not enough to make a marriage work." Meg shook her head, frowning a little. "She was in love with Blackie. She couldn't have married another man."

"Even if that other man would take better care of her? Even knowing that Blackie was going to spend five years in prison and would probably be the same lying, cheating crook when he came out?"

"She loved him," Meg said stubbornly.

"And love conquers all?" Ty asked, his mouth twisting cynically.

"I think so." Meg lifted her chin, refusing to back down even if he did think her a foolish romantic. How much more foolish would he think her if he knew she was halfway to being in love with him?

"It would be nice if you were right." His expression softened in a smile that held real affection, making Meg's heart ache. She'd have given anything to be able to read something deeper into that look.

"Of course I'm right." She smiled up at him, wishing with all her heart that love really *did* conquer all.

Ty's smile faded, replaced by a small frown. "What happened to your mouth?" He touched the tip of one finger to the faint trace of swelling still visible in her lower lip.

Meg pulled back, lifting her own hand to touch her lip as if she didn't quite know what he were talking about. It had been two days since her stepfather had hit her, and the swelling was almost gone. If she hadn't been standing in the spill of light from Barnett's window, Ty couldn't possibly have noticed anything wrong.

"This? It was so silly, I hate to admit it." She hoped he couldn't hear the forced note in her laughter. "I dropped my napkin under the dinner table and hit my mouth when I leaned down to pick it up again. Isn't that ridiculous?"

"You must have hit it pretty hard," he said, still frowning.

"Not really. I think I must have hit it just right. You know how things like that are." She hoped he *didn't* know, hoped he'd accept the excuse she'd thought up just in case she had to explain the swelling to anyone. If he knew that her stepfather had hit her because he'd seen her with Ty, she might not even have these last few precious days with him.

"It's almost completely healed now," she said, seeing that he still looked concerned. "I'd almost forgotten it."

"You should be more careful."

"I should be less clumsy," she corrected lightly.

"That, too." He grinned and she was relieved that he'd apparently accepted her explanation. "Buy you a sundae?" he asked, just as he had every Saturday for the past three months.

"That would be nice," she said.

It took all her willpower to keep from looking over her shoulder at her stepfather's hotel as they walked up the brightly lit steps of Barnett's. It seemed as if she could almost feel his small eyes boring into her back, counting up the imagined sins he could charge her with when he got home.

She pushed the memory of their last confrontation away,

determined to enjoy her sundae and Ty's company. Later she'd pay whatever price she had to with her stepfather.

"Hiya, Meg. Ty." Eddie's cheerful greeting helped chase away Meg's dark thoughts.

"Hello, Eddie." She slid onto a stool and smiled at him. "How's business?"

"Can't complain, I guess. Ask me in a coupla weeks and I might not say the same, though."

"Why?"

"Folks just don't eat as much ice cream when the weather starts cooling off. Things'll start slowing down pretty soon, I imagine, what with summer pretty well over."

"I'd guess they would." Meg heard the flatness in her own voice and she felt Ty glance at her, but she kept her attention on Eddie's cheerful face. "I'll have a Miami Flip," she said, forcing a smile she didn't feel.

"Miami Flip you got," Eddie promised. "Usual for you, Ty?"

"Coffee soda," Ty confirmed.

"Coffee and Miami, comin' right up."

Eddie's departure left a silence that seemed strangely awkward.

Summer *was* almost over. No matter how much she wanted to pretend otherwise, nothing was going to make time suddenly reverse its march and make the leaves bright green and the flowers bloom again.

Or make Ty stay in Iowa.

"Hard to believe it's September already," she said softly. "I guess summer really is gone."

"I guess so." He didn't seem to be overjoyed by the thought.

"Your parents should be back from Europe soon, shouldn't they?" she continued, trying to sound as if she were simply making polite conversation.

"The boat will dock any day now." Ty stirred restlessly on the shiny red stool.

"Then you'll be going back to California soon." She

couldn't have said just why she felt the need to rub salt into her wounds, but the compulsion was there.

"Yes." Ty frowned at the shiny marble counter and then turned his head to look at her. "Jack Swanson got into town a couple of days ago. He says he thinks there's a couple of jobs waiting for us when we get back to Hollywood."

"That's wonderful." Meg felt herself bleeding inside, the pain sharp and hard in her diaphragm, making her wonder that she could still breathe. "I guess I'll still be seeing you at the theater. Only you'll be on the screen this time," she said lightly.

"Maybe." Ty's gaze was searching on her face. Meg didn't know what he was looking for, but she presented him with a serene expression. Not for anything would she let him see that her world was crumbling around her.

"One coffee ice cream soda and one Miami Flip, as ordered." Eddie's cheery voice cut through the silence like a hot knife through butter.

Ty looked away and Meg pulled the sweet citrusy concoction toward her, her appetite gone as she wondered if she'd imagined the question she'd seen in his eyes.

"Ty! What a surprise to see you here." Ty turned at the sound of Jack's voice.

"Jack. What are you doing here?"

"Buying a bottle of perfume for Beryl. Her birthday's coming up, you know."

Ty didn't know anything of the kind. Last he'd heard Jack's sister's birthday was sometime in April. September seemed to be a bit early to be buying gifts. But then Jack's eyes swung to Meg and he knew exactly what his friend was up to.

"Introduce me?" Jack suggested, raising his eyebrows in Ty's direction.

"Jack, this is Meg Harper. Meg, this is Jack Swanson, a former friend of mine," he added ominously.

"Pleased to meet you, Meg." Jack ignored Ty's scowl and slid onto the stool on the other side of Meg. "Pay no attention to Ty. He's just jealous because I'm better looking than he is.''

"And a bigger buffoon, too," Ty said.

"See?" Jack lifted his brows and grinned at Meg. "Jealousy, plain and simple." He sighed. "People don't realize how difficult is life for someone of my good looks and talent."

"It must be very hard for you," Meg said, her solemn look spoiled by the tuck that appeared in her cheek.

"Yes." Jack's lugubrious expression was pathetic to behold. "But I bear up under the pressure rather well, don't you think?"

"You're very noble," she agreed.

"You see, Ty, *someone* understands the burden I bear." Jack's laughing green eyes met his across Meg's head.

"It isn't the burden you bear that bothers me, Jack. It's the burden you *are*."

He sipped glumly on his coffee soda, listening with half an ear as Jack went out of his way to be outrageously charming. And from the sound of Meg's soft laughter, it was working. The thought annoyed him in some way he couldn't quite define. If he hadn't known better, Ty might have thought he was jealous. But the idea was so ridiculous that he dismissed it instantly.

"Fill it up, Joe."

"Goin' someplace, Ty?" Joe made no immediate move toward the gas pump, lingering to question his customer's purchase with the familiarity of someone who'd had to help that same customer pull his first flivver out of a ditch less than a week after he got it.

"Nowhere in particular. Just like having a full tank." Ty didn't mind the question. It was the kind of thing he expected in this town, where everyone seemed to feel they had not just an interest in but a right to know everyone else's business.

"It's a good feeling," Joe agreed. He pulled a rag from the pocket of his overalls and rubbed a faint smudge from the roadster's gleaming finish. "Not as many filling their tanks these days."

"Business must be slow."

"Not too bad." Joe rocked back on his heels and squinted up the road. "Folks're keeping their automobiles 'stead of gettin' new ones. I keep pretty busy doin' repairs. Still, can't say as how it wouldn't be nice to see things lookin' up for everybody."

"I'll second that," Ty said.

"Reckon most of us would," Joe said, his grin revealing a gap where a front tooth was missing.

"The worst thing about small towns is that everyone is so friendly," Jack commented as Joe finally departed to fill the gas tank.

"I much prefer people to be unfriendly," Ty agreed solemnly.

"You know what I mean. You order a chicken dinner and you get a lecture from the waitress on the latest government study that says it's important to eat plenty of red meat to keep your blood healthy. You ask for some gas and instead of getting a full tank and paying your eighteen cents a gallon and going on your way, you have to have a philosophical discussion about the current state of the country."

"Get up on the wrong side this morning?" Ty asked, grinning at Jack's disgruntled expression.

"Every morning I'm in this town." Jack hunched his shoulders under his jacket. "The place gives me claustrophobia."

"You're right. Big cities are so much more wide open," Ty commented dryly.

"You know what I mean. In a city, you may be surrounded by people but not one of them is going to walk up to you and comment on how they once helped your mother diaper you. Or how you were their worst pupil in second grade or . . ."

But Ty lost the thread of Jack's complaints. Half aware of a feeling that someone was watching him, he turned his head and found his eyes colliding with those of a man sitting in the rusty black Model T on the other side of the pumps. It took Ty a moment to put a name to the round face and pale eyes.

Harlan Davis might run the only hotel in Regret, but Ty's path had rarely crossed his.

This was Meg's stepfather; the man she'd said was small in mind as much as body. The knowledge sharpened his interest, making his gaze linger on the other man. Davis's skin seemed almost unnaturally pale but perhaps that was to be expected. After all, a man who owned a hotel probably didn't have much chance to spend time in the sun.

Ty brought his eyes back to the older man's and was caught off guard by the cold hatred that made his eyes the color of heavy ice. Surprised, he looked away, and when he looked back, Joe's nephew, who worked with him at the filling station, was standing in front of Davis, blocking Ty's view.

"You know, the least I expect from my friends is that they listen to me when I whine." Jack's disgusted complaint dragged Ty's attention back to him, but he was acutely aware of the sound of the Model T's engine as Davis pulled away from the gas pump. He watched as the car pulled onto the road and headed toward the center of town.

"Someone you know?" Jack asked, following Ty's gaze.

"Harlan Davis," Ty said, still watching the car.

"Davis. Owns the hotel?"

"Yes. He married Meg's mother after her father died."

"He didn't look as if he was particularly fond of you," Jack commented, having seen the exchange of glances between Ty and the other man. "Does he know you've been seeing Meg?"

"I don't know. And I haven't been 'seeing' Meg," Ty said, exasperated.

"What do you do? Close your eyes when you're with her?" Jack lifted his hand in apology at the less than amused look his friend threw him. "Okay, okay. You're not 'seeing' her. But for someone who's not seeing her, you spend a lot of time with her."

Joe's reappearance prevented Ty from responding to Jack's comment. Not that it deserved a comment, he thought irritably. For some reason, Jack insisted on making something out of his relationship with Meg, as if it couldn't possibly be what it was, which was nothing more than a casual friendship.

"She's a nice kid," he said as he pulled away from the gas pumps. He was aware of the doubt in the look Jack slanted him but he ignored it. Jack just didn't understand.

"I had a wire from my parents yesterday." Ty heard the soft catch of Meg's breath and realized that he'd spoken too abruptly, firing the words out as if they were bullets.

"Has their ship docked?" They'd just left the theater and, for once, neither of them had any interest in talking about the picture they'd just seen.

"A few days ago."

Now why was he so reluctant to admit that? Ty wondered irritably. His parents were back, he'd fulfilled his promise to his mother. He'd survived a summer in his hometown, and now he could get on with his life with a clear conscience.

"Are they going to stay in the city or come straight home?" There was nothing but polite interest in the question. So why did he seem to think that her voice wasn't quite steady?

"A little shopping, I think."

"That will be nice for your mother," Meg said politely.

Instead of walking to Barnett's, they'd crossed the street to the small park. They hadn't discussed the change in their routine, but both seemed to feel the need to avoid bright lights and people. It was growing dark earlier these days, a sure sign that summer was well and truly over, as was the chill in the evening air. Ty shoved his hands in the pockets of his trousers as they stepped onto the grass.

"Then you'll be leaving soon?" This time there was no mistaking the tightness in her voice, and Ty felt something twist tight and hard in his chest.

"Yes."

"So I guess this is good-bye," she said with a forced good cheer that fell abysmally flat.

Ty stopped abruptly, catching her hands in his and turning her to face him, trying to see her expression in the faint light from the streetlamps. Big maple trees blocked most of it, but there was enough for him to see the pale oval of her face and the glitter of her eyes.

It wasn't supposed to be this hard to say good-bye, he thought resentfully. This wasn't the way he'd told himself it would be. "I'm going to miss you, Meg."

"I'll miss you, too." Her smile was little more than a shadowy movement in the dark, but he didn't need bright lights to know that it didn't reach her eyes.

Damn, the last thing he'd wanted was to hurt her. She was such a sweet kid.

"You're a sweet—" Her fingers pressed against his mouth, stilling the final word.

"Don't." Her lips twisted in a half smile. "Please don't call me a kid, Ty. Not now."

Hardly aware of the movement, he reached up to close his fingers around the hand at his mouth. He pulled her hand away but kept his fingers curled around it.

"You've made this summer a pleasure," he said. "Can I tell you you're a sweet girl?"

"Yes." Her voice sounded muffled and he caught the sheen of moisture on her cheek.

"Ah, Meg." He lifted his free hand, brushing his fingers across her skin, feeling the dampness of her tears. "The last thing in the world I wanted to do was hurt you."

"You haven't. I just have something in my eye." He caught the white gleam of her teeth as she tried to smile and felt that odd pain in his chest again.

"Ah, Meg," he said softly, unable to express the feelings all tangled up inside him.

Acting on instinct, he let his fingers slide from her cheek into the soft golden length of her hair, tilting her head up to his. *Just one kiss,* he told himself. *He was leaving soon. What harm could one kiss do?*

It was just like before. Only this time her mouth opened to him without any coaxing. Without giving himself time to think, to question, Ty deepened the kiss, letting his tongue taste the delicate inner surface of her lip before sliding into the welcoming warmth of her mouth.

She melted into his arms, her hands coming up to clutch his shoulders, her slender body pliant as a young willow in his embrace. Her breasts pressed against his chest, her hair sifted through his fingers, and her mouth was his—only his.

A light breeze drifted over the grass, blowing the soft rayon of her skirt against his legs, seeming to wrap their embrace still tighter until it seemed that not even a shadow could have slipped between their entwined figures.

A few yards away, Regret went about its business, a few couples braving the evening cool to stroll down the street, peering in the windows of the closed stores. A truck rattled by on the street, the smell of manure drifting from its rusted bed. But for all the notice Ty and Meg took, they could have been alone in the middle of the prairie with nothing but the sky and earth for company.

Feeling the sweet surrender in her, it took every ounce of Ty's willpower not to pull Meg deeper into the sheltering trees, to press her down into the soft grass, and— He slammed a mental door shut on what might come after. This was Meg, not some loose woman he'd met in a bar next to the airfield. This was sweet, *innocent* Meg.

He dragged his mouth from hers but it was more than he could do to release her completely. Leaning his forehead against hers, he tried to steady his breathing, tried to remember all the reasons something that felt so right was so wrong.

"Maybe it's just as well I'm leaving," he said ruefully. "You make it awfully easy to forget what's right."

Then forget. Meg had to swallow the words back. *This is right,* a part of her wanted to shout. Being here in his arms was right. It had to be.

But it wasn't, of course. She might be young, as he was so fond of reminding her, but she wasn't too young to know where this could lead. If he were staying, if she'd had even the slightest hope that he could love her, then she could have ignored every moral precept she'd ever known for the chance to be his.

But he was leaving. She might never see him again. And she wanted, on some deep visceral level, for him to remember her with affection and not with the regret he'd feel if they gave in to the need that tugged at them both. Drawing on all her self-control, she stepped back. Ty's arms fell away from her and she immediately felt chilled in a way that had nothing to do with the temperature.

"I shouldn't have done that," he said.

"No," she agreed bleakly. Because it had only served to remind her, yet again, of everything she could never have. Feeling his eyes on her face, sensing his concern, she forced a smile. "But there's no harm done. Maybe we could blame it on spring fever."

"It's not spring," Ty reminded her.

"Autumn fever, then," she conceded. She tugged her thin jacket closer around her slender body, unable to suppress a small shiver.

"You're cold," Ty exclaimed. "I should get you home before you catch a chill."

The cold she felt was deep inside but Meg didn't correct him. Neither did she mention that they were forgoing their usual visit to Barnett's soda fountain. She was torn between conflicting urges—the need to prolong the evening, to hold on to every moment, and the need to be alone so she could let go of the tears burning behind her eyes. So she said nothing.

She walked beside Ty to where he'd parked the roadster. The silence between them was thick with things unspoken. Meg wished she could think of something light and witty to say to diffuse the tension, but all she could think of was that this was probably her last evening with him, and the knowledge closed her throat.

When he took her arm to help her step into the roadster, Meg felt a shivery awareness of his light touch. She glanced at Ty, her eyes meeting his, and knew he felt the same awareness; knew also that it didn't change anything. She was still too young. He was still leaving. This time her shiver was caused by a deep inner chill.

"Shall I put the top up?" Ty asked, looking concerned.

"No. I like it down." She tilted her head to smile up at him, hoping that the light from the nearby streetlamp was too dim to reveal the shadows in her eyes.

"It's really too late in the year to have it down," Ty muttered as he slid behind the wheel.

"I like it," Meg said firmly. She didn't care if the wind carried a distinct edge to it. With the top down, it was almost as if summer hadn't quite ended.

Neither of them spoke on the short drive to Meg's home. No matter how she tried, Meg couldn't come up with a snappy topic of conversation. All she could think of was that this might very well be the last time she saw Ty. The thought was so painful that she was forced to admit to herself that her feelings went much deeper than they had any business doing. She'd slipped from a girlish crush into love with hardly a whisper of warning.

He stopped the car in front of the plain little house and got out. She watched him walk around the front of the car to open her door. She felt his hand close over hers as he helped her from the car, and it took a conscious effort for her to keep her fingers from clutching his.

Vaguely she was aware of her stepfather's car parked beside the house, and some part of her registered that he'd undoubtedly be furious that she'd been out with Ty again. But she couldn't feel any real concern. She couldn't feel anything but the terrible pain in her chest as she looked up at Ty. She'd always known this would happen, that they'd have to say goodbye, and she'd thought herself prepared for it. But nothing could have prepared her for this kind of pain.

"Well, I'll see you around," he said after a moment, just the way he always did when they parted.

"Sure." Meg forced herself to smile, determined that he wouldn't remember her with tears in her eyes. "I'll be watching for you on the big screen," she said lightly.

"Right."

The moment stretched. Meg's eyes clung to his face, drinking in as much as she could see in the shadowy light that spilled from the porch. She needed this memory to last a long time.

"Well, I'll see you around," he said again.

Meg realized that he felt awkward about walking away from her, that the first move would have to come from her. Though she could have stayed right where she was for the rest of her life, she loved him enough to make this parting easier for him. Swallowing hard, she forced a casual smile.

"See you," she said lightly.

Feeling as if a knife were lodged in her chest, she turned and walked away from him. Behind her, there was a moment's silence and then she heard his footsteps, quick and impatient, as if he were anxious to put the moment behind him. She flinched at the sound of his car door closing. Her knees were shaking so badly that she reached out to catch one of the supporting posts to pull herself onto the porch. And then the solid roar of the engine froze her in place.

Every instinct screamed at her to turn and watch him leave, but she didn't move. If she didn't actually see him go, then maybe he hadn't really gone. But she couldn't close her ears. She heard the slight hesitation as he reached the end of the lane and glanced both ways before pulling onto the road. And then the sound of the engine rapidly fading away as he headed back toward Regret.

He was gone.

Meg sagged against the post but she didn't cry. The feeling of loss was too deep for tears. Later, perhaps, she'd be able to cry, but for now, her eyes were dry.

Forcing herself upright, she crossed the narrow porch and pulled open the screen. She pushed open the front door, hearing the familiar whine of the hinges, remembering that she still hadn't soaped them. It was not much warmer in the house than it was outside. Harlan Davis didn't believe on wasting money on firing up the coal heater in the basement any earlier in the year than was absolutely necessary, which meant that, for a few weeks every year, it was necessary to layer on sweaters to stay warm. But Meg barely noticed the temperature. The chill she felt was deep inside.

"Margaret. Come in here at once." Her stepfather's voice was a nasal bark and Meg closed her eyes for a moment. She'd nearly forgotten that he was home.

She pushed the front door shut with a soft thud and turned to walk into the living room. She knew what was going to happen. This time she couldn't count on her mother to interfere, just as she'd never counted on her to interfere when her father got out his belt.

She felt completely numb. Whatever physical pain Harlan Davis inflicted couldn't possibly compare to the ache she already felt. Bruises and belt marks eventually faded. But the ache in her heart—that was something she'd carry with her for the rest of her life.

Chapter 7

Saying good-bye to Meg had been harder than Ty had expected. He kept seeing her face, the pain she'd tried to hide. He'd told himself that a friendship wouldn't do any harm, that Meg wouldn't get hurt. But she had and it was his fault. And he'd have to live with that knowledge for a long time to come.

He'd done his best to ignore the feelings he saw in her eyes. He'd convinced himself that friendship was all Meg felt, that she didn't want any more from him than that. But he'd been lying to himself. What was worse: He'd known she was getting in too deep, and he hadn't done anything to stop it.

All the truisms about water under the bridge and not crying over spilled milk didn't serve to soothe his aching conscience. He'd made the wrong decision, and because of it, someone he liked had ended up hurt. It did no good to tell himself that Meg was young enough to recover quickly from a bruised heart. Whatever she felt for him—or thought she felt— was real to her, and the pain was just as real.

The fact that it had begun raining not long after he left Meg did nothing to improve Ty's mood. He'd put the top up on the roadster when he got home, darkness making the job twice as hard as it normally would have been. It had been foolish to leave the top down as long as he had—common sense said it should have been put up days ago, when it became obvious that summer was over. Only he hadn't wanted to admit that undeniable fact.

The rain started out as a light shower, steadily increasing as the night wore on until somewhere near midnight, it became a downpour. Ty hadn't bothered going to bed, knowing that sleep would be impossible. The noise of the rain beating against the windows would have made it so even if his guilty conscience hadn't already done the job.

He tried to read, settling into his father's big leather chair next to the radiator and picking up an issue of *The Saturday Evening Post* from the stack that had accumulated over the summer. But he couldn't concentrate on the printed words. He couldn't get the image of Meg's big blue eyes out of his mind. Or forget the way her mouth had softened under his, her slim body warm in his arms.

"Dammit!" Ty shot to his feet, tossing the magazine aside. "Dammit, dammit, dammit!"

He strode restlessly to the front window, twitching aside the curtains to stare out into the rain-drenched darkness. How long before his parents came home? A week ago he'd been half hoping they'd decide to extend their stay in New York for a few days. Now he could hardly contain his impatience. Maybe once he left Regret, he'd be able to stop thinking about Meg and get on with his plans for the future. Plans that did not include a girl with hair the color of sun-ripened wheat and eyes as blue as a summer sky.

If she were older . . . Or he hadn't already planned things out . . . But she wasn't and he had and that's all there was to it. She'd get over whatever infatuation she might have felt for him, and he'd eventually stop feeling lower than a snake's belly and get on with his life.

He'd learned one thing for certain: The next broken bone he suffered was going to have to heal without benefit of Iowa sunshine.

Ty started to turn away from the window when something caught his eye. A half-glimpsed movement, a pale shape in the blackness outside. Ty narrowed his eyes, trying to see through the rain and darkness. There it was again, a little clearer this time, closer. Was that someone standing next to the low hedge that separated the McKendricks' property from the Vanderbilts'?

The figure, hardly more than a lighter shadow in the darkness, moved again, edging closer to the house and then stopping. Ty felt a shiver run up his spine as all the childhood tales of banshees and ghosts flashed through his mind.

"Idiot," he muttered. If there was anyone out there at all, they were probably lost—maybe their car had stalled and they were seeking shelter from the rain. They'd probably seen the light in the window.

He let the curtain fall and walked to the front door, pulling it open and flipping on the front light. The moment he stepped out onto the porch, cold, damp air cut through his shirt. He hadn't realized how the temperature had dropped, another sign that summer was well and truly over.

"Hello?" He peered out into the darkness, seeing the figure more clearly now. A woman, he thought. "Do you need help?"

There was no answer unless he counted the fact that she swayed slightly and took a hesitant step forward. A gust of wind blew rain in under the overhang of the porch roof, making Ty shiver.

"Do you need help?" he asked again, thoughts of ghosts drifting through his mind, despite his best efforts to put them from him. There was something a little eerie about the slim, silent figure standing on the lawn at midnight.

"Ty." His name was barely audible over the sound of the rain. Ty felt the hair on the back of his neck stand on end. Meg. She'd been so much on his mind that, for a moment, he thought she might be a hallucination brought on by a guilty conscience.

"Meg?" He heard the disbelief in his own voice as he stepped off the porch. What on earth would she be doing here at this hour of the night?

He was wearing only heavy socks, which were soaked through the moment he stepped onto the wet grass. But he didn't notice the discomfort. Nor did he pay any attention to the cold rain that found its way through his shirt and slid icy fingers under his collar.

"Meg?" he asked again, still not completely certain she was real.

Again there was no response. She didn't even lift her head when he stopped in front of her. She had no umbrella, nothing to shield her from the weather. Unless he counted the faded rose-colored sweater that looked several sizes too big.

"Meg?" A convulsive shiver ran through her, but she didn't lift her head or speak.

"What's wrong?" He stretched one hand toward her, needing to touch her to confirm the reality of her. His fingers brushed her shoulder and she shied back like a frightened animal, her fingers twisting deeper into the wet wool of the sweater. He caught a glimpse of her face as she jerked back from him. They were just beyond the pale glow from the porch, but he didn't need light to see the fear in her eyes. It radiated from her. He let his hand drop, feeling a chill that had nothing to do with the rain.

"What are you doing out here?" he asked, trying to make his voice low and soothing. She was silent so long, he thought she wasn't going to respond.

"I didn't know where else to go," she said just when he'd given up hope of getting an answer. Her voice was so soft that he had to strain to hear it over the gurgle of water that ran through the rain gutter overhead.

She didn't know where else to go? What the hell did that mean?

"Come inside."

He stretched his hand out to her, moving slowly, trying not to startle her. She didn't shy away this time but neither did she respond. He wasn't sure she'd even heard him.

"Come inside," he said again, more firmly this time. He took hold of her elbow, feeling her jerk at the light touch. But he didn't release her. "It's cold and wet out here. We can talk inside." Fear was a hard, cold lump in his gut, but his voice was soft and soothing, coaxing her to trust him.

"I shouldn't have come here," she said. "But I didn't know where else to go. I tried to think of somewhere but I couldn't." Her voice was dazed, as if she were talking to herself. She seemed unaware of the icy rain that plastered her hair to her head and soaked through her clothes.

But Ty was not so oblivious. Rain dripped off his hair and soaked his shirt so that the soft flannel clung to his shoulders and back. He'd only been outside a few minutes and he was thoroughly chilled. God alone knew how long Meg had been out in the rain, but she had to be chilled to the bone.

"You have to come inside now," he told her. When she made no move to obey either his voice or the urging of his fingers on her elbow, Ty's patience snapped.

Taking a quick step toward her, he bent and slid one arm under her knees, the other around her shoulders, and swept her into his arms. She cried out, a harsh, wordless sound of fear, and her body jerked in a quick, convulsive attempt to escape, but Ty had no intention of letting her go. His arms tightened around her, controlling her struggles effortlessly as he turned toward the house.

Whatever had happened, she was so lost in the terror of it that the fear lapped out to encompass him. The thought that Meg was afraid of him was as sharp as a knife in his chest. But as he reached the top of the steps, she suddenly went limp in his hold, her slender body collapsing against him as she turned her face into his damp shirt. Ty's arms at once tightened and gentled around her, and he felt something hard and painful twist in his chest.

He maneuvered his burden into the house, kicking the door shut behind him. He felt Meg's body jerk in response to the thud of door meeting the frame and murmured soothingly, his arms cradling her in wordless reassurance.

The warmth inside the house contrasted sharply with the cold outside. Ty felt a shiver work its way up his spine. He carried her into the kitchen, which was the warmest room in the house. The first thing to do was to get her warm and dry, and then he could work on finding out what had happened to bring her to him in the middle of the night.

He hooked his foot around the leg of a chair and pulled it out from the table, scooting it close to the warmth of the stove. The smell of coffee lingered in the room from the pot he'd made earlier. It was probably black as sin by now, but he could heat it up and get some of it down Meg.

Meg's fingers clung to his shirt when he tried to set her down, and Ty felt his heart contract painfully.

"It's all right, honey," he said, unaware of the endearment. "Let me go so I can get some towels and get you dried off."

Her face still buried in his chest, she shook her head, her slender fingers knotted in his shirt as if clinging to a lifeline. For a moment Ty considered just sitting down with her in his lap, but he was nearly as wet as she was.

"Come on, Meg," he coaxed. "I'm cold and you must be nearly frozen to the bone. We're both going to catch our death of colds. I won't go far."

Whether it was the promise to stay close or the comment that he was cold, too, Ty didn't know, but Meg's fingers slowly relaxed their panicked grip, and she allowed him to set her on the chair.

"I'm going to get some towels," he said. "You stay right here."

She kept her head bent, her dripping wet hair falling forward to conceal her face, but she nodded slowly to indicate her understanding. Ty hesitated a moment longer, reluctant to leave her alone, wanting to demand explanations. But the goose bumps that rose on his skin reminded him that explanations had to wait.

He took the stairs three at a time, snatching an armful of towels from the linen closet and a wool bathrobe from his bedroom before hurrying back downstairs. He didn't realize how worried he'd been that Meg might have disappeared back out into the rain until he stepped into the kitchen and saw her sitting just where he'd left her.

She was shivering convulsively, her slender body shaking with cold. Thinking it couldn't do any harm to start warming her from the inside out, Ty turned the heat on under the aluminum percolator. Though the room was warm, he lit the oven and left the door open. At this point, he didn't think there was such a thing as too much heat.

"You need to get out of those wet clothes," he said briskly. "There's a stack of towels so you can dry off and then wrap up in the robe. I'm going to go change into dry clothes and then we'll get some hot coffee down you and get you warmed up. Okay?"

There was no response from her. She sat there, her head bowed, water dripping from her clothing to puddle on the floor. Rain had taken the warm gold from her hair. It clung to her skull in dull brown strands and fell around her face, so that all Ty could see was the top of her head and the curtain of wet hair.

"Meg?" The only response was the convulsive shiver that shook her shoulders.

What the hell had happened? Ty swallowed down the fear that threatened to choke him and sank back on his heels in front of her chair. She didn't react to his nearness, unless he counted the shivers that trembled over her.

"What's wrong, Meg?" he asked softly. "What happened?"

But the only response was that her fingers tightened their hold on the faded sweater, her knuckles showing white under her skin.

Moving slowly, Ty reached out and slid his hand under the curtain of wet hair that concealed her face. She started and pulled her head back, trying to avoid the light touch, but he caught her arm, holding her still with gentle but implacable fingers.

"Let me see," he said quietly, cupping his fingers under her chin. Though she remained stiff under his touch, she stopped trying to pull away, letting him tilt her face up and brush the strands of wet hair back. Though he'd been half expecting what he saw, Ty sucked in a sharp breath when he saw her face.

"My God." The quiet words were more prayer than profanity.

Bruises marked both cheeks and there was a scrape high on one cheekbone, an angry red streak across the pallor of her skin. Her mouth—the soft lips he'd kissed a few hours before —was puffy and tender looking, traces of blood on her chin telling of a split lip. There was the beginnings of a dark bruise along her jaw, as if she'd been punched. And her left eye was swollen partially shut, blue and purple shadows just starting to show around it.

"Who did this to you?" Rage made his voice thick, and his fingers unconsciously tensed against her chin.

"I'm sorry," Meg whispered, reacting to his anger, quick, unreasoning fear flaring in her eyes. "I'm sorry." She twisted her head away from his touch. "I didn't mean . . . I shouldn't have come here."

"It's all right, Meg." Ty made an effort to soften his voice, to tamp down the anger that churned in his gut.

"I'm sorry."

"It's all right," he soothed. "Just tell me what happened."

But she shook her head, her eyes wide and frightened. "I can't. Please. I can't."

"Okay. It's okay, Meg." Ty smoothed her hair back from her face, trying to reassure her with words and touch. "We can talk about it later, okay?"

She nodded uncertainly, leaving Ty to wonder how much she understood of what he was saying. She lowered her head, her hair swinging forward to conceal her bruised face again. Ty stared at her in silence for a moment, feeling completely out of his depth.

"Here, let's get you out of those wet clothes," he said finally, trying to sound calm. But when he reached for the front of the sweater, she shook her head violently, her fingers tightening until the knuckles gleamed white under her skin.

"It's soaked through, Meg." But she only shook her head again, her whole body tensed for flight. He caught a glimpse of her eyes, wild and frightened, and decided that it wasn't worth fighting her to get her clothes off.

"Okay. You can keep the sweater for now," he said

soothingly. She couldn't possibly get any wetter or colder than she already was, he decided.

He stood up and looked around the kitchen, trying to decide what to do next. His gut churned with the need to know who had hurt her; to find whoever it was and kill the son of a bitch. But taking care of Meg came first. Ty thrust his fingers through his wet hair, combing it back from his forehead with a quick, impatient gesture.

Glancing down at Meg, he saw that she still hadn't moved, unless it was possible that she'd somehow shrunk deeper into the dubious protection of the dripping sweater. Remembering the blood on her mouth, he decided that he could at least clean up her injuries. Maybe after that he'd be able to persuade her to change into something dry.

A few minutes later he pulled a chair out from the table and sat down. A gray graniteware basin sat on the table, full of gently steaming water, and a soft linen towel lay next to it. He slid his hand under Meg's chin, urging her head up. "Let's wash some of the dirt off your face. Okay?"

After a moment's hesitation, she nodded, though her eyes remained lowered, refusing to meet his. Ty moistened the cloth in the warm water and dabbed it gently against the scrape on her cheekbone.

"What happened here?" He kept his tone easy and conversational, wanting to reassure her. She lifted one hand to the scrape as if she needed to touch the injury to identify its source.

"I fell," she said finally. "I was running and I fell."

"Did you hurt yourself anywhere else when you fell?" He carefully didn't ask about the other injuries—the bruises on her cheek, the split lip, the black eye—that were clearly *not* the result of a fall.

"My hands," she said, after thinking a moment. Her voice was slow and flat. "And my knees. I think I scraped my knees."

From the looks of her knees and the palms of her hands, Ty guessed she must have fallen, not once but several times. The hem of her dress was torn and muddy, the dirt ground into the fabric, as if she'd been so frantic to get away from something—or someone—that she hadn't been watching her footing and had tripped repeatedly.

Though he knew he must be hurting her, she said not a word as he cleaned the dirt and tiny bits of rock out of her skin.

By the time he'd washed and bandaged her knees, Ty's jaw ached with the effort of holding back his rage. He wanted to break something, preferably Harlan Davis's miserable little neck. Because he knew, on a deep gut level, who had done this to Meg. Unless she'd gone back out after he took her home, who else could it be?

He wanted to shout aloud his anger that anyone could have hurt Meg—his Meg—as she'd been hurt. The idea that someone had dared to lay their hands on her made him feel almost light-headed with rage.

By the time he'd finished cleaning her bruised knees, Meg's shivering was almost nonstop. Whether it was cold or shock, Ty didn't know. He did know that he couldn't let her sit around in sopping wet clothes. But when he reached for the sweater, she grabbed the faded wool and pressed her spine so hard against the back of the chair that Ty suspected she'd have new bruises from the pressure.

"You're going to catch pneumonia if we don't get you out of those clothes," he told her.

She shook her head, her eyes haunted. It hit him suddenly that her refusal was more than an irrational desire to cling to the perceived comfort of the old sweater. There was a reason she didn't want him to take it from her.

"Let me see, Meg." He hardly recognized his own voice, made raspy by the anger he couldn't tamp down. He stopped and closed his eyes, struggling for control. When he opened them again, she was watching him with a wary expression that made his chest ache.

"Whatever it is, it's all right," he said quietly. "You don't have to be afraid of me. You know that, don't you?"

There was a heart-stopping hesitation and then she nodded slowly.

"You can't keep the sweater, Meg. It's soaking wet." He kept his eyes on hers as he put his hand over her fingers and began gently prying them loose.

"No. Please." The soft plea stabbed straight through him, but he hardened his heart and continued to loosen her hold.

"You need to get warm and dry," he said, speaking calmly. "It's all right, Meg. Whatever it is you don't want me to see, it's all right."

She shuddered as he pried her fingers loose, but she didn't continue to fight him. Instead, she closed her eyes and turned her face to the side as he pushed the sweater back off her shoulders and dragged it away from her. The garment hit the floor with a damp splat.

She was still wearing the same dress she'd worn to the movies—God, was that only a few hours ago? But the soft blue and white print was splattered with mud from where she'd fallen and the pretty white lace collar was torn away, hanging by a few threads. One shoulder seam was ripped completely open and the sleeve had slipped down to expose her upper arm, revealing a set of blue bruises that were obviously the result of someone grabbing her.

She'd lifted her hand to hold the torn bodice in place but Ty closed his fingers around hers, dragging her hand gently but inexorably down. She shuddered but didn't fight him.

There was a plain white slip beneath her dress, but both straps were broken and the soft, damp cotton barely clung to the curves of her breasts. There were bruises on her shoulders faint blue marks that would be purple by morning. A pair of ugly red scratches traced across her pale skin, starting at her collarbone and ending just above her breast, as if someone's nails had scraped across her skin as the dress was torn away. But it wasn't the bruises or the scratches that drove the color from Ty's face and made his hand tremble as he reached up to brush aside the torn lace at the top of her slip.

On the upper swell of her right breast, plainly visible and absolutely unmistakable, was a set of sharp little bruises. Ty hadn't seen bruises like that since he'd been a boy and the neighbor's toddler had sunk her set of shiny new teeth into his arm. But there was no mistaking that distinctive circular mark for anything else.

Someone had bitten Meg. The same someone who'd hit her, who'd left bruises on her arms, who'd torn her dress. Who'd . . . Ty swallowed against the bile that rose in his throat, threatening to choke him. He felt as if he'd just stepped off the top of a staircase only to find nothing but air under his foot.

"Who did this to you?" The voice that issued from his throat was one he'd never heard, a harsh, angry growl, more animal than human. He felt Meg wince away from him, trembling. Ty closed his eyes and rubbed one hand over his face, aware that his fingers were trembling, aware that he hovered on the knife edge of losing control and frightening her even more than she already was. He drew a deep breath, gathering all the threads of his self-control.

"It's all right, Meg." He opened his eyes and looked at her. "Just tell me who did this to you," he said gently.

Her teeth worried her swollen lower lip and she shook her head slightly, whether in denial of his question or of what had happened, Ty could only guess. And what the hell *had* happened? She started to pull her torn dress back into place, but Ty caught her hands in his, holding them until her eyes met his.

"Meg, you've got to tell me what happened. Did he . . . did he rape you?" The ugly word scraped his throat.

Her eyes dropped to where their hands were linked and color rushed into her face, but to Ty's infinite relief, she shook her head.

"Are you sure? You can tell me the truth."

"I'm sure," she whispered. "He . . . I think he would have but she stopped him."

"Who stopped him, Meg?" She didn't answer and Ty drew a deep breath before probing further. "Was it your mother?"

She shook her head uncertainly, less in answer than in denial of everything that had happened. She couldn't seem to lift her eyes to his face, though her fingers clung to his. Ty freed one hand and brought it up to cup her chin, tilting her face to his, searching her eyes.

"Tel me, Meg. Tell me who did this." When she didn't say anything, he asked, "Was it your stepfather? Is he the one who hurt you?"

She didn't say anything. She didn't have to. The answer was in the tears that suddenly filled her eyes, in the trembling of her mouth. Though he'd already known what the answer would be, Ty still felt as if he'd been kicked in the stomach.

"Oh, Meg." Afterward he didn't remember scooping her up off her chair and settling her on his lap. The move was born of a deep instinctive knowledge that what she needed more than anything else right now was to be held and soothed.

For a moment only, she was stiff in his hold. Then a long shudder shook her slender body, and she curled into his embrace as tears broke past the control she'd fought so hard to maintain and she began to cry.

"It's going to be all right," Ty told her, hoping it was true.

He stroked her damp hair back from her forehead and held her while the cleansing tears shook her body. He'd thought that he couldn't get any angrier, but listening to Meg cry, he found his rage shifting from white hot to something hard and cold and dangerous. If Harlan Davis had been standing in front of him at that moment, Ty could have killed him without feeling a second's remorse.

Meg cried until she had no more tears left to shed. She cried until her breath was ragged with hiccoughs, until she was drained of fear and incapable of movement. She was aware of Ty holding her, of the soothing murmur of his voice, the rumble of it beneath her cheek.

When the last of the tears had finally been cried, she lay against him like a tired child, drained and exhausted. She let him dry her cheeks with a towel and then took it from him and obeyed his order to blow her nose. It had been a long time since someone had held her and cared for her.

She could remember Patsy soothing her bruises when she

was a little girl, telling her that Daddy didn't really mean to hurt them, that everything was going to be all right in the morning. Meg hadn't believed her but she'd been comforted by the love in her sister's eyes, by the awkward gentleness of her childish hands as she dried Meg's tears and tried to make everything all right again.

But this wasn't one of her father's whippings and Ty wasn't Patsy. She shouldn't have come here, Meg thought tiredly. She should have gone somewhere else. Only, when she'd stumbled out of the little house into the rainy darkness, all she'd been able to think about was getting to Ty, that she'd be safe with him. She closed her eyes, afraid to see the contempt that must be in his eyes, the disgust he must feel.

"I'm sorry." Tears had left her voice little more than a husky whisper.

"For what? For crying? I think you've earned that."

He was being kind, of course, pretending he didn't know what she meant, pretending that he wasn't disgusted. Ty had always been kind, she thought. Even when he was a boy, he'd been kind.

"You were nice about Mary," she said fuzzily, fighting the urge to close her eyes and sleep.

"Mary?" Ty dampened one corner of the linen towel in the basin of water and stroked it over her flushed cheeks, his touch so gentle it would have made her cry again if only she'd had any tears left.

"My doll," she mumbled. "You said a prayer."

"The only one I could remember," he said, his voice laced with amusement. "And then I wondered if I'd go to hell for praying over a doll."

"I didn't think you remembered." She was so tired that her lashes seemed weighted, dragging her eyelids down.

"I remember." Meg felt his hand on her forehead, his fingers brushing her cheek.

She could have stayed just where she was for a lifetime. The steady beat of Ty's heart under her cheek, the warmth of his arms around her—as long as he was holding her like this, it was almost possible to believe that the scene with her stepfather had been no more than a nightmare. Only it had been real and terrible and nothing could make it go away, not even Ty.

Feeling the shiver that ran over her and mistaking its cause, Ty's arms tightened around her for a moment. "You're chilled to the bone. How long had you been standing outside?"

"I don't know."

"You should have knocked," he told her. A kind of anger laced his deep voice, and Meg heard herself apologizing even though she knew that his anger wasn't really directed at her.

"I'm sorry. I didn't want to be any trouble." Still holding her in his arms, Ty stood up. "Let's get you into a hot bath and some dry clothes."

The thought of being clean was enough to still Meg's instinctive urge to protest. She was suddenly aware of a need to wash that had less to do with getting rid of the traces of mud that still clung to her skin than it did with scrubbing away the memory of her stepfather's touch.

The hot water washed away the mud and warmed her body, but it wasn't so easy to wash away the feel of her stepfather's hands on her skin or to warm the chill that seemed to have crept into her bones. When the water started to cool, Meg climbed out of the big claw-footed tub and reached for the towels Ty had left for her. They were larger and softer than any she'd ever used before, but she was oblivious to the luxury.

She felt numb and her movements were lethargic as she toweled herself dry. Too much had happened in too short a time. She'd thought she was completely drained after watching Ty drive away, knowing he was taking her heart with him. She'd believed that there was nothing Harlan Davis could do to her that would even come close to the pain she already felt. But she'd been wrong.

Meg shivered and dropped the towel to reach for the flannel pajamas Ty had given her. They were his, he'd said, outgrown before he left home. The blue-and-white striped fabric was soft against her skin and the knowledge that the garments were Ty's made them seem warmer, almost as if he were holding her.

She left the bathroom and padded down the hall, shuffling slightly as she tried to keep her feet in the thick socks he'd given her. She halted at the top of the stairs, wondering uncertainly whether she should go back downstairs. The simple decision seemed suddenly overwhelming.

Before she could make up her mind, Ty came into the downstairs hall. As if sensing her presence, he looked up, his somber expression disappearing in a smile when he saw her. Meg backed away from the staircase as he started up the stairs, his long strides taking them two at a time.

"Warmer?" he asked as he reached the upper hall and stopped in front of her.

"Yes." It was a partial truth. The chill she felt was deep inside, and it would take more than hot water to drive it away.

"Good. Let me put something on those scratches and then we'll get you into bed."

Meg started to protest—she didn't want anything on the scratches. Just thinking about them made her stomach churn with shame. But before she could tell him not to worry about her injuries, he'd taken her arm and was herding her gently but firmly back down the hall and into the bathroom.

And somehow, Meg found herself sitting on a low-backed brass stool with Ty crouched in front of her dabbing Mercurochrome on the scratch across her cheekbone. She kept her eyes lowered as he undid the top two buttons on the pajama top and brushed it aside so that he could dab the antiseptic on the scratches across her chest.

She suddenly remembered the way her stepfather had grabbed the front of her dress, ripping it open, so eager to strip it from her that he hadn't cared that he was hurting her. It was too easy to remember the terrifying hunger in his small eyes, the soft wetness of his mouth on her skin.

The memory washed over her and she shuddered, unaware of the soft moan of fear that escaped. And then Ty's arms were around her, hard and strong, holding back the terror.

"He can't hurt you anymore, Meg," he told her, his voice

fierce and angry—anger *for* her, she realized as she pressed her face against the soft warmth of his sweater. Ty was angry *for* her, not *at* her. She couldn't ever remember anyone being angry on her behalf.

She told herself she was going to sit up, straighten her spine, and stop acting like a frightened child. But that was just what she felt like, a frightened little girl. And the solid strength of Ty's arms was all that kept the fear from swallowing her completely.

So she clung to him, too weary to pull away, wishing she could simply close her eyes and go to sleep and wake up to find that this had all been a terrible nightmare.

"Thing will look better tomorrow," Ty said, almost as if he'd read her thoughts. "Let's get you to bed."

"I don't think I could go to sleep."

"Sure you can." He stood up and then bent to lift her in his arms.

"I can walk," she mumbled.

"Of course you can." But he didn't put her down and Meg didn't offer another protest.

Ty carried her into his bedroom, and when he set her on the bed, Meg had to force herself to release him. It was bad enough that she'd thrust herself on him like this. Clinging to him like a child could only add to the disgust he must surely feel toward her.

"I want you to try to get some sleep," he told her, pulling the covers up to her chin.

"I didn't mean to be so much trouble," she whispered, feeling exhaustion wash over her in relentless waves. She let her head sink back against the soft pillow.

"You're no trouble," he said gruffly.

She stared up at him, seeing the frown that creased his forehead, the concern in his dark eyes. He reached out to brush her damp hair back from her forehead and she closed her eyes, absorbing the warmth of his touch.

"Go to sleep," he told her again. "Things'll look better in the morning."

She doubted that he believed that any more than she did,

but she nodded. She kept her eyes closed as she heard him move away, curling her fingers into her palms against the urge to reach for him, biting her tongue to hold back the need to beg him not to leave her. He hesitated in the doorway and Meg felt him looking at her, but she didn't open her eyes, afraid of what they might reveal.

"If you need me, just call," he said.

And then he was gone and she was alone. And she wanted nothing more in the world than to call him back, to beg him to hold her until the fear went away.

Chapter 8

Somewhere around two in the morning, the rain began to taper off. Ty tilted his head toward the window as the sound of it changed. The steady pounding became a gentle patter. He lifted his coffee cup and took a swallow of the lukewarm contents, grimacing at the bitter taste. He'd reheated it for Meg and then never even poured her a cup. Once he'd seen that she was hurt, he'd forgotten all about the coffee.

His jaw tightened until the muscles ached. There was a knot in his stomach that had nothing to do with lack of sleep or the fact that he was guzzling bad coffee at an hour when most sane people were asleep. If sleep had been elusive before Meg's appearance, it had vanished completely since then.

If only he had Harlan Davis in front of him. He'd like to see the other man's eyes bulge, his face turn purple as Ty's fingers tightened around his throat. But before he strangled him, he wanted to pound his fists into his pasty complexion, give him a sample of the abuse he'd doled out to Meg. And that wasn't even the worst of his crimes.

Unable to sit still, Ty shot to his feet, reaching out to catch the chair as it teetered on the brink of falling backward. He paced restlessly back and forth across the kitchen, needing to release the nervous energy that filled his body. He still couldn't absorb what had happened—what had *almost* happened. God, what if she hadn't managed to get away? She'd said that her mother stopped Harlan. What if her mother hadn't been there? His hands clenched into fists and he swallowed against the choking sensation that rose in his throat.

He had to stop thinking about what might have happened. It hadn't and Meg was here now and safe. And she was going to stay that way. If he had anything to do with it, nothing would ever hurt her again.

The fierceness of that thought might have given him pause if he hadn't heard a sound that drove everything else out of his mind. He was out the door and taking the stairs two at a time before the echoes of Meg's cry had faded. She cried out again as he reached the upper hall, a frantic sound that was not quite a scream nor yet a word.

Ty's heart was pounding as he pushed open his bedroom door and crossed the room in two long strides. The light that spilled in from the hallway provided enough illumination for him to see that she was tangled in the bedcovers, her face twisted with fear.

She whimpered softly as he reached the bed, a sound so full of quiet despair that it tore at his heart. He bent down and took hold of her shoulder, intending to shake her awake. The moment he touched her, her eyes jerked open and she screamed, the sound seeming ripped from the very depths of her being.

"Meg. It's all right. It's me." Ty caught her hands as they flew up as if to defend herself. "You're safe."

"Ty?" Her voice was ragged and uncertain.

"It's okay. I've got you safe." Seeing awareness in her eyes, he released her hands and sank down on the edge of the bed, reaching out to brush her hair back from her forehead. He wasn't surprised to see that his fingers were not quite steady. "You had a bad dream, that's all."

"It was him," she murmured, her eyes staring past him at an image only she could see. "It was happening all over again."

"It was a dream, Meg."

"He was so angry," she said, seeming not to hear him. "I knew he'd be mad but I thought it would be like the last time."

"The last time?" Ty's hand stilled against her hair. It hadn't occurred to him that this might have happened before.

"When I went to the fair with you. Mama told me he wouldn't like it."

"Wouldn't like you going to the fair? Or wouldn't like you going out with me?" Ty probed quietly.

She blinked and seemed to suddenly become aware of him, as if the last traces of sleep had finally disappeared and she remembered where she was and whom she was talking to. Ty could almost see the walls go up as she shook her head.

"It's not important. I don't want to talk about it anymore. Please."

Who was she protecting? Herself? Or him?

"Tell me, Meg. Tell me why your stepfather was angry."

"It doesn't matter anymore," she said, her eyes shifting away from his.

"It matters to me." The more she tried to avoid the question, the more he was convinced that it wasn't her own feelings she was trying to spare.

Meg felt tears spring to her eyes as Ty brushed his fingers over the bruises on her face, his touch soft as a butterfly's wing.

"Was he angry because you were seeing me?" he asked.

She'd never realized it was possible for someone to sound at once infinitely gentle and completely implacable. She shook her head, knowing that he'd be upset if she told him the truth, that he'd blame himself for what her stepfather had done.

"Please," she whispered.

"You can tell me, Meg. Did he hit you when I brought you home from the fair?" She shook her head wordlessly but he sucked in a quick breath, a look of realization flooding his face. "Your mouth. You told me you'd hit it on the table. Did he do that to you?"

She said nothing but he must have read the answer in her

face, because a sudden, terrible rage burned in his eyes, making them black as coal.

"Did he do anything besides hit you?" he asked fiercely.

"No," she said quietly, closing her eyes as she realized that she'd just admitted that his suspicions were right, that it had been her relationship with him that had sent her stepfather into a rage.

"Why didn't you tell me?"

"Why should I have?" she asked, hearing the weariness in her own voice. She opened her eyes and looked at him. "There wasn't anything you could have done. Besides, I thought I could handle it on my own. Just like I did with my father. It wasn't that big a deal."

"He *hit* you!" Ty said furiously.

"I've been hit before. The only thing you could have done was to stop seeing me, and I didn't want that."

Ty opened his mouth and then closed it again without speaking, a silent admission that what she'd said was nothing more than the truth.

"You still should have told me," he said finally.

Meg lifted one shoulder in a half shrug, wincing as the movement pulled her bruised flesh. "I chose not to."

"Now that I know, will you tell me what happened?"

She hesitated but there didn't seem much reason not to tell him what he'd asked. After all, what he already knew was far worse than anything else that had happened.

"He was furious that I'd gone out with you—with any man, I think. He said I was a . . . He said things that weren't true," she finished awkwardly, unable to tell him just what Harlan had called her. "I told him he was wrong; that you hadn't . . . that we didn't . . . that we didn't do anything wrong, but he didn't believe me. I don't think he even listened to me."

"What happened?" Ty asked.

"He hit me," she said simply. "I think he'd have hit me again but Mama said that she was sure I hadn't done anything bad and that he shouldn't get so upset. And then he said that he'd taken her and her daughters in and that he wouldn't see any shame brought down on his name."

"Did he . . . Was he upset about the same thing tonight —last night?" Ty corrected as he glanced at the clock and saw that a new day was not far off.

"Yes. He kept saying that we'd done things that we hadn't." She stared past him, seeing her stepfather's flushed face, the insane rage in his eyes, the flecks of saliva that had shown at the corners of his mouth as he shouted at her. Her mother had been huddled in a chair, curled into herself as if trying to disappear.

Meg had tried to reason with him, tried to tell him he was wrong, that she hadn't done anything to bring shame to his precious name. But that had only seemed to make him angrier. He'd slapped her, the blow hard enough to make her stagger, but he'd caught her arm, holding her for the next blow and the one after that. She'd felt her lip split, her teeth snapping together as his hand connected with her jaw.

She'd been shocked by the ferocity of his anger. This was nothing like the beatings her father had given her. George Harper had been a mean drunk and he'd taken that meanness out on his family. But there'd been an oddly impersonal feel to his anger, a feeling that it was a rage at himself and the world that drove him more than anything she'd done. But the look in Harlan Davis's eyes was different. There was an anger she didn't understand, something that approached hatred.

She'd tried to bring up her hands to push him away, but he'd brushed them aside. And then his fist struck her eye and pain had exploded through her head, dazing her. She'd fallen then, her knees hitting the thin carpet with a force that jarred her body. Vaguely she'd heard her mother whimpering, but then her stepfather grabbed her arm, dragging her upright, his fingers digging cruelly into her flesh.

She wasn't sure what had happened then. Had he deliberately torn her dress, or had his hand caught in the collar when she tried to pull away? She didn't know. But she did remember the feel of air on her skin and the sudden change in her stepfather's eyes.

For a split second, time had stood still. Meg had stared at Harlan, her head ringing with pain, the salt taste of blood in her mouth. And he'd stared at the skin bared by her torn dress at the prim white cotton of her slip.

"He—he reached out. I thought he was going to hit me again, but then he put his hand on me." Meg stopped and swallowed the nausea that rose in her throat. She'd forgotten where she was and whom she was talking to. She was looking backward, reliving the terror of that moment, oblivious to Ty's pale face and the sick look in his eyes.

"I tried to get away but he was stronger than I was. He kept touching me and he tore my dress again."

"Don't." Ty's voice was choked but Meg didn't hear him.

"I couldn't get away," she said. "And then Mama started pulling on him, telling him he had to stop, that he didn't know what he was doing. He didn't seem to hear her but she kept pulling at him and crying, saying he had to stop. Finally he shouted at Mama to stop her whining and I was able to get away from him. He started toward me but Mama kept hanging on his arm and crying. And then he said it was my fault for tempting him and that I was a . . . slut and that he'd deal with me later. So I ran."

Meg hadn't realized she was crying until she felt Ty's fingers brushing the tears from her cheeks. She lifted her eyes to his, suddenly aware that she was bone-deep tired and strangely numb, as if the scene she'd just described had happened to someone else, someone she barely knew.

"I came here because I didn't know where else to go," she said slowly.

"You did just what you should," he told her, his voice tight with some emotion Meg was too tired to put a name to.

"I'm so tired," she whispered.

Ty shifted his position, moving so that his back was against the headboard, his arms coming around her, cradling her against the lean strength of his body. Meg let her head settle on his chest, her eyelids drooping. The beat of his heart was strong and steady under her ear, as reassuring as the feel of his arms holding her.

"I've got you safe," he said softly. "Go to sleep."

As if that command was all she'd needed, Meg relaxed into his embrace and let sleep's heavy curtain fall across her consciousness.

Ty held her lax body, feeling the gentle rise and fall of her breathing and cursing himself for being the most selfish bastard in all of creation. How had he managed to cause so much harm to the one person he knew who deserved it least?

Why had he believed her story about bumping her mouth on the edge of the table? Was he blind that he hadn't seen the truth?

Nothing was ever going to hurt her again, he thought fiercely. He'd told her that he'd keep her safe, and come hell or high water, he was going to keep that promise. No matter what it took.

Ty dozed off near dawn but he slept only a short while, waking to find pale sunlight sliding through the thin curtains. There was no period of confusion about where he was or what had happened the night before. Meg's body was a soft weight against his side, her head pillowed on his shoulder, one slender hand on his chest, the fingers curled around a fold of his sweater as if clinging to a lifeline.

The room was chilly, a reminder that he'd forgotten to shovel coal into the furnace the night before. He'd slept propped against the headboard, and the awkward position had put a crick in his neck and made his back ache. Moving slowly, he eased off the bed, shifting Meg gently, careful not to wake her. But she was so deeply asleep that she didn't even stir.

Ty winced as he straightened his spine. Putting one hand on the back of his neck, he rolled his head, trying to work the kinks out. Away from the warmth of the bed, the chill in the room was even more noticeable, but Ty lingered next to the bed, his eyes on Meg.

The pale sunlight revealed the bruising on her face with

merciless clarity. The blue that circled her eye had darkened to purple, the swelling making it doubtful that she'd be able to open it more than a slit when she woke. Her lower lip was still puffy, and the swelling along her jaw seemed worse. She lay on her back and the pajama top had twisted around her so that the neck pulled open, revealing the fragile line of her collarbone. He could just see the beginnings of the scratch that ran across her chest—the scratch Harlan Davis had put there when he tore her dress open.

Ty's jaw tightened until it ached, his eyes grim and cold as he thought of what Davis had done to her—and of what he'd tried to do. Ty shook his head. There was no sense in running over it again and again, imagining what might have happened.

He turned away from the bed, leaving Meg to what he hoped was a healing sleep. After going downstairs, he dumped out the dregs of last night's cold coffee and filled the percolator with water before setting the freshly filled basket in the pot and putting it on the stove to heat. The most important necessity taken care of, he went down into the basement to feed the furnace a ration of coal.

Ty was halfway through his second cup of coffee when he heard Meg stirring upstairs. He hesitated a moment before setting his cup down and leaving the kitchen. He wasn't sure how she would feel about him this morning. He might be the last person she'd want to see. He couldn't blame her if she held him at least partially responsible for what had happened. God knew, he held himself responsible.

He tapped on the bedroom door and obeyed Meg's muffled invitation to enter. She was out of bed and standing unsteadily beside the wing chair that sat a few feet away. Ty had draped his heavy robe across the chair when she'd gone to bed the night before, and she'd apparently been attempting to put it on. She had one arm through the sleeve, but the rest of the garment eluded her.

"Let me help." Ty was across the room in a moment, reaching for the soft wool and pulling it into position.

"Thank you." She eased her arm into the sleeve, her

movements stiff and painful. He tugged her hair from under the collar, feeling anger churn anew in his gut.

"I've got coffee downstairs, if you'd like some," he said, allowing none of what he was feeling to color his voice.

"No, thank you." She kept her head bent, her voice muffled as she tied the belt around her.

Ty stared at the top of her head a minute, caught between the need to respect her privacy and the feeling that, if he let her, she'd close herself away—from him, from the world.

"How are you?"

"Fine." The answer was automatic, polite. And a lie.

"Meg." Her fingers had been tugging nervously at the fabric belt, but the soft command in his voice made her hands still, her whole body tensing in a way that reminded him a doe scenting danger but uncertain of its direction.

Ty reached beneath the tangled curtain of her hair, his fingers gentle on her chin as he tilted her face up to his. The daylight illuminated her battered features with cruel clarity, but Ty refused to let her duck her head.

"This is me you're talking to," he reminded her quietly. "You don't have to lie to me."

"I'm sorry," she whispered, her eyes shifting away from his face.

"And you don't have to apologize either. Just tell me how you feel."

"I'm all right," She caught the lift of his eyebrow and flushed. "A little achy," she admitted reluctantly. "It hurts when I move. But it's not near as bad as it probably looks." She lifted one hand to her face, gingerly touching the swelling around her eye.

"Maybe I should ask Dr. Corey to come over and take a look at you," Ty said slowly, his eyes worried.

"No! No, please." It was the first spark of real emotion she'd showed that morning, but Ty would have preferred that it be something other than pure panic.

"You could be hurt inside somewhere," he argued. "Maybe have a couple of cracked ribs or something."

"No." So great was her distress that she reached out and

caught hold of his wrist, her fingers digging into his skin. "Please, Ty. I'd be so ashamed if he found out what happened. If anyone knew what he tried to do."

"The shame isn't yours," Ty protested angrily. "Your stepfather's the one who should be ashamed."

But she shook her head, her fingers digging pleadingly into his arm, her eyes begging him to understand. "Please. Don't call Dr. Corey. I'm not hurt bad. Just a little bruised, that's all."

A little bruised didn't begin to describe her injuries, and Ty hesitated, the desire to make sure she was all right warring with the need to banish the fear from her eyes once and for all.

"Please, Ty," she whispered, the despair in her voice telling him that she didn't expect him to pay any attention to what she asked. He wondered suddenly if anyone had ever paid attention to what Meg wanted—what she needed.

"All right. I won't call the doctor."

"Thank you." Meg sagged with relief, her eyes filling with quick tears. She didn't know how she'd bear the shame if anyone else were to find out what her stepfather had tried to do. It was bad enough that Ty knew. It seemed almost miraculous that he could even stand to look at her.

"But that means you've got to rest," Ty told her. His stern tone was a contrast to the gentleness of his fingers as he touched her bruised face.

"I can't do that," she said, her relief changing to uneasiness. She let her hands fall to her waist to begin twisting at her belt again.

"Why not?"

"I have to go home."

"Like hell you do," Ty snapped. "You're not setting foot in that house."

It didn't occur to either of them that he had no real right to dictate what she would or wouldn't do. Nor to wonder just what she'd do if she didn't go home eventually.

"I left Mama alone with him. There's no telling what he

might have done. He was so angry." She twisted her hands together in distress.

"You're not going back there," Ty said flatly.

"I've got to see that she's all right," she said, trying to make him understand.

"I'll go."

"You can't."

"Why not? I'll go over there and just make sure your mother's all right," he said as if it were the most reasonable thing in the world.

Meg rubbed her fingers over her forehead, trying to soothe the pounding ache that was lodged just above her eyes. It was so hard to think clearly, nearly impossible to make even the simplest decision.

"I don't think you should be involved," she said at last.

"Meg, I'm already involved." His voice was gentle. He reached out to stroke her forehead and the ache seemed to recede a little.

"I shouldn't have come here," she whispered. "I didn't mean to cause you any trouble."

"You're not causing me trouble."

He said it so firmly that it was almost possible to believe him. Almost.

"I think you should go back to bed," he said briskly, as if the question of him going to see her mother was settled.

And perhaps it was, Meg admitted, feeling the wobble in her knees. The fact was, she doubted she could walk down the stairs without help, let alone make it home. And the possibility of seeing Harlan Davis was enough to make her feel cold and clammy, as if someone had just run skeletal hands across her gravestone.

So she let Ty ease the robe from her shoulders and help her back into bed, and she took the headache powder he insisted on giving her. Meg lay back against the pillows and watched Ty walk out the door, feeling weak tears spring to her eyes.

She wondered what her mother would think when Ty showed up. What had Ruth thought when Meg disappeared the night before? Had she worried? Or had she just been grateful that there'd be no more trouble? Would Harlan have turned his rage on his wife? What if he was there when Ty arrived?

Ty will take care of it, she thought, feeling the pounding in her head ease as the medication took effect. She didn't believe there was anything that he couldn't deal with.

Ty knocked on the door and then waited. Though the rain had stopped sometime before dawn, the air was still cold and damp, making him wish he'd worn a heavier jacket. He turned away from the blank door to frown at the neat front yard. The tidy flower beds held the tattered remnants of summer color, tired and brown now with the change of seasons.

He heard footsteps inside and turned toward the door. He'd debated all the way over here just what he should say to Ruth Davis when she answered the door, and he was no closer to knowing now than he had been when he left. The door opened with a squeal of hinges and he was looking at Meg's mother through the fly-specked screen.

"Mrs. Davis?"

Her eyes widened when she saw him, her already pale complexion going a shade whiter. Ty had met her only the one time when he'd picked up Meg, but he'd seen her in town a few times over the years. It struck him suddenly that he couldn't remember a time when she hadn't looked old and worn, ground down by life. Yet she could not be much more than forty, hardly old by anyone's standards.

"Could I talk to you?" he asked when she didn't seem willing to speak.

"I doubt we've much to say to one another."

She began to shut the door.

"Meg asked me to come," Ty said quickly.

That brought her head up and she eyed him uneasily through the screen. "When?"

"This morning. She came to me last night, Mrs. Davis."

There was a moment when he thought she might shut the door in his face anyway, but she seemed to change her mind, reaching to pull open the screen instead.

"Best you come inside," she offered.

"Thank you."

If he'd expected the little house to be warmer than the outdoors, he was disappointed. If anything, it seemed colder but that could have been his imagination.

Ruth tugged her heavy gray sweater closer about her shoulders and nodded her head toward the parlor, which was dominated by her quilting frame, just as it had been the last time, though the quilt stretched in it was a different one from the one he'd seen before. This one was flowers of some kind, done in bubble-gum pink and Nile green. It provided the only spot of color in the drab room.

"How is Meg?" she asked as soon as Ty had seated himself on the uncomfortable horsehair sofa. She sat down at the quilting frame and picked up her needle.

"She'll be all right," he said, hoping he was telling the truth. "She was worried about you."

"Me?" Ruth glanced up from her quilting, her faded blue eyes surprised, the surprise quickly fading as she shook her head. "Meg always was a worrier. Patsy, now, she never worried about a thing. She always figured she'd turn a corner and everything would work itself out. But Meg was always worrying about things, trying to take care of other people."

"Seems to me she's the one who needs someone to take care of her," Ty said. "After last night."

Ruth's eyes shot to his face and then back to her quilting. The needle rocked in and out of the fabric automatically, but Ty didn't think she was paying much attention to what she was doing.

"I can understand Meg being upset," she said slowly, seeming to pick her words. "Her stepfather was real upset and maybe he shouldn't have slapped her like he did, but there was no real cause for her to run off—"

"Slapped her?" Ty's incredulous question interrupted her. "Slapped her? Mrs. Davis, Meg has a split lip, a black eye, and more bruises than I can count."

"Harlan lost his temper. Maybe he was a bit rougher than he should—"

"Meg told me everything that happened."

The flat interruption stopped her cold. Though she didn't look at him, Ty saw her flush and then pale and her fingers suddenly began to tremble around her needle.

"I told her he'd be upset," she whispered, seeming to speak more to herself than to him. "I tried to tell her he'd be angry."

"I don't think anger justifies what your husband tried to do, Mrs. Davis."

"He just lost his temper," she said, shooting him a pleading look. "He's not a bad man." Seeing Ty's incredulous expression, she flushed again and looked away. "What happened last night—it won't happen again."

"Damn right it won't," Ty snapped. He stood up, offering no apology for his language. His expression held more than a trace of contempt when he looked at her. "Because Meg isn't going to be in a position where it *could* happen. She's not coming back here."

"Where's she going to stay?" Ruth rose to face him. "Who's going to take care of her? You?" Seeing that Ty had no answer, it was her turn to look contemptuous. "I wouldn't go casting any stones too quickly, Tyler McKendrick. You think I don't care about my girl, but I've done what I had to to make sure that she had a roof over her head and food on the table."

"There's more to taking care of a child than feeding her."

"You can say that because you've never gone hungry, never had to wonder whether or not you'd be able to scrape up enough pennies to buy food to fill your children's bellies or enough to pay the rent so's there'd be a roof over their heads come winter. Don't you judge me until you've stood in my shoes."

Ty looked at her, seeing a trace of the spirited girl she might once have been. For the first time he noticed a resemblance to Meg, in the thrust of her jaw, in the passion in her eyes. But it was gone the next moment as Ruth looked away, her shoulders slumping inside the shapeless sweater.

"I told Meg no good would come of her seeing you. The McKendricks live on the Hill, I said. And she'd always be George Harper's youngest. You were only here for the summer and then you'd be going on with your life, leaving her behind. I knew she'd end up hurt."

"I'm not the one who hurt her last night."

"Aren't you?"

The simple question silenced him as nothing else could have done. He stared at her for a moment, seeing himself through her eyes and not liking what he saw.

"She's not coming back here," he said finally, turning to leave.

"Good enough." Ruth followed him to the door. "See that you take care of her."

"I will." Ty ducked his head in farewell, feeling an odd respect for her. As far as he was concerned, she'd made the wrong choices in her life and Meg had suffered for them. But he was willing to concede that perhaps the choices had seemed right to her at the time.

He got into the roadster and backed it around to head out the driveway. The sky to the north was thick and dark with clouds, hinting at another storm on the way, but Ty paid them no attention. He had one more stop to make before going home.

The Davis Hotel was a square, three-story brick building situated in the middle of town. It was completely without any pretensions to architectural greatness. It looked like exactly what it was: a plain hotel that had seen better days in a small midwestern town that had also seen better days.

Ty had been inside the hotel only a few times, generally when an out-of-town relative visited and chose the marginal luxury of the hotel over staying at his parents'. From what he could recall, the lobby hadn't changed since the last time his great-uncle Millard had stayed there, which had been at least fifteen years ago. The same carpet covered the floor, the floral pattern more faded than he remembered. Overhead was the same crystal chandelier, gleaming like a diamond in a shabby velvet case.

But Ty wasn't particularly interested in the subtle evidence that the Davis Hotel, like the rest of the country, had fallen on hard times. His attention was on the small man standing behind the front desk, his head bent over a ledger.

At the sound of the bell over the door, Harlan Davis looked up, his professional smile fading when he saw Ty. His face twisted in a look of such hate that Ty paused, momentarily thrown off balance. But only momentarily. He continued toward the desk with long strides, taking some satisfaction in seeing the hatred fade, to be replaced by a look of alarm.

"Mr. McKendrick." Harlan's greeting was an automatic courtesy.

"I want to talk to you about Meg," Ty said, skipping the courtesies. As far as he was concerned, the fact that he hadn't punched Harlan on sight was stretching his manners to the limit.

At the mention of Meg's name, Harlan's spine stiffened, his caution fading as his face twisted in a look that mingled anger and frustration.

"I should have known the little slut would go straight to you," he said with a sneer. "Her lover. I told her I wouldn't have her ruining my good name in this town and I meant it. You tell her to get—"

His sentence was choked off midword as Ty reached across the desk and caught him by the front of his shirt, dragging him halfway across the gleaming mahogany surface.

"If you say one more word, the only thing I'm going to be telling Meg is the news of your untimely death."

"You can't—" Whatever Ty couldn't do was lost as he twisted his hand deeper into Harlan's shirt, causing the collar to tighten alarmingly.

"I can do anything I want, Davis." His voice was low and hard, audible only to Davis. "If you're so concerned about your good name, I'd suggest you consider the fact that I know exactly what you are and what you tried to do to Meg."

Davis's eyes bulged, whether out of fear or lack of air, Ty

didn't know. Nor did he care. Strangling Davis offered only marginal satisfaction. What he really wanted was to plunge his fist into the other man's face, to feel the bones in his nose crunch under the impact, to inflict on him a small portion of the hurt he'd given Meg.

"What do you think it will do to your precious reputation in this town if people find out you tried to rape your own stepdaughter?"

Davis paled, his skin nearly as white as the ledger that lay open between them. "She's lying." He gasped. "I didn't touch her. No matter how much she flaunted herself, I didn't—"

Ty twisted his hand until Davis's collar dug viciously deep. Rage made him light-headed. He saw Davis through a red haze, could almost feel the pleasure to be gained from choking the life out of him. Davis batted feebly at his wrists, his pasty complexion taking on a purple hue.

Ty was oblivious to the half-dozen people who stood in the lobby, watching the scene with shocked gazes. His fingers tightened momentarily and Davis began to make wheezing noises as his air was cut off. Just before the other man blacked out, Ty eased his grip, allowing him to draw a deep, gulping breath of air. He watched Davis coldly until he saw reason replace the blind terror that had filled his eyes, then he leaned down until only inches separated their faces. Feeling the fingers on his shirtfront tighten, Davis squeaked with alarm.

"I'm not going to kill you now, Davis." Ty's voice was low and hard. "I just wanted to be sure I had your attention. Now, I want you to listen to me carefully. If you ever lay another hand on Meg, I'll kill you. In fact, if you so much as look at her, I'll break you in half."

Ty released his hold and Davis dropped to the floor like a sack of badly packed flour. Davis lifted his hands to his throat, patting nervously at his creased collar as he eased back, out of Ty's reach.

"You can't threaten me," he blustered, his voice hoarse and quavery.

"I just did. And I'd suggest you take my words to heart.

You're a small man, Davis. All the way to the core. And if you take me on, you're going to bite off a lot more than you can chew.'' He leaned forward and Davis backed hastily away. Ty grinned, enjoying the other man's fear. "Stay away from Meg.''

He turned and walked away without waiting for a response, feeling better than he had all morning.

Chapter 9

J ack was playing solitaire at the kitchen table when the doorbell rang. He laid the nine of spades on the ten of hearts before setting the deck down and pushing his chair back. If the doorbell had awakened Meg, Ty was likely to have his skin. He glanced up the stairs as he entered the hall, but there was no sign of her. He opened the door.

"Mrs. Vanderbilt." Jack smiled as if nothing pleased him more than to find the town's biggest busybody standing on the doorstep. "You look younger every time I see you."

"You're such a flatterer, Jack Swanson." Edwina giggled, a girlish sound that contrasted oddly with her solid, matronly frame.

"Just telling the truth," he protested, wondering if it was possible that she'd aged ten years in the five since he'd last seen her. "What can I do for you?"

"Well, actually, I wondered if there was something I could do for you," she said.

"For me?"

"Well, for you or Tyler, perhaps. I just happened to be looking out my front window and saw him leave a few minutes ago. He looked rather grim. And of course, I recognized your mother's car so I knew you must be here. Is there anything wrong?'' She craned her neck in what she fondly believed was a subtle fashion, trying to see past Jack into the hallway.

"Not a thing, Mrs. V. But it's neighborly of you to be concerned.'' *Nosy old bat.*

"Well, I did tell his mother that I'd keep an eye on Tyler, make sure he was all right.''

"And I know Ty appreciates that.'' *About as much as he'd appreciate another broken leg.*

"You're sure nothing is wrong?'' she asked, edging a little closer. Jack shifted subtly, blocking the doorway. Edwina was notorious for walking into her friends' houses uninvited.

"Nothing's wrong.'' *Except the fact that you're still standing on the doorstep.*

"It just seems odd, Ty leaving you here while he goes out.'' She edged closer still, tilting her head in an effort to see around him.

"He ran out to get some coffee,'' Jack improvised quickly, knowing that if he didn't provide an explanation she was likely to keep prying, hoping to find some juicy tidbit with which to burn up the party-line wires. And God knew, there were plenty of juicy tidbits lying around right now.

"Well, that silly boy. I told him if he needed anything at all, he should just let me know.'' She pursed her lips and shook her head, setting several of her chins into motion. "I could have loaned him some coffee.''

"I'm sure Ty didn't want to bother you.'' Jack hoped his smile didn't look as strained as it was starting to feel. *What was it going to take to get rid of her?*

"Well, if you're sure there's nothing wrong.''

"Everything's fine, Mrs. V. But I'll tell Ty you were concerned. I know he'll want to thank you.''

"Well, I guess I'll just run home then,'' she said reluctantly.

"You do that, Mrs. V.''

She lingered a moment longer, casting an almost wistful look over his shoulder, like a cat being forced to abandon a hole where it knew a mouse was hiding. Jack had heard of people having a nose for news, and he was starting to believe it. If the *New York Sun* knew about Mrs. Vanderbilt, they'd recruit her onto their staff at once. And he'd pay her train fare, if it would serve to get her off the porch any faster.

Only when she was safely on her own side of the hedge did he shut the door. As he turned away, a small sound brought his head up and he saw Meg standing at the top of the stairs. With her slight figure wrapped in a robe that was miles too big for her and a pair of heavy socks trailing off the ends of her toes, she looked like a waif out of a Mary Pickford film.

"Hello, Meg."

"H-hello." The word came out hesitantly and she made no move to come downstairs, hovering at the top of the staircase like a small animal reluctant to get too far from safety.

"Ty called and asked me to come over and stay with you while he went to see your mother." Jack offered the explanation to reassure her. "He said you'd had a little trouble at home last night." "A little trouble" hardly began to describe what Ty had said, but it would suffice.

"He didn't have to do that," she said. "I would have been all right alone."

"Well, Ty didn't agree. He tends to be a little overprotective of people he cares about." Jack gave her a coaxing smile. "I make a mean cup of hot chocolate, if you feel up to it."

"I don't know."

"It's famous in three states."

"Three?" That drew a half smile and she eased a little closer to the top stair.

"Well, maybe only two and a half," he conceded. "I don't make it for just anybody, you know."

Meg hesitated a moment longer, uncertain about leaving the safety of the dimly lit hallway. But ever since Ty left, she'd been lying in bed, the events of the night before playing over and over in her mind. Every time she closed her eyes, she saw her stepfather's face, twisted with rage and a terrible lust. The image of him bending over her, the feel of his hands on her—those things were burned into her mind, refusing to leave her in peace.

"My grandmother always believed that hot chocolate is good for what ails you," Jack commented, smiling up at her.

Meg knew it would take considerably more than a cup of warm milk and chocolate to soothe her ills, but she suddenly didn't want to be alone anymore. She started down the stairs, taking them one at a time as the bulky socks threatened to trip her.

Jack was glad that Meg was concentrating on her footing as she came down the stairs. If she'd been looking at him, she would surely have seen his appalled expression when she got close enough for him to really see her face.

Ty had told him the basics, that her stepfather had been angry because she'd been out with him, that he'd blacked her eye, left bruises on her face and arms. But Ty's description hadn't prepared him for the actual sight of Meg's bruised face or for the careful way she walked, which told of other hurts. It made him want to find Harlan Davis and string him from the nearest tree.

Meg reached the bottom of the stairs and looked at him uncertainly. "I look awful," she murmured, lifting her hand to touch the swelling around her eye.

"I've seen worse," he told her. Privately he thought she looked as if she'd been on the losing end of a bout with Max Schmelling, but he'd have cut his tongue out before he said anything to add to the uncertainty in those soft blue eyes. "You should have seen Ty the time he fell out of my father's prize apple tree. Now *there* was someone who looked awful."

"You've known Ty a long time, haven't you?"

"All my life." Jack followed her as she moved toward the kitchen, shuffling slightly to keep from tripping on the socks.

"Have you been friends always?"

"Pretty near." He pulled a chair out for her and saw her settled. "Of course, there was the time when we were eight and he lost my best shooter."

"A cap gun?"

"A marble." Jack shook his head, his expression reminiscent. "I never found another one half so good and I didn't speak to Ty for a week after he lost it. And when we were fourteen, we fought over Clara Anne Oglethorpe.''

''Was she very pretty?'' Meg asked, her tone wistful.

''Not particularly. But her mother made the best apple pie in the state, and Clara Anne always brought an extra slice of it to school in her lunch bucket. She'd share it with whoever she ate lunch with.''

''You fought over her because of a piece of pie?'' Meg asked, looking incredulous.

''Her mother won prizes with it at every state fair,'' Jack protested, as if that explained everything.

Meg's laugh was uncertain and it didn't last long, but it *was* a laugh. Jack couldn't remember when he'd last been quite so pleased with himself.

At first Meg had worried about what Ty might have told his friend. If he'd told Jack everything . . . But there was nothing in the way Jack looked at her to indicate that he knew anything more than what the visible bruises would tell him. Sitting in the warm kitchen, watching him heat milk for his famous-in-two-and-a-half-states hot chocolate, Meg was surprised to realize that she felt as comfortable with him as if she'd known him for years.

''Do you cook anything besides hot chocolate?'' she asked.

''A few things. When you do a lot of traveling, the way Ty and I have these last few years, you get pretty sick of eating in restaurants.''

''Does Ty cook?'' She couldn't quite imagine Ty puttering around the kitchen.

''Not exactly.'' Jack poured steaming milk into a thick mug and stirred it briskly before setting it down in front of her. ''Ty won't starve to death, if left to his own devices. He does okay as long as he can slap something between a couple slices of bread. The height of his culinary skill is putting mustard on the bread first. I won't say he's dangerous in the kitchen, but if you value your stomach, I don't recommend eating anything he's cooked.''

Meg smiled, finding the idea that Ty was less than skilled in the kitchen oddly endearing.

"Tell me what happened when Ty fell out of the apple tree," she asked him.

It was the first time in Jack's memory that he'd been in the company of a pretty girl and done nothing but talk about another man. He told her about some of their childhood adventures, pleased with himself whenever he drew a smile from her. When she smiled, she reminded him of her sister, a thought he pushed away as soon as it occurred to him. He'd done a pretty good job of not thinking about Patsy Harper for almost five years. He wasn't going to break the habit now.

"Telling tales out of school?" Ty's voice came from the doorway, startling the two people seated at the kitchen table. Jack had been telling Meg about the time Ty put his pet frog in the teacher's desk and they hadn't heard the door open.

"In school, actually," Jack said. "I was just explaining why Miss Jones taught only one year before retiring to marry a distant cousin."

"I suppose you didn't bother to mention just whose idea the frog was, did you?" Ty asked, casting him a mock threatening look as he hung his coat on a peg near the back door.

"I don't know what you're talking about," Jack protested innocently. "I was a model student."

"Model hellraiser, you mean. How are you, Meg?"

"I'm fine," she said, unaware of the absurdity of that claim coupled with her battered features. "My mother?"

"She's just fine. She was worried about you but now that she knows you're safe, she's fine."

Ty walked to the stove, brushing his hand lightly over the top of Meg's head in a quick, reassuring touch. The casual gesture made Jack's brows climb.

"You're sure she's all right?" Meg asked, still anxious.

"I'm positive." Ty poured himself a cup of coffee and carried it to the table. Meg was turning her empty mug around with quick nervous gestures. Ty reached out to take one of her hands in his, and Jack's eyebrows nearly disappeared into his hairline.

"I wouldn't lie to you, Meg."

"I know. Thank you for checking on her, Ty. I'm sorry to be so much trouble but I was so worried. He was so angry," she whispered, her eyes dark with memory.

"You can stop worrying," he told her firmly. "About your mother *and* about your stepfather. I went to see him."

"You shouldn't have!" Meg's shocked protest drowned out Jack's murmur of approval. Not that it would have mattered if it hadn't, he thought. The two of them had quite plainly forgotten all about his existence.

"I couldn't just let him get away with what he did to you."

"You shouldn't have talked to him."

"All I did was tell him he'd have me to answer to if he ever tried to hurt you again."

"Now he'll be angry with you," she said, obviously distressed.

"I can live with that."

Jack said nothing, watching the two of them, his eyes alert and curious. Did Ty know Meg was in love with him? he wondered. Seeing the gentleness in his friend's touch, the tenderness in his face as he soothed her fear, perhaps it was more to the point to question whether Ty had yet realized the strength of his own feelings toward Meg.

"How is she?" Jack asked as Ty entered the kitchen.

He'd been upstairs, making sure that Meg followed orders and went back to bed after taking another of his mother's sleeping pills.

"Asleep," Ty answered. He dumped out his cold coffee and refilled it from the pot. He cradled the cup in one hand, rubbing the other over the back of his neck, trying to ease the tension in his muscles. "If I'd known it would upset her so much to know that I'd talked to Davis, I wouldn't have told her."

"She's worried about you."

"Yeah. Ironic, isn't it?" Ty's mouth twisted with bitter humor. "He beats her to a pulp and she's worried that he'll be angry with me."

"I suppose it's too much to hope that you fed Davis his teeth?" Jack gave him a hopeful look but Ty shook his head.

"I wish. I'd have wrung his neck if I hadn't thought that it might cause her more problems." He pulled out a chair and sank into it, more tired than he could ever remember being in his life.

"Has this happened before?"

"I don't think so. Not like this, anyway."

"What kind of a bastard is Davis, that he could hurt her that way?"

Ty stared at the cup in his hand, thinking that Jack only knew the half of what Davis had done. He hadn't even told him the worst of it.

"I don't know. But he's not getting a chance to hurt her again. She's not going back to that house."

"Sounds like a good idea."

The only idea, Ty thought. He took a swallow of coffee, feeling his stomach churn as it went down. He hadn't eaten since sometime the night before, he realized. But he made no move to get up and get something to eat.

"What's going to happen to Meg when you leave?" Jack asked slowly.

Ty felt the momentary feeling of peace disappear like a popped balloon. It was the same question Meg's mother had asked. He'd had no answer then and he didn't have one now.

"I don't know." He set his cup down and stood up, moving to the window to stare out at the gray landscape outside. "But she's not going back there."

"Well, she's going to have to go somewhere because it's a cinch your mother won't let her stay here."

Ty didn't need Jack to tell him that. His mother was not without her sympathetic side, but taking Meg in would be as foreign to her nature as going out to get the mail in her nightdress. It just wasn't done. No, having Meg stay with his family was out of the question.

"What about her sister?" he said suddenly, turning to look at Jack. "Maybe Meg could stay with her."

"Patsy?"

"Why not?" Ty asked, warming to the idea. "Meg and I saw her when we went to the fair this summer."

"How did she look?" The question seemed to come without his volition, his tone enough to shake Ty out of his preoccupation with Meg.

"Why? I thought you didn't really know Meg's sister."

Jack shrugged, his expression controlled as he got up from the table. "We dated a time or two."

"When?" Ty's interest was caught. Something in Jack's tone said that there was more to it than just a casual date or two.

"A few years ago. The winter Dad died, actually. You remember, I came home for a couple of months to take care of things, get Mom and Beryl settled."

"I remember. But you never said anything about dating Patsy Harper." Ty moved out of the way so that Jack could rinse his cup in the sink.

"There wasn't much to say. We went out a few times, then I took Mom and Beryl to Europe for a few weeks. By the time I got back, Patsy had gotten married." He shrugged. "End of story."

Ty doubted that. Something told him there was considerably more to the story than Jack was admitting. But the problem of settling Meg was more urgent than Jack's past involvement with her sister.

"Do you think Patsy would take Meg in?" he asked.

"How would I know? I haven't seen her in almost five years. She seemed fond of Meg. But even if Patsy is willing, there's no saying how Patsy's husband would feel."

"True." Ty frowned into the middle distance. He didn't want Meg living where her presence was only tolerated. She deserved more than that.

"Look, you don't have to make any decisions this minute." Jack set his cup down and crossed the room to take his jacket from the coat hook beside the door. "I'm going to go home and see if Beryl has a few things she can loan Meg."

"Things?" Ty had only been listening with half an ear, his thoughts still circling the need to get Meg properly situated.

"Clothes," Jack clarified. "Or do you expect her to continue living in your pajamas indefinitely?"

"No, of course not." Clothes. Why hadn't he thought to ask her mother to pack some of her things? "Ask Beryl not to mention Meg to anyone, would you? If people find out she's staying here with me, there'll be hell to pay."

"Speaking of which, Mrs. Vanderbilt was over this morning, a few minutes after you left. Said she was worried that something might be wrong when she saw you leave."

"Busybody," Ty muttered as he followed Jack to the front door.

"I don't think it's fair to say that, Ty." Jack paused in the doorway and shook his head. "She's carried gossip to a new high. It's almost an art form with her. Give credit where it's earned, Ty. She's gone far beyond such a common term."

"You're right. They ought to invent a new word for someone like her."

"It's raining again," Jack commented, frowning at the light drizzle that was falling.

"Looks like." Ty thought of the storm the night before, of how wet Meg had been when he brought her inside.

"You know it's really too bad Meg isn't a little older," Jack commented, apropos of nothing.

"Why?" Ty shifted his attention from the lowering sky to Jack's face. "What's her age got to do with anything?"

"Well, if she were just a little older, you could marry her. That would solve all her problems. I'll bring some clothes by later." He lifted one hand in farewell before hurrying down the steps and into the rain.

Ty watched him dash across the wet lawn to the black Studebaker parked at the curb. It was a good thing he hadn't waited for a response to his comment, because Ty doubted he could have said a single word at that point.

Marry Meg? Jack was off his rocker. Shaking his head, he pushed the door shut, closing out the damp afternoon. Meg was just a kid. *Please don't call me a kid, Ty.* The words she'd spoken—my God, was it only last night?—came back to him.

Heaven knew, she didn't feel like a kid in his arms. When he was holding her, she was all woman and a desirable one at that. But that wasn't the point. She was too young for him. Besides, he had no intention of getting married. He had neither the money nor the inclination to be taking on a wife. Jack must have been joking. That was it. Jack had been jerking his chain.

Ty stopped and stared up at the door of his room, just visible at the top of the stairs. Marry Meg? The idea was ridiculous.

Meg came downstairs for supper and ate some of the soup Ty fixed, though he suspected it was more to please him than because she felt hungry. After supper, they sat in the living room and listened to the radio. Meg seemed wrapped in her own thoughts, so withdrawn that not even Amos and Andy managed to draw more than a vague smile from her.

Seeing her so subdued, noticing the way she tended to jump at the smallest sound, Ty found himself bitterly regretting the lost opportunity to plant his first squarely in Harlan Davis's face.

It was barely nine o'clock when Meg stood up and asked if he'd mind if she went to bed. Ty followed her upstairs and rifled the medicine chest for another of his mother's sleeping pills, which he insisted on Meg taking before she lay down. She looked so small and fragile lying there. Her hair tumbled over the white linens like warm gold silk and her skin was nearly as pale as the pillowcase. The blue of her eyes seemed dull, the life drained away.

"You'll feel better tomorrow," he said, making the words at once reassurance and command.

"I know." She made an effort to smile for him but her eyes remained shadowed.

"You don't ever have to be afraid of Davis again."

"I keep thinking about him," she admitted. "The way he looked at me. The way he . . . touched me."

"Try to put it out of your mind." He gave in to the urge to stroke his fingers across her forehead, brushing her hair back from her face. "I'll keep you safe, Meg. Trust me."

"I do." The soft words were solemn as a prayer.

It occurred to Ty suddenly that he was responsible for someone else's life in a way he'd never been before. He'd promised her that he'd take care of her and she believed him.

It was a promise he'd keep, come hell or high water. All he needed was a few days to figure out how to go about it.

Unfortunately, he wasn't going to have those few days.

With all that had happened, Ty had all but forgotten his parents' imminent arrival. Since their wire had simply said that they'd be home in a few days, giving no specific date, it had been easy to shove it from his mind. Which was exactly what he'd done.

The first time he thought of them was when the front door opened the next morning and he heard his mother's sharp voice telling someone to be careful with the luggage because it wasn't made of granite. His eyes flew across the table to where Meg sat, a cup of coffee steaming in front of her. She stared at him in dismay and not a little fear.

"Don't worry," he said automatically.

"Tyler? Where are you, dear?" His mother's voice preceded her as she apparently decided to check the most likely spot for him to be at eight-thirty in the morning.

He stood up, half thinking to stop his mother before she got to the kitchen and saw Meg, though he could hardly conceal her presence for more than a few minutes. But he'd taken only one step toward the hall before his mother sailed through the door, her still-pretty face wreathed in a smile.

"Tyler! It's so wonderful to see—" She broke off as she registered the scene before her.

Ty closed his eyes, knowing exactly how it looked, exactly how she'd interpret it. Damn, but this was the last thing Meg needed. When he opened his eyes again, he saw the color rush up under his mother's smooth skin as she took in the sight of her son, in his shirtsleeves, standing next to the table where he'd obviously been sharing breakfast with the girl still seated there. A girl who was not only young and beautiful but who just happened to be wearing that same son's bathrobe.

"Oh!" She put her hand to her chest and staggered back as if from an actual, physical blow.

"What's the matter, dear?" Elliot McKendrick, as always, trailing behind his wife, put his hands on her upper arms to steady her and peered over her head. "My, my," he murmured, a masterpiece of understatement if ever Ty had heard one.

He opened his mouth to offer some explanation, something to diffuse the scene before it got started. But what came out was: "How was your trip?"

Chapter 10

Not surprisingly, no one was interested in discussing the McKendricks' recent European jaunt. In fact, for a moment, Ty wasn't sure there'd be any discussion at all, since his mother looked as if she might faint. But he underestimated her. After a moment of stunned silence, she straightened away from her husband's support and drew herself up to her full, if not particularly impressive, height.

"What is the meaning of this?" she demanded, in a tone that left no doubt in anyone's mind that the meaning of it was perfectly clear. And appalling.

"Calm down, Mother," Ty said. He stepped forward so that he stood between her and Meg, instinctively trying to protect Meg from the scene that was sure to follow. "There's nothing to get upset about."

"Nothing to get upset about?" she repeated. Her voice rose questioningly. "I come home to find my son—my only remaining son—having breakfast in my kitchen with some . . . some floozy who's wearing his bathrobe and you tell me I shouldn't be upset. How could you, Tyler!"

"Meg is not a floozy. And this isn't what it looks like."

"Then what is she doing in my kitchen wearing *your* bathrobe?"

"She's not doing what you obviously think she is." He

thrust his fingers through his hair, wishing he'd had a chance to prepare for this. "I wish you'd let me know when you were coming," he said, speaking his thoughts out loud.

His mother gasped indignantly. "We certainly didn't think there was any reason to warn you of our arrival!"

"That's not what I meant." He hadn't thought it possible that things could get worse, but he seemed to be doing a pretty good job of insuring that they did.

"I was so looking forward to coming home," she said, her voice breaking. "I thought you'd be glad to see us." She searched through her purse to come up with a handkerchief with which to dab at her eyes, though Ty saw no sign of tears.

"Of course I'm glad to see you, Mother. It's just that, if I'd known when you were arriving, I could have picked you up at the station and . . . explained things to you so that you wouldn't jump to conclusions about Meg's presence."

"Then why don't you explain it now," she snapped, clenching the linen handkerchief into her fist. Before Ty could respond, her eyes widened and the narrowed. "Meg?" She seized on the name, her finely plucked brows drawing together. "Not George Harper's daughter?" Her appalled tone made it clear that she was hoping for a denial.

"Yes, as a matter of fact she is." Ty was vividly aware of Meg sitting behind him, listening to what was being said. The last thing she needed at this point was this encounter with his mother's razor-edged tongue.

Helen started to say something, caught the blaze of warning in her son's eyes, and changed her mind abruptly.

"I must say, I'd thought better of you, Tyler. I know a boy's expected to . . . sow some wild oats," she said delicately. "But to bring a woman into your own home . . . I just can't believe you'd do something so . . ."

"Ty didn't anything wrong." Ty turned as Meg stood up. "Meg—"

She ignored his half-spoken protest and came to stand beside him. She was pale as a ghost but determined to come to his defense. "Ty was helping me, Mrs. McKendrick. He hasn't done anything wrong." There was a moment's silence and Ty wondered if it was possible that her words had gotten through to his mother.

"What happened to her face?" Helen snapped, looking at Meg but addressing the question to Ty.

"Her stepfather beat her," Ty said bluntly. "She came to me for help."

Shock flickered through her eyes and he thought he saw a trace of sympathy, but perhaps it was his imagination because an instant later, her mouth firmed into a disapproving line.

"I've always thought that a family's problems should stay in the family," she said. "Decent people don't go about airing their dirty linen in public." Without saying it, she managed to imply that she'd have expected no better of George Harper's offspring.

Meg flushed at the criticism and Ty felt anger rush over him. Damn his mother's sharp tongue. Meg didn't need this. He drew a deep breath but forced down the sharp response that rose in his throat. It wasn't going to do anybody any good to turn this into yet another argument between him and his mother.

"We're not going to get anywhere this way," he said, keeping his tone even but with an effort. He turned to Meg. "Why don't you go upstairs and get dressed."

She hesitated, glancing from him to his mother, and Ty knew that she was concerned for him, worried that her presence was going to cause a problem between him and his mother. If he could have, he would have told her that the problems between the two of them went back a long way and had nothing to do with her.

"Go on. We'll get this straightened out when you come back down."

"Yes, perhaps it would be best if you put on something besides my son's robe." Helen managed to make it sound as if the heavy robe were as scandalous as Sally Rand's feather fans.

"Mother." Ty's voice held a warning. His mother sniffed but didn't say anything more.

She drew pointedly out of the way as Meg approached the

door, and Ty's fingers curled into his palms as he struggled to restrain the urge to grab her and shake her until her teeth rattled—a most unfilial urge. He waited until Meg was on her way up the stairs before speaking.

"I'd appreciate it if you didn't say anything to upset Meg, Mother. She's been through a very difficult time."

"*She's* been through a difficult time. I'd like to know what you think you're putting me through." The handkerchief came into play again. "Coming home to find that . . . that girl in my house, alone with my son, doing heaven knows what. It's a wonder my poor heart didn't just give out right on the spot. Think how you'd have felt then."

"I'd have been very sorry if your heart had given out, Mother. Especially over nothing."

"Nothing! Nothing!" Her voice rose indignantly. "Well, I like that!"

"Now, Helen, let's not jump to conclusions." Elliot McKendrick, who'd been silent and nearly forgotten, spoke soothingly. "Before you start saying things you might regret, why don't you let the boy explain?"

"I don't see how he can possibly explain what I saw," she snapped.

"No harm in listening," he pointed out with all his usual calm.

"Well, I guess so." But she sniffed to make it clear that she doubted the possibility of any explanation being good enough to soothe her.

She was right.

"I still don't understand why she came to you." Helen waved one hand to emphasize her lack of understanding.

She addressed the question to Ty, just as she had done with every word she'd spoken. Though Meg sat not six feet from her, she'd yet to acknowledge her existence. Meg wondered if Mrs. McKendrick was hoping that she'd disappear if she simply refused to look at her. She saw Ty's jaw tighten but his mother's attitude didn't upset her. She could even understand it. If Ty had been her son, she might have felt much the same.

At Elliot McKendrick's suggestion, the discussion was being conducted in the comfort of the living room. But if he'd been hoping that softer surroundings would be conducive to soothing tempers, he must have been disappointed, she thought, feeling oddly detached from the whole discussion.

"I already explained that, Mother," Ty said in a voice that spoke of thinning patience. "Meg came to me because we're friends."

"Friends?" A lift of one thinly plucked eyebrow carried the implication of the question.

"Friends," Ty said flatly. Meg saw a muscle work in his jaw and knew that he was holding his anger in check only with considerable effort.

"Well, if the two of you have developed some sort of 'friendship,' I suppose I can understand why she'd feel she could impose on you in this manner," Helen conceded, sounding as if she didn't understand it at all. "But you say she's been here since night before last. Perhaps the first night was understandable," she said, sounding doubtful. "But what about yesterday? And last night? The two of you have been here, alone, for nearly two days. Have you given a thought to the scandal it would be if anyone found out she was here?"

"No one knows she's here, Mother. I know what it would do to Meg's reputation if people knew she'd spent the night here."

"It's not just Meg's reputation at stake here, Tyler." Clearly she thought that was already beyond the pale. "It doesn't look good for any of us," she said earnestly.

"Would it have looked better if I'd sent her home immediately?" he questioned, lifting one dark brow in angry question.

"Well, perhaps that would have been best." She lifted one manicured hand when he started to speak. "I'm not saying that her stepfather wasn't at fault, Tyler. But after all, he is, for all intents and purposes, her parent. Perhaps he was a bit too harsh," she admitted, slanting an uneasy look at Meg's face.

"Of course, I don't know the whole story, but perhaps if Meg tried a little harder, this kind of thing wouldn't happen again. You can't run away from your problems," she finished with the air of having just said something profound.

"If Meg tried a little harder?" Ty's voice rose. "You think she should try harder to please that son of a bitch?"

"Tyler!" His mother's gasp of shock was drowned out by his father's stern reproof at the profanity.

"I'm sorry." He stood up, as if unable to stay still. "If you knew," he muttered, pacing restlessly to the window and then back to the sofa. His frustration and anger was palpable.

His eyes met Meg's and she read in them a plea to let him tell his parents the whole truth, to make them understand. If they knew what Harlan had tried to do . . . Meg shuddered, feeling her stomach churn with shame. She couldn't bear for anyone to know. Ty must have read the fear in her eyes because he muttered something under his breath and turned away, his hands clenched into fists at his sides.

"I couldn't send her back there," he said flatly.

Meg huddled deeper into her corner of the sofa, feeling as if she'd failed him yet unable to bear the thought of anyone else finding out what had happened.

"She has to go back sooner or later," Helen said in a tone of utmost reason.

"No, she doesn't. She's not going back, ever."

"Not going back?" His mother's eyebrows rose into thin arcs. "Of course she's going back. What else can she do?"

"I don't know but she's not going back to that house." Meg felt his determination warm her.

"You're not making any sense," his mother snapped, her patience strained to the limits. "She has to go home. There's simply no other choice. Mr. Davis may have been a bit harsh, but that's not your problem."

"I don't happen to agree." Ty turned to face his mother directly and their eyes clashed. Meg saw a muscle working in his jaw, saw his mother's chin firm. They looked on the verge of coming to blows. All over her, she thought, distressed.

"Oh, please, don't fight about this." She stood up, her

hands twisted together in front of her as she looked from one to the other. "I'm not important enough for you to quarrel over."

"We certainly agree on that," Helen snapped.

"That's enough, Mother. You've no right to speak to her like that."

"No right? In my own home?"

"Meg is my guest," Ty said furiously. "That entitles her to common courtesy, if nothing else."

"Please." Meg put her hand on Ty's arm. "Please don't be angry," she begged, nearly in tears. She could feel the tension in the muscles under her fingers, feel the anger coursing through him. She sensed that the anger between Ty and his mother went deeper than the current situation, but she simply couldn't bear to see him at loggerheads with his family. She'd caused enough trouble for him without this.

"Meg's right." For the first time, Elliot McKendrick spoke up, his calm voice almost shocking in the tension filled room. "There's no good to come of the two of you getting into a squabble."

"Squabble?" Helen turned on her husband, her face flushed with anger.

"A squabble," he said firmly. "All this fussing isn't getting anybody anywhere. Sit down, Tyler. Meg."

Ty hesitated before sinking onto the sofa, whether in response to his father's command or to the pleading tug of her fingers on his sleeve, Meg didn't know. She sat down next to him, linking her hands together in her lap.

Elliot reached into his pocket and drew out his pipe, letting the silence stretch while he filled it from the ribbed glass jar that sat on the table next to his chair.

"That's better," he said, glancing at the room's occupants as he tamped the tobacco down with his finger. His wife shot him an annoyed look but she didn't speak. Elliot lit the pipe and took a few leisurely puffs so that the warm fragrance of tobacco wafted into the room.

"I don't hold with any man doing what Harlan Davis did to you," he said, speaking directly to Meg. "No man should have a right to do that, whether or not he's the head of the house, and I'm real sorry about it happening to you."

"Thank you," Meg murmured. She lowered her eyes to conceal the tears that rose at his kindness.

"And I'm proud of you, Tyler, for taking her in and seeing to her needs."

"Proud of him?" Helen burst out. "I suppose you'll still be proud when we're in the midst of the biggest scandal this town has ever seen!"

"I'd guess we'll survive," he said placidly. "Scandal or no, Tyler did the right thing and you know it."

"Thank you, Dad."

"Well, I still don't see why this is any of our affair," Helen said, not at all pleased to have her husband side with their son. "And I'd also like to know just what you plan on doing with her if she's not going home where she belongs."

"I'll think of something," Ty snapped.

"Well, now, there's where I see a problem," Elliot said quietly. "It seems to me that you could have some trouble there. What if her folks want her to come home?"

"She's not going. I don't care what they want."

"You may not care, son. But I think the law would see it different." Elliot sounded regretful. "She *is* underage, isn't she?"

Meg sucked in a quick breath. The gentleness of his tone gave the words more impact. Why hadn't it occurred to her that her stepfather could force her to go back? Instinctively her eyes flew to Ty's face, seeking reassurance but seeing only her own shock reflected there. She looked away before he could see the fear that swept over her in an almost paralyzing wave. She caught a quick glimpse of the triumph in Helen McKendrick's eyes, but the spiteful look had no meaning. She was already envisioning what her future could be.

To be forced to live in her stepfather's house, seeing him every day; to try to sleep at night knowing that only her bedroom door stood between her and the sickness she now knew existed in him. She couldn't do it. No matter what, she couldn't go back there.

"She's not going back," Ty said again, but this time his words offered no reassurance.

Meg shivered, her fingers twisting painfully together in her lap as she fought to swallow the scream of denial that rose in her throat. If they tried to force her back into that house . . . She'd run away. The one thought was crystal clear inside her. She didn't know where she'd go or how she'd live, but she knew she wouldn't go back to that house, no matter what the law said. She thought briefly of her sister. Patsy might take her in, but she couldn't be sure. She didn't really know her sister anymore.

"If the law says that's what she must do, you can't fight that," Ty's mother said, her tone sympathetic now that she saw victory in her grasp.

"I don't care what the law says."

"I know it's upsetting," she said. "But you can't argue with the law."

The argument continued but Meg was no longer listening. If the law said she had to go back, there was nothing Ty could do to prevent it. She knew he'd meant it when he said he'd keep her safe, but neither of them had given a thought to the possibility that her stepfather might have a legal right to make her go home. And she wouldn't let Ty break the law on her behalf. She'd been trouble enough to him already.

She let the argument roll over and around her, knowing it was pointless. If there was a way he could force her back, Harlan Davis would use it. She knew that on some deep, gut level that she couldn't explain. Just as she knew that he'd take pleasure in her fear, in the power that fear would give him over her.

Ty's mother was saying something about someone named Dickey and how he'd never have done this to her when a new voice entered the picture.

"Yoohoo! Anybody home?" Edwina Vanderbilt's voice sailed in from the entryway, freezing the living room's occupants as effectively as an arctic blizzard. "I know it's naughty of me to just come right in but you know how I am. And I just *had* to see my dear friends and hear all about your trip."

She was talking as she walked into the living room, seemingly oblivious to the thick silence she encountered. "You've been gone so long and I— Oh!" Her gaze fell on Meg and she broke off in midsentence, her small mouth forming a little round O of surprise. Her eyes widened as she took in the condition of Meg's face. The swelling along her jaw had gone down, but the scratch on her cheek was still an angry red streak across her pale skin and there was no concealing the fact that she had a black eye.

"Oh, my!" There was shocked delight in the exclamation. Here was a juicy piece of gossip if ever she'd seen one. Not that she was one to gossip, of course, but telling her three dearest friends wasn't the same thing at all. "Am I interrupting something?" she asked hopefully.

"Not at all," Helen said, rising to greet her. "How are you, Edwina?"

"I'm fine." The two women bumped cheeks. "How was your trip?" Edwina's eyes darted around the room's occupants, taking in Meg's huddled misery, the palpable anger that surrounded Ty, and the fine lines of tension in her friend's face.

"We had a lovely trip," Helen said, as calm as if they were chatting over a cup of tea. "I hope we can have a nice chat later." She took Edwina's arm and began herding her toward the door.

"Well, I certainly didn't mean to come at a bad time," Edwina said, throwing a longing look over her shoulder.

"Not at all, my dear. But I would like to unpack and freshen up." There was iron under the polite tone and Edwina sighed, recognizing defeat.

"Of course. But you must tell me everything." Clearly, "everything" included the interesting little tableau in the McKendricks' living room.

"Of course." Helen had managed to get her almost into the entryway when the front door opened again. This time it was Jack who walked in unannounced.

"The door was open so I came in," he said as he entered the living room.

"Seems like we're getting quite a little gathering," Elliot commented, speaking to no one in particular.

"I think it's going to get even larger," Jack said, throwing Ty a worried look. "I passed Sheriff Marlon on the way here and he had Harlan Davis with him."

Jack's announcement left silence in its wake, a silence Edwina Vanderbilt was more than happy to break.

"Whatever would Sheriff Marlon being doing coming here?" she questioned. With a deft move at odds with her size, she slipped away from her hostess's grasp and came further into the living room. "And why is he bringing Mr. Davis with him?"

She fixed a bright-eyed look on Meg, not even troubling to conceal her curiosity. With a sound that approached a moan, Helen McKendrick lifted her hands, whether in prayer or simply to say that she gave up, Meg wasn't sure. Elliot continued to puff his pipe, though his dark brows drew together in a worried frown. Ty said nothing, but a muscle began to tick in his jaw.

As for Meg, she wasn't sure what she felt. In the last forty-eight hours, she'd been dealt a number of blows, both physical and emotional. There was, she realized, a limit to the amount of pain and fear an individual could absorb. She'd reached that limit. The news of her stepfather's imminent arrival caused only a sluggish stir of alarm.

She leaned her head back against the sofa and closed her eyes, wanting nothing so much as to crawl in a dark hole somewhere and lie there until the world returned to normal. Only she wasn't even sure she knew what normal was anymore, she thought wearily.

"Don't worry." She felt Ty take her hand, his fingers tense around hers. She opened her eyes to look at him. She thought that perhaps a soldier facing a battle he knew he was fated to lose might look much the same. "Don't worry," he said again.

She wanted to tell him that she'd gone beyond worry to a not unpleasant feeling of numb acceptance, but before she could say anything, the doorbell rang.

"Well, at least *some* people still ring the bell," Helen said tartly.

"I'll get it." Ty squeezed Meg's hand one last time before getting up to answer the door.

"Hello, Sheriff."

"Tyler." Ben Marlon touched the brim of his khaki hat. His expression was pleasant but official enough to make it clear that while he might be a friend of the family, he was here on business. He was a large man, with the kind of build that people always said came of having big bones. He was nearly sixty and had constituted Regret's only law enforcement for as long as Ty could remember. "I need to talk to you."

"I guessed as much." Ty looked past him to where Harlan Davis stood. He felt a certain satisfaction at the way the smaller man paled when their eyes met. And a definite regret that he hadn't buried his fist in Davis's mouth.

"You think we could continue this inside?" the sheriff asked. "It's a bit chilly out here. Besides, I never did like conducting official business in full view of God and anybody else who happens to be looking."

Ty's hesitation was imperceptible. The last thing he wanted was to let Davis into the house. He didn't want the man within fifty feet of Meg. But he didn't think the sheriff would agree to letting Harlan stand on the porch. He stepped back without a word.

"Thank you, Ty." Ben stepped inside, reaching up to doff his hat and tuck it under one arm. Ty was pleased to note that Davis nearly sidled through the door, attempting to keep as much distance between them as possible.

Since there was no way to avoid it, Ty led the way into the living room. While the necessary courtesies were being observed, he crossed the room to stand next to Meg, who was still huddled in one corner of the sofa. He wouldn't have been surprised to see her trembling at the sight of her stepfather, but he could see no reaction at all.

"Well, now, I guess we might as well get to the point of all this," Ben said, having greeted Ty's parents and Edwina

Vanderbilt, who'd planted herself in a chair with an expression
that said it would take considerable effort to persuade her to
leave. He nodded to Jack and glanced at Meg, who hadn't
lifted her head since he'd entered the room. He settled his
attention on Ty.

"Mr. Davis here, he claims that you threatened to kill
him, Tyler. Said you came into the hotel yesterday and, without any provocation whatsoever, threatened to do him bodily
injury. Says he can produce witnesses who'll say the same. Is
that true?"

"Of course not," Helen said sharply. "Tyler wouldn't do
any such thing and you know it!"

"I've got to hear it from Ty, Mrs. McKendrick," Ben
said, his smile holding both apology and determination. "Ty?"

"I told him I'd kill him if he came near Meg," Ty admitted slowly.

"Well, of course, it's one of those things one says but
doesn't really mean," Helen said quickly. "If the police were
called out every time someone threatened to kill someone, they
wouldn't have any time for catching real criminals. Which is
exactly what you should be doing right now, Ben Marlon. Not
standing in my living room questioning my son as if he were a
common thief!"

"I'm sorry to intrude, Mrs. McKendrick. If you'd rather,
I could ask Ty to come down to the courthouse and we could
settle it all down there," he suggested gently.

Under other circumstances, Ty would have been hard
pressed not to laugh out loud at seeing his mother so neatly
silenced. At the mention of the courthouse, she blanched, the
color draining from her face, leaving two neat spots of rouge
standing on her cheeks. Ty knew, as if he could read her mind,
the picture she'd immediately conjured: Ben Marlon leading
him into the courthouse in handcuffs while the entire town
looked on.

"That's quite all right, Sheriff," she said in a weak tone.
"I'm sure this can all be settled here."

"I hope so." He turned back to Ty. "You want to tell me

why you felt the need to threaten to kill Harlan Davis if he came near his own stepdaughter?"

"Because he beat her."

"*Beat* her?" Ben's shaggy eyebrows rose as if to chase his receding hairline. "That's a pretty serious word, Ty. I know you and the Harper girl have been real friendly this summer and I can understand you getting a mite upset about someone layin' a hand on her, but a man's got a right to run his family as he sees fit and—"

His voice trailed off as Meg lifted her head and looked at him. Where she was sitting, weak sunshine spilled through a nearby window to illuminate her bruised face. Ty had had nearly two days to get used to it, and it was still a shock each time he looked at her. Clearly it had an even stronger impact on Ben Marlon. He stared at her for a moment, his face tightening, and then he turned to fix a steely gaze on Harlan Davis.

"I didn't hurt the girl," Davis said, stumbling in his haste to get the denial out. "She fell and did that to her eye. She's lying if she says I ever laid a hand on her."

Hearing Davis deny what he'd done when the evidence of his brutality was plain for everyone to see fanned Ty's smoldering anger to a red-hot blaze. He heard a low growl and was surprised to realize that it came from him.

"Ty." Jack's low-voiced warning stopped him from doing what every instinct urged, which was wrapping his hands around Davis's throat and choking the life from him, to hell with whoever was watching.

With an effort, he stayed where he was. It wasn't going to do anyone any good if he lost his temper. The important thing was to take care of Meg, not to satisfy his need for revenge. It was his fault Davis was here at all. If he hadn't gone to see him yesterday, hadn't humiliated him . . . But he had and now all he could do was try to deal with the consequences.

"It must have been quite a door to do that kind of damage," Ben was saying. He loomed over the smaller man but Davis didn't back down.

"It was a door and you can't prove different."

"Apparently the girl says otherwise," Ben pointed out.

"She's lying. She's done it before." Seeing no change in the sheriff's ominous expression, he abandoned that line of defense. "It doesn't matter whether you believe me or not. Long as she's a minor, she's in my charge. I don't care what you think I did. I want McKendrick arrested and I want my stepdaughter back home where she belongs."

Ty felt Meg shudder and he put his hand on her shoulder, trying to reassure her, though God knew he'd precious little reassurance to offer.

"Well, now, as far as arresting Ty, I wouldn't feel right about doing that. Like his mama pointed out, people say a lot of things they don't mean when they're all in a lather. I'd feel pretty silly arresting him." He paused, looking thoughtful. "Of course, if he actually was to kill you, then that'd be another story altogether," he said, seeming to consider the point. "I reckon I'd have to arrest him then."

Jack's snorted laughter was drowned out by Harlan's gabbled protest, which the sheriff ignored.

"However, as far as Miss Harper going home . . ." He paused and shook his head regretfully. "I'm afraid I'd have to agree that Davis has the right of it. Until she's eighteen or married, the law says she belongs at home."

"You'd send her back there after what he did to her?" Ty protested.

"Not me, son. But the law says a minor belongs with her folks."

"What does the law say about this kind of abuse?" he demanded, gesturing to Meg's bruised face.

"You'd have to go to court to do anything about that," Ben said. His look was regretful but firm. "I'm not saying it's right. I'm just saying that's the way it is."

"Well, she's not going back there. That's all there is to it."

"Now, son, I sympathize with how you feel, but the law is the law." Seeing the set of Ty's jaw, he sighed. "I'll tell you what, how about if I promise to keep an eye on her? And if there's any more trouble, she can come direct to me and I'll deal with it." The look he turned on Harlan Davis said he wouldn't be averse to "dealing" with him. "How about that, Meg?" he asked kindly.

"I . . . That's very kind of you, Sheriff," she whispered without lifting her eyes from her lap.

But Ty knew she wouldn't go to the sheriff, not for the kind of abuse Davis might deal out; not after the way she'd begged him not to tell anyone what had happened, that she couldn't bear the shame if anyone were to find out the truth. If he told Ben what had really happened, the sheriff would come down on their side and Meg would be safe.

But she'd never forgive him. And if he was willing to risk that, he still wasn't sure it was the best thing for her. Even if he kept her away from Harlan, what was she going to do? Where was she going to live?

"Actually, there's a very good reason Meg can't go home, one I haven't mentioned yet."

"Ty, no!" Meg's protest was horrified. Obviously she thought he was going to tell them that Davis had tried to rape her.

"It's all right, honey. We're going to have to tell them sooner or later."

"Tell us what?" That was his mother, sounding impatient. "I don't see how anything you say can change the facts, Tyler. The law says she belongs with her people, and that's all there is to it."

"Ty, please," Meg whispered.

He gave her shoulder a playful squeeze and laughed, wondering if anyone else heard the strained sound of it, wondering if he'd lost his mind to be doing what he was about to do; unable to see any other way.

"There's really no question of her going anywhere with anyone but me, actually. You see, Meg and I were married yesterday."

Chapter 11

The words hung in the air and Ty had the urge to look around to see who had uttered them. It couldn't have been he. It was, as he might have expected, his mother who recovered first.

"You wouldn't have gotten married without telling us," she said, the words more a plea than a statement.

"I'm sorry, Mother. If we'd known you were going to be home today, of course we would have waited. Wouldn't we have, dear?" He gave Meg a look that was both warning and promise.

She nodded dazedly, obviously responding more to his tone than to his words. She looked as if she were in shock. Ty gave her a reassuring smile, hoping it didn't look as desperate as it felt.

"A wedding. Isn't this exciting!" Edwina clapped her hands together, giving the "newlyweds" an indulgent look.

She'd been so quiet throughout the proceedings that Ty had nearly forgotten her presence. But he was suddenly glad she was here. With Edwina sure to spread the news about their "marriage," it could make Davis hesitate before causing any real trouble. Considering his concern for his precious name, he might think twice about creating a full-blown scandal.

"But you can't be married," Helen protested. "Not to Meg Harper."

"Careful, Mother." Ty kept his smile in place with an effort, wondering what she'd say when she found out that she was right—he wasn't married but that he had every intention of making the lie a reality.

"I can't believe you've done this." For the first time, genuine tears sprang to her eyes, and she groped for the handkerchief she was never without. "The airplanes were one thing. I thought you might grow out of those, but now you've thrown your life away on a—"

"That's enough now, Helen." Elliot's placid voice cut through his wife's shrill protest. She looked as if she might continue but caught his eyes and subsided into soft sobs instead, muffling them with a lace-edged handkerchief. "Congratulations, son." Ty met his father's look and knew that at least one person in the room was not in the least fooled by his hasty announcement.

"He's lying!" Davis was so agitated that he momentarily forsook his safe position behind Ben Marlon, bumping into the other man in his haste to come forward. "He's lying to keep me from getting what's rightfully mine."

"Meg isn't a piece of property," Ty snapped, taking a quick step forward. Seeing the look in his eyes, Davis retreated, putting Sheriff Marlon's bulk between himself and Ty.

"He's lying," he said again, giving Ty a venomous look. "It's not possible that they're married."

"I was a witness," Jack said calmly, speaking for the first time since the whole scene had begun. "It looked pretty possible to me."

Ty didn't even look at him. He'd known he could count on Jack to back him up. His attention was all for Harlan Davis, whose face twisted with anger.

"You're his friend," Davis snapped furiously. "Of course you'd lie for him."

"I don't much like being called a liar," Jack said, all his usual good humor gone, leaving him looking cold and hard.

"Now, hold on a minute." Ben Marlon raised one large

hand in a gesture that commanded silence. "I want all of you to be quiet while I get things sorted out." He paused to make sure his order was being heeded and then turned his attention to Ty. "So, the two of you were married yesterday. Mind telling me where?"

"In Herndale. Meg's sister lives there. She was our other witness."

"What about a license?" Davis demanded, pushing himself forward again. "You can't get one of those overnight."

"I've had the license for a couple of weeks," Ty said easily. Inwardly he was amazed by his hitherto undiscovered talent for lying. "We'd planned to wait until my parents returned from Europe, but when Meg was forced to run away, we decided that we shouldn't delay any longer."

He ignored Davis, keeping his eyes on Ben Marlon's face. If Ben believed him, even halfway, he'd have managed to buy some time.

"Ask him for the marriage certificate," Davis demanded. "Ask him and you'll see he's lying."

"Harlan, if you don't stop telling me how to do my job, I'm going to arrest you for interfering with an officer in the performance of his duty." Ben turned and looked down at the smaller man with an expression that suggested he wouldn't mind an excuse to do just that.

"You can't do that." Davis's eyes were nearly popping with outrage.

"And just who do you think is going to stop me?"

"It wouldn't be legal."

"It's a fine legal point, all right," Ben said, stroking his chin thoughtfully. "We'd probably have to have a judge decide whether or not you were guilty. And that would mean setting a date for a hearing. And, after I'd arrested you, I'd feel obliged to put you in jail, leastwise till you raised the bail."

Aghast, Harlan stared at the sheriff, reading the calm threat in his eyes. He opened his mouth to offer another protest. Ben lifted one eyebrow. Harlan's mouth shut with a snap. It was all Ty could do to keep from laughing out loud. His good humor faded when Ben turned back to him.

"How about it, Ty? If you can show me a marriage certificate, I reckon we can end this whole thing right here."

Ty hesitated, knowing that it could all fall apart right here. Where his hand still rested on her shoulder, he felt the tension in Meg's frame.

"I don't suppose you'd like to show me the marriage certificate," Ben repeated, sounding as if he already knew the answer to that question.

"I left it in the judge's chambers." The tissue of lies was growing thin enough for the sun to shine through it, Ty thought, but he didn't drop his eyes from the sheriff's.

"He doesn't have it," Harlan said triumphantly. "He doesn't have it because there isn't a certificate."

For once the little weasel was speaking nothing but the truth. The question was, would Ben believe him? Ty had almost given up the game for lost when help came from an unexpected quarter.

"Well, I can't say for certain that they're married, of course." Edwina hadn't said anything since her comment about them being newlyweds and Ty had nearly forgotten her. Now he swung his eyes in her direction. "But Ty did come over yesterday afternoon and ask me if he could pick a few of my roses for a wedding bouquet. My roses bloom later than most people's, you know," she said, looking smug. "Some people have said it's because they have a sheltered location." She cast a pointed look in Helen's direction. "That may have something to do with it, I suppose. But I also take the most particular care of them and I do think that makes a difference."

"And you *gave* him the roses," Helen asked, as if, without the roses, Ty couldn't possibly have gotten married.

"Well, I didn't see any reason not to, Helen. After all, I did tell you that I'd keep an eye on him and make sure he had everything he needed."

"So you're saying Ty told you he was going to get married?" Ben asked, ignoring the interruption and expressing no interest in how late Edwina's roses bloomed or what the cause might be.

"Well, he said he wanted roses for a wedding bouquet," she lied without a blink. "I didn't ask *whose* bouquet, of course. I'm not one to pry," she added mendaciously.

Ty didn't have it in him to wonder why Edwina Vanderbilt had just lied through her teeth for him. For the moment he didn't care. All that mattered was that she'd helped patch a few of the holes in his story, at least for the moment.

Sheriff Marlon looked from Edwina to Ty to Jack and back to Ty again before dropping to Meg. Her head was lowered, her hair swinging forward to conceal her face in a golden curtain. She wore a dress that belonged to Jack's sister, a subdued gray and blue print, the cut as conservative as a nun's habit, which was one of the reasons Beryl had been quite happy to part with it.

As if sensing the sheriff's gaze on her, Meg lifted her head, meeting his eyes with a blank look that asked for nothing, expected less.

"Well, I guess I've heard all I need to." Ben spoke abruptly, taking his hat out from beneath his arm and dusting it against the side of his pants.

"I'll be taking Meg home with me," Harlan said, sensing victory in his grasp. Ty felt the shiver that ran over Meg and tensed.

"Just a minute, Davis." Ben's beefy hand caught his arm. "Far as I'm concerned, Meg stays right where she is. With her husband."

It was all Ty could do to keep from sagging with relief. Now that Ben had shown himself willing to accept the story he'd spun, it was possible to admit just how little he'd believed the desperate lie would work.

"Husband!" Harlan's mouth gaped. "You can't believe this . . . this lie they're telling, Sheriff. They don't even have a marriage certificate."

"Well, now, I'll admit that's a concern, but I figure, as long as Ty agrees to bring the certificate by my office in the next day or two, there's no real problem." He gave Ty a shrewd look, his eyes holding a warning. "You ought to be able to get a copy of that certificate by then, Ty."

"I'll have it," Ty said steadily.

"Be sure you do." Ben clapped his hat on his head and nodded his farewells. "Sorry to interrupt your day like this, folks."

"That's quite all right, Sheriff," Elliot said, setting his pipe down and rising. "We understand you have to do your duty. Let me see you to the door."

For a moment Ty thought Harlan Davis was going to refuse to leave. He stood there, nearly quivering with frustrated anger, his mouth working as he struggled to find the words that would turn the situation his way. Before he could say anything, Ben clapped a heavy hand on his shoulder.

"Let's go, Davis. We've taken up enough of their time."

With a last furious glare in Ty's direction, Harlan turned and followed the sheriff out. Ty didn't make the mistake of thinking Davis had given up. He'd be hovering like a vulture waiting for any opportunity to snatch Meg back into his keeping. It was up to him to see that Davis didn't get that opportunity.

The sound of the front door closing behind the sheriff and Davis seemed to echo oddly. There was a moment's silence and then Meg rose, pressing one hand to her stomach.

"Excuse me, please," she muttered, and then hurried from the room, passing Elliot McKendrick without seeming to see him. Ty started after her.

"Don't you dare leave this room, Tyler Douglas McKendrick!" His mother had spent the last ten minutes dabbing at her eyes with a hanky, but her voice sounded more drill sergeant than grieving mother. Ty would have ignored her command but his father caught his eye and shook his head.

"Let her have a little time alone, son. I'd guess that's what she needs more than anything."

Ty hesitated and then nodded reluctantly. Perhaps his father was right.

Meg rinsed her mouth out and splashed cool water on her face, trying to drive away the clammy chill that had crept over her whole body. She'd lost what little breakfast Ty had insisted she eat, but her stomach still churned. Forcing her trembling knees to support her, she turned away from the sink, careful to avoid her reflection in the mirror above it.

Moving slowly, Meg made her way down the hall to Ty's bedroom, giving a brief thought to his mother's indignation should she find her there. She made it across the room before her knees gave out and she sank onto the welcoming surface of the bed. Meg sat there for a moment, staring at the gently faded pattern in the carpet beneath her feet.

She made a concerted effort to keep her mind a complete blank. When that proved impossible, she sighed and lifted her head. Looking at the clock, she was shocked to see that it wasn't even ten o'clock in the morning yet. So much had happened, it seemed as if it must be midafternoon, at least. Yet here it was, not even lunchtime.

There were, she thought, a hundred things she needed to think about, to decide. Ty had bought her a little time with his crazy story about them being married. She had to try to make some decisions about her future. But all she could think about was Ty's voice saying *Meg and I were married yesterday.* If only that were true. Freedom from her stepfather and her dearest wish all in that one little sentence.

She was still sitting there, her thoughts drifting aimlessly, when Ty tapped on the door and then pushed it open. He seemed surprised to see her sitting up and Meg wondered if he'd expected to find her in a state of collapse. Heaven knew she'd given him little reason these past two days to expect anything else.

"How are you?" He stepped into the room and pushed the door shut behind him.

"I'm fine. I'm sorry I ran out like that."

"That's okay. It was a . . . difficult morning."

"Yes." She sighed and reached up to push her hair back from her face, giving him an apologetic look. "I've been a lot of trouble the past couple of days. I'm sorry."

"You don't owe me an apology."

"Don't I? I've dragged you into the middle of this mess with my stepfather and now I've upset your parents and forced you to tell that ridiculous lie. I think the least I owe you is an apology.''

''My parents will recover,'' he said. He walked over to the wing chair and sat down. ''I'm just sorry you've had to go through all of this.''

''It's not your fault.''

''No?'' He looked doubtful.

''Of course it's not! I know you think you're to blame somehow because my stepfather was upset about me seeing you, but you couldn't know that. Besides, it could have been anything that set him off. There's a . . . sickness in him,'' she said more quietly. She clasped her hands on her elbows, hugging her arms close against her midriff. ''Something dark and twisted inside. It has nothing to do with you.''

''Maybe.'' He still sounded doubtful but Meg didn't protest any further. Given time, he'd realize she was right.

''I want to thank you for what you did, lying to the sheriff like that, telling him we were . . . married.''

''I'd like to think of it as an exaggeration rather than an outright lie,'' Ty said.

''It's a considerable exaggeration.'' Meg managed a half smile, trying not to show how much it hurt to be casually discussing something that meant so much to her.

''Maybe I should have called it a premature announcement.'' His eyes were intent on her face as he spoke.

It took Meg a moment to sort out what he'd said, to understand the implication. When his meaning hit her, she sucked in a quick breath, feeling the blood drain from her head so quickly that she felt suddenly dizzy. Perhaps she swayed, because Ty was beside her in an instant, his hand firm on the back of her neck as he pressed her head down to her knees.

''Take deep, slow breaths,'' he ordered.

With her forehead pressed to her knees, there wasn't much else Meg could do. She must be worse off than she'd thought. She could almost have sworn that he'd just implied that they were getting married.

''I'm all right,'' she mumbled into her skirt. When Ty released his hold on her neck, she raised her head slowly, relieved to find the dizziness gone. She didn't look at him, afraid of what he might see in her eyes. Instead, she stared at the print of an airplane that hung on the wall opposite.

"Look, I know it's a shock," Ty said when the silence had gone beyond comfort. "But I'm not sure I expected the first girl I proposed to to be struck dumb by the idea." It was a strained attempt at humor, but it told Meg, more than anything else could have, that she hadn't imagined his words of a moment ago.

"Premature announcement?" she said hoarsely. "You mean you really plan on . . . on . . ." She couldn't get the word out.

"On marrying you," Ty finished calmly. "Yes, I do. If you'll have me, that is."

If she'd have him? Was there any question? Wasn't this the secret dream she'd hardly dared admit having? Hadn't she spent the entire summer wishing she were older, smarter, more sophisticated, prettier? Anything at all that would make her more attractive to him? That would make him feel half as much for her as she felt for him? Of course she'd have him! She opened her mouth to tell him as much.

"Why do you want to marry me?" she heard herself ask.

"It's the only possible solution," he said.

"Solution? To what?" Solution? That hardly sounded like he was madly in love with her.

"To everything."

"You mean to the problem of my stepfather?" she asked bluntly.

"What else are we going to do?" he asked, his dark eyes serious.

"You can't marry me just to protect me from him." Meg felt the tentative flicker of hope that he might love her die.

"It's not just that." He frowned as if he were having trouble finding the right words. "I . . . like you. And I want to take care of you. If you marry me, you can come to California with me. You'll be far enough away from your stepfather to be safe there. It might be different if you were eighteen, if you could be on your own. But you're not. And right or wrong, I feel responsible for what happened.''

"You don't have to," she protested, knowing it wouldn't change how he felt. She played his words over in her mind. He liked her and wanted to take care of her. She could go to California with him and be safe. And when she turned eighteen in a few months? What then? An annulment? Was that what he had in mind?

She smoothed her fingers over the fabric of her borrowed skirt, wishing she knew what was right, wishing she didn't feel so overwhelmed by everything that had happened. No matter what she said, Ty was going to carry a burden of guilt for her stepfather's attack. If she agreed to marry him, that guilt would be eased. In a few months, they could have the marriage annulled and he could go on with his life, assured that he'd kept his promise to take care of her.

And in the weeks between now and your birthday in December? a sly voice asked. *Is there a chance that he'd fall in love with you? That the marriage wouldn't be annulled after all?*

"Is it that difficult a decision, Meg?"

She turned to look at him, her head spinning with questions. Was she being selfish to even consider his proposal? Would he be relieved if she said no?

"I don't know," she whispered.

"I do." He brought his hand up to stroke his fingers across her cheek, his touch gentle. "Trust me, Meg. This is the best thing for you. For both of us. Say yes."

Meg sighed, wishing she weren't so tired, so overwhelmed by everything that had happened, wishing she didn't want what he was offering so badly that she couldn't trust her own judgment.

"Trust me," he said again, looking deep into her eyes.

"I do."

"Then say yes. Say you'll marry me."

And with a soft sigh, she gave him the answer he seemed to want. "Yes. I'll marry you, Ty."

She pressed her face against the pleasantly scratchy wool

of his sweater as he put his arms around her and pulled her close. Closing her eyes, she drew a deep breath, inhaling the mixture of soap and coffee that clung to him. God help her for being too weak to say no, she thought tiredly. God help them both.

It was early afternoon the day after the scene at the Mc-Kendricks' house when Jack turned his mother's Studebaker into the drive that led to Patsy Harper's house. No, it was Patsy Baker now, he reminded himself. Patsy Baker, who had a husband. He didn't want to forget that.

He turned off the engine and sat staring at the house for a moment, wanting nothing so much as to turn around and leave and yet wanting to see her again. Five years was a long time. Had she changed?

What difference did it make if she had? He was here only because Ty had asked him to come. He'd thought it would be nice if Meg had someone there for her wedding. And since Ty was busy trying to finagle his way into a wedding license, Jack had been detailed to fetch Meg's sister. That's all she was, he reminded himself as he pushed open the car door. Just Meg's older sister.

The clouds had finally dispersed the night before, and pale sunshine bathed the damp countryside. The Baker home was on the edge of Herndale, some thirty miles from Regret. It was not a large house but it was pleasant and neatly kept. There were flower beds on either side of the door, dotted with bright mounds of chrysanthemums, which looked as if they were starting to recover from the heavy rains they'd endured.

Jack stepped up onto the porch but he didn't ring the bell immediately. He was surprised and annoyed to find that he was nervous. In the seat of a plane, he could challenge heaven itself without so much as a twinge of nerves. Yet the thought of seeing Patsy again made his palms damp.

"Fool," he muttered under his breath. Without allowing the memories to creep any closer, Jack rang the doorbell. He heard it buzz inside the house, then the sound of footsteps coming toward the door. And there was suddenly a knot in his stomach.

The door was pulled open and he found himself looking through the screen at the girl he'd once planned to marry. Only she wasn't a girl anymore. She must be twenty-three now, a woman by any standards.

"Jack!" The soft exclamation told him that she hadn't been expecting him. Ty must not have mentioned who would be picking her up. Jack found himself unreasonably pleased by her shocked surprise. Always before it had been Patsy who'd caught him off guard, who'd surprised him in some way. Right up until the last big surprise of finding out that she'd married someone else.

"Hello, Patsy. It's been a long time."

"Yes. Yes, it has." She drew a quick breath and gave him a forced smile before reaching out to push open the screen door. "Won't you come in?" she asked formally. "I'll just be a minute."

"Thank you."

Patsy shut the door behind him, and he could smell beeswax and soap. The inside of the house was as neat as the outside. He found it hard to imagine Patsy—his Patsy—polishing a table or mopping a floor. She'd always said that housework was pure drudgery and *she'd* never get caught in that trap. She was going to marry a man rich enough to hire a maid. Or maybe go to Hollywood and become a motion-picture star in the one of the new talkies. Of course, she'd also planned to marry him and said that she could be happy in a garret, as long as they were together. The cozy little house was far from a garret, but it was hardly the mansion she'd once dreamed of, he thought, looking around.

"How have you been?" The question brought Jack's eyes back to Patsy's face.

"Fine. You?"

"Oh, not bad." She gave him a nervous smile, her eyes skittering away from his. She seemed to be searching for something else to say and coming up blank. Jack had no such problem.

"Is your husband home?"

"Eldin?" She looked at him, her blue eyes wide and startled.

"If that's his name." Jack was pleased to hear the cool indifference in his voice; even more pleased to see her flush and then pale, her eyes darting away again.

"No. He travels quite a bit. Selling farm equipment, you know."

"No, actually, I didn't know." *And didn't care,* his tone said.

She flushed again and Jack felt his conscience twinge. When had he become such a bastard? he wondered. *The day he found out she'd married another man* came the prompt response. But that was five years ago, water under a bridge that should have been long forgotten.

"I'll just get my coat," Patsy said.

She was gone less than a minute and was already shrugging into the garment when she reappeared. She was probably just as anxious to get him out of her home as he was to leave, he thought as he opened the door. Not that he blamed her. He hadn't exactly been overwhelmingly friendly so far.

He opened her car door and offered his hand in automatic courtesy. She seemed to hesitate a moment before setting her fingers in his. She was wearing gloves, but the soft gray kid couldn't mask the shock of awareness that jumped between them. Patsy's breath caught and her eyes met his for an instant, telling him that she'd felt the same thing, and then she looked away, drawing her fingers from his as she settled onto the leather seat.

Jack shut the door and walked around the front of the car to the driver's side. If it had been anyone but Ty who'd asked him or if the circumstances had been anything other than what they were, he would have gone back to California rather than see Patsy again. Five years wasn't nearly long enough to forget.

"I saw Meg with Tyler at the fair a few weeks ago," Patsy said as he backed onto the road. Obviously she'd decided that polite conversation was preferable to strained silence. "I had no idea they were planning on getting married, though."

"It was a rather sudden decision," Jack said, his tone as bland as hers.

"I had that impression, what with Ty calling me just yesterday and all."

If she wondered why it was a sudden decision, she didn't ask. She stared out the window, her hands lying quietly in her lap. That was another thing that had changed, Jack thought, glancing at her. The Patsy he'd known had rarely been still for more than a few minutes. She'd been bubbling over with energy, always looking for some new adventure.

There were things that hadn't changed, though. Like the silky cap of pale-brown hair. She'd worn it the same way five years ago and he'd loved the way it molded her head, the feel of it sifting through his fingers. She'd gained a little weight, enough to soften the line of her jaw a little. But the mouth was the same, and it was all too easy to remember the way it had felt under his, warm and hungry.

His jaw tightening, he looked away, focusing his attention on the road. Five years, he reminded himself. He'd gotten over her a long time ago. It was absurd to think otherwise. She was simply the sister of the girl his best friend was going to marry. She meant nothing to him beyond that.

"Patsy!" Meg had been making a halfhearted effort to pin her hair up, but she let it tumble to her shoulders when she saw her sister's reflection in the mirror. "What are you doing here?"

"Ty said you were getting married." Her smile faded when Meg turned toward her. "My God, Meggy, what happened to your face?"

Meg brought her hand to touch the swelling around her eye. Funny, in the midst of everything else, she'd almost forgotten about her face. Seeing the shock in Patsy's eyes, she found herself lying automatically.

"I ran into a door," she said, forcing a smile. "Stupid of me, wasn't it?"

"A door?"

"Yes. You know what an oaf I can be. It was so sweet of Ty to think to ask you," she said, making an obvious change of subject. "Everything is happening so quickly that I hadn't even thought about asking anyone to the wedding."

Her voice sounded brittle, even in her own ears. Perhaps Patsy heard the same thing because she looked as if she were about to say something and then seemed to change her mind. When she spoke, her tone was as light and almost as false as Meg's.

"Well, I'm glad Ty thought of it."

"So am I." Meg turned back to the mirror, keeping her head bowed so that Patsy couldn't see her expression in the reflection. For an instant she'd had the urge to throw herself into her sister's arms and spill out the whole miserable story, just as she had when they were children. But it had been a long time since they'd been that close. The Patsy standing behind her was not the big sister she'd known.

"Did Eldin come with you?" she asked.

"No. He's out of town. He travels a lot, you know."

"I'd forgotten." Meg picked up the brush again and began brushing her hair, needing something to occupy her hands. There was an awkward silence.

"Do you have your something old and new and borrowed and blue?" Patsy asked, her cheerful tone forced.

"No. I hadn't even thought about it."

"Well, you can't get married without those things," Patsy protested. "You want to get your marriage off to a good start, don't you?"

"Of course." Privately Meg thought that it was going to take more than a few sentimental tokens to get this marriage off to a good start. But then again, they couldn't hurt.

"Here. I brought some things just in case." She began pulling things out of her purse. "I have a pretty hanky that Eldin brought home from his last trip to Chicago. It's Irish linen and I've never used it. That can be your something new."

"I couldn't take that from you," Meg protested, turning to look at her sister. "It was a present from your husband."

"Don't be silly. Eldin always brings me a few little trinkets when he comes home from a trip."

"Oh, but—"

"Please, Meg. I'd like you to have it."

There was no arguing with the plea in her sister's eyes. Meg took the hanky, admiring the almost silklike feel of the linen and the delicate lace that trimmed it. "Thank you."

"Don't thank me yet," Patsy said with forced gaiety. "I'm not through. I have a pair of earrings for you that can be your something blue. I hope they'll go with your dress," she added, looking worried.

"I don't really have a dress." Meg took the pretty enameled earrings, curling her fingers around them. "I mean, nothing fancy. There wasn't really time to get anything."

"You don't need a fancy dress to have a happy marriage," Patsy said briskly, looking as if there were nothing in the least odd about a wedding being arranged so quickly that the bride didn't have time to get a dress.

"Now, for the something old and something borrowed, I brought this." Patsy drew a small gold locket out of her purse. "It belonged to Eldin's grandmother and he gave it to me when we got married."

"It's lovely, Patsy." Meg was surprised to see that her hand wasn't quite steady as she reached out to touch the locket with one finger.

"Here. Turn around and let me put it on you."

Meg obediently turned around, watching in the mirror as Patsy set the necklace in place and then bent close to work the clasp. It struck her suddenly as ineffably sad that they'd grown so far apart. She wanted to turn and put her arms around her sister, to try to recapture some of the closeness they'd once known.

"There." Patsy straightened and gave the locket an admiring look. "Whatever you're wearing, this will look nice with it."

"Thank you."

"Not yet," Patsy said playfully. "One more thing." She dived into her purse again, dug around for a moment, and then drew her hand out, a penny triumphantly clutched between thumb and forefinger. "And a penny for your shoe. Now you're set."

"Yes." Meg had to clear her throat to get the word out. "Can I say thank you now?"

"Yes, you may."

"Thank you." The words didn't begin to express how much it meant that Patsy had not only come here but that she'd thought of the old tradition and made sure Meg had the appropriate lucky tokens.

"You're welcome." Patsy looked at her for a moment, her eyes, the same blue as Meg's own, questioning. Then she smiled and reached around Meg to pick up the hairbrush. "Let me do your hair. You never did learn how to put your hair up. If you do it, you'll put so many pins in, you'll end up looking like a porcupine," she said teasingly.

At Helen McKendrick's insistence, Meg had been moved into Ty's sister's old room the night before. Louise had moved to New York City five years before, scandalizing her mother by becoming a career woman. She hadn't been back since, and the room had the slightly musty smell that came from lack of use. Meg missed the comforting feeling of being surrounded by Ty's things, but she couldn't have even hinted at such a thing to her soon-to-be mother-in-law. Now she sat at Louise's pretty vanity and tried not to think about the step she was about to take.

The feel of the brush stroking through her hair was familiar. How many hours had they spent brushing each other's hair? Talking of all the small unimportant things that had been so important at the time. Meg closed her eyes when she felt the sting of tears. That all seemed like so long ago.

"You have hair just like an angel in a picture book," Patsy said softly. "I always wished my hair was like yours, all warm and golden, instead of plain brown. Do you remember the time I bleached my hair with that bottle of peroxide Mama kept in the kitchen for skinned knees?"

Meg nodded, her jaw aching with the effort of holding back the threatened tears. The sound of Patsy's voice and the slow rhythm of the brush through her hair were like drops of water on stone, slowly eroding her control.

"Mama nearly had a heart attack when she saw what I'd done to my hair. She said I looked like a skunk, the way it had streaked and all. That was the year before Pa died and I thought he'd whale the tar out of me when he got home, but he just laughed and laughed." Her voice was soft and reminiscent. "Funny, how, when I look back, Pa doesn't seem so bad, least not when he was sober. And we had some good times together, didn't we?"

Meg didn't say anything. Seen through the window of memory, the good times seemed much clearer than the bad. But she couldn't get anything out past the huge lump in her throat. She clung to the fragile threads of her control, telling herself that no good could come of falling apart now. But she'd forgotten that Patsy had only to look in the mirror to see the struggle reflected in her face.

When the brush faltered and then stopped moving, she opened her eyes, meeting Patsy's worried gaze in the mirror.

"Oh, Meggy, tell me what's wrong," she begged softly. "Why are you and Tyler getting married all in a rush like this? Where's Mama? Why aren't you at home?"

Meg started to reassure her sister that nothing was wrong; that there was nothing strange about her hasty wedding; that she was really happy as could be. But when she opened her mouth, what emerged was a sob that seemed ripped from the bottom of her soul.

"Oh, honey." The brush thudded to the floor and then somehow Patsy's arms were around her and Meg was sobbing out the whole story. Or almost all of it. She couldn't bear to tell even Patsy everything.

"So Ty's marrying you to keep you from having to go home? Because Harlan did this to you?" Patsy touched the tips of her fingers to Meg's bruised face.

"Yes." The word came out on half sob. The two of them sat on the edge of the narrow bed, their knees touching as they

faced each other. Meg twisted the handkerchief Patsy had dug
out of her apparently bottomless purse. "I know it's wrong to
marry him. I shouldn't let him do this."

"I don't really know Ty but he doesn't strike me as the
kind of man who'd do something if he didn't want to."

"Oh, he wants to marry me," Meg said. "But it's because he feels guilty about . . . about Harlan hurting me. He
thinks it was his fault."

"Why would it be Ty's fault?"

"It's not. But he was angry because I was seeing Ty. He
thought we were . . . doing things we weren't," she finished,
flushing at the memory of her stepfather's accusations.

Patsy sucked in a quick breath, and when Meg looked at
her, she seemed paler than she had been. She reached and
caught Meg's hands in hers, her fingers tense.

"Did he— Did Harlan . . . hurt you, Meg? I mean, did
he do anything besides this?" She touched the bruising around
Meg's eye with a fingertip. "Is that *all* he did?"

There was urgency in her voice, tension in the hands that
gripped Meg's. And there was a look in her eyes that seemed
to ask Meg to say yes, that the hurts Patsy saw were the only
ones. Which was exactly what Meg intended to say, but she
hesitated too long. Or perhaps Patsy could read the answer in
her eyes.

"Oh, Meg. Not you." Her eyes filled with tears. "Please,
not you, too."

"Too?" Meg stared at her sister as the shock of realization struck her. "Too? Patsy, did he . . ."

Tears streaming down her face, Patsy nodded. Seeing the
anguish in her eyes, Meg knew, with a certainty she didn't
question, that, for Patsy, there'd been no one to stop him, no
one to run to for protection.

"Oh, Patsy." It was Meg's turn to put her arms around
her sister, to offer her comfort.

Meg had no idea how long they stayed that way, each
giving and receiving comfort. They didn't talk about what had
happened. Words weren't necessary. They simply sat there,

drawing comfort from their shared pain, until the sound of someone tapping on the door made them draw apart.

"Yes?" Meg had to clear her throat to get the word out.

"Ty says to tell you he'll be ready to leave in about half an hour, if that's all right with you." Jack's voice was muffled by the wooden door.

Meg felt her throat close up. Half an hour. She was to be married in half an hour and she still didn't know if she was doing the right thing.

"She'll be ready," Patsy called back, her voice husky with tears but the words clear.

"I'll tell Ty."

Patsy stood up and brushed her fingers impatiently under her eyes, wiping away the last of her tears. "Come over here and let me get your hair up."

Meg rose obediently and went to the vanity, staring at her reflection as Patsy picked up the brush. "I'm not sure I should marry him, Patsy."

"You love him, don't you?"

"Yes." There was no hesitation in her response.

"And he obviously cares for you or he wouldn't be willing to marry you to keep you safe."

"But he doesn't love me," Meg protested.

"Love can come after marriage," Patsy said briskly. "Hand me a hairpin."

"How do you know?" Meg obediently handed her a pin, watching as Patsy deftly rolled her hair up and began pinning it in place.

"Because it did for me." She caught Meg's surprised look in the mirror and smiled ruefully. "Oh, Meg, do you think everyone who gets married is madly in love? I married Eldin because he was a kind man who said he'd love me and take care of me. And I—I had to get away from home." Her fingers trembled slightly as she smoothed a stray lock of hair into place.

"Do you love him now?" Meg asked.

"Yes." There was no hesitation in the response. "Maybe not a grand passionate kind of love, but a fond kind of love."

She smiled, her eyes meeting Meg's in the mirror. "You marry Ty and be the best wife you know how to be. Give it a little time and he'll see how lucky he is to have you. Now, what are you going to wear?"

Meg didn't argue any further but she wondered privately which would be worse: If Ty never loved her at all? Or if he someday felt a "fond kind of love" for her?

Chapter 12

It wasn't exactly the wedding of Meg's childhood fantasies. No church full of friends, no familiar pastor giving them indulgent looks. No white wedding dress that she'd pack away afterward to save for the day her own daughter might wear it. Instead she was married in a plain room at a courthouse in a town she'd never been in before today. The only witnesses were Jack and Patsy.

Instead of the lace-trimmed wedding gown of her dreams, Meg wore another outfit provided by Jack's sister. She didn't know what Jack had told Beryl, but she'd graciously plundered once more and come up with a smart tweed suit in a pale heathery shade of gray. She'd even included a matching hat, a pair of soft kid gloves, and a pair of shoes.

Since they were to catch a train for Los Angeles directly after the wedding, it was a perfect choice. Never mind that the suit was a little too big and so were the shoes, which slipped on her heels, promising to raise blisters by the time she was settled on the train. At least she didn't have to attend her wedding in her husband-to-be's pajamas, she thought with a touch of hysteria.

She tuned out the judge's voice and looked down, focusing her gaze on the small bouquet of roses she held. Edwina Vanderbilt had given the flowers to her, rushing out of her house to catch them before they drove away and thrusting the pink and white blooms into Meg's hands.

"Can't lie to the sheriff, you know," she'd said, puffing a little from hurrying. "I said I'd given you a wedding bouquet and so I have. Now my conscience is perfectly clear." Her eyes had been bright with laughter, and Meg had felt tears rise in her throat at the small kindness.

"Meg?" Ty prompted, and her head came up. The judge was looking at her expectantly and she realized it must be time for her to say "I do."

She swallowed hard, feeling panic rise up inside her. This was it. Unless she stopped this now, in a few minutes the judge would declare them husband and wife. How long after that before Ty started to hate her? Even if they got an annulment in a few months, how could he do anything but despise her for letting him do this?

Her heart was beating much too quickly and she felt light-headed. This was all wrong. No matter what Patsy said, she could never make this work. She couldn't possibly go through with it.

She looked at Ty, intending to tell him that she'd changed her mind, that she'd rather do almost anything rather than trap him into a marriage he didn't want. But in his eyes she read understanding, reassurance, and determination in equal measure. It was as if he'd read her thoughts and was telling her without words that her fears were unfounded. And oh, how she wanted to believe him.

"Miss Harper?" the judge prompted, sounding both puzzled and impatient.

"I do," she whispered, her eyes clinging to Ty's, her heart filled with a prayer that she was doing the right thing.

It seemed hardly more than a heartbeat later that the judge was declaring them man and wife. Ty's expression was solemn as he bent to press a chaste kiss on her mouth, and then Patsy was hugging her, her eyes filled with tears.

"You did the right thing, Meggy."

Meg only wished she were half as sure.

* * *

After the brief ceremony, Jack insisted that the four of them go out for an early dinner. Meg appreciated his effort to give the somewhat stark proceedings a more festive air, but she found it very difficult to play the role of the happy bride.

It might have been easier to pretend that this was a normal wedding if it hadn't been just the four of them, but the absence of Ty's parents made that impossible. His mother had taken to bed with a sick headache the day before when she'd realized that, while Ty had lied to the sheriff about marrying Meg, he planned to make the lie a reality immediately.

Mercifully, Meg hadn't been there for most of the discussion that had ensued, but she could imagine what Helen McKendrick must have said, how she must have argued against the marriage. When Ty had refused to change his mind, she'd retreated, sobbing, to her room, which she hadn't left since. There'd certainly been no question of her attending the wedding.

Though he'd chosen to stay home with his wife, Elliot McKendrick had been much kinder, welcoming Meg to the family with a gentle smile and wishing the two of them a safe journey. But she'd seen the worry in his eyes and knew that he thought Ty was making a disastrous mistake.

She was grateful when the time came for them to catch the train that would take them to Los Angeles. It had been Ty's decision to catch the train from Herndale, rather than going back to Regret. Jack had agreed to take a copy of their marriage certificate to Sheriff Ben Marlon. He'd also be driving Ty's car to the West Coast for him.

Saying good-bye to Patsy was bittersweet. Meg felt as if she'd just found her sister again, only to lose her once more. But the physical distance could be bridged with letters in a way the emotional distance could not have been. Standing on the platform, the sisters clung to each other. It would have been difficult to say just who was offering comfort to whom.

And then it was time to go. With a few last minute promises to write and a quick good-bye, the newlyweds boarded the train. Meg settled onto her seat with Ty beside her. Only he wasn't just Ty anymore; he was her husband now. And she wasn't Meg Harper. She was Mrs. Tyler McKendrick. Mrs. Tyler McKendrick. If she said the name a thousand times, she still couldn't imagine it applying to her.

She pressed her cheek to the window to catch a last glimpse of Patsy as the train pulled away from the station. As her sister's figure grew smaller with distance, Meg felt tears sting her eyes. She was starting off on a new life, one that was, in many ways, exactly what she'd dreamed of. So why did it seem less a dream than a nightmare?

It had been a mistake to accept Jack's offer to drive her to her old home, Patsy thought. With Eldin not due home for another two or three weeks and her with no car, it had seemed like a sensible idea when he suggested it. After all, the sooner she picked up Meg's things, the sooner she could get them to California for her.

But she wished now that she'd waited until Eldin could have brought her. If it had been Eldin sitting across from her instead of Jack she wouldn't have had this nervous lump in her stomach or the niggling worry that she had a smudge on her chin or lipstick on her teeth.

She could have asked one of her neighbors, she thought, exasperated that it hadn't occurred to her until now. Mr. Reardon was a thousand years old and more suited to controlling a pair of reins than a steering wheel, but he was a sweet old thing and he'd have been more than willing to drive her to Regret.

But it was too late now because Jack was already turning the Studebaker into the driveway. And the nerves in her stomach were suddenly caused by something else entirely. Since her marriage five years ago, she'd come home only a handful of times and not at all in nearly two years. Looking at the small white house, she felt all the old, terrible memories wash over her, all the things she'd almost convinced herself she'd forgotten and put behind her forever.

"Are you all right?" Jack's question made her realize that he'd stopped the car some time ago. Patsy tore her eyes away from the house and looked at him. The sun was nearly gone but there was enough light left for her to see the concern in his eyes. For a moment she had the wild urge to tell him to start the car and turn it around, to take her as far from this house and the memories it held as it was possible to get.

"I'm fine." She forced a quick smile. "Just day-dreaming."

"No law against it."

"I guess not." She looked at him a moment longer, remembering a time when all her daydreams had centered around him, around a future that held the two of them together. No, there was no law against daydreams, but it was so painful to see them die that perhaps there should be.

He got out of the car and came around to open her door. Reluctantly Patsy stepped out onto ground still damp from the rain of two days before.

"Shall I come in with you?" he asked.

"No." She saw Jack's brow go up and quickly softened the abrupt response. "It will be easier for me to do it alone, I think."

"All right." Jack shrugged and leaned one hip against the Studebaker's fender, reaching into his pocket to pull out a pack of cigarettes.

There was no sense in putting it off, Patsy thought. Straightening her shoulders, she walked up to the house, her heels clicking on the wooden steps as she climbed them. She rang the bell, hearing the echo of it through the door and then hearing the sound of her mother's footsteps. Though the weather was hardly balmy, the shiver that ran through her had nothing to do with the temperature.

Given a choice, she'd have preferred to walk barefoot through the Arctic rather than return to this house. Just standing on the porch, she could feel the old, suffocating fear rise up in her throat. She wanted to turn and run, to beg Jack to take her away from this awful place.

But she'd told Meg she'd get her things for her and she wasn't going to go back on that promise. She'd already failed her little sister so many times. This wasn't going to be another.

The door opened with a mournful squeal of hinges and

there was her mother. The two women eyed each other through the screen for a long moment without speaking.

"You'd best come in," Ruth said at last, and reached down to push open the screen door.

Patsy stepped inside, feeling her stomach roll at the familiar smell of the little house. It wasn't beeswax or baking or laundry soap, though all of those were there. But for her, those pleasant odors couldn't banish the smell of fear and despair. She put her hand to her throat, feeling as if she might choke.

"You've come about Meg," Ruth said, the words both question and statement. Patsy dragged her eyes to her mother's face, struggling to control her emotions.

"I've come to get her things," she said, pleased to hear that her voice was steady. She turned and walked toward the back of the house, pushing open the door to the room she and Meg had once shared.

Like everything else, it was the same as she remembered it. The same faded wallpaper, the same cheap curtains. Even her bed was still there, still pushed under the window. In the winter, there'd always been a nasty draft through that window, but she'd liked waking up with the sun shining in on her, liked the promise the morning always seemed to hold.

Hearing her mother's footsteps following her down the hall, Patsy shook off the old memories and turned to the scuffed pine dresser that she and Meg had shared. After pulling open the top drawer, she began to empty it, piling things on the bed.

"Harlan told me about the McKendrick boy saying they were married." Ruth stopped in the doorway, watching as Patsy emptied another drawer. "He didn't believe it and neither do I. It won't do for her to be living in that house with him."

"It won't do?" Patsy felt good, healthy anger burn away the memories. She straightened and looked at her mother. *"It won't do?* I suppose you think it *would* do for her to stay here? With *him* in the same house?" The contemptuous question made her mother flush and look away. "Meg told me what happened, Mama. If she and Ty were to set up housekeeping

and live in blatant sin together, it would certainly *do* much better than what happened here.''

"That wouldn't happen again," Ruth said.

"Why not? It's happened before."

Silence followed her words, a silence so complete she could hear the rhythmic tick-tock of the grandfather clock in the hall.

"I don't know what you're talking about," Ruth whispered.

"Don't lie to me, Mama. On top of everything else, don't lie to me now." Hot, cleansing anger boiled up inside her. She'd denied that anger for five long years, but denial hadn't changed the reality of what she felt. "You know exactly what I'm talking about."

"No, I don't." But Ruth's protest was weak, her eyes sliding away from her daughter's face. She pulled her cardigan sweater closer about her thin body. "I don't know at all."

"You knew then." The words were an accusation.

"I didn't." Ruth's eyes slid to Patsy's and then away. "Not for sure," she whispered, her shoulders slumping in defeat.

"You knew and you stayed with him anyway." The old feeling of betrayal made her voice harsh, and Ruth seemed to shrink and age before her eyes.

"I didn't know for sure. You never said."

"I shouldn't have had to say," Patsy shot back. "And what good would it have done me? Would you have taken me away? Would you have left him?"

She saw the answer in her mother's eyes and spun away. Jerking open another drawer, she snatched her sister's clothing out, aware that her hands were trembling, feeling sick to her soul.

"He's my husband," Ruth said, as if that explained the choices she'd made. "For better or worse, I promised."

"Not good enough, Mama. Not nearly good enough." Patsy didn't trust herself to look at Ruth. She dragged a cheap suitcase from the rickety chifferobe that stood in one corner and began stuffing Meg's clothes into it.

"You weren't the one living the 'or worse' part of it. You stayed with him because you were too much of a coward to make any other choice."

"You've no right to talk to me like that."

Patsy spun to face her, her face twisted with anger and betrayal. "I've every right. You're my mother. You were supposed to keep me safe, protect me. But you protected yourself instead."

"I made sure you had a roof over your head and food to eat," Ruth protested.

"There's more to caring for a child than feeding them and keeping them dry, Mama." Unknowingly, she echoed Ty's words.

Ruth flinched but straightened her stooped shoulders, drawing dignity around her. "You don't know what I've gone through—"

"I know what *I* went through. And I know what *Meg* went through. I don't care what you went through. You at least had a chance to make your own choices. Meggy and I didn't have that chance, did we?"

Ruth seemed to wilt beneath the fierce demand in her older daughter's eyes. Her shoulders slumped, age settling on her like a coat, worn and heavy with dust. Watching her, Patsy felt no sympathy, no pity. She turned back to the packing, moving quickly, anxious to get the task done and leave this house. This time she wouldn't be coming back.

"How—how is she?" Ruth asked quietly.

"How do you think she is?" Patsy snapped.

"Harlan says the sheriff will have to make her come back here," Ruth said. "I told him it'd be best to leave well enough alone."

She said it like a child pointing out that they'd cleaned up the glass after hitting a baseball through the window. As if there were any possible way to make up for what had happened —what she'd allowed to happen.

"Ty married her this afternoon and they're already on their way to California," Patsy said shortly, not bothering to look up.

"He said, even if they did get married, it wouldn't be legal because she didn't have permission from her parents."

Patsy said nothing. She shoved the last of Meg's clothes into the suitcase and slammed the lid down. She snapped the latches into place before giving the room a quick once-over, looking to see if she'd missed anything. Assured that she had everything, she hefted the heavy case off the bed. Ruth moved out of the doorway, allowing her to pass and then following her to the front of the house.

"If anyone asks, I'll say I gave her permission to get married."

Patsy had her hand on the doorknob when her mother spoke. She wanted only to leave this place and the memories it held, but the plea in her mother's voice, more than her words, made her stop. She let her hand drop from the knob and turned slowly to look at her mother.

Had she always been so small and worn looking? Hadn't there been a time when she'd been young and pretty? Patsy could no longer remember. All she could remember was that, since she was a tiny girl, she'd known that she couldn't count on her mother to take care of her, to protect her or Meg.

Now she was offering to stand up to her husband, to lie to the law if necessary. Patsy searched inside herself for some gratitude on Meg's behalf, for some appreciation of what Ruth was willing to do. What she found was emptiness. The anger and bitterness were gone and there was nothing to fill the void they'd left.

It was too little, too late. One act of courage couldn't make up for the years she'd buried her head, pretending not to see first George Harper's then Harlan Davis's abuse. It was far too little, offered much, much too late, Patsy thought wearily. If Ruth expected her to say thank you on Meg's behalf, she was doomed to disappointment. She owed Meg—owed both of them—so much more than she could ever repay.

"Good-bye, Mama."

She turned and pulled open the door before picking up the heavy suitcase and walking out into the fresh, clean air.

* * *

Seeing Patsy come out, Jack dropped the cigarette he'd been smoking and ground it out with a quick twist of his foot before hurrying forward to take the suitcase from her.

"Thank you."

"You should have called me to come in and get it," he told her, feeling the weight of it pull his arm.

"I managed."

Over her shoulder, Jack saw Ruth Harper through the screen, watching them. He hesitated, wondering if he should say something to her, but Patsy was already walking past him to the car. He turned to follow her, hearing the slow whine of the hinges as Ruth shut the door behind him. He put the suitcase in the car and slid behind the wheel, shooting a questioning glance at his companion.

"Everything all right?"

"Fine."

It didn't take a mind reader to know that "fine" was not exactly the truth. But the time when he'd had the right to probe for answers was long past, five years past. She'd taken that right from him when she'd married another man. His jaw tightening at the memory, Jack started the car, letting the sound of the engine fill the silence between them.

Neither of them spoke until they'd left Regret behind. Jack had promised himself that he wouldn't be the one to break the silence. They could drive all the way to Herndale without saying a word if that was the way she wanted it.

"Thank you for taking me to get Meg's things," she said quietly.

"You're welcome." Jack glanced at her, wishing it wasn't too dark to see her face. "Did you tell your mother about the wedding?"

"Yes. She said, if there was any question, she'd say she'd given Meg permission to get married."

"Good. That should put a stop to Davis trying to make any more trouble."

"I hope so." She sounded doubtful.

"You think he'll still try?" Jack asked.

"I don't see what he can do, what with them being in

California.'' But there was something in her voice that said she wouldn't be surprised if he found a way, even across that distance.

"Well, even if he tries, he has Ty to deal with now.''

"Yes. He'll take care of Meg.''

She fell silent and Jack wished again that he could see something of her expression, read what she was thinking. But all he could see was the pale cameo of her profile against the darkness outside the window and the restless movement of her hands as she smoothed her gloves over her fingers.

"Did he . . . did Davis ever . . . hurt you?'' he asked, voicing a suspicion he hadn't fully worked out in his mind.

"What do you mean?''

The fear in her voice surprised him. What had he said to frighten her?

"Did he hit you, the way he did Meg?''

"I don't think that's any of your business,'' she said tightly, giving him the answer he'd sought.

"Why didn't you tell me?'' There was anger in the question and a hurt that he hadn't realized he felt. But it did hurt to think that she'd have concealed something like that from him.

"What could you have done?'' she asked tiredly, not trying to deny that her stepfather had abused her.

"What could I have done?'' Jack shot her a quick, angry look. "What the hell do you think I'd have done? I'd have gotten you out of there so fast that Davis's head would still be spinning.''

"Would you have?'' There was a kind of wistful pain in her voice.

"You know I would have. My God, Patsy, I wanted to marry you. Do you think I'd have let that bastard hurt you?'' His hands tightened the steering wheel as if it were Harlan Davis's neck. "You should have told me.''

"And then what? You'd have ridden in on your white charger and swept me away?'' There was no sarcasm in her question.

"We'd have gotten married right away,'' he snapped.

"Your father had just died. You were trying to settle his

affairs. Your mother had collapsed with grief and your sister was depending on you to take your father's place, to give them both someone to lean on.'' She recited the circumstances of five years ago in the flat tone of someone who'd gone over the same facts a thousand times. ''In the midst of all that, do you think I should have added my problems to the list?''

''Yes,'' he said without hesitation. ''I'd asked you to marry me. That made your problems mine. I would have taken care of you.''

I would have taken care of you. Patsy closed her eyes for a moment. Five years ago she'd have given her soul to have been able to let him do just that. But it never would have worked. She'd known it then and there was no reason to think she'd been wrong.

She opened her eyes as Jack turned into the drive in front of her house. He shut the engine off. In the sudden silence, he turned to face her, resting his arm along the back of the seat. Patsy kept her head down, her eyes on the restless movement of her fingers.

''Why didn't you tell me, Patsy? Didn't you know I'd have done anything to keep you safe?'' There was old pain in his voice, five years of wondering, and Patsy's heart ached.

''I know you would have tried. But there were . . . things I couldn't tell you,'' she whispered.

''Like what?''

''It doesn't matter anymore.'' If she hadn't been able to tell him then, she certainly wasn't going to now.

She felt Jack's eyes on her down-bent head and knew he was cursing the darkness that prevented him from reading her expression. She should say good-bye, get out of the car, and walk away without looking back. Jack Swanson was part of her past. No good could come of pretending otherwise.

''These 'things' you couldn't tell me. Could you tell your husband about them?'' There was a bitter edge to his voice, a jealousy that told her that she wasn't the only one who hadn't quite managed to put the past behind them.

''I told him,'' she admitted softly. She lifted her head to

look at him. She'd left the front porch light on and there was just enough illumination inside the car for her to see the impact of her words. Or did she just feel his pain?

"Why?" He sounded bewildered. And hurt. "Why could you tell him something you couldn't tell me?"

She stared at him, searching for the right words, for a way to explain why she'd made the choices she had. And found it remarkably simple, after all.

"Because I didn't love him the way I loved you."

She gasped and put one hand to her mouth, dismayed to hear what she'd said, what she'd revealed. In one sentence, she'd explained why she'd been able to tell Eldin Baker what her stepfather had done, able to tell him everything that had happened. Because she hadn't loved him enough for it to matter whether he turned away from her. But if she'd had to see the love in Jack's eyes turn to disgust—that would have destroyed her.

"Patsy—"

"I have to go in." She fumbled for the door handle and jerked it open.

"Wait." Jack reached for her but she scooted out of the car, nearly falling in her haste to get away from him—but even more to escape the echo of her own words.

"Thank you for the ride. Give my love to Meg when you see her in Los Angeles," she babbled. She saw him reach for the door on his own side. "No!" She realized that she was nearly shouting and repeated the word in a more moderate tone. "No, don't get out."

"We need to talk."

"No. No, we don't." She clung to the edge of the door, staring at him across the width of the car. "It was all a long time ago, Jack. There's nothing to talk about."

"But—"

"I'm married now. And I love my husband." She saw his hand drop from the door handle and told herself that she was relieved. "Good-bye, Jack."

Patsy pushed the car door shut without waiting for a reply. She could feel his eyes on her as she walked up the porch steps and she willed strength into her trembling knees. After pushing open the front door, she stepped inside and closed it behind her, leaning back against it. Seconds ticked by and she finally heard Jack start the car. It wasn't until she'd heard him pull out of the drive that she allowed the tears that filled her eyes to spill over.

Sliding down against the door, Patsy sank to her knees on the polished floor, wrapping her arms across her stomach as hard, painful sobs shook her frame.

Chapter 13

Meg worried at the wedding ring on her left hand, turning it restlessly around and around her finger. She'd been wearing it for three days and it felt no more natural now than it had when Ty had slipped it on her finger in Iowa.

Ty. She stole a glance across the table at him, allowing her eyes to linger when she saw that he was reading the menu. Her husband. No matter how hard she tried, she couldn't make the words stick. She simply couldn't make her marriage seem real. Of course, it wasn't completely real. Not yet, anyway.

Her wedding night had been spent on a train rocking its way across the country. She'd slept alone in the cramped upper berth that was all Ty had been able to secure at the last minute. It was a measure of her exhaustion that she'd slept through most of the night. The second night had been spent much the same as the first except that she'd been rested enough to worry about where her new husband was sleeping. Assured that he had a berth in another car, she'd climbed into her own bed and lain awake half the night, listening to the rhythmic clack of the train as it skimmed over the steel rails and trying to absorb the reality of her new circumstances.

They'd arrived in Los Angeles a few hours before. Meg had been enthralled by her first glimpse of slender palm trees outlined against the blue sky. There'd been so much to look at that, for a few minutes, she'd forgotten their situation. Ty had smiled at her excitement and laughed when she'd asked if he thought they might actually see a movie star. And for a few minutes, she'd been comfortable with him, the way she had been all summer.

But then they'd reached the hotel and she'd heard Ty ask for a suite. It had suddenly occurred to her that she'd be spending tonight alone in a hotel room with her husband—her wedding night, for all intents and purposes. But was there going to *be* a wedding night? Did she even *want* there to be a wedding night?

As if sensing her gaze, Ty looked up, his eyes meeting hers. Meg flushed and looked down at her menu, half afraid he could read her thoughts. They hadn't talked about what was going to happen after they were married. Did Ty intend for this to be a real marriage? Or was he planning on getting an annulment once she turned eighteen and was beyond her stepfather's reach?

Meg wasn't sure which frightened her most at the moment: The thought of having her marriage annulled in a few months or the thought of sharing a room, not to mention a bed, with him.

"See anything you like?" Ty asked.

At his question, Meg looked up at him and Ty found himself wondering just what was going on behind those big blue eyes. She'd been studying the menu with an intensity that suggested that the fate of nations might rest on her gastronomic decision, but he doubted she'd read a word of it.

"I'm not very hungry," she said.

"You haven't eaten much since the . . . since we left home." His tongue stumbled clumsily over the word "wedding." The look in Meg's eyes said that she knew exactly what he'd started to say, and Ty wished the word had come more readily to his tongue.

"I'm not a very big eater," she said, answering his comment.

"How about a bowl of soup and a roll?" he coaxed,

thinking that there were hollows in her cheeks that hadn't been there a week ago.

"All right." She gave him a quick smile and shut the menu. Ty knew she'd eat the soup to please him rather than because she wanted it. But dammit all, she'd eaten barely enough to keep a kitten alive these past few days. He'd married her to take care of her, not to watch her waste away.

He gave their order to the waiter, who took their menus and disappeared, leaving Ty with nothing to do but look across the table at his bride. Meg stared out the window, as if enthralled by the traffic outside the hotel. She was twisting the ring on her finger again—her wedding ring, he reminded himself. The one he'd given her barely three days ago, the one that said that she was his wife. His wife. Little Meg Harper, his wife.

"If the ring's too big, I can take it to a jeweler's," he said, seeking a distraction from his thoughts.

Meg's fingers jerked away from the ring as if it were suddenly hot to the touch and her eyes flew to his face. "It's fine," she said quickly.

"It's not a problem to have it sized," he said.

"It doesn't need to be sized," Meg insisted. It was the truth, but even if the ring had been on the verge of dropping off her finger, she wouldn't have admitted it. It was silly, but she had the feeling that, if she let the ring off her finger, she wouldn't be married anymore. As if the gold band were the only thing that made their marriage real.

"If you're sure." Ty reached across the table and took her hand, running his thumb across the surface of the ring. "It was my grandmother's, you know."

"No, I didn't." Though she'd jumped like a startled deer when he touched her, Meg was soothed by the feel of his hand holding hers.

"My grandfather gave it to me not long before he died. Said he hoped it brought half as much luck to me someday as it had brought to him."

And he'd given it to her. Meg felt something stir inside

her, something she was afraid to examine too closely. Something that could have been, if she was very, very foolish, a renewed hope that this marriage was more to him than just a means of protecting her.

"It fits just fine but I'm not used to it," she admitted apologetically.

"Not used to the ring? Or not used to being married?" Ty asked.

"It does feel a little strange, still." She kept her eyes on their hands, his fingers enfolding hers.

"To me, too. How long do you think it'll take to get used to it?"

There was a trace of laughter in his voice that brought her eyes to his face. The laughter was in his dark eyes, too, inviting her to smile at the absurdity of the two of them finding themselves married. Meg felt a small shaft of pain stab her chest, but she smiled, wanting desperately to get back something of the comfortable relationship they'd had—Lord, was it only a few days ago?

"I don't know," she said, wondering if they were going to be married long enough to worry about getting used to it. But she couldn't ask him that—not when she wasn't at all sure she wanted to hear his answer.

"I guess most couples must feel like this, at first." Ty squeezed her hand one final time before releasing it.

"Yes," Meg agreed, even as she thought that there couldn't be very many marriages that started out quite like theirs had.

"I imagine we'll get used to it," he said. He leaned back to allow the waiter to set a plate of steak and still-sizzling fried potatoes in front of him.

Meg stared down at her bowl of cream of tomato soup and wondered if she should take his words to mean that there would not only be time for them to get used to being married, but a reason to do so. Was she to have a real marriage, after all? A real wedding night?

* * *

Meg smoothed her hand over the soft cotton of her pajamas—Ty's pajamas, actually. Jack was bringing her things to California with him, but until he arrived, her wardrobe was limited, to put it mildly. Hanging in the spacious closet was one dress and the suit in which she'd been married. Her only night attire was the striped pajamas Ty had provided. She'd grown quite fond of them, actually, but she couldn't help but wish for something just a little more feminine to wear on her wedding night. Or what she thought might be her wedding night.

Ty had left her alone in their suite, saying he'd be back later. After their conversation at dinner, when it had seemed so clear that he intended their marriage to last, she thought he was being considerate, giving her some privacy in which to get ready for bed.

Meg lifted her head and looked at her reflection. It wasn't exactly the motion-picture image of a girl on her wedding night. And the bride wore yellow and blue, she thought, touching the bruises that still circled her eye. The swelling was gone and the marks were starting to fade, but she doubted that her appearance was going to start a craze for brides with black eyes this season.

She patted her cheeks to bring color into them, aware that her fingers were trembling. She might not be wearing a white silk nightgown, but she'd brushed her hair until it shone golden in the soft light. She wanted desperately for Ty to think she looked pretty. He *had* thought she was pretty, before they were married. He'd kissed her and he wouldn't have done that if he hadn't thought she was attractive.

The frightened girl in the mirror had no answers to give her, and Meg turned and left the bathroom. Holding on to her courage with both hands, she crossed the soft carpet to the bed. Abandoning dignity, she dived into the bed and pulled the covers up to her chin. She was trembling a little, shivers of nervous tension running down her spine.

Staring up at the pale-pink ceiling, she asked herself if she was afraid. The answer was a very definite maybe. The consummation of her marriage was something she wanted, dreaded, longed for, and feared. Like most unmarried girls, she had only a rough understanding of just what happened between a man and a woman in the privacy of a marriage bed. What little she did know was neither encouraging nor reassuring.

But against those vague bits of knowledge, she had the memory of the way she'd felt when Ty held her, kissed her. There'd been nothing frightening about that, unless it was the sheer wonder of how he'd made her feel.

Briefly she considered whether her stepfather's brutal attack had left any lingering traces of fear. The memory of his hands on her body, the twisted lust in his eyes were enough to bring the acrid taste of bile to her throat. But it simply wasn't possible to compare the horror of that moment with the sweet memory of Ty's arms around her.

When Ty held her, kissed her, she'd felt a warmth that started in the pit of her stomach and spread outward to encompass her entire body. His touch made her want things she didn't understand, made her hungry for something she couldn't quite define. Just thinking about those feelings made her blush.

When Meg heard the outer door to the suite open, her breath caught. A quick spurt of panic had her hand shooting out to snap off the lamp, plunging the room into darkness. The outer door shut and Meg held her breath, her eyes glued to the narrow band of light just visible under the bedroom door. She could hear vague noises as Ty moved around in the sitting room that comprised the other half of their suite. Tired and nervous as she was, Meg had been impressed by the sophisticated decor, everything done in shades of peach and black lacquer. There was a built-in bar and she heard the faint clink of a bottle against glass as Ty poured himself a drink.

She wondered suddenly if it was possible that he was nervous about tonight, too. The thought that he might need a little Dutch courage was oddly reassuring. She lay watching the thin bar of light beneath the door, trying to guess what Ty was doing from the faint sounds that reached her.

Minutes ticked by and the door remained shut. She could hear Ty stirring in the other room, but he didn't come to the door. Should she have left the light on? she wondered. Maybe he thought she was asleep. Her teeth worried at her lower lip. Should she turn it back on or would that look absurd?

Her nerves were stretched near to breaking point when the light under the door vanished. Meg caught her breath, thinking that Ty would be coming to the bedroom now. Her fingers clutched the sheet with white-knuckled force, and she could feel her every thud of her heart as it pounded against her breastbone.

The room was so quiet, she could hear the seconds ticking off on the clock next to the bed. Seconds that stretched into a minute. Two minutes. *What was he doing?* Five minutes. *What could be taking him so long?* Ten minutes.

He wasn't coming.

The realization crept over her slowly as the minutes ticked away. Her fingers relaxed their hold on the sheet and the nervous anticipation drained away, leaving her shaky and feeling almost sick. She didn't have to worry about not having a white silk nightgown or whether her husband thought she looked pretty for her wedding night or not.

Because there wasn't going to be a wedding night.

Would there ever be? Or was she going to be signing annulment papers in a few months, standing before a judge and admitting that her marriage had never really been a marriage; that there was no reason that the court shouldn't wipe it from the record books as if it had never happened?

Without thinking, Meg swung her legs off the bed, feeling the soft pile of the carpet beneath her bare feet as she crept toward the door. She turned the knob slowly, holding her breath as she tugged the door open and peered out into the sitting room. The curtains were open and there was enough light coming in through the windows for her to make out the lines of the furniture.

She tiptoed forward until she stood next to the sofa. From outside, she heard the faint hum of traffic, the buzz of the city that never completely disappeared, no matter how late the hour. But the room was quiet enough for her to hear the steady sound of Ty's breathing. He was asleep.

Meg stared down at him. The sofa was nearly a foot shorter than he was and his feet hung off the end of it. He'd taken off his shirt but left his T-shirt on. A blanket was draped over his legs and a pillow was bunched under his head. All in all, it looked like a thoroughly uncomfortable place to spend the night. But he'd apparently preferred it to sharing a bed with her.

Staring down at him, Meg forced herself to accept reality. He'd married her to protect her. No more dreams, no more telling herself that they could build a solid marriage on the unorthodox beginning they'd had. Ty had married her because he'd wanted to keep her safe. He didn't want her and there was no sense in thinking he did.

When she turned eighteen and was beyond Harlan Davis's reach, her marriage would end. If Ty didn't ask her for an annulment, she'd offer it. She loved him enough to make it easy for him. And in the few weeks between now and her birthday, she'd do her best to be a good wife, to make him happy. If possible, when she walked away, she'd leave him with nothing but good memories.

With a last look at Ty's sleeping figure, Meg turned and went back into the bedroom, closing the door quietly behind her. She crept back into the bed, letting the smooth linen pillowcase absorb the slow tears that dampened her cheeks.

Ty heard the barely audible *click* of the bedroom door closing and drew a deep, ragged breath. He opened his eyes and stared at the faint gleam of lights just visible between the open drapes. Sometime in the past, he must have committed a sin for which he was now being punished.

It wasn't enough to know that Meg was his wife, his by laws of man and God, and yet know that she was out of reach. And it apparently wasn't enough to have spent the past several hours thinking about the wide bed in the other room, a bed just made for sharing, and yet know that he was going to be spending his night on a sofa that fell a foot a short of comfort.

Those things weren't punishment enough. Meg had to come tiptoeing out of the bedroom, smelling of soap and tooth powder, wearing his old pajamas and looking more desirable than any woman had a right to do. He'd watched her through slitted eyes, careful to keep his breathing steady. She'd hovered next to him for a moment, and Ty had curled his fingers into his palm, fighting the urge to reach out and catch her hands in his, to pull her down to him.

He'd cursed the need he felt, the hunger that burned in his gut. He'd married Meg to protect her, to keep her safe.

She wouldn't fight you, a sly voice whispered. *Remember the way she kissed you?*

No, she wouldn't fight him. Knowing Meg, he figured that she'd probably think her virginity was the least she owed him. She just couldn't seem to see that he was to blame for what had happened, that *he* was the one who owed her. All the pain and humiliation she'd suffered had been his fault. If he hadn't let their friendship develop; if he hadn't ignored the growing affection he'd seen in her eyes, she wouldn't have found herself hurt and alone, turning to him because there was nowhere else she could go. For once he was going to do the right thing and keep his distance from Meg.

She's your wife.

She was also a sweet, innocent girl who'd come to him for protection, who'd married him out of fear. Considering all that she'd gone through, he couldn't imagine that she'd welcome sharing her bed with him. Maybe she'd had a bad dream and that was why she'd come to him. But offering comfort was beyond him tonight. Tonight he couldn't forget how good she'd felt in his arms, how sweet her kisses had been. Or the fact that she wore his wedding ring.

So the argument went, need battling conscience, hunger fighting decency. And then Meg turned away, going back into the bedroom, leaving him to stare at the city lights and wonder just what he'd done to deserve such punishment.

The newlyweds breakfasted in their room the following morning. They'd shared other meals and always had plenty to discuss, whether it was a movie they'd just seen or whether or not Thelma Nathan was going to let her husband move back into the house or make him stay in the barn where he'd been ever since coming home roaring drunk one night and breaking all the china dogs she'd inherited from her mother. But this time conversation seemed difficult to come by. Once Meg had commented on the bright sunshine outside and how it was hard to believe that it was nearly October, and Ty had agreed that the weather was certainly different from Iowa and would she mind passing the marmalade, they seemed to run out of conversational gambits.

"Did you sleep well?" Ty asked, aware that he sounded like a host rather than a husband.

"Yes. The bed is very comfortable."

Ty bit into his toast and tried not to picture her in that comfortable bed. What was it about getting married that had made him so suddenly aware of her as a woman? But it wasn't just the marriage, he thought, remembering the delicious softness of her mouth under his, the feel of her in his arms. He'd wanted her long before he married her.

"How did you sleep?" Meg inquired politely.

"Like a baby," he lied without hesitation. The truth was, he felt as if Bill Robinson had spent the night tap-dancing up and down his body. Muscles he hadn't even known he possessed were aching and he doubted his spine would ever completely straighten.

"The room is lovely," Meg said, giving him a smile that didn't reach her eyes.

"Great hotel," Ty said heartily. He already hated the place.

"Yes. Great." She dabbled her fork in her scrambled eggs for a moment.

Another long silence while they both devoted their attention to their food. Ty chewed a slice of perfectly cooked bacon, which could have been shoe leather for all he tasted of it. He'd never realized how difficult marriage would be, he thought sourly. Were they go to stare at each other over the breakfast table like this for the next fifty years?

"Who's Dickey?"

Ty has just picked up his coffee cup. The unexpected

question made him take too large a mouthful of the hot liquid, scalding his tongue.

"Dickey?" The cup hit the saucer with a distinct *click* and he stared at her.

"Your mother mentioned him," she said, looking as if she regretted the question already. "I don't remember what she said."

"Probably something about how he'd never cause her the sort of anguish I always do," Ty said, and then was surprised to hear the bitter edge to the words. "He was my brother."

"I knew you had a sister but I didn't know you had a brother," she said, surprised.

"He was killed in the Great War. In France."

"Oh, Ty. I'm sorry." She reached across the small table and touched the back of his hand, making him realize that his fingers were clenched. "I shouldn't have asked."

"It's all right." He turned his hand, catching her fingers in his. "It was a long time ago. I was only ten when he died."

"You must miss him a great deal," Meg said, her eyes smoky blue with sympathy.

"I did. But like I said, it was so long ago." He stared at their joined hands, searching for the words to express what he was thinking. "Sometimes I wonder what he'd be like, if he were still alive. I wonder if we'd be close. If my mother would see him as a real person instead of as a model of perfection."

"It must have been very hard on her," Meg said with compassion, apparently able to overlook Helen McKendrick's cruelty toward her.

"It was hard on all of us. But she didn't get out of bed for over a week after we got the news," Ty said slowly. He remembered how frightened he'd been. His beloved older brother was gone, never to come home again. His mother seemed to have vanished almost as completely, staying in her bedroom with the blinds drawn, out of reach. His sister, Louise, had cried for days, great noisy sobs that had echoed through the unnatural quiet of the house. Only his father had continued to go about his business, but his face had been gray and drawn, all the life gone out of his eyes.

"It must be terrible to lose a child," Meg said.

"She didn't lose him. She keeps him very much alive so she can hold him up in front of me as a never-to-be-achieved ideal." His mouth twisted with half-angry, half-rueful humor as he met Meg's eyes across the table. "Anytime I disappoint her, she always tells me that Dickey would never have done such a thing. I guess one advantage of dying young is that you don't have time to be less than perfect."

"I'm sure she knows he wasn't perfect," Meg said, looking distressed for him.

"Does she?" Ty doubted that. After eighteen years of hearing his mother refer to Dickey as having been an angel, he doubted she could separate reality from her fantasy anymore. Dickey was, and would remain, her perfect son.

Before either of them could say anything more, there was a knock on the door. Ty hesitated a moment, reluctant to break the moment. It was the first time since their marriage that they'd managed to recapture something of the comfortable relationship that had grown over the summer.

The knock came again and Meg gave him a quick smile— the first he'd seen in days that didn't seem to hide any shadows —and pulled her hand away from his.

"You'd better see who it is," she murmured.

With a mental curse, Ty got up and went to the door. A young woman in a crisp blue maid's uniform stood on the other side of the door, her arms full of pillows and blankets.

"I have the extra linens you requested, Mr. McKendrick." When Ty gave her a blank stare, she smiled uncertainly. "You *did* order extra linens, didn't you?"

"Yes, of course." After spending the night on the sofa, he'd decided the floor couldn't be any worse and had called down to the desk to request pillows and blankets.

"Shall I put them in the bedroom, for you?"

"Sure." He stepped back so that she could enter the room, and his eyes sought out Meg. She was looking at the maid. He saw color come up in her cheeks when she saw what the girl carried. She dropped her eyes to her half-eaten breakfast, not lifting them again until the maid had deposited her burden in the bedroom and left the suite.

Ty shut the door behind the girl and came back to the table. Just as he'd suspected, the ease that had been between them while they talked about his brother was gone.

"I forgot to tell you that I'd called housekeeping this morning," he said as he sat down again.

"The service is certainly prompt," she said, giving him a quick, meaningless smile.

"Yes." Ty took a swallow of his coffee, which was now lukewarm and held a bitter edge.

Meg's eyes skimmed over his face, settled on the sofa for a moment, and then returned to her plate. She took a small bite of her scrambled eggs and chewed without enthusiasm. "How long will we be staying here?"

"Until I can find us a place to live, I guess. I thought I'd see about finding a bungalow, maybe. The rents are reasonable and I thought you might like that more than an apartment."

"Whatever you like," she said, giving him that meaningless smile again.

Ty could read nothing from her face but he could sense her discomfort, feel her unhappiness. That was the last thing he wanted. She'd known enough unhappiness in her life, enough pain. She had a right to a little peace and happiness for a change. "Look, Meg, maybe we should have talked about this before we got married." Ty put down his fork and looked across the table at her.

"About renting a bungalow or an apartment?" She looked surprised.

"No. About us. About this marriage." He hadn't thought it was necessary to put it into words, thinking that she'd know that she had nothing to fear from him, but perhaps it was better to say it, to remove any doubts that might linger in her mind.

She seemed to pale a little. Her fork settled against her plate without the slightest sound and then she dropped her hands into her lap. The eyes she lifted to his face were guarded and Ty found himself wondering if she'd ever be able to look at him—or at any man—with the same openness and trust she once had. Or had Harlan Davis managed to kill that trust forever?

"Meg, you don't have to worry about anything. I mean, about us being married."

"Why would I worry?"

"Well, about . . . about me being your husband or anything." She stared at him blankly and Ty drew a deep breath. "You don't have to worry about me wanting to make this a real marriage. I don't expect us to share a room," he said bluntly.

He'd expected her to look embarrassed or relieved or grateful, maybe some combination of the three. But there was not so much as a flicker of expression in those wide blue eyes. No embarrassment at his blunt announcement, no relief that she wouldn't be asked to share her bed. Nothing he could read at all.

"I know," she said calmly. Her eyes shifted to her plate as she picked up her fork again. Ty wondered if it was his imagination that put a barely visible tremor in her fingers. She began to eat again, her attention apparently all for her breakfast.

I know? That was all she was going to say? *I know?* Shouldn't there be more to it than that? Ty picked up his own fork but his appetite had deserted him.

They ate in silence for a few minutes. Meg pushed her plate away first, and Ty was perversely annoyed to see that she'd eaten everything on it. There was no logical reason for his annoyance. Unless he'd been hoping she'd protest, say she wanted their marriage to be real? He stared down at the eggs congealing on his plate, wondering just how long it would be before she was ready to be a wife. A month? Three months? A year? Just how many cold showers could a man take and survive?

Not a real marriage. Meg sipped at the glass of fresh-squeezed orange juice that had come with the breakfast—an unthinkable luxury back home, now no more appealing than a cup of cold coffee. *Not a real marriage.* It was no more than she'd expected.

A little over two months until her birthday—two months to be a wife without ever really being a wife. Two months to store up memories to last the rest of her life. She set the glass down abruptly and looked across the table to give Ty a smile dazzling in its bright insincerity.

"So, what are we going to do today?"

Ty seemed startled by her bright tone and then almost relieved, and Meg knew she'd made the right choice. Not for anything in the world would she have him know just how much she would have given for their marriage to be real.

"I thought you might want to do a little sightseeing. Then, in a couple of days, we could start looking for a place to live," Ty said.

"Why don't we find a place to live first? I'm sure you've seen all the usual tourist spots and don't particularly want to see them again. There'll be plenty of time for me to be a tourist later."

"Are you sure? Wouldn't you like to look around a bit first? Get your bearings?"

"I can get my bearings later," she said, giving him another bright smile. "I'm sure you want to get me settled so you can get back to work. I heard Jack tell you that he had a couple of job possibilities lined up. Maybe we can be settled in by the time he gets here with your car."

Ty hesitated and then shrugged. "If it's what you want."

"It is." What she didn't want was for him to feel as if he had to baby-sit her. He might be stuck with her for a while, but she didn't want him to feel tied down.

It took them a week to find a place to rent. It was one unit in a small bungalow court settled snugly in the hills above Hollywood. The rent seemed appalling to Meg but Ty insisted that thirty-five dollars a month was not unreasonable for four furnished rooms and a fireplace. There was even a garage for the Chrysler.

She hadn't given any thought to finances, but she'd assumed that they'd be on a very tight budget until Ty could find some work flying. But he explained that he had a small trust fund left to him by his maternal grandfather. It wasn't a lot of money, but the investments had weathered the crash fairly well and the income was enough so that she didn't ever have to worry about finding herself in a bread line.

Meg was less concerned with finding herself in a bread line than she was with the fact that he was spending money because of her. If this had been a real marriage, rather than a temporary arrangement, she might not have minded so much. A smaller place in a cheaper neighborhood would have suited her just fine. But Ty refused to consider it.

"I want to know you're safe when I'm not here," he told her. "This is a good neighborhood. I won't have to worry about you here."

And since she felt she'd been far too much of a worry to him already, Meg bit her tongue to hold back more arguments and agreed that it would be nice to have a tiny patio all their own and that the view really was lovely. It was nothing more than the truth. The bungalow was charming and she could hardly imagine a more wonderful place for any couple to begin their married life. If they'd been beginning something rather than just marking time, she'd have been thrilled with her new home.

So Ty paid out the first month's rent and the woman who managed the bungalow court promised to give the place a good cleaning that afternoon so that the newlyweds could move in the following day. Which was another thing that kept Meg from protesting too much about the rent. She knew Ty had to be as anxious to move out of the hotel as she was. After all, the floor couldn't possibly make the most comfortable of beds.

But worse than the discomfort of their sleeping arrangements was the fact that the suite that had seemed so spacious when she'd first seen it was starting to take on all the aspects of a jail cell. After that first breakfast, they'd taken all their meals elsewhere. And they'd spent most of their days looking at places to rent. But there still seemed to be far too much time spent in the hotel room with nothing to do but read or sit and look at each other. The ability to hold a conversation seemed to have evaporated with the stroke of the pen that had made them husband and wife.

Which was why they both were relieved when Jack's arrival in Los Angeles ended their enforced companionship. A week of honeymoon that wasn't really a honeymoon was more than enough for them.

"Jack!" Ty couldn't have sounded more pleased to see him if Jack had just returned from the dead. He thrust out his hand, taking Jack's and pumping it as if they hadn't seen each other in years. "You made good time. Great to see you. Come in." Since Ty was already pulling him inside and closing the door, the invitation was a formality.

"Look, Meg. Jack's here." Ty made the announcement as if she might have forgotten who Jack was in the week since he'd witnessed their wedding.

"Hello, Jack." She rose from the sofa, setting aside the magazine she'd been reading. "It's good to see you."

"Hello, Meg. It's good to see you, too. California living up to its advertising?"

"Yes. It's very nice." It was the right answer, but there was no real enthusiasm in her voice and the smile she gave him seemed strained. Jack's eyebrows climbed a notch. Obviously all was not as it should be.

"I've got your things with me. Patsy packed everything up."

"Was there . . . any trouble?" A worried frown pleated her forehead and the fingers she'd linked in front of her were suddenly tense.

"No trouble," he assured her. "Your mother was there and she helped Patsy get everything together." Considering the stiff anger in Patsy's face when she'd exited the house, Jack suspected that was stretching the truth more than a bit, but Meg didn't have to know that.

"I'm glad."

"Did you show the license to Ben Marlon?" Ty asked.

"Sure did. He didn't say a word about the date being off by a day or two. Asked me to wish the two of you luck."

"Good." There was a moment's silence and then Ty rubbed his hands together. "We should have a drink to celebrate," he announced in a cheerful tone that rang false to Jack's ears. "What'll you have?"

"I didn't plan on staying," Jack said. "I just dropped in to let you know I was here and that I had Meg's stuff. Three's a crowd and all that."

"No!" He had the feeling that Ty just restrained himself from grabbing his coat sleeve in case he tried to make a break for the door. "We can't let you go without a drink, can we, Meg?"

"Of course not." Something in Meg's tone said that she was no more anxious to be alone with Ty than he apparently was to be alone with her. Curious, Jack allowed himself to be persuaded to sit on the sofa, a glass of Scotch in his hand.

It seemed as if they were both anxious to hear every word Ben Marlon had said. Then there were the details of his drive across the country in Ty's car. Where he'd stopped, what he'd eaten, practically every mile seemed to enthrall them. By the time he'd recounted all the minutia of the journey, Jack was torn between amusement and concern.

What on earth had happened? Neither Ty nor Meg looked at the other if they could avoid it. Though Meg's bruises had faded and the color had come back into her cheeks, there was a subtle air of sadness about her, something haunting in her eyes even when she smiled. And he'd known Ty too long and too well not to see the signs of strain in his face.

"I stopped by the airfield this afternoon, asked if anyone had seen you," he said to Ty once the subject of his trip had been exhausted. "Joe said you hadn't been around."

"We've been pretty busy looking for a place to live," Ty said.

"Any luck?"

"We paid the first month's rent on a place this afternoon. We're moving in tomorrow."

They talked a little while longer before Jack left. Ty gave

him the address of the bungalow and Jack promised to meet them there the next afternoon, bringing Ty's car and Meg's clothes. As he was leaving, he had the feeling that, if it hadn't been for the lateness of the hour, Ty would have urged him to stay longer.

Jack's expression was thoughtful as he stepped into the elevator. He stared at the ornate grillwork on the door and wondered just what was going on in his friend's brand-new marriage.

Not that it was any of his business, he reminded himself the elevator stopped and the operator opened the doors. He was oblivious to the graceful palms and the plush banquettes discreetly placed among them as he strode across the pink marble floor. Whatever the problem was, he was in no position to give advice to Ty or anyone else, he thought bleakly. Not when it came to marriage—or love, either. He'd never experienced the former and he'd done a miserable job of hanging on to the latter.

Pushing the memories aside, Jack stepped out into the warm night air and turned right to reach the lot where he'd left the Chrysler. Funny, he'd thought the past well and truly behind him until he saw Patsy again. Which just went to show that he could lie to himself as well as anyone.

Chapter 14

Meg saw the familiar lines of the roadster as soon as the cab pulled up in front of the bungalow court. Jack was leaning against it, his lean frame completely relaxed. When he saw them, he dropped his cigarette and ground it beneath his shoe as he walked toward them.

Meg was glad to see him, not just because she liked him, which she did, but because when he was around, the silence between her and Ty was not quite so noticeable. Other than a few simple courtesies, they'd barely spoken all morning. It was hard to remember how easy conversation had been during the summer. And the silences had been just as easy.

"Great view," Jack said by way of greeting as he opened the cab door for her.

"Yes. And it's just as nice from inside." Meg turned to look down the twisty road the cab had labored up, admiring the city spread out beneath them. "It must be very pretty at night, with all the lights," she said.

"Yep." Jack turned from the view to look down at her. "How do you like California so far?" he asked. "Not much like Iowa, is it?"

"Not much," she agreed, laughing a little. "I haven't seen much of it yet but I like it, so far."

"If offers a few advantages over Iowa," Jack said. "Not many beaches in Iowa."

"I haven't been to the beach yet."

"You've been here a week and haven't seen the Pacific?" Jack couldn't have sounded more shocked if she'd just confessed to having kidnapped the Lindbergh baby. "You haven't taken her to see the beach?" he asked, his eyes going over her head to Ty.

"We wanted to find a place to live first," Ty said. He set down the suitcases he'd unloaded from the cab while they were talking.

"You couldn't take time out to go twenty miles to see the largest body of water on the planet?"

"We were busy," Ty said, flushing a little beneath Jack's look.

"I really wanted to get settled," Meg said quickly. She didn't want Jack to think that it was Ty's fault they hadn't done any sight-seeing.

"The Pacific's been there a long time, Jack," Ty said dryly. "It's not going to disappear in the next couple of days."

"I guess not." But Jack's expression said that wasn't reason enough to postpone seeing it.

"Hello." The word was dragged out into three syllables and came from the doorway of the nearest bungalow. All three turned to watch Millie Marquez slink across the grass toward them. The slink would have been effective if she'd been tall and thin and mysterious looking. Since she was short and plump and had the open face of a child, the effect was lost on her audience.

"I wondered when you two would be arriving," she said, stopping on the walk in front of them. "I was hoping it would be soon because I have an audition in an hour. It's for a new movie with Clark Gable. They're looking for someone to play a femme fatale. What do you think? Do I look the part?" She struck a pose, throwing back her head and giving them what Meg assumed was a sultry look from under her lashes.

In the brief silence that followed, Meg stole a glance at Jack's face, biting her lip to hold back a smile when she saw him staring, openly fascinated, at Millie's hair, which was dyed a particularly virulent shade of red. This was Meg's second encounter with their new landlady, and the impact of that hair wasn't lessened by familiarity.

"I don't see how they can resist hiring you," Meg said, when both Ty and Jack appeared to be at a loss for words.

"Gee, thanks." Millie dropped the vampish pose and gave Meg a wide smile, revealing the gap between her two front teeth. "Let's get you two settled in. I just know you're going to love living here. We're just like one big happy family." She turned and bustled up the walkway. Jack and Ty picked up the suitcases and followed along behind Meg. Millie was still talking, her voice floating back to them.

"When Larry and I were divorced—that was my husband, you know—I said, Larry, I don't care what you do with the cute little yacht or the cottage on Long Island—which wasn't really a cottage at all, you know, he just called it that. All I want, I said, is that cute little bungalow court—and a reasonable alimony, of course. Because even though I'm an actress, I'm not stupid, you know, and a girl's gotta have something to fall back on. So I've got a place to live and I can rent out the rest of these cute little places and have enough to live on. Only I don't really need to live on it because Larry's real good about keeping up with the alimony. He's a real sweet guy and we'd probably still be married if it hadn't been for his mother thinking an actress in the family might dilute some of that blue blood of theirs. If I'd wanted to be really nasty about it, I'd have kept my married name as a stage name, which would have given the old biddy a heart attack. But Millie Smith just wouldn't look so great on a marquee, you know. I think Millie Marquez has a much better ring to it."

She'd reached the tiny porch of their new home and turned to look at her three companions, oblivious to their lack of response and the slightly glazed look in their eyes. "I really loved Larry, you know, but I couldn't give up my career. After all, like my friend Betty Rickenbacher—no relation to Eddie, you know—once said, Talent comes with a responsibility, and I wouldn't be living up to my responsibility if I was to hide my light under a bushel, even if it did mean giving up the man I love. You know?''

There was a moment's silence while her small audience sorted through possible responses to this sea of revelations. It was Meg who came up with the safest reply.

''I know,'' she said, putting enough feeling into it to satisfy Millie.

''Yeah. Life's a tragedy sometimes.'' Millie sighed and looked as pensive as her round cherub's face would allow. ''But I shouldn't be going on about my problems,'' she said, brightening. ''What with the two of you moving into your first home. It's a swell place.'' She unlocked the door and then handed the key to Meg with the air of one proffering the keys to the city.

''Thank you.'' Meg started to walk through the door but Millie's shriek of dismay froze her in place.

''He's got to carry you inside,'' Millie said, in answer to the startled looks she received. ''It's bad luck otherwise. Larry didn't carry me into our first home together, what with him having a bad back and all, and look what happened to us.''

''Oh, I don't think it's necessary,'' Meg started to say, thinking that the last thing Ty would want was to carry her over the threshold as if they were real newlyweds.

''Can't have you thinking there's anything wrong with my back,'' Ty said lightly as he set the suitcase down. Meg caught her breath as he caught her beneath shoulders and knees and swept her off her feet. Her arms came up to circle his neck.

His arms felt strong and hard around her. Meg could feel the steady beat of his heart, the warm pressure of solid muscles against the softness of her breast. A tiny shiver of awareness slid along her spine, and she suddenly remembered how it had felt when he held her in his arms and kissed her. That seemed so long ago, as if in another lifetime, but it had been less than two weeks. Two weeks ago she'd thought she was saying good-bye to him forever. Now they were married and he was lost to her in a way she'd never imagined.

As Ty stepped through the door and into their new home,

Meg lifted her eyes to his face. Their eyes met and, for a moment, she thought she read the same awareness, the same memories. Ty's arms tightened around her, his head lowered, and she caught her breath, thinking he was going to kiss her.

"Isn't that romantic?" Millie's voice preceded her as she entered the small living room just a step behind them.

The moment was broken—if there'd really been a moment to break. Ty's arms relaxed around Meg, his eyes leaving her face as he lowered her to the floor. Her knees felt just a little weak but she refused to cling to his arm. It was time she grew accustomed to standing on her own two feet.

"People think actresses are shallow, you know," Millie was saying. "Because we cry so easily." She dabbed at her heavily made-up eyes with a scrap of linen. "But the truth is that we feel things more deeply than other people. Sensibilities, you know. I'm just loaded with them. All great actresses have tons of sensibilities. I'm real sensitive to atmosphere, too," she continued.

"Oh, really?" Meg was incapable of a more profound response, and neither Jack nor Ty seemed interested in filling in the gap. But it didn't matter. Millie didn't need much encouragement.

"Oh, yes. I can always tell what people are feeling. I just sense things. Like a sponge, you know."

"Yes, I can imagine," Jack said.

Despite the ache in her chest, Meg had to bite her lip to hold back a smile at his dry tone.

"Sensibilities," Millie said, nodding wisely and setting her red curls bobbing. "You either got 'em or you don't."

"That's very true," Meg agreed, careful to keep her expression solemn.

Millie beamed. "I knew we were going to get along famously. Soon as I saw you two, I just knew you were the folks who'd rent this cute little bungalow. You see what I mean about sensing things? I mean, how else would I have known you were going to be the ones?"

No one seemed to have an answer to that. After a moment's silence, which Millie seemed to take to mean they were all stumped by the profundity of her question, she beamed impartially on the three of them and took her leave.

"Don't want to be late for my audition, you know. I've got a feeling this could be my big break."

"I wouldn't bet the farm on it," Jack muttered as the door closed behind her.

"Oh, I don't know. I think she's rather impressive in an odd way," Ty said thoughtfully.

"With the emphasis on *odd*," Jack agreed.

The three of them looked at each other and grinned, and for a moment, all the tension was gone.

"I'll get your things out of the car," Jack said to Meg.

After he was gone, Meg turned slowly, admiring her new home. It wasn't large or fancy but it was clean and bright and it was hers, at least for a little while. She wasn't going to think about the future, about annulments and of a life without Ty. Those things could be dealt with in their own time.

"You like it?" Ty had been watching her slow inspection.

"Yes."

"Think it's worth thirty-five a month?" he asked teasingly, reminding her of her concern about the cost.

"It still seems like an awful lot of money, but it's a wonderful place." *And would be even more wonderful if they were really starting a life together.*

"Where do you want this?" Jack asked as he shouldered open the door and carried in a big suitcase that Meg recognized as having been her father's.

"The bedroom's through there," she said.

Jack bent and grabbed one of Ty's suitcases on his way to the bedroom. Meg opened her mouth to protest but her glance collided with her husband's and she said nothing. There was no reason for Jack to know that she and Ty weren't sharing a bed. The situation was humiliating enough without other people knowing about it. Since Ty picked up the other suitcase and followed Jack into the bedroom, she assumed he felt the same.

She wandered into the small kitchen and opened the refrigerator, marveling that the coil that sat on top of it like a hat was to take the place of having ice delivered. What a convenience that would be. It was empty now, of course. She'd have to find out about buying food—where the nearest store was, how she could get there. She was a better than average cook. She might not be a wife in every sense of the word, but Ty would certainly never go hungry. It was nice to think that she'd be able to do something for him.

Meg was making a mental list of the things she'd need to start preparing meals when someone knocked on the front door. Thinking it was Millie, with some new tidbit of personal information she wanted to reveal, Meg started toward the door. She'd barely made it out of the kitchen before the knocking came again, louder this time, and a masculine voice came through the door.

"No sense trying to hide, Tyler McKendrick. We know you're in there."

Meg stopped short, one hand coming up to rest on the base of her throat, her pulse suddenly beating much too quickly. Her first thought was that it must be the police. That even from two thousand miles away, Harlan Davis had found a way to set the law on them. Her eyes flew to Ty and Jack, who had just walked out of the bedroom.

"I suppose I have you to thank for this," Ty said, throwing Jack a disgusted look.

"I might have happened to mention your address to one or two people," Jack admitted with a shrug.

Neither of them seemed concerned and Meg dared to draw a shallow breath. As if sensing her anxiety, Ty gave her a quick, reassuring smile as he opened the door. The room filled with people in the space between one heartbeat and the next. Not just people, but large, masculine people—dozens of them, or so it seemed. They were all laughing and talking at once, and it took her a minute or two to sort them out and realize that there were only six of them.

"Jack here just happened to mention that you were back in town. Not only back but that you'd gone and got yourself married and were moving into a new place and that you hadn't bothered to tell any of your friends about it." The man who was speaking was tall and lanky, with a lean, serious-looking face and a head of thick, dark-brown curls. His voice had a long, Texas drawl to it.

"Jack seems to have been busy," Ty said, giving Jack a mock annoyed look.

"Some folks would think that you bein' back in town and not tellin' us and all meant that you wanted some privacy," the man continued. "But we discussed the matter and decided you were just bein' polite, not wanting to bother your friends with a housewarming."

"So, naturally, you decided to come over and warm my house whether I like it or not," Ty said, grinning.

"That's about it. Besides, none of us could sleep last night just wondering what kind of a girl had managed to throw a rope around your neck. We figured she'd have to be something pretty special."

"I'll let you decide that yourself." Ty turned to where Meg stood with her back pressed against a wall and held out his hand. "Come and meet these apes who call themselves friends of mine. They're not as bad as they look. Most of them are even housebroke."

Meg came forward hesitantly, taking Ty's hand and feeling his fingers close reassuringly strong over hers. She caught only about half of the introductions. They were all pilots Ty had worked with at one time or another. The Texan was Joe Long, a name that was more than appropriate, considering his size. His hand swallowed hers but his smile was open and friendly. There was Billy Lawrence, who had white-blond hair and pale eyes and a smile that revealed slightly buck teeth. Then there were two brothers who looked so much alike that Meg could only remember that one was Clive and one was Clint and she hadn't the faintest idea which was which.

The final introduction was Max Sinclair, the youngest of the bunch, not more than two or three years older than Meg herself. He had a shock of blazing red hair and blue eyes that smiled at her with such shy admiration that Meg found herself blushing as she shook his hand.

"Very pleased to meet you, Mrs. McKendrick," he said.

* * *

"Please, call me Meg. All of you," she added, encompassing the others in her smile. "I don't think I'd know who you were talking to if you called Mrs. McKendrick."

"We'd all be honored," Joe said. He seemed to be the spokesman for the small group. "I figured any gal Ty married would be right pretty, but I shoulda known he'd find himself an out-and-out beauty. And a smile like an angel. You're a lucky dog, Ty."

Meg blushed to the roots of her hair, barely hearing Ty's agreement. Of course he'd agreed. What else could he do? He could hardly tell these men the truth about his marriage. It was starting to occur to her that this whole situation was much more complex than she'd imagined. She hadn't thought about the fact that she'd be meeting Ty's friends and that they'd naturally assume that their marriage was a real one. It was going to make it that much harder to untangle their lives when the time came. But it was much too late to worry about that now. For now she could only play the role of Ty's wife and try not to forget that it was only a temporary part.

The weeks that followed were some of the happiest that Meg had ever known. It wasn't long before Ty was working on a more or less steady basis—some of it stunts for the movies, some more mundane trips carrying passengers or small cargo. But Meg didn't have a chance to be lonely. She wasn't quite sure how it happened, but the bungalow seemed to become a kind of unofficial clubhouse for temporarily grounded pilots. Most evenings two or three of them dropped by to play cards or listen to the radio—*Amos and Andy* was a prime favorite.

At first, she'd assumed it was friendship for Ty that brought them. But on the rare occasions when he was gone in the evening, she still had plenty of company. Jack, of course—she noticed that he made it a point to be there when Ty couldn't be. But Max Sinclair was there almost as often, along with Joe and Billy Lawrence and half a dozen others who'd dropped by to introduce themselves the first week they were in the bungalow.

When she thought about it, Meg assumed that her cooking

was a good part of the attraction. Pilots, she came to realize, were generally broke. They spent money faster than they made it, on everything from the pair of ivory-handled Colts that had earned Joe the sobriquet of "Tex" to the shiny new Lincoln on which Max had spent most of a year's earnings.

They were like no one else she'd ever encountered. Fun loving, freewheeling, prone to practical jokes and taking wild chances. All of them loved flying with a passion that bordered on obsession, leaving them just a little awkward when they weren't in the air, like birds that didn't know quite what to do with themselves on the ground.

She was a little surprised that she was so comfortable around them since she'd never thought of herself as someone who made friends easily. But it occurred to her that she'd always liked children, and that, in many ways, it was like having a houseful of overgrown boys most of the time.

What she didn't realize was that it wasn't her cooking that brought them. It was the feeling of home she created. For some of them, it was a chance to glimpse the home they'd left behind months or years before. For others, it was a look at a warmth they'd never known. But for all of them, Meg McKendrick provided something solid and comforting in the crazy spin that was the life they'd chosen to lead.

Meg could have been completely happy if only her marriage had been everything she'd once dreamed.

Ty was pleased to see Meg settle so easily into her new life. Life in southern California was quite a change for a girl raised in rural Iowa. But Meg seemed to take to the sunshine and the more casual atmosphere like a duck to water. She seemed happy, and there'd been too little of that in her life. He'd never had any doubt about how his friends would take to her, but he hadn't been as sure about her liking them. But within a matter of a couple of weeks, she'd become a combination mascot and den mother.

He was glad to see her so happy. Really he was. But he'd have been more glad if he'd been able to go to sleep at night without thinking of her in the wide bed that took up more than its fair share of the small bedroom. Or if he hadn't been able to imagine just how she'd look while she was bathing in the claw-footed tub that dominated the bathroom.

Ty would sit on the sofa and listen to the water run, picturing her pinning her hair up on top of her head. Then she'd turn the water off and his mouth would go dry as he imagined the plain white terry robe sliding from her shoulders to pool on the blue linoleum. She'd be stepping into the water now, sinking down so that it lapped around her bare shoulders, maybe closing her eyes with pleasure . . .

His own eyes would close as hunger dug sharp claws into his gut, threatening to overwhelm his determination to give her time and space to heal. Only an insensitive lout would make demands before she was ready. Unfortunately, he was beginning to wonder just how long his self-control would hold out. Living in the same house with her day after day, seeing her all sleepy-eyed and tousled in the morning, watching her laugh with his friends, Ty found himself wanting her more and more.

Cold showers and stern mental lectures did little more than sharpen his temper. He took to spending more time at the airfield, taking on jobs that would keep him away from home overnight, trusting to Jack to keep an eye on her. Lord knew, he wasn't sure he trusted himself anymore.

Early in November, the rainy season arrived with an unseasonable cloudburst that put a halt to most flying for three days. Deprived of their usual occupation, half a dozen pilots descended on the McKendrick bungalow every afternoon and evening. The faces changed from time to time as someone left and someone else arrived, but there were rarely fewer than three large, restless men parked on the sofa or at the table, playing poker or talking or staring gloomily out at the rain that was keeping them grounded.

On the afternoon of the first day, Meg made cookies, thick, soft sugary rounds that sparked memories of baking day back home, whether home was Texas or Maine or Georgia. The glum mood was somewhat lifted and the cookies vanished in record time. Max made a wistful comment about the doughnuts his mother had made when he was a boy and Meg promised that, if it was still raining the next day, she'd make doughnuts.

Word got out and it seemed as if half the city managed to cram itself into the tiny bungalow the next afternoon. Ty watched sourly as Meg put Joe to work patting out the soft dough on the table while she kept a careful eye on the kettle of oil she was heating on the stove. To Max was given the honor of cutting the first round with a glass and then carefully cutting the middle out with a thimble. After that, there was considerable jockeying to cut the doughnuts and several scorched fingers as the hot treats were pulled out of the sizzling oil and set to drain before being dipped in sugar.

She certainly looked happy enough. Not like someone who had any desire to change the status quo. Not like a woman who thought there was anything wrong with her marriage. There was a burst of laughter from the group huddled in the kitchen and Ty felt his mood sink still lower.

Someone shifted enough to give him a clear view of his wife. Her hair was caught back from her face by a pair of clips. Her cheeks were flushed from the heat generated by the stove, and she was smiling. He'd never seen her look happier. Never wanted anyone more in his life.

His gaze shifted to Max, who was standing next to her, his eyes on her face. Seeing his expression, Ty felt as if someone had just kicked him in the stomach. The boy was in love with her, he realized. The look in his eyes was nothing short of worship. And Meg? Did she feel the same way about him? If she did, Ty couldn't see it. But then, he knew, better than most, just how good she was at concealing what she was thinking, what she was feeling. What if she'd transferred her feelings for him to Max? That wouldn't be so hard to imagine. Max was closer to her age. He was a nice kid, clean cut, clean living. The perfect husband for a girl like Meg.

Except Meg already had a husband.

The strength of that thought startled Ty. Max reached out to brush a smudge of flour from Meg's cheek and Ty found himself on his feet. He was halfway to the kitchen when Jack was suddenly in front of him.

"Talk to you a minute, Ty?"

"Not right now," Ty said, starting around him. He wasn't sure what he planned to do but he wanted Meg away from Max, away from the whole damned bunch of them.

"It's important," Jack said. He set one hand on Ty's shoulder and steered him toward the French door that led out onto the tiny patio.

"It's raining," Ty protested, glancing over his shoulder to see what Meg was doing.

"There's a roof." Jack pushed open the door and all but shoved him out into the cool, damp air.

Since Jack was standing between him and the door, Ty pushed his hands in his pockets and frowned at his friend. "What's so important?"

Jack reached into his jacket pocket and pulled out a pack of cigarettes, shaking one out before reaching for his lighter. "Never thought you were a dog in the manger, Ty."

"What are you talking about?"

"Meg." Jack lit the cigarette and then flipped the lighter shut and put it back in his pocket. "I'm talking about Meg. And Max."

"What about them?" Ty snapped.

"He's in love with her," Jack said, as if there were nothing wrong with that.

"She's my wife," Ty said, feeling angry color run up under his collar.

"The way you treat her, no one would ever guess it," Jack said bluntly. "You act like she's your kid sister. You can't blame someone for thinking that's all she is to you. Can't blame them for thinking the way might be open for somebody who felt a little stronger about her."

"Well, it isn't open. She's my wife and she's going to stay that way."

"Then why don't you treat her like she's your wife?" Jack snapped, dropping his air of cool indifference.

"It's nobody's business how I treat her." Ty moved restlessly, turning to frown down at the tangle of foliage on the hillside below the bungalow. "Besides, she's too young. She's not even eighteen yet."

"Since when is eighteen the magic age of maturity? You and I were a hell of a lot less mature at twenty-four than she is at seventeen. And she's damn well old enough to wonder why her husband is sleeping on the sofa."

Ty spun to face Jack, his eyes wide with shock.

"She told you that?" He sounded as stunned as he felt.

"Hell no." Jack tossed his half-smoked cigarette into the soggy grass next to the patio. "You just did," he said wearily.

There was a long silence while the two men stared at each other.

"If we hadn't been friends for so long, I think I'd feed you your teeth right about now," Ty said slowly.

"If we hadn't been friends for so long, I'd deserve it," Jack responded evenly.

"Friendship doesn't extend to interfering in my marriage, Jack." There was a warning in Ty's voice as well as in his words.

"You're right. But since I've already stepped out of line, I'll go one step further. That's a damn fine girl in there, Ty. No matter what your reasons were for marrying her, you're a fool if you let her go."

"I have no intention of letting her go," Ty said angrily.

"Does she know that?" Jack stopped abruptly and reached up to thrust his fingers through his hair. He shook his head. "Ah hell, it's none of my business."

"We agree on that."

"Just forget I said anything," Jack said. He turned away and pulled open the door, stepping back into the living room without another word.

Ty stayed where he was, ignoring the rain that blew in under the overhang. Obviously the builders had assumed that the bungalow's occupants would be smart enough to stay inside when the weather was inclement.

He stared through the glass door at the group inside. Jack said something to Meg and then departed without so much as a glance in Ty's direction. Ty watched him leave and then found his gaze drawn back to the gathering in the kitchen. Meg was smiling, seemingly unaware that her husband was standing out in the rain like an idiot. Max was standing as close to her as good manners allowed, which was considerably closer than Ty liked. He was watching her, his expression reminiscent of a hungry puppy's.

But Ty didn't feel the anger he had earlier. He knew Max well enough to know that he wouldn't step out of line, no matter how strong his feelings for Meg were.

As he watched Meg with the group of men, what struck him was how comfortable they all were with her and she with them. They were laughing and talking, teasing each other like they were one big happy family. Ty felt like a kid with his nose pressed to the candy store window. He'd been that comfortable with her once. Not so long ago, either.

He wanted Meg but he didn't just want to share a bed with her. Dammit, he missed her. He missed the friendship they'd had, missed the easy companionship. He wanted her to smile at him again without shadows in her eyes. He'd thought he was doing what was best for her in giving her time, keeping his distance. But what if Jack was right? Were the walls between them of his building? And did Meg want them torn down?

A trickle of water worked its way through a crack in the boards over his head and found a target in the back of his neck. The icy drop startled a curse out of Ty and he reached for the door. Maybe he'd spent enough time on the outside looking in.

Chapter 15

I t was warm inside. Warm and welcoming. Ty hesitated a moment, oddly reluctant to approach the cozy little group that stood near the plate of cooling doughnuts. Watching them, he took a step toward the sofa, thinking maybe he needed more time to consider the idea that any lack in his marriage was of his own doing. But then he saw Max touch Meg's arm to get her attention and he changed course abruptly.

"Any doughnuts left?" he asked.

"I think there's one or two that don't already have my name on it," Joe said as he bit into a sugar-coated ring.

The group shifted to allow Ty to move to his wife's side. "They smell terrific, Meg." He set his arm casually around her shoulders, giving Max a friendly nod as he pulled her against his side.

"Thank you." Meg's response was a little breathless and Ty looked down at her, catching her surprised look. Surprise but not rejection, he decided, and kept his arm where it was as reached for a doughnut.

It was every bit as delicious as it looked, but Ty wouldn't have cared if it had tasted like an old tire. He wasn't as interested in food in the moment as he was in the feel of his wife against his side. He contributed his bit to the conversation, which picked up where it had left off when he joined them, but he was vividly aware of Meg.

The initial stiffness slowly eased from her and she relaxed in his hold, her body curving to his so that she was a soft weight along his side. She felt so right there that it was suddenly hard to remember why he'd been keeping his distance. As she relaxed, it seemed natural for his arm to slide downward, his hand settling in the gentle curve of her waist.

Ty could feel the warmth of her skin through the layers of fabric that separated them. The warm, brown smell of the doughnuts overlaid a fresh, clean scent that he finally realized must be Meg's shampoo. Perhaps sensing his attention, she glanced up, her eyes questioning. Ty smiled at her. His fingers shifted, opening over the curve of her hip. Her breath caught a little at the casual intimacy. He saw a delicate wave of color fill her cheeks in the moment before she looked down, but she didn't stiffen or move away.

Ty felt someone watching them and dragged his attention from the soft curve of Meg's cheek. His eyes met Max's for an instant before the other man's gaze shifted to the blatantly possessive arm at Meg's waist. After a moment, he lifted his eyes to Ty's face again. Ty met his look calmly. There was no need to say anything. The way he held Meg said it all. She was his. And if anyone had thought otherwise, he needed to re-think.

Perhaps Jack was right, Ty admitted. If Max had any idea that the way might be clear with Meg, there was no one to blame but himself. He *had* been treating Meg like a sister, and it was understandable that someone might have gotten the wrong idea. He didn't blame Max and wouldn't embarrass him by saying anything. But Max must have read something in his eyes, something that told him that Ty recognized his feelings for Meg. The younger man flushed and looked away. With Meg pressed so snugly along his side, Ty found it in himself to sympathize.

He wasn't surprised when, a few minutes later, Max commented that he ought to be going. Ty didn't urge him to stay, and he was unreasonably pleased that Meg didn't, either. One of the others said that he'd catch a ride back to the airfield with Max. After the two of them left, it wasn't long before the others began to drift away with muttered comments about the rain maybe easing enough to let them get off the ground tomorrow. Still, it was past dark before Ty was finally alone with his wife.

He closed the door behind the last of his friends and turned to lean against it for a moment, his eyes seeking out Meg. She was in the kitchen, gathering up the coffee cups and plates and setting them in the sink. She was wearing a pink dress with a neat white collar and had a soft blue apron wrapped around her waist. Her cheeks were flushed and there were baby fine curls of warm gold laying in soft tendrils against her forehead. He'd never seen her look more beautiful and he'd never wanted anyone more.

Just how did a man go about seducing his wife?

Meg was conscious of Ty watching her, and she found her fingers trembling a little. She was careful not to look at him, not sure what she might see. For the past few weeks he'd barely looked at her and never touched her if he could avoid it. Yet tonight he'd put his arm around her, held her the way he might have if they'd really been married. And now—the way he was just standing there, looking at her . . .

"Here. Let me give you a hand with those."

Ty's voice came from right behind her, and Meg jumped and spun to face him. He was smiling at her, an open friendly smile, the kind of smile that had been all too rare since the wedding. Her fingers tightened over the cup she held until her knuckles ached.

"That's okay. There's not that much to do. And the kitchen is so small."

If it occurred to Ty that, less than an hour ago, the kitchen had been big enough to hold five men as well as herself, he didn't say as much. He nodded, still smiling.

"Okay. Why don't I start a fire while you finish up in here?"

"A fire?"

"In the fireplace," he said gently. "Maybe we can open that bottle of wine Billy gave us for a housewarming gift."

"All right." If he heard the hesitation in her response, he chose to ignore it. With another smile, he turned and went back into the living room.

Meg set down the cup she'd been clutching. For weeks they'd done their best to politely avoid each other, not an easy task in the small bungalow. Now it sounded as if Ty actually wanted her company. What on earth was going on?

She was no closer to an answer twenty minutes later. By the time she'd finished the dishes, Ty had a fire going in the stone-lined fireplace. He'd turned the radio to a music program, and the soft sounds of strings blended with the crackle of flames. He handed her a glass of wine and gestured casually to the sofa. Not feeling casual at all, she sat on the edge of the seat.

"I've never tasted wine," she admitted, giving her glass an uneasy look.

"Think of it as grape juice with a kick," Ty said. Looking at him, she had the odd impression that he was pleased that she'd never tasted wine.

"Mind if I turn off a few lights?" he asked. Since he was already doing just that, Meg's agreement seemed unimportant. He snapped off all the lights except a floor lamp in one corner, leaving the room in soft gloom. "This way we can really appreciate the fire," he said as he came back to where she was sitting and the sofa cushion dipped as he sat down.

The mournful sound of violins filled the silence that followed. Meg stared at the fire and tried to think of something to say.

"The doughnuts were certainly a hit," Ty said, when it seemed as if the silence might continue indefinitely.

"I think just about anything edible is a hit with pilots."

"They enjoy your cooking," Ty agreed. "But they enjoy your company, too."

Something in his voice brought Meg's eyes to his face. But there was nothing in his expression to imply that the comment was anything more than a casual remark.

"I like your friends," she said, returning her attention to her untouched wine.

"They're a pretty good bunch." Ty took a sip of wine. "Max is a nice kid."

"Yes." She glanced at him and smiled. "They all are."

If it hadn't been crazy, she'd have thought that a subtle tension seemed to go out of Ty, as if there was some importance to her answer.

"Try the wine," he said, gesturing to her glass. "It won't bite."

She took a cautious sip, her nose wrinkling slightly at the odd, heavy taste of it. "It doesn't taste much like grape juice."

"Give it time to grow on you," Ty said, seeing her hesitation. "You can't really appreciate it until you're on your second glass."

Left to her own devices, Meg would have poured the remainder of the wine down the sink, but she'd have drunk kerosene as long as Ty kept smiling at her the way he was now.

An hour later she was partway through her second glass of wine and starting to think that Ty might have been right. The second glass certainly did seem to taste better than the first. In fact, the world in general was starting to take on a slightly rose-colored glow. But that wasn't because of the wine. It was because, for the first time in weeks, she didn't have the feeling that Ty was counting the minutes until he could be free of her.

They'd talked, though what they'd talked about, she couldn't have said. And they'd sat without talking, listening to the patter of the rain on the roof and the crackle of the fire in the fireplace. It had been almost like it was last summer, Meg thought wistfully. Before her stepfather's attack, before Ty had married her to protect her. She took another swallow of wine, feeling it slide down her throat, warming her from the inside out.

"You have the most beautiful hair." Ty's voice was husky. Turning to look at him, Meg was surprised to see him right next to her. Had he been sitting so close before?

"Thank you," she whispered.

She jerked, startled, when she felt his fingers in her hair,

loosening the tortoiseshell clips. Her hair tumbled forward as
the combs slid loose, soft golden tendrils caressing her flushed
cheeks.

"It's so soft," Ty murmured. He gathered a handful of it,
his fingertips brushing her scalp.

"I—I brush it a lot." She hardly knew what she was
saying. She couldn't take her eyes off his face and suddenly
seemed difficult to breathe.

"Your skin is soft, too." His thumb brushed across her
cheek in a touch that could have been accidental. But he did it
again, his hand lingering this time. His thumb stroked her
lower lip and Meg felt the breath shudder from her. His head
dipped toward hers and she realized he was going to kiss her a
split second before his mouth touched hers.

His lips were just as she remembered, firm and warm,
coaxing a response from her. Meg closed her eyes, feeling her
senses spin as his tongue stroked across her lower lip, just as
his thumb had done a heartbeat before. Her mouth opened
hesitantly and he slipped inside, his tongue touching hers
lightly, coaxingly until it came up to twine with his.

Meg felt dizzy and she brought one hand up rest against
his chest, her fingers curling into his shirtfront, clinging to him
as the world dipped and spun around her. Her other hand still
clutched the glass of wine but, without breaking the kiss, Ty
took it from her, setting it on the table behind them and then,
flattening his hand against her spine, drawing her closer still,
deepening the kiss until Meg felt almost faint with the sensations rushing over her.

Just when she was sure she couldn't bear another moment, Ty ended the kiss, his mouth softening against hers,
lingering for a moment before he slowly lifted his head. For
the space of several slow heartbeats, Meg didn't move. She
wasn't even sure she was still breathing. Feeling his eyes on
her, she forced her incredibly heavy eyelids to lift, staring up
into his eyes.

His gaze was intent, questioning. Meg understood neither
the questions he asked nor the answers he sought. The wine
had left a not-unpleasant muzziness in her brain, making co-

herent thought difficult. Not that she cared. Her body tingled with an awareness she'd never known. He'd kissed her before but it hadn't been like this. She'd never even imagined anything like this.

"Do you trust me, Meg?" Ty's voice was little more than a husky whisper and she felt tension in the hands that held her.

Trust him? Did he have to ask? But his eyes demanded an answer.

"Always."

"You know I'd never hurt you." It wasn't quite a question but she answered him anyway.

"I know." She brought her hand up to trace the lines of tension that bracketed his mouth. "I trust you and I know you'd never hurt me," she said, giving him the words he seemed to want.

Her fingertip touched the corner of his mouth and a shudder ran through him. His hand came up to catch hers, pressing it to his lips, and Meg shivered as she felt the soft brush of his tongue against her palm. He bent her hand back, exposing the delicate length of her wrist, tasting the soft skin there, sending wild shivers down her spine.

And then his mouth was settling on hers again. There was less gentleness in this kiss and more demand. It was as if he'd been keeping a careful rein on his hunger and was letting just a little of that control slip. Meg opened her mouth to his, her hands clinging to his shirtfront, giving herself to him without reservation.

Ty's conscience stirred as he felt Meg's surrender. She was too innocent to recognize the deliberate seduction he'd set up. The fire, the dim lights, the wine—he'd set the scene with care. He should stop this now, before it went too far, he thought. And then his hand found the soft weight of Meg's breast, heard the shallow catch of her breath, and he knew it was already too late. Much, much too late.

It took every ounce of his self-control not to rush her. It would have been easy to forget her inexperience, especially when she seemed to burn in his arms. But even more than he

wanted an easing of his own hunger, Ty wanted her first experience to be as perfect as he could make it. Everything had to
be just right for her.

Meg was so lost in the power of Ty's kiss that she was
hardly aware of his fingers deftly loosening the buttons down
the front of her dress. She obeyed his unspoken request and
shifted to allow him to push the garment from her shoulders. It
was only when she felt the strap on her slip slide down her arm
and then the brush of his fingers against the side of her breast
that she felt a sudden rush of panic.

She dragged her mouth from his, her hand coming up to
catch his fingers. Wide-eyed, she stared up at him. "I don't
want you to touch me there," she said breathlessly.

Ty held his hand where it was, unmoving, while his eyes
searched her face.

"Why not?"

She swallowed hard, remembering the feel of her stepfather's hand on her, the wetness of his mouth against her skin.
"I just . . . don't," she whispered finally.

"You said you trusted me," he reminded her.

"I do." It had nothing to do with trust, she wanted to
protest. It was something else, something she couldn't explain.

"Then trust me now," he whispered. In his eyes was the
knowledge of what she was remembering. "Let go of my
hand, Meg," he said softly.

"I . . ."

"Please, Meg."

Trembling, she let her hands drop into her lap. She sat
before him, her back stiff, her eyes closed as Ty lowered the
straps of her slip, baring her to the waist. She flinched when he
trailed his finger gently across the upper slope of one breast.

"You're so beautiful. Open your eyes and look."

She shook her head, squeezing her eyes tight shut. She
was so tense, she felt as if she might faint.

"Open your eyes, Meg. Do it for me," he coaxed.

She'd have walked barefoot across hot coals for him, but
that wouldn't have taken as much willpower as it did to open

her eyes. She stared into his face, reading the understanding there. Understanding and determination.

"Look at how beautiful you are," he whispered, his eyes shifting downward.

"I can't." But even as she protested, her eyes were following his command.

Ever since her stepfather's attack, she'd avoided looking at herself in the mirror, not wanting to see the shameful evidence of what he'd done. Now she was shocked to see the marks he'd left were gone. Somehow, even though weeks had passed, she'd expected to see the scratches and bruising still dark and angry on her skin. But there was not a trace left to see, nothing but the creamy expanse of her own skin. And Ty's hand.

The sight of his fingers on her breast made her feel dizzy and flushed. It was shocking. It was undoubtedly sinful, even if he was her husband. And she couldn't take her eyes away.

"See how beautiful you are? Look how pale your skin is compared to mine." He moved his fingers and Meg caught her breath as he cupped one breast, his thumb brushing across the dusky rose of her nipple.

Her hand came up to close around his wrist but she didn't pull him away, didn't lean back out of reach, didn't look away from the stunning sight of his hand on her body. He stroked her nipple until it stood up taut and aching beneath his touch and then repeated the action on her other breast. By that time Meg's eyes were closed again, but it wasn't from shame.

She'd never imagined such sensations, never dreamed she could feel such things. She felt the light touch of his hand at her breast throughout her body, bringing her to tingling life. She felt him move and opened her eyes as he flattened one hand across her spine, arching her back against his supporting arm as he lowered his head.

"No!" She gasped out the protest as she realized what he was going to do. She couldn't bear it if he— She felt his breath against her skin and she stiffened, her hands pressing against his shoulders, her body tensed against the anticipated pain.

And then his mouth closed over her and her breath left her

on a rush of sound that was nearly a sob. His mouth was warm and moist. His tongue laved her nipple with gentle strokes, painting it to shivering awareness before he drew it deeper into his mouth. Meg's fingers were suddenly digging into his shoulders, clinging to him as the world rocked around her.

She felt the rhythmic drawing of his mouth at her breast but she felt it deeper still, at the very core of her. Heat pooled in the pit of her stomach, warm, molten liquid that pulsed in time to the motion of Ty's mouth. When he shifted his attention to her other breast, lavishing it with the same sweet torture, she whimpered. She pressed her knees together, responding to an ache she'd never felt before. She wanted—needed—something she couldn't define.

Ty lifted his head, smothering her protesting moan with his mouth. Meg's lips opened for him, her fingers clinging to him as his tongue thrust inward, retreated, then entered again. She was too innocent to recognize consciously the primal rhythm, but her body reacted to it like a finely tuned instrument responding to a master's touch.

Ty murmured something against her mouth and then he was moving, standing up. Before she had a chance to miss him, he leaned down and lifted her off the sofa, cradling her against his chest as he carried her from the living room.

Meg was grateful for the darkness of the bedroom when Ty set her down next to the bed and eased the rest of her clothes from her. She stood before him, naked and trembling with a mixture of fear and anticipation. He started to unbutton his shirt and she felt her heart suddenly beating much too fast. She could feel his eyes on her but she couldn't lift her gaze past his hands.

He shrugged out of the shirt, letting it fall to the floor, and then his hands dropped to the waistband of his trousers and Meg swallowed hard. She closed her eyes when she heard the rasp of his zipper. She wanted to turn and dive into the bed and bury her head under the pillows. She wanted to open her eyes and look at him as openly as he'd looked at her.

"Meg?" She jumped when she felt his hands settle on her shoulders, drawing her a step closer so that she could feel the heat radiating from him. "You can open your eyes." Gentle amusement laced his voice. "It's too dark to see anything anyway."

She might not be able to see but she could certainly feel. Opening her eyes, she stared up at him as he slid his hands down her back, urging her closer still. A shudder of pleasure went through her as she felt the broad muscles of his chest against her breasts for the first time. The crisp mat of black curls was a delicious abrasion against her skin.

"You are so beautiful," he whispered against her hair.

His hands were not quite steady on her shoulders, and she realized suddenly that he wasn't as calm as he seemed. The knowledge was oddly reassuring. She lifted her hands to his chest, smoothing her palms over the muscles there, marveling at the hard strength beneath her fingertips. She felt him shudder at the light touch and was awed that she could make him tremble.

It took every ounce of willpower at his command for Ty to stand still beneath the sweet torment of Meg's delicate exploration. He clenched his teeth, fighting the urge to tumble her back onto the bed and finally sate the hunger that had been gnawing at him for so long. But not for the world would he do anything to frighten her.

Just when he thought his control was stretched to the breaking point, Meg tilted her head back, her lips parting in unmistakable invitation. With a groan, Ty lowered his mouth to hers. Despite his determination to take things slow, the kiss was avid and hungry. To his delight, she responded without hesitation, her tongue twining with his, her slender body curving into his.

Without breaking the kiss, he eased her back onto the bed, bracing one hand against the plain cotton sheets as he lowered her. He followed her down, letting her feel the fullness of his arousal for the first time. He tasted the quick, shocked breath she drew, felt the sudden uncertainty in her. He lifted his head, staring down at her in the darkness as his legs slid between hers.

"Trust me, Meg." The words were both command and plea.

"I do," she answered without hesitation.

But trust wasn't enough to still the tremor of fear that ran through her at the first touch of him against the most feminine part of her. Feeling her hesitation, Ty forced himself to stop, though every drop of blood in him screamed with the need to complete their union.

His eyes had long since adjusted to the dimness of the room. He could see Meg staring up at him, her eyes wide blue pools. He waited, sensing the battle between fear and desire that was waging inside her. Slowly, so slowly he could almost have imagined it, he felt some of the tension go out of her. Her hands stirred restlessly on his shoulders and there was a slight, almost imperceptible movement of her hips.

Biting his lip to hold back a smile as he felt curiosity edge out fear, Ty deepened the contact. The smile became pained as he felt her close around him, all soft heat and moisture. He felt the thin barrier that marked her virginity, heard Meg's shallow gasp of pain as it yielded to him, and then she was holding him in the most intimate of embraces.

Meg had thought she had a basic understanding of what happened between a man and a woman, at least the mechanics of the act. But nothing she'd thought she knew had prepared her for the incredible intimacy of sharing her body with a man. What little she knew hadn't covered the remarkable feeling of . . . fullness, of completion.

She gasped as Ty shifted, withdrawing, then easing forward again, repeating the movement until she began to echo it. Though it hardly seemed possible, the sensation intensified. Her skin felt hot to the touch. And so tender. Every brush of Ty's body against hers brought new nerve endings to tingling life, added to the liquid heat that pooled deep inside her.

Her hands clung to his shoulders as heat threatened to consume her. She couldn't possible stand it another moment, she thought, and yet it continued, the tension coiling tighter and tighter within her until she thought that its release would surely be her destruction.

Meg cried out, her nails biting into Ty's damp skin as the tension suddenly grew unbearable. She gasped in shock, in pleasure tinged with just a little fear. Ty murmured something —reassuring her even as he refused to let her retreat from the blinding intensity that threatened to swallow her whole.

And then she felt him tremble against her, felt the shudders of pleasure racking his long body. She wrapped her arms around him, clinging to the only solid thing in her world as the tension inside her suddenly snapped and she seemed to shatter into a thousand tiny fragments of sensation.

It was a long time before Meg became aware of her surroundings again. She floated back to awareness. Her body tingled with life yet felt heavy with a kind of exhaustion she'd never known. Though he was supporting most of his weight on his elbows, Ty's frame was warm against her. She could feel him still inside her and she shifted slightly, marveling at the incredible sensation of sharing her body with the man she loved.

Her movement, slight as it was, drew a groan from Ty and a husky order to hold still. Meg froze, wondering if she'd hurt him somehow. Moving slowly, as if it took considerable effort, he lifted himself away from her. Meg caught her breath on a mixture of discomfort and regret as he left her body.

Without the heavy, masculine blanket of his body, the air in the room seemed chill. But before she could do more than register the discomfort, Ty had settled next to her and was dragging the covers up around them, creating a warm cocoon.

Outside, Meg could hear the rain pattering against the roof. From the living room came the soft crackle of the fire, and she could see its flickering light on the bedroom door. She felt warm and secure. Complete in a way she'd never known possible.

Ty's fingers slid through her hair, stilling as he felt the dampness at her temples, the result of tears Meg hadn't even been aware of shedding. He tilted her face up to his, his forehead creasing in a frown.

"Did I hurt you?"

"No." She caught his disbelieving look and corrected herself. "A little," she admitted.

"I'm sorry." He frowned as he dried the traces of her tears with his fingertips. His touch was so tender that Meg had to close her eyes against the threat of fresh tears. The pain had been so fleeting that it was easily forgotten, lost in the wonder of what had come afterward.

"I'm not sorry," she whispered, blushing at her own boldness. Ty's hand stilled. She felt his surprise and her blush deepened, wishing she could take the words back. He slid one hand under her chin, ignoring her slight resistance as he tilted her face up to his.

"I'm sorry it had to hurt you," he said. And then she saw the white slash of his smile in the darkness. "But I'm certainly not sorry about anything else."

Though he couldn't possibly have seen her fiery cheeks, he laughed softly, causing her blush to deepen. Taking pity on her embarrassment, Ty brushed a kiss across her forehead before settling her more solidly against his side, her head tucked into the curve of his shoulder.

Meg's hand rested against his chest and she threaded her fingers through the crisp mat of dark curls there. She could feel Ty's heartbeat under her cheek, the length of his body pressed to hers. She thought vaguely that she should be embarrassed to be lying here with him, both naked as the day they were born. But what she felt was a deep contentment, a feeling of completion she'd never known, a feeling that went much deeper than the delicious physical languor that filled her.

She was Ty's wife. Meg savored the thought. Her marriage was no longer just a few lines of print on a piece of paper. It was a reality. Later she might question the why of what had happened. But for now, it was enough that she was really and truly Ty's wife.

Chapter 16

I n her more superstitious moments, Meg worried that she might be *too* happy. What if God looked down on her new life and decided that she simply had more happiness than any one person deserved? The way she felt right now, she couldn't have argued the point. But not even the threat of divine outrage could keep the smile from her face.

The past few weeks had been like a small glimpse of heaven. She had friends, laughter, sunshine, and most of all, Ty. Not just the Ty who'd been her friend over the summer, but a Ty who was also her husband. Her lover. Just thinking the word made her flush, but that's what he'd become. Her lover.

And if she worried that she being too happy might be a sin, she was almost positive that the pleasure she took in their new intimacy had to be grounds for divine punishment. Over the years, she'd heard women of her mother's acquaintance make veiled references to the duties of the marriage bed. There'd always been something vaguely ominous in their tone of voice. When she was small, Meg had had a blurry impression that such duties were rather like taking castor oil or eating spring's first bitter greens—one of those things that had to be endured. As she grew older, her understanding of just what "marital duties" were grew only slightly less blurred, but she began to doubt that anything that happened between a man and a woman who loved each other could be quite as unpleasant as it had been made to sound, especially not if it resulted in anything as delightful as a baby.

Then she'd seen the lust in her stepfather's face, felt the terrible, wicked hunger in him as he tore at her clothes, and she hadn't been quite so sure about what happened between a husband and wife. The one thing she'd clung to was the knowledge that Ty would never hurt her. She'd believed that with all her heart and soul. And she'd been right.

In the warmth of his touch and the gentle strength of his body, Meg had found nothing but pleasure, that night and all the nights since. She'd learned to know her body in ways she'd never dreamed. Far from finding her marital duties something to be endured, she found herself anticipating the nights with an eagerness that seemed downright sinful. Which brought her full circle to her original thought that it might be possible to be *too* happy.

"What're you doing?" Millie's voice preceded her across the courtyard, interrupting Meg's thoughts. She looked up from her sewing, watching as her landlady made her way down the concrete path. Millie was wearing a pair of black feathered mules, the likes of which Meg had never seen outside a theater, and her plump form was draped in pink satin lounging pajamas. The color clashed so magnificently with her hair that Meg found herself almost admiring the effect. She also carried a cigarette in a long ivory holder, but Meg had yet to see her actually take a puff on it.

"I'm mending one of Ty's shirts," Meg said, in answer to Millie's question.

"Isn't that nice. I can't sew a stitch, you know." Meg occupied one of the two metal chairs on the small porch. Millie sank into the other one. "I had an aunt that tried to teach me to sew one time. She did all kinds of fancywork, and she figured every girl needed to know how to sew on a button, at least. So she tried to teach me, but I just couldn't get the hang of it."

"It's handy to know," Meg said, while she tried to imagine how anyone could have trouble learning to sew on a button.

"It drove Aunt Millicent crazy—she's the one I'm named for, you know. Can you imagine sticking a poor innocent little baby with a name like Millicent Abigail Dorfman?"

"It does seem a mouthful," Meg admitted. She'd had time to become accustomed to Millie's parenthetical mode of speech and was no longer disconcerted by the abrupt jogs in the conversation.

"That's why I changed my name to Marquez." Millie tapped ash off her cigarette into the flower bed that bordered the bungalows. "I thought of changing my first name, too. To something more dramatic, maybe like Myra. Myra Marquez would look real good on a marquee, you know?" Meg made a noncommittal noise and kept her eyes on her sewing. "But then I thought, What if the director calls me Myra and I don't remember that's my name? I wouldn't do what he said and then I'd get a reputation for being poison to work with and my whole career could be ruined, all because I didn't remember I was Myra." The outlined scenario made Millie's eyes widen in horror. Meg bit her lip and concentrated on putting the next stitch in the seam she was mending.

"So I changed the Dorfman and kept the Millie. Of course, I was Millie Smith when I was married to Larry. That's a dull name, if ever there was one. Sometimes I wonder if maybe I'd have tried a little harder to keep his mother off our backs if he'd had a different name. Like maybe I knew, deep in my heart, that I just wasn't meant to go through life as Millie Smith, you know?" She seemed to interpret Meg's mumbled response as sympathetic, because she sighed and tapped the ash off her cigarette again. "Anyway, Aunt Millie never did manage to teach me to sew," she finished, as if the intervening digressions had never occurred.

"It's not all that difficult," Meg said. She finished up the seam, took a small back stitch, and knotted the thread before breaking it off. "My mother made quilts for other people and made most of our clothes. My sister and I both learned to sew when we were small."

"My aunt Abigail made quilts—she's the Abigail in Millicent Abigail, you know. I remember being sick at her house once and there was a quilt on the bed—no pattern, you know, just all kinds of scraps. And I spent hours trying to match up the different pieces of fabric.''

''I can remember doing that, too,'' Meg said. Her mouth curved at the memory of lying in bed, the sun slanting through the window onto the quilt that covered her. Not one of the ''good'' quilts that her mother made to sell but a hastily put together affair made up of scraps of clothing, lined with an old blanket, and tied together with bits of yarn.

''Do you miss your family a lot?''

Millie's question made Meg realize that she'd been staring out into the sunshine, her hands idle in her lap. She picked up the mended shirt and began to fold it, buying time to formulate a response. Did she miss her family? There was no simple answer to that.

Though she felt guilty for thinking it, she couldn't honestly say she missed her mother. Meg loved her but they'd never really been close. Perhaps it was because Ruth had always been too busy struggling to stay afloat in the turbulent waters of life to have much time for the quiet moments that went into building closeness with another human being.

And Patsy? It was ironic that she'd had to move two thousand miles away to find her way back to something of the old closeness she'd once known with her sister. They'd already exchanged several letters, and Meg felt closer to her than she had in years.

Aware that Millie was still waiting for an answer to her question, she shook herself out of her thoughts and smiled at the other woman.

''My sister and I have been writing,'' she said finally, sidestepping the question. ''And I certainly don't miss the weather,'' she added, nodding to the warm sunshine that spilled into the courtyard. ''With weather like this, it's hard to believe that Thanksgiving is next week.''

''You get used to it,'' Millie said, flicking ash off her as-yet-untouched cigarette and giving the sunshine an indifferent look. ''I been out here four years now, ever since the divorce, and after a while you begin to crave a change of seasons. I mean, there's hardly any difference between summer and winter, except it rains in the winter.''

"I guess that could get a little tiresome," Meg said politely, but she didn't believe it. It seemed as if she'd known more than enough winters. The warmth of the California sunshine seemed to sink all the way to her bones, driving out a lifetime of cold. Of course, maybe it was Ty that was doing that, she thought, flushing a little.

"You two going back to Indiana for Thanksgiving or Christmas?" Millie asked.

"Iowa. No, we're not going back." She suspected that Ty's parents would rather have invited Bonnie Parker to share the holidays with them than their new daughter-in-law. "A few of Ty's friends are going to join us for Thanksgiving."

"They seem like a swell bunch of guys," Millie said. There was a wistfulness in her tone that made Meg lift her eyes from the button she'd been replacing. "It's almost like you were all a family, the way they show up here at all hours."

"I guess it is." Meg hadn't thought about it but she realized Millie was right. They had become a kind of family, more of one in some ways than anything she'd ever known.

"That kid, Max, seems real stuck on you."

"Max?" Meg glanced at her in surprise. "Stuck on me?" She chuckled. "I think you've been an actress too long, Millie. You're starting to see dramatic potential where it doesn't exist."

"Maybe you're right." The reference to her being an actress was a stroke to Millie's ego that she couldn't bring herself to turn away. "But like I said before, I do have strong sensibilities when it comes to people. Max is real fond of you."

"I'm fond of him, too," Meg said comfortably, returning her attention to her sewing.

There was a period of silence, something of a rarity when Millie was around. Since auditioning didn't seem to fill up much of Millie's time, she was often home during the day. When she grew bored with her own company, she sometimes sought Meg out. She was not like anyone Meg had every known before. Her wardrobe and makeup seemed taken right from a movie screen. And her conversational style was unique, to say the least. But once Meg got past Millie, the actress who was filled with sensibilities, she found there was a surprisingly genuine and unexpectedly nice woman beneath the surface.

"That fellow, Joe Long, is he going to be coming over for Thanksgiving?" Millie's tone was elaborately casual. When Meg looked at her, she was placing a fresh cigarette in the holder, her movements languid.

"Last I heard, Joe was planning on being here. It's too far for him to go home to Texas. Why do you ask?"

"Oh, no particular reason." Millie lifted one shoulder in an indifferent shrug that would have done Greta Garbo proud. "I just wondered."

"Oh." Meg's needle made another trip through the button.

"Is he seeing anyone that you know of?" Millie couldn't have sounded less interested.

Meg bit the inside of her lip to hold back a smile. If this was an example of Millie's acting skills, it was no wonder she hadn't been hired.

"I don't think so."

"Hard to imagine a man like that running loose," Millie said wistfully. "I mean, a girl just can't help but notice a guy like that. So tall and that cute little accent."

Meg wasn't sure Joe would appreciate hearing his slow Texas drawl called cute but she didn't argue. She was occupied with trying to imagine Millie Marquez and Joe Long as a couple and finding it wasn't as hard to do as she had thought. Joe's slow-talking style might be just the right balance to Millie's occasionally empty-headed chatter. Besides, in her current state of wedded bliss, she was not averse to dabbling a little in matchmaking.

"Would you like to join us for Thanksgiving dinner?" she asked guilelessly.

It had been quite the nicest Thanksgiving she could remember, Meg thought. She ran a dish towel over a solid blue plate, part of the hodgepodge of plates and cups that made up her dinnerware. Nothing matched anything else, but no one seemed to mind. After setting the plate in the cupboard, she reached for another, this one orange and chipped on the edge. She smiled as she dried it. She couldn't imagine that the holiday dinner would have tasted any better if it had been served on the finest Havilland china.

Millie had been right—they had created a kind of family. Joe and Max and Billy, Clint and Clive, though she still wasn't sure she could tell them apart, even Millie had become part of their little circle. They'd crowded around the table, eating the food they'd all chipped in to pay for, and for the first time in her life, Meg had felt as if she had something for which to be truly thankful. A family in the best sense of the word.

And Ty. Most of all, she was thankful to have Ty. The few weeks since she'd become his wife in fact as well as in name had been wonderful. And if she sometimes thought, wistfully, that life could be perfect if only Ty loved her as much as she loved him, she quashed the thought as soon as she became aware of it, telling herself not to be greedy. For now it was enough that Ty cared for her. That could grow into love, given time and patience. She had plenty of both.

Meg tried not to remember Patsy's comment that a marriage could be based on a "fond kind of love." Or to wonder how she'd feel if five years from now or ten years, all Ty could give her would be that sort of love.

Leaning against the doorjamb, watching her, Ty wondered what thoughts were going through her head. Expressions flickered across her face like images on a screen, a soft smile giving way to a frown. The frown in its turn replaced by a slight firming of her chin that might have meant she'd made her mind about something, and then that expression fading into a vaguely anxious look.

"What are you thinking about?"

At the sound of his voice, Meg gasped and jerked her head toward him, her eyes wide and startled.

"I thought you were starting a fire," she said.

"It's started. So I came to see if you needed any help with the dishes."

"It's all done." She turned to hang the damp towel over the edge of the sink. "Besides, the dishes are my job."

"I've been known to wash a dish or two since leaving home."

"It's not a man's job." Meg reached behind her to untie the blue gingham apron she wore.

"There were a lot of times when Jack and I couldn't afford to hire a maid," he said idly, his gaze admiring the soft thrust of her breasts beneath the pale-yellow cotton of her dress.

"Well, you have a wife now. You don't have to do dishes."

"But wives are good for so many more interesting tasks." Grinning, he reached out and slid one arm around her waist, pulling her up against him. He bent his head and nuzzled the side of her neck.

"Ty, we're in the kitchen!" Meg protested breathlessly.

"What better place to find out that you taste delicious," he said with a growl, nibbling on her ear.

"If you're hungry, maybe you should have another piece of pie," she told him primly, her hands braced against his chest.

The only thing he was hungry for was her, but when Ty lifted his head and saw the pinkness in her cheeks, he didn't say as much. Sometimes he forgot how innocent she still was.

"Come admire the fire," he said, deciding that there could be worse things than having to seduce his wife. Though she'd never said as much, he had the feeling that she suspected there was something more than a little sinful about the way she enjoyed his lovemaking.

He'd been careful not to rush her. The way Meg had blossomed these past few weeks was more than ample evidence that he'd been a fool to think she wasn't ready to make their marriage a real one. Though he'd thought Jack was crazy when he said it, maybe Meg *had* wondered why he didn't share her bed; maybe she had thought he didn't want her. But she couldn't have any doubts on that score now.

"Did you notice the way Joe and Millie hit it off?" she asked as they settled on the sofa in front of the fire. "I think they'll make a nice couple."

"Joe and Millie?" Ty's eyebrows climbed in surprise. "That's like pairing Gary Cooper and Betty Boop. Only I think Betty Boop is smarter."

"Don't be mean," Meg protested, elbowing him in the ribs. "Millie's very nice when you get to know her."

"What makes you think Betty Boop isn't?"

"She likes Joe." Meg ignored his facetious question. "And I think he likes her."

Ty opened his mouth to argue then closed it, remembering the way his friend's eyes had seemed to linger on Millie's brilliant red hair. He'd assumed Joe was as blinded by the color as everyone else was but, now that he thought about it, there'd been admiration in that look.

"Well, I'll be darned," he muttered.

"I think they'll do very well together," Meg said smugly. She snuggled a little closer to his side.

"Maybe." Ty was losing interest in Joe and Millie's potential as a couple. Of far more immediate concern was finding the pins that held Meg's hair in a soft bun and pulling them out.

She murmured something, not quite a protest, not yet a plea, as Ty threaded his fingers through her hair and tilted her face up to his. She stared up at him and Ty thought he'd like to drown himself in the blue of her eyes. With one hand supporting her head, he let the other drop to the row of neat buttons that marched down the front of her dress.

"Did I ever tell you how much I like dresses that button down the front?" he whispered. He saw her throat work as she swallowed.

"No." The word was little more than a breath.

"I do." He slid his hand under the loosened fabric of her dress, flattening his palm against her stomach, feeling the warmth of her beneath the cotton slip. "We're not in the kitchen anymore," he said huskily.

"I know." She lifted her hand, her fingers threading through the thick blackness of his hair as he lowered his head to hers.

If this was a sin, it was surely the sweetest he'd ever known, Ty thought as he tasted her response.

The weeks between Thanksgiving and Christmas seemed to fly past. Meg's birthday came in early December. In years past, the occasion had been marked by her mother baking a cake and if there was money to spare, which was rare, a small gift of some kind, usually something practical, like underwear or a new pair of shoes. She saw no reason to think that this birthday would be any different from the seventeen birthdays that had preceded it.

When Ty came home in the middle of the afternoon and presented her with a beautiful bouquet of eighteen pale-yellow roses, Meg was thrilled. It was the first time anyone had given her flowers, and to receive roses in December seemed particularly wonderful.

"Oh, Ty, they're so beautiful." She set the bouquet on the table, as carefully as if the flowers had been made of spun glass, and then turned and put her arms around his neck, rising on her toes to kiss him. His hands caught her around the waist, pulling her close, and the kiss became a much more thorough thank-you than she'd intended. When he finally let her go, she was flushed and breathless.

"If I'd known I'd get that reaction, I'd have brought you flowers sooner," Ty said, grinning wickedly. Meg's blush deepened but she was pleased to see that his breathing was just a little faster than it had been.

"Thank you for the roses, Ty. They're the best birthday present I've ever had," she said shyly.

"Well, I hope you're not going to think that for very long," he said, taking her hand and pulling her toward the door.

"Wait. I've got to put my roses in water."

"They'll be fine," he told her, not slowing his pace. "Your other birthday present is outside."

"*Another* birthday present?" The roses were so much more than she'd expected that Meg couldn't imagine what else he could possible give her.

It was another in a seemingly endless parade of warm, blue-sky days, a far cry from the cold and snow of an Iowa December. As she hurried along behind Ty, Meg could feel the tension in the hand that held hers. Whatever her other present was, he was excited about it. The idea that he was excited about giving something to her seemed so amazing that she nearly walked into him when he stopped abruptly.

"What do you think?" Ty asked.

Meg looked but there was nothing to be seen except grass and shrubs and the cars parked at the curb. She caught Ty's expectant look and bit her lip, her eyes scanning the area again.

"Do you like it?"

"Do I like what?" she asked, bewildered.

"The car." Ty stepped forward to pat the roof of a black Ford coupe. Meg stared at him. "It's a few years old but it's in pretty good shape. I went through the engine and it's in tiptop condition. Billy banged out a dent in the fender and found new bumpers, and Max touched up the paint where it needed it."

When Meg said nothing but only stared at the car, her hands clasped together between her breasts, Ty cleared his throat. "It's not fancy but it's solid, and it will do to get you around town."

Meg moved closer, afraid to blink for fear the car would disappear. He'd bought her a car. She'd only half heard his explanation of who had done what to it. She couldn't quite grasp the basic idea that he was talking about a car for her.

"If you don't like it, we'll get something else," he said when the silence just continued.

"Like it?" Meg reached out one hand and touched the fender, more than half expecting it to disappear in a puff of smoke. When that didn't happen, she pulled her hand back, clasping it with the other as she stared at the car. "You bought me a car?"

"Well, I thought it would come in handy, what with the buses not coming up this far and me gone all day. It'll make it easier for you to go shopping or whatever."

"A car." It was slowly sinking in that the car was really for her.

"Do you like it?" he asked, sounding a little anxious.

"Oh, Ty. I—I don't know what to say." She felt the sting of tears.

"Say you like it," he suggested, only half jokingly.

"Like it?" The word was hopelessly inadequate. "It's the most incredible thing. I never imagined. I wouldn't have dreamed. I can't believe you did this."

The choppy half sentences were all she could manage, but they seemed to be enough to reassure him that she most definitely liked her birthday present. He grinned at her, looking boyishly pleased with himself.

"I thought you might like it," he said modestly.

"I love it!" Coming out of her state of shock, Meg threw her arms around him, hugging him. "I love it!"

Though not a fraction as much as she loved him, but she couldn't tell him that.

A week before Christmas, Ty took Meg to an air show in which he and Jack were to be flying. Meg hadn't been up close to a plane since that never-to-be-forgotten occasion when she was a child and Ty had taken her flying. She was dismayed to find that the planes seemed much smaller and more fragile than she'd remembered. Looking at the shiny red Curtiss aircraft of which Ty was so obviously proud, all Meg could think of was that the thin framework of metal and wires didn't look like nearly enough to keep her husband safe thousands of feet up in the air.

She couldn't say as much. She smiled and admired the plane, listening as Ty told her about the engine, the rate of climb, maximum speed, and assorted other bits of information that went in one ear and out the other. None of those things sounded as if it had anything to do with keeping him alive.

Meg reminded herself that Ty had gone up hundreds of times and come down again safely. Of course, it was a crash that had resulted in the broken leg that brought him home to Iowa for the summer. But she wasn't going to think about that. Ty was a good pilot and there was no reason to worry.

Max was the only one of the pilots in their small circle of friends who wasn't to be flying that day. Meg attributed Ty's seeming reluctance to leave her in Max's care to the fact that she hadn't been feeling well that morning. She'd been warmed by his concern, oblivious to the completely male look that passed from Ty to Max.

The weather couldn't have been more beautiful. Meg was beginning to think that Los Angeles didn't have anything but beautiful weather, as if a Hollywood director orchestrated everything from above, allowing only an occasional shower to clear the air. Meg picked her way up the wooden bleachers, grateful for Max's hand at her elbow to steady her.

"Thank you, Max." She turned her head and smiled at him as he sank onto the bench seat beside her. "It's a terrific seat."

"You should be able to see about everything from here," he agreed. "Can I get you anything? There's hot dogs and Coke."

Meg felt her stomach roll at the mention of hot dogs. She swallowed hard and forced a smile, hoping the shadow cast by the brim of her hat would be enough to mask her sudden pallor. "A Coke would be nice, I think."

"Sure thing." Pleased to be able to get her something, Max bounded off down the bleachers.

Just watching him made Meg feel tired. She drew a clean handkerchief from her purse and dabbed at the fine beads of perspiration along her upper lip. She'd been tired a lot lately. Even Ty had commented on it. She'd laughed and told him he was imagining things, unwilling to say anything about her suspicions as to the reason for her sudden lack of energy. It was too soon, she thought.

"Here's your Coke, Meg." She took the paper cup Max handed her, smiling her thanks before taking a sip of the sweet, iced liquid. It seemed to settle her queasy stomach, and she was able to give her companion a more natural smile.

"Just what I needed," she said.

Max stared at her a moment, a look in his eyes she couldn't quite define. Abruptly he flushed and ducked his head to stare at his own drink. Meg shrugged off his odd behavior, attributing it to shyness. Though he was a few years older than she was, he sometimes seemed much younger, making her think of what it might have been like to have had a younger brother.

"There's Ty and Jack now," Max said.

Meg turned her head in the direction he was pointing, feeling her heartbeat increase as she watched the planes taxi onto the field. They were identical, making it impossible to know which one Ty was in.

"Ty's the one in front," Max said, as if reading her thoughts. She felt him glance at her but she couldn't take her eyes off the first plane. "He's a terrific pilot, you know. One of the best."

His words soothed a little of her anxiety. Still, she couldn't stop her teeth from worrying her lower lip as she saw Ty's plane leap into the air, Jack seemingly only a heartbeat behind. She did not enjoy the act that followed. It was one thing to know what Ty did for a living. It was something else altogether to watch him doing it.

Almost immediately, she lost track of which plane was which as they ducked and dived around each other, performing midair acrobatics with an ease that belied the danger of what they were doing. It was a breathtaking display of skill, and Meg found herself feeling both proud and terrified. She neck ached from the strain of watching the sky, but not even for an instant did she take her eyes from the planes. So intent was her gaze that it was almost as if she thought the sheer force of it would be enough to keep Ty's plane in the air.

The display seemed to go on forever, and Meg was just starting to relax when first one plane and then the other rose high in the air and then turned to plummet toward the ground nose first. The sound of the engines grew louder, taking on a whine that grated at her nerves. They'd pull out in a second, she told herself. But the whine grew louder, almost a scream now. Around her, the crowd was murmuring in sudden concern as the bright red planes arrowed downward. Meg didn't even realize that she was on her feet, her hands clasped in front of her, her whole body taut as a finely stretched wire.

She heard Max speaking but the words had no meaning. Nothing had any meaning except the howl of the planes' engines. At the last possible second, just when it seemed inevitable that both aircraft would smash into the ground, the nose of the first one and then the other jerked up and they leveled out, skimming along in front of the bleachers.

But the roar of approval from the crowd was drowned out by the sudden rushing sound in Meg's ears. She heard Max say her name, his voice urgent, and then she closed her eyes and, for the first time in her life, collapsed in a dead faint.

When she came to, it was in the cool shadows of the hangar where Ty's plane had been. There was a cot against one wall, for the use of the pilots who sometimes worked late into the night on a plane. The first thing she saw was Max's face, looking nearly as pale as she felt, his blue eyes worried. There was a sopping rag across her forehead. Water from it trickled into her ear and she reached up to brush it away, surprised by how much effort the simple movement took.

"Are you okay?" Max asked, his voice as hushed as if he were at a funeral. *Funeral.*

"Ty?" She sat up abruptly and dizziness spun through her, nausea rising in her throat.

"He's fine," Max hastened to assure her. His hands were gentle as he eased her back against the wall of the building. "Here, drink some of this."

"This" was a paper cup half full of lukewarm water. Meg sipped it, feeling her stomach sullenly begin to settle.

"I fainted," she murmured, shocked by the realization.

"You sure did. Scared the life out of me." Max crouched in front of her, still looking more than a little scared. "I darn near didn't catch you. I brought you down here, figured you'd be more comfortable.''

''Thank you.'' She sipped the water again and managed a weak smile. ''Sorry to be so stupid.''

''Not stupid at all,'' he said, rising to her defense with a speed that would have warmed her if she hadn't been so weak. ''That stunt's meant to scare people. A lot of what brings people to air shows is the idea that some pilot may get himself killed.''

''That's horrible!''

''Just human,'' he said, shrugging. ''It isn't that they exactly *wish* anybody dead, but there's a thrill in thinking something like that might happen. If it wasn't dangerous, no one would want to watch.''

''I still think it's horrible,'' she muttered, knowing he was right but repulsed by the thought that some of those people out there had been waiting to see Ty or Jack crash.

''Maybe. But you don't have to worry about Ty, you know. He's about the best darn pilot I've ever seen.'' Max's eyes shone with admiration. ''He and Jack between them have more skill in their little finger than I'll ever have. I couldn't ever do a dive like that. I get dizzy and pull up too soon.''

''I wish they had pulled up sooner,'' Meg muttered.

''They knew just what they were doing,'' he assured her. ''But I know they'll both be sorry they scared you.'' He started to stand up but Meg reached out to grab his arm.

''Don't tell Ty I fainted,'' she said urgently.

Max looked from the slender hand on his sleeve to her face, his expression torn. ''He'd want to know, Meg.''

''I don't want him to worry. I was silly to react like that. It was just the heat and the excitement. If he knew, he'd think I worried about him and that would worry him. Please, Max.''

He stared at her a long moment. ''You love him a lot, don't you?'' he said slowly.

''More than anything in the world.'' Her eyes had gone past him to where she could see the first of the planes approaching the huge open door so she missed the wistfulness in

Max's eyes as he looked at her. He set his hand over hers, squeezing her fingers gently.

"I won't say anything," he promised quietly.

Unlike Thanksgiving, Christmas was quiet. Most of the pilots managed to find their way home for this holiday, though Joe and Millie were to join them for Christmas Day. Meg had looked very smug when she gave Ty this piece of information, and he'd conceded that, unlikely as it seemed to him, the tall, quiet Texan and the bubbleheaded actress seemed to suit each other.

But Christmas Eve was to be just the two of them. Meg took special pains with the meal for more reasons than just the obvious one that this was their first Christmas together. They were getting a gift neither of them had planned, and she hoped Ty would be as pleased about it as she was.

Ty stared into the flickering flames in the fireplace and felt himself drifting on a hazy cloud of contentment. He couldn't ever remember enjoying a Christmas as much as he had this one. When he was a boy, he could remember thinking Christmas by far the most exciting time of the year. But after Dickey had been killed, there'd been several years where the main thing he remembered was his mother crying for her lost son.

But this year there were no memories to intrude, no old griefs to spoil the quiet pleasure of the evening. A small tree sat in the corner near the door, its twinkling lights providing the only source of light other than the fire. Delicate strands of tinsel dripped from its boughs and framed the delicate glass ornaments. Everything on it was new, purchased by Meg and himself less than a week ago.

New traditions, he thought drowsily. Exactly right for a new family, which was what he and Meg were. A family. Funny, he'd have said that family was the last thing he needed. Had said just that, in fact. He hadn't wanted a wife and certainly would never have dreamed of acquiring one under the circumstances he had. But no matter how rocky their beginning, he rather liked what they were building together.

"Ty?" Meg's voice broke into his lazy thoughts.

"Hmmm?" He didn't turn his head to look at her, too content to move. He was sitting on the floor, his back propped on the sofa, his long legs sprawled toward the fire. Meg was sitting on the sofa, her knee almost brushing his shoulder. She was knitting something, apparently able to work by feel as much as sight.

Her hands were rarely idle, he thought, his eyelids drooping. She always seemed to be knitting or sewing bits of fabric together to make a quilt. The sweater he was wearing now was a result of her busy hands, her Christmas present to him. He hoped she was half as pleased with the silver-backed dresser set he'd given her as he was with the heathery gray crewneck.

"Ty?" She spoke again, making him aware that he was hardly providing her with the most alert of conversational companions.

"What?" He forced himself to sit straighter and turned his head to look at her.

"I have something I want to tell you." Her knitting needles flashed rapidly in and out of the yarn, the smooth ivory making almost no sound.

"Okay." He was watching her face, admiring the soft glow of the firelight on her skin.

"I wasn't sure before but I'm practically sure now," she said without looking at him.

"Sure about what?"

Meg didn't answer immediately but only continued to knit at the same frantic pace. Ty realized that her fingers were trembling and his lazy contentment slipped a notch. She was upset. Shifting his position so that he sat on the sofa next to her, he reached out to put his hand over hers, stilling her movements.

"Is something wrong?"

"No. Yes. I don't think so." She kept her head down, staring at his hand where it covered hers. "I've thought it might be but then I thought it was too soon. And maybe it's still too soon but I'm sure. Almost sure, anyway."

"Meg, what is it? What's wrong?" Her nearly incoherent

speech alarmed him, coming as it did from someone who was usually calm to a fault. "What's the matter?"

"Nothing. At least, *I* don't think anything's the matter, but I don't know how you'll feel."

"Meg." There was both warning and plea in the way he spoke her name.

She drew a deep breath, lifting her eyes to his face. "Do you know what I'm making?"

The apparent non sequitur threw Ty off balance. But she was looking at him so intently, as if the answer really mattered to her. He looked at the mass of pale-yellow yarn in her lap.

"A sweater?" he guessed. It could have been a circus tent for all he knew. Or cared.

"It's a blanket," she said. When he continued to stare at her blankly, she drew a quick breath and then clarified. "It's a baby blanket."

It took several seconds for the import of her words to sink in on Ty. His first thought was that she must have a friend who was going to have a baby, and why did she feel it necessary to tell him about it now? Hard on its heels came the truth.

"A baby blanket?" His eyes widened and then dropped to the pile of yarn, seeing it in an entirely new light. "*Our* baby blanket?" he asked in a hushed tone.

Her teeth tugged at her lower lip as she nodded. "I'm almost positive. I know it hasn't been that long since we . . . since you . . ." She flushed and abandoned that line of speech, but Ty knew exactly what she meant. It hadn't been that long since their marriage had become more than writing on a piece of paper.

"Six weeks or so," he said, as much to himself as to her. "Isn't that too soon?"

"It could be for some, I guess, but I . . . I've always been very . . . regular. And I've missed twice now." The red in her cheeks rivaled the flames in the fireplace at the necessity of alluding to something so personal.

It struck Ty that, for all they'd shared a bed, there were still levels of intimacy they'd yet to reach. It had never occurred to him to wonder about the absence of certain events.

But then, he'd never been married before, never been privy to the private rhythms of a woman's body.

"Are you feeling all right?" he asked, hoping he didn't sound as dazed as he felt.

"A little tired but other than that, I'm fine." Meg's eyes searched his face. "Are you upset?"

"No. Of course not." *Stunned, maybe, but not upset.*

"Are you . . . are you pleased?" she asked hesitantly.

"Of course. This is wonderful," he said, conjuring an enthusiasm he didn't feel, at least not quite yet. She needed reassurance, even if his mind was still reeling with the impact of her news. He put his arms around her and drew her close.

"I can hardly believe it," he murmured, hoping it sounded like more than the bald-faced truth.

"We didn't talk about having children," Meg said without lifting her head from his shoulder.

"No. I guess we didn't."

Ty stared over her head at the steady glow of the Christmas tree. How could he have been such a fool, not to have even given a thought to this possibility? Of course she was pregnant. He hadn't done anything to prevent her from getting that way.

A baby. In a few months, he was going to be a father. He'd always assumed he'd marry someday, but he'd never given much thought to the idea of children. He supposed, if he'd thought about it, he'd have assumed he'd eventually be a father. He just hadn't anticipated "eventually" coming quite so soon.

Hardly aware of his actions, Ty flattened his hand over Meg's stomach, trying to absorb the idea that she carried a new life inside her. A baby. His son or daughter. A son to play ball with, to teach to fly. Or a daughter who'd play with frilly dolls and kiss him good-night.

The shock lingered but there was a feeling of rightness starting to creep through it, a sense of completion. Meg's small hand settled over his as if completing the link between the three of them—her, him, and their child. Ty felt his mouth curve in a smile. A baby. Maybe that was a pretty nice Christmas present, after all.

Chapter 17

The weather continued warm and sunny after Christmas and into the New Year. Sometimes, when Meg was reading one of Patsy's letters, which described the cold, snowy weather besetting Iowa, she'd look out the window at the blue sky arcing over Los Angeles and find it hard to believe that she and Patsy were even on the same planet, let alone in the same country.

Iowa and the life she'd known there seemed impossibly distant, both in time and space. Two thousand miles and a few short months and her life had changed beyond all recognition. A husband she loved and who cared for her, even if he didn't love her the way she longed for him to. Friends who'd become more of a family than she'd ever known. And a baby on the way. Life was so nearly perfect that it scared her.

The first weekend of the New Year, there was another air show. The bulk of Ty's work was in ferrying passengers and packages up and down the coast, a relatively dull routine that kept money coming in. And it was certainly better than not flying at all, he'd told her. But his real love was for the aerobatics he and Jack performed as a team. One or two jobs for the movies and the occasional air shows were the only opportunity they had test the limits of their skills.

As far as Meg was concerned, if she never saw Ty loop

another loop or fly again, it would be just fine with her. Max's assurance that Ty was one of the best pilots he'd ever seen went only so far in assuaging her fears. After all, even the best could make mistakes.

But she'd rather have cut her tongue out than say anything to Ty about her fears. So when he asked if she wanted to come to the air show, she did her best to look thrilled. Of course, nothing short of death could have kept her home. The only thing worse than being there to watch him would be to stay home and wonder if he was all right.

Since Joe had asked Millie to go to the show, the two women went together, with Meg driving the little Ford Ty had given her. Millie chattered nonstop all the way to the airfield. Meg let the words roll over her, merely contributing the occasional comment that was all Millie needed to carry on a conversation.

She wasn't feeling particularly well, hadn't been for a couple of days. It was nothing definite, just a general malaise that left her tired and vaguely nauseated. It seemed as if it were going to take awhile for her body to make peace with its new condition. If she could have, she would have curled up in bed and slept the day away. But if she'd said as much to Ty, he would have been worried about her. He'd want to take care of her, just as he had time and again over the past few months. More than anything, Meg wanted him to see that she could take care of herself. If there was any chance of Ty loving her the way she loved him, it wouldn't happen as long as he thought of her as a helpless child.

So Meg blended on a little extra rouge to conceal her pallor and determined to enjoy the air show. If turning somersaults in a plane was what made Ty happy, then she'd just have to learn to live with it.

She found a place to park the car and she and Millie made their way to the bleachers, finding seats about halfway up. Meg was amused to see the looks thrown in Millie's direction. She wore a trim little knit suit in her favorite shade of bright pink, and the contrast between the suit and her hair was eye-catching, to put it mildly. A dashing little hat in the same pink completed the outfit, complete with a black feather that angled back jauntily from the brim.

"You see, Meg, people pay attention when a girl knows how to dress," Millie said as she sank onto the wooden bleacher. She preened a little, like a movie star accepting adulation from her public. "It's like I was telling you, if you'd just let me take you shopping, liven up your wardrobe a little, give it some spice." She paused to give a cool smile to a teenage boy who was staring at the dead fox she'd tossed around her shoulders to complete her ensemble.

"I don't think I'm the spicy type, Millie."

"Nonsense. Every girl's the spicy type. All it needs is somebody with the right touch to bring it out. Now, for me that was my aunt Gussie. She was my father's sister, only the family didn't like to admit it because she went on the stage, back in New York, you know—the real stage 'cause they didn't have movies in those days. Aunt Gussie—her real name was Augusta but everybody called her Gussie, which really suited her much better than Augusta, which is a stuffy kind of name and nobody was less stuffy than Aunt Gussie. Anyway, she told me when I was thirteen that she saw great things in my future and that I should move to Hollywood because she thought I had 'It.' You know, like Clara Bow, only now that everybody's making talkies, I'm not so sure she's really got 'It' anymore. You know what I mean?"

Thus taxed, Meg mumbled something noncommittal and hoped that Millie wouldn't ask for a more specific opinion. She needn't have worried.

"I knew you'd understand," Millie said. She adjusted the fox stole around her shoulders. "Anyway, Aunt Gussie said that I—"

The start of the show prevented Meg from finding out exactly what words of wisdom Aunt Gussie had bestowed on her niece. Ordinarily, she didn't mind Millie's nonstop chatter, but today it was getting on her nerves. Probably just the combination of worry about Ty and the tiredness that seemed to be an unavoidable symptom of pregnancy was making her feel a little cranky.

She tensed as the first plane went up and hardly drew a breath until it landed safely again. But as time passed and each plane went up and came down again just the way it should, Meg began to relax. Max might have been right that part of the excitement of such demonstrations was the danger inherent in them, but these were all experienced pilots and the chance of a crash was undoubtedly not nearly as great as it seemed.

"Oh, look, there's Ty," Millie said, about an hour into the show.

Meg followed her pointing finger to see Ty and Jack standing on the ground, heads tilted back as they searched the crowded bleachers.

"I bet they're looking for us," Millie said. Without waiting for Meg's response, she stood up and waved her arm, oblivious to the annoyed complaints of the people behind them. Flushing, Meg grabbed one corner of her friend's jacket and tugged firmly enough to topple her back into her seat.

"There now, they saw me," Millie said as Jack and Ty began climbing toward them. "It's a talent of mine, being able to get people's attention. Star power, Aunt Gussie called it."

Privately Meg thought that it would have taken a blind man to miss that bright pink suit and the punctuation of dead fox and red hair. Millie stood out like a stoplight. The magnificent clash of colors might cause a few people nightmares, but it had served to get Ty's attention. She tilted her head to smile up at him as he and Jack reached them.

"I wasn't sure you'd be here," he said, smiling his thanks as the man sitting next to Meg slid over to make room for him. Jack found a seat on the other side of Millie.

"I said I would be." Meg slid her hand through his arm, wondering if she'd ever lose the feeling of amazement that he was hers.

"Yes, but you didn't look like you were feeling very good this morning," he said, his eyes searching her face.

So much for not worrying him, she thought wryly. "I feel fine." She smiled to prove it. "Your son is just using up all my spare energy, that's all."

"Maybe you should have stayed home to rest," he said, concern lingering in his dark eyes.

"I'm fine," she insisted.

"Aren't you two going to fly today?" Meg was grateful for the distraction of Millie's question. "I was looking forward to seeing Joey do all those tricks you boys do in those cute little airplanes, but then he had to fly to Phoenix today and I was so disappointed, but then I figured that it would be nearly as good to see you two do tricks, because I know you. It won't be the same as if Joey was up there but wishers can't ride horses, you know."

There was a long moment of silence. Meg saw Ty glance at Jack over her and Millie's heads and wondered which part of the speech had been the biggest shock—hearing Millie refer to their friend as "Joey," the idea that they were doing "tricks" in their "cute little" airplanes, or her final sage comment that wishers can't ride horses.

"We're flying a little later," Jack said finally, making the safest choice by simply answering the initial question.

"Jack and Ty are the climax of the show," Meg said, proud even though she wished they were the highlight of something a little less terrifying.

"There's Max," Ty said. Meg turned her attention to the orange and black plane soaring past the bleachers. "He's been working on some new stunts."

"Is he a good pilot?" she asked, thinking of Max's admiration for Ty's skill.

"Pretty good. He hasn't been flying as long as most of us and he sometimes pushes too hard, takes chances he shouldn't to prove himself. But he's got a good feel for it, and he'll get less anxious as he gets older."

Afterward Meg was ashamed to admit that she paid only minimal attention to Max's performance. It felt so nice to be sitting next to Ty, with the warm sunshine bathing over her, that she let her attention wander to other things, even as her eyes followed the rolls and dives of the little plane.

But her attention sharpened when the plane turned its nose toward the ground and began to spiral down. She hated the dives. It didn't matter that she'd seen them several times now and nothing ever went wrong, she still hated them. She felt the attention of the crowd sharpen and abruptly remembered Max's words about people half hoping for a crash. Meg pushed the thought away, telling herself that there was nothing to worry about.

"He's coming in too fast." Jack's taut comment shattered the layer of security she was trying to build.

Her hand was resting on Ty's arm and the muscles in it were suddenly as hard as steel. She glanced at Ty's face. His attention was riveted to the orange and black plane spinning toward the earth. Meg read the truth in the rigid line of his jaw, and the last thing she wanted to do was to look back at the plane. But it was like a magnet, drawing her eyes.

"Pull out," Ty muttered. His hands were clenched into fists on his thighs. "Pull out, goddammit."

Time seemed to move in slow motion, seconds taking hours. Meg was unaware of the rising murmur from the crowd as the plane spun closer and closer to disaster. She didn't feel Millie's scarlet-painted fingernails digging into her arm. All she could see was the plane, spinning downward, the engine screaming in protest, the velocity so great it seemed impossible that the wings were still clinging to the fuselage.

Someone screamed but the sound was immediately swallowed by the stunning impact of the plane hitting the ground at full speed. There was a split second of near silence and then the air was shattered by noise—screams from the crowd, the shriek of the fire trucks kept waiting at the edge of the field for just such an event, the wail of an ambulance as it rushed toward the burning plane.

Despite all logic, Meg was reassured by the sound of those sirens. The firemen would pull Max from the plane and the ambulance would take him to the hospital and he'd be all right. They'd all tease him about the crash and—

The explosion as the fire reached the gas tanks was deafening. A wall of flame engulfed the plane, obliterating the twisted wreckage. The fire truck and ambulance stopped a little distance away, the men on them unable to do anything more than watch the fire burn.

Max's family asked that his body be shipped home to Vermont for burial. On the day the train carrying his casket left Los Angeles, the balmy weather disappeared. The temperatures lowered and the skies turned gray. A light, drizzling rain began to fall. The rain continued into the next day and the next, rarely strong enough to be called a shower, more an omnipresent dampness that wore at the spirits.

The weather chilled Meg all the way to her bones. There was a meanness about the rain, a pervading kind of cold that had little to do with the temperature. She found herself longing for the crisp iciness of an Iowa winter. It seemed a cleaner cold, the kind that could be chased away by a hot cup of coffee and a warm fire. But there didn't seem to be anything that could drive out this cold.

Rationally, she knew the chill she felt was more emotional than physical. Max had been a friend and it was difficult to accept that she'd never see his crooked smile or hear him laugh again. Though he'd been older than she, he'd seemed younger, hardly more than a boy. And now he was gone forever, his sweetness lost in one split second of error.

For a week she relived the crash in her dreams. Every night she woke, trembling and frightened, her cheeks wet with tears, her mind seared with vivid images of flames. Only in her dreams, it wasn't Max who piloted the doomed plane, it was Ty.

She didn't know if she cried out her denial and woke him or if Ty wasn't sleeping any better than she was, but he always seemed to be awake, pulling her into his arms and holding her close. Feeling the strong beat of Ty's heart beneath her cheek, his strong arms around her, and hearing him tell her there was nothing to be afraid of, Meg was able to shove the nightmare away, tucking it out of sight, afraid to look at it too closely, for fear that might make it real, somehow.

But the fear was not that easily dismissed. She'd always known that flying was dangerous, but knowing it and actually seeing the horrible reality were two different things. She was haunted by the image of Max's death, haunted by the knowledge that it could easily have been Ty in that plane. A tiny error in judgment, a reflex that came a little too slow, a mechanical failure, and it would be Ty's body being shipped home.

During the day she managed to put her fears aside, filling her time with housework and sewing, trips to the library and shopping. But each time Ty left to go the airfield, she fought the urge to cling to him and beg him not to go. She knew her fears were exaggerated. Ty had been flying for years. He was a good pilot, one who didn't take foolish chances. But she couldn't shake the thought that accidents happened, even to good pilots.

Perhaps if she hadn't been plagued with a nagging physical weakness, Meg would have been better able to keep her fears at bay. But it seemed as if she was not one of the lucky women with whom pregnancy agreed. She was tired and half sick most of the time. The persistent weakness made it harder to keep the fears in check.

Like her fear about his safety, she did her best to hide her illness from Ty, not wanting him to worry about her. When he commented on her pallor, she laughed and said it was just that she'd been spending too much time indoors. And when he asked if she'd lost weight, she lied and said it was just that the dress she was wearing made her look slimmer. She was sure the sickness was just a symptom of early pregnancy. If she could endure a little while longer, she'd develop some of that glow that pregnant women were supposed to have. In the meantime, there was no reason to worry Ty.

Unfortunately, the decision was taken out of Meg's hands near the end of January. She'd gone to a fabric sale at The May Company. When they'd moved into the bungalow, Ty had given her money to fill in any gaps in the furnishings or housewares. One of the things she'd purchased had been a sewing machine. Though it had seemed a bit of an extravagance, she knew it would pay for itself many times over. She'd already made new curtains for the kitchen, dresses for herself, and shirts for Ty.

Though she hadn't felt much like going out, the sale was simply too good to pass up. The store was crowded with women looking for bargains, but Meg was well pleased with her purchases and she was smiling as she paid for them. The smile had faded by the time she reached the car. She sank into the seat, feeling weak and a little sick. Her stomach had been upset that morning, and all she'd managed to choke down was a cracker and some weak tea. It was just hunger, she told herself though her stomach churned sluggishly at the thought of food. Still, she had to eat, for the baby's sake, if not her own. As soon as she got home, she'd heat up some soup.

She sat in the car for a little while, waiting for the dizziness to fade before she started the engine. Taking extra care, she drove home slowly. Meg parked the little Ford in front of the bungalow court and slid out of the car. Immediately a wave of dizziness washed over her, so powerful that she had to brace one hand on the edge of the car door to keep from falling. When it passed, she decided that the fabric could stay in the car until she felt a little better. Clutching her purse in a white-knuckled grip, she made her way around the car and stepped up onto the curb.

By the time she reached the walkway, beads of cold sweat were breaking out across her forehead. Though the day was cool, she felt hot. The rayon fabric of her dress was sticking to her back and the skirt seemed to cling to her legs, making it hard to walk. Just a few more yards, she told herself. And then she could lie down. Ahead of her, the bungalows seemed to dip and roll as if the ground under them were rolling.

One of the famous earthquakes? she wondered vaguely, concentrating on putting one foot in front of the other. She thought she heard someone say her name. Millie, perhaps? But she couldn't turn her head. A few more steps and she'd be in the blessed privacy of her own home. It would be cool and dark inside and she could lie down until she felt better. Just a few more steps.

She was a few yards away from the door when Meg felt

her knees start to buckle and the sky tilted wildly. There was a roaring in her ears that she'd heard once before. And her last thought was that Max wasn't there to catch her this time.

"She's exhausted." The doctor summed up Meg's condition in one succinct sentence.

"Is she going to be all right?" Ty asked, glancing past the doctor at the closed bedroom door.

"I'd say so." Dr. Winston was on the wrong side of fifty, a thin gray-haired man with a piercing gaze and a no-nonsense way of speaking. "I gave her a sedative and I'll leave a bottle with you. She needs plenty of rest and a bit of feeding up. Is there someone who can keep an eye on her during the day?"

"I don't know." Ty ran his fingers through his hair, trying to push aside his fear long enough to think. There was Millie. She was the one who'd gotten another tenant to carry Meg inside when she fainted. And then she'd called the airfield and asked someone to find him. She'd also called the doctor, who'd been here when Ty arrived. Meg liked her, but somehow Ty couldn't picture Millie as a nurse, not even in the loosest sense of the word.

"Well, it's not vital that she have someone with her," Dr. Winston said reassuringly. "Your wife seems a sensible girl and she wants this baby so I'd guess she'll do as she's told and rest. And it's very important that she not worry about anything. Right now she needs to concentrate on taking care of herself and that baby."

"But she is going to be all right?" Ty asked as the doctor picked up his bag and started toward the door. "Her and the baby?"

"As long as she gets some rest and eats three solid meals a day. Make sure she eats plenty of good red meat to build up her blood, and she should drink plenty of milk. It's important for a young woman in her condition. And you do your best to make sure she doesn't have anything to worry about." Seeing the worry still in Ty's face, Dr. Winston set his hand on Ty's shoulder and gave it a reassuring squeeze. "With rest and proper care, I think Mrs. McKendrick should be just fine."

Ty saw the doctor out and then quietly entered the bedroom. Meg was sleeping. It was midafternoon but the drawn curtains blocked most of the light, leaving the room pleasantly dim. He approached the bed quietly and stood beside it, looking down at his sleeping wife.

She was lying on her back, her breathing light and even. Her face was nearly as pale as the pillowcase. The only touch of color came from the soft rose of her mouth. The covers were pushed back to her waist and her nightgown was twisted beneath her, the neckline tugged aside just enough to bare the upper curves of her breasts. They were fuller now and fine blue veins showed beneath the milky skin. And though she hadn't said anything, he'd noticed that her breasts had grown more tender, so that he took care to use only the gentlest of touches when he held her at night.

She looked so fragile lying there. And so young. He still couldn't quite shed the thought that she was too young to be a wife, let alone a mother. No matter how many times he told himself that other girls married and had children at an even younger age, he just couldn't silence the nagging voice that whispered that he should have given her more time. At the very least, time before she faced motherhood.

But he hadn't. Now he had to make sure she got the care she needed.

Ty reached down to pull the covers up to her shoulders but stopped when he saw the grease on his hands. He'd been working on the Curtiss when Millie called and said that Meg was ill. He hadn't taken time to clean up, only rubbing the worst of the grease from his hands on the way to the car.

Grimacing, he straightened away from the bed. Since his face was probably almost as greasy as his hands, maybe he'd better clean up before Meg woke and thought there was a stranger in the bedroom. He'd change into fresh clothes and then heat some soup for supper. Maybe when Meg woke up, he could coax her to eat a little.

It was almost ten o'clock before Meg stirred. Ty had

brought one of the kitchen chairs into the bedroom and set it next to the bed where he could keep an eye on her. He had a book open in his lap, but he hadn't turned more than half a dozen pages in two hours. For the most part, he'd sat and stared at nothing in particular, listening to the rhythm of Meg's soft breathing and thinking. Sitting in the dim room, with nothing to do but think, Ty found himself taking a hard look at himself and not liking some of what he saw.

He'd married Meg to keep her away from her stepfather. He'd been motivated by guilt as much as anything else. He hadn't been able to shake the feeling that it was his friendship with Meg that had triggered Davis's twisted rage. He'd married her to protect her and, at the same time, to assuage the guilt. He'd even, God help him, felt vaguely noble for doing it. Like the hero in one of the movies Meg so loved, he'd done the right thing, putting her needs before his own. And he'd slyly patted himself on the back for doing it.

He'd brought her to California—land of dreams—installed her in a cozy bungalow, and then gone about his life, living much as he had before the crash that had resulted in his trip home last summer, only now he had a wife at home to see to his comforts, a wife who had every reason to feel grateful to him for saving her from a terrible situation.

Ty shifted uneasily on the chair, but he couldn't escape his thoughts. It struck him suddenly that he hadn't spent as much time as he might have wondering how Meg felt about the abrupt change in her circumstances. He'd decided that marrying him was her only way out and he'd given her little chance to disagree.

Once married, they'd never really talked about the future. Again, he'd simply assumed they both had the same idea. Now he suddenly wondered if Meg might have had very different plans for their marriage. What if she'd been hoping to get an annulment once she turned eighteen and would be legally beyond Harlan Davis's reach? It hadn't even occurred to him to ask Meg how she felt about making their marriage real in every sense of the word. He'd set out to seduce her, setting the stage very carefully and succeeding in his intent. What if she hadn't protested because she thought she owed him her virginity as a kind of payment for keeping her out of Harlan Davis's clutches?

The thought was so repulsive that Ty shot to his feet. Oblivious to the soft thud of his book as it fell to the rug beside the bed, he strode to the window. Brushing aside the curtain, he stared out into the moon-washed chaparral that covered the hillside behind the bungalow court.

As he thought back over the past couple of months, he felt relief edge out self-recrimination. He might deserve to feel guilty about some aspects of his marriage, but not about that. It wasn't obligation or duty that made Meg melt in his arms. Not that first night nor any of the nights since. Her response was too warm and passionate, her hunger too real.

"Ty?"

He spun from the window, crossing quickly to the bed. "Hey, sleepyhead."

"What time is it?" Meg's voice was soft and thick with sleep.

"Nearly ten o'clock," he said, glancing at the clock beside the bed. He sat down on the edge of the bed and reached up to brush her hair back from her face with gentle fingers. When it began to grow dark, he'd lit the small brass lamp that sat on top of the dresser. It now provided enough light for him to read the dismay in her expression.

"So late?"

"You needed the rest. How do you feel?"

"Silly. I don't know why I fainted like that."

"The doctor says you're run down and that you need to eat more. He says you're too thin."

"I guess I haven't been eating like I should," she said. With a guilty look, she pressed her hand against her stomach, as if apologizing to the child she carried. "I haven't had much appetite since . . ."

"Since Max died," Ty finished for her.

"I keep seeing the crash," she admitted after a moment's silence.

"It's tough to forget something like that. But making yourself sick won't bring Max back."

"I know that." Her sigh quivered on the edge of tears.

But that didn't change how she felt, Ty thought, finishing the sentence for her. She'd seen a friend die and it was going to take time to put it behind her.

"Do you think you could eat some soup?" he asked, changing the subject.

"I guess."

"You guess?" Ty repeated, raising his brows in mock offense. "I slave over a hot stove and all you can offer me is 'I guess'? I don't cook for just anyone, you know."

The teasing had the desired effect. Meg smiled up at him. "In that case, I'd love some soup. But I really don't need to be pampered like this, you know."

"Let me decide that." Unable to resist, Ty leaned down to brush a soft kiss across her mouth. There was more color in her cheeks than there had been earlier, but she still looked more fragile than he liked.

But not for long, he thought as he stood up from the bed. He was going to make sure that she got the care she needed. His jaw was set as he left the bedroom. It was time—and past —that he took care of his family the way he should have from the start.

"I just saw Joe." Jack's voice preceded him as he walked around the nose of the red Curtiss.

"Yeah?" Ty didn't look up but simply continued with the task of polishing the fuselage.

"He says you sold him your plane." Jack stopped a few feet away and pushed his hands into the pockets of his leather jacket, his eyes on his friend.

"You've been out of town this past week," Ty said by way of answer.

"If I'd been out of town a year, I wouldn't expect to come back and find out that you're quitting flying and moving back to Iowa." Jack's tone was casual but Ty could feel the intensity of his look, sense the questions he wasn't asking.

"It's time I settled down," he said, concentrating on rubbing out a minute spot that marred the bright red paint.

"How's Meg?" Jack asked. Meg's fainting spell had happened the day before he'd left for Seattle.

"She's doing all right." Satisfied that the paint gleamed as brightly as it ever would, Ty threw down the rag he'd been using and turned to look at his best friend. "The doctor said she'll be fine but she needs rest and no worry."

"And you think she'll get those things in Iowa?" Jack asked, his tone noncommittal.

"I don't know. But I know she's not getting them now." Now that he was no longer working on the plane, Ty was aware of the chill inside the hangar. He lifted a worn brown leather jacket from the bench where he'd tossed it and shrugged into it. Jack hadn't said anything but Ty felt the pressure of his concern. He shoved his hands in his pockets.

"She's scared to death every time I go up," he said, staring at the three-year-old calendar that hung, forlorn and yellowing, on the wall above the bench. "She never says anything but I can see it in her eyes. She thinks I'm not going to come back."

"Like Max," Jack said softly, his green eyes dark with the memory of the crash.

"Yeah. She thinks the same thing's going to happen to me." Without taking his hands from his pockets, he lifted his shoulders in a shrug. "I can't tell her it won't. How many pilots do we know who aren't around anymore?"

It was a rhetorical question, and Jack didn't try to come up with an answer. They both knew the number was depressingly high.

"You can get killed crossing a street," Jack said instead.

"Yeah, but you've got to cross the street anyway. I don't have to fly."

"Don't you?" Jack asked quietly. "Can you really give it up, Ty?"

Ty had asked himself the same question a hundred times this past week, and he always came up with the same answer. He gave it to Jack now.

"I have to." He shook his head slowly. "It's not just Meg. It's me. I've got a son on the way, Jack. I want to be around to see him grow up. Giving up flying won't guarantee that, but it increases my odds a hell of a lot."

There was a moment of silence and then Jack spoke. "So, what are you going to do when you get to Iowa? Make your mother a happy woman and go into politics?" The change of topic told Ty that Jack understood his decision and that he wouldn't try to talk him out of it.

"Not likely." Ty grinned wryly, thinking that if there was anything his mother could hate more than flying, it was what he was about to do. "I'm going to try and get my grandfather's farm going again."

"Farming?" Jack raised his eyebrows in disbelief. "Haven't you heard we're in the midst of a depression? Farmers pouring milk on the ground because it's too expensive to ship it—that sort of thing? Ring any bells?"

Ty grinned at his expression, feeling a measure of Jack's incredulity. The truth was, he thought he was more than half crazy himself. "At least I'll be able to feed my family," he said, shrugging.

He glanced at the Curtiss and his smile slipped a notch. Since making the decision to move back to Iowa, he hadn't let himself think too much about what he'd be giving up. What was it Meg had said all those years ago? That flying was the closest thing she'd ever known to heaven?

"I'm getting tired of flying anyway," Ty said abruptly.

It was a measure of Jack's friendship that he managed to look as if he believed the blatant lie; as if he didn't know that selling the plane had torn out a piece of Ty's heart.

"I guess everybody has to settle down sooner or later" was all Jack said.

"Yeah."

They were silent for a long moment. Ty drew in a deep breath, savoring the familiar scents of grease and rubber, the indefinable combination of smells that filled the hangar. God, he was going to miss this, he admitted with stark honesty. Not just the flying itself but the other pilots, the camaraderie, working with Jack.

"You know, I've been thinking about going home for a little while," Jack said slowly. "All this sunshine is starting to get old."

"I can imagine," Ty said with a pointed look out one of the dirty windows at the rain that fell outside. "What the hell would you do in Iowa in February?"

Jack shrugged. "Maybe I need a break. I could lend you a hand getting the farm into shape. Maybe look up a few old friends."

"Like Patsy Harper?" Ty asked shrewdly.

Jack gave him a startled look. "What makes you think of her?"

"Only a fool could have missed the tension between the two of you. What goes on?"

"We dated for a while," Jack said slowly.

"You've dated a lot of girls."

"Not like Patsy." The simple statement revealed more than he might have liked.

"She's married, Jack." There was no condemnation in Ty's words, just a quiet warning.

"I know." Jack shrugged. "I'm just thinking of having a little vacation, that's all."

"Iowa in February is certainly one of the vacation hot spots," Ty said with heavy irony. But he didn't argue any further. Jack was old enough to make his own decisions.

The silence stretched until Ty forced himself to admit that he was just trying to put off leaving.

"You can still change your mind," Jack said, reading his mind with the ease of a long time friend.

"No." Ty shook his head. "I'm not going to change my mind. This is the right decision for Meg and the baby. And for me." He shrugged, his mouth twisted in a wry smile. "I guess I've finally figured out that you can't have everything. I think I'm going to like being a father. I'm willing to do what I can to make sure I'm around long enough to find out."

Ty looked at the Curtiss, now polished to within an inch

of its life. Joe would take good care of the plane. He had other responsibilities now. A wife, a new baby. And a farm. Life certainly did take some interesting twists.

"I could use a drink," he said abruptly. Turning away from the plane, he walked away without a backward glance.

Chapter 18

Snow flurries greeted Ty and Meg's return to Iowa, but the weather was no colder than Helen McKendrick's welcome. If Meg had harbored any hopes that the news about the baby would have softened her mother-in-law's feelings toward her, she realized immediately how foolish they had been. It would take more than the news that she was to be a grandmother to soften the older woman's implacable dislike.

"You may use Tyler's old room," she said with little enthusiasm.

"Thank you," Meg whispered, thinking she'd rather sleep in a toolshed than accept her mother-in-law's reluctant hospitality. But, of course, that wasn't an option. Until the farmhouse could be made habitable, this would be her home and she'd just have to make the best of it. "It's very kind of you to allow us to stay here," she said, forcing a smile.

"When Tyler told us he was coming home, naturally we couldn't have him staying anywhere else. This is *his* home," Helen said, the delicate emphasis making it clear that, while it might be Ty's home, it would certainly never be his wife's.

If she hadn't been so tired, Meg could almost have admired the skill with which she'd just been put in her place. But she *was* tired. The train trip had left her shaking with exhaustion and far from ready to deal with her mother-in-law. There hadn't been room in the taxi for all of their things, so Ty and his father had gone back to the station for the remaining luggage, leaving Meg alone with the other woman.

"It's very kind of you," Meg repeated, unable to come up with another response. "We'll try not to be any trouble."

"*Tyler* would certainly never cause trouble," Helen responded with that same careful emphasis that implied that the same could not be said of Meg. If she'd been hoping that she could provoke her daughter-in-law into defending herself, she was disappointed.

After a moment's silence, she sniffed and rose from the chair where she'd been seated since Meg's arrival half an hour before. Like a queen awaiting the arrival of her subjects. Or a spider awaiting the approach of a fly, Meg's less charitable side suggested.

"I'm sure you'd like to clean up before supper," Helen said. "I'll show you to your room."

Meg opened her mouth to say that she remembered where Ty's room was but caught the words before they spilled out. It was probably not a good idea to remind her mother-in-law that this wasn't her first stay in the McKendrick house. She followed the other woman upstairs, thinking longingly of a warm bath and a soft bed.

When they reached the upstairs hall, Helen stopped and turned to look at her. Meg was surprised to find that their eyes were on a level. Somehow she thought of Ty's mother as being a much bigger woman.

"I hope you understand that I am not running a hotel," Helen said, sliding the gloves off just a fraction to allow Meg a glimpse of the iron beneath.

"Of course not," Meg said, shocked. "I certainly don't expect you to wait on us. I'd appreciate it if you'd allow me to help with the cooking and the housework."

"We'll see." Meg's eagerness to help didn't seem to mollify the older woman. "I'm very particular about how things are done," she said icily.

"I understand." But she didn't really. It had been Meg's observation that there was always more than enough work to go around. She'd have thought that her mother-in-law would welcome an extra pair of hands. But it was becoming clear that the only thing Helen McKendrick would welcome would be her disappearance from Ty's life.

"The two of you will use the bathroom down the hall," Helen was saying as she pushed open the door to Ty's room. Meg followed her inside, feeling the familiar room embrace her. "Mr. McKendrick and I have a separate bath off our bedroom." There was justifiable pride in the way she announced this incredible luxury.

"It's a lovely house," Meg said, offering a shy smile as she set her purse on the dresser and turned to look at her mother-in-law.

"I've worked to make it so." Helen acknowledged the compliment with a regal tilt of her head.

Meg wondered vaguely if she should say something to fill the silence that followed. But the truth was, she was so tired she could barely remember her own name. Perhaps she swayed a little or maybe she looked as pale as she felt. Her mother-in-law's eyes narrowed slightly.

"Tyler tells me you're not carrying well," she said, the first reference she'd made to the fact that Meg was carrying her grandchild.

"I've just been a little tired," Meg said, forcing another smile. "Ty worries too much."

"I have an extremely delicate constitution. But I managed to carry three children without causing any fuss." There was blatant condemnation in the look she gave Meg.

Meg felt weak tears start to her eyes, but she forced them back. She knew instinctively that tears would only compound her sins in Helen McKendrick's eyes.

"I'm sure, now that I'm home, I'll start feeling better right away," she offered.

"I certainly hope so. It would be a pity if Tyler were to have sacrificed his career for nothing." Without giving Meg a chance to reply, she turned and left, closing the door behind her with the air of one closing out a bad odor.

Meg sank onto the edge of the bed, grateful for the support her knees were no longer willing to provide. Hot, angry tears burned her eyes and spilled over onto her cheeks. She didn't need to be reminded of what Ty had given up to bring her home. Meg fully appreciated the irony of his mother's reproach, considering the way she felt about her son's career. But that didn't change the underlying truth in her words. Ty had given up something he loved a great deal in order to bring her home to Iowa.

The sound of a masculine voice downstairs had her quickly wiping the traces of tears from her cheeks and straightening her shoulders. When Ty pushed open the bedroom door a moment later, she was standing next to the bed. She turned toward him with a smile.

"That was quick," she said, though being left alone with her mother-in-law had made it seem like a week.

"The snow's easing up." Ty set down the suitcases he was carrying and stripped off his gloves. He cupped his hands in front of his mouth and blew on his fingers. "I'd forgotten how cold it could get. How are you?"

"I'm fine," Meg said, hoping her smile didn't look as forced as it felt. "I wish you'd stop worrying about me." She moved forward to help him off with his coat.

Ty caught her chin in his fingers when she started to turn away with the garment. His hand was cold against her skin, but the concern in his eyes warmed away the chill. He looked at her searchingly.

"It's part of my job to worry about you," he said in a light tone at odds with the intensity of his eyes.

"Well, it's not necessary." *A job? What that how he looked at being married to her?* "I'm just fine."

"Did my mother . . . say anything?"

"Only that this was your home and that you were always welcome here." She was careful not to use the same emphasis her mother-in-law had, not wanting Ty to know that it had been made clear that welcome did not include his wife.

"I know my mother can be . . . difficult, Meg. You don't have to pretend she isn't."

"She was very kind," she lied without hesitation. He

looked doubtful. "I'm not as helpless as you think I am," she protested. Her smiling exasperation covered a very real need for him to see her as something more than a responsibility.

"I don't think you're helpless. But you need a little extra care right now." He brushed a kiss across her mouth, and Meg let herself relax into his arms. "We moved back here so you could rest and take care of yourself. I don't want you to worry about anything. If you have any problems with my mother, I want you to tell me."

"I'm fine, Ty." Her fingers tightened around the fabric of his coat. "We didn't have to move back here and you didn't have to give up your flying."

"We already talked about this," he said, setting her from him and bending to pick up the suitcase.

With a sigh, she draped his coat across the back of a chair and went over the bed to begin unpacking while Ty went downstairs to bring up the rest of their things. Perhaps, once the baby was born, she could convince him to go back to flying. Though it made her shudder to think of risks he took, the last thing she wanted was for him to give it up because of her. In time, he'd surely come to hate her for it. But there'd be no changing his mind until the baby was born.

It wouldn't be so bad, Meg told herself. Spring was only a few weeks off and then summer would be just around the corner. Holding a stack of Ty's clothing, she paused to look out the window. The snow had stopped falling but it left behind a landscape all done in gray and white, as if the cold had somehow drained the color from everything. But if she narrowed her eyes a little, she could see the deep green of grass, the pale, clear green of spring's first leaves on the trees, the bright splashes of early flowers. A little more imagination and she could feel the warmth of the sun against her face, smell the heavy fragrance of the roses that bloomed along Edwina Vanderbilt's front porch.

Her expression grew dreamy. She'd fallen in love with Ty last summer. Maybe this year the summer sun would work its magic on him.

"Supper's almost ready," Ty said as he carried in a suitcase and the arched wooden cabinet that held her sewing machine. Meg turned from the window still wrapped in the warmth of her dream.

"I'm almost ready." She set the clothes down, her pleasant mood vanishing at the thought of having supper with her in-laws.

Her expression must have revealed more than she'd intended, because Ty came over and put his arm around her shoulders. And despite her determination to show him that she was not helpless, Meg couldn't resist the temptation to lean against his strength.

"I know this isn't the best arrangement, Meg, but it's only for a little while, just until Jack and I can put the farmhouse in a livable condition."

"I'm just a little nervous," she said, forcing a smile. "I know your parents didn't approve of you marrying me."

"I'm a little too old to be asking their permission," Ty said, his voice dry.

"I know, but—"

"No buts about it," he said firmly. He dropped a kiss on the end of her nose. "Everything's going to be fine."

"Of course it is," Meg said, wishing she believed it.

Ty started to lead her out the door and then hesitated. "You'll tell me if you have any problems?" he asked, making it obvious that he didn't believe his reassurance any more than she did.

"Of course," she lied. The last thing she'd do was bring him any more problems.

"Good." Meg hoped her smile looked more sincere than his. "We probably shouldn't be late," he said. "No sense starting off on the wrong foot."

In the days that followed, Meg came to the conclusion that there was no "right foot" when it came to her mother-in-law. At least not when it involved her son's wife. Meg's attempts to help with the cooking and cleaning were rebuffed without hesitation or courtesy. Helen made it clear that she didn't trust Meg's ability to do even so menial a task as dust the furniture.

The morning after she and Ty arrived, Meg washed the breakfast dishes, thinking to make it clear that she was more than willing to shoulder her share of the work. She dried them but didn't put anything away since she didn't know where things went and sensed that Helen wouldn't want another woman going through her cupboards. She came downstairs an hour later to find her mother-in-law carefully rewashing each plate and cup.

"I'm very particular about how things are done," Helen said, stretching her lips in a thin smile.

When Meg swept the floor, Helen swept it again. "I'm sure you just didn't notice the dust in the corners," she said with that same cold smile.

"I doubt you're accustomed to handling delicate things," Helen told her when Meg offered to help her hostess dust the cabinet full of knickknacks in the living room. "Some of these things are quite valuable," she added, making it clear that Meg couldn't be trusted to handle anything worth more than a dollar or two.

So each day went, with Meg's every effort rebuffed. She accepted each implied criticism without comment, relinquished each task with a quiet apology, and retreated to the bedroom she shared with Ty where she stood in the center of the room with her fists clenched, trying to control her frustration and anger.

What did the woman want from her?

What Helen McKendrick wanted, of course, was a reaction. Tears or anger—either would have satisfied her. If Meg had lashed out, it would have proven to Helen's own satisfaction that her son's wife was the low-class product of white-trash parents that Helen knew her to be.

What she couldn't know and wouldn't have understood was that life had taught Meg that the best response to anger and hostility was passivity. When she was a child, the best way to avoid a beating from her father had been to be as nearly invisible as possible. Her instinctive dislike of her stepfather had only encouraged this natural tendency. Like a fawn's camouflage, Meg used a calm facade to protect herself, unaware that she was only adding to her mother-in-law's anger.

As the days passed and Meg failed to react to Helen's veiled criticisms, the veiling grew thinner in direct proportion to the older woman's growing frustration. Hints that someone of Meg's background couldn't be trusted to handle anything of value became open statements.

When Meg failed to point out that the dishes were already clean or the laundry adequately washed, the insincere smiles started to disappear and the blame was laid squarely at Meg's feet. Or rather, at the feet of her poor upbringing. And always, Meg accepted the criticism without giving the smallest hint as to what she was really feeling.

It was almost two weeks before Helen finally found something that drew a reaction from her daughter-in-law.

"What are you doing?"

At the sound of Meg's voice, Helen glanced over her shoulder. Meg stood in the bedroom doorway, still wrapped in the coat she'd worn as protection against the blustery weather while she was hanging the clothes on the line.

"The door was open and I happened to notice the bed," Helen said, turning her back on Meg to continue fussing with the sheets. "Tyler always liked his bed made in a particular way. Of course, he'd never say anything to you about it, but—"

She broke off with a start of surprise as Meg suddenly appeared beside her and took the pillow she'd been fluffing from her hands.

"Thank you for your concern, but the least I can do is take care of our room." Seeing the other woman in *her* room, touching the bed she shared with Ty, Meg felt a depth of anger she hadn't known she was capable of. This was the one place she was able to escape to, the one place she didn't have to listen to Helen McKendrick's smooth voice telling her what a failure she was, how Ty's life had been ruined when he married her.

"I know you try," Helen said insincerely. "But coming from the kind of background you do, I'm sure it's difficult—"

"I am capable of making a bed, Mrs. McKendrick." Meg offered no apology for interrupting. Anger rose thick and hard in her throat. She forced it back, knowing that she couldn't possibly win an open confrontation with this woman. "*I* will take care of this room. You have more than enough to do taking care of the rest of the house."

"I'm very particular—"

"Yes, I know. But this room isn't your responsibility. It's mine."

Her tone was polite but implacable. Helen couldn't have looked more shocked if the pillow had addressed her.

"I refuse to allow you to take on yet another chore," Meg said, forcing a smile every bit as insincere as those her mother-in-law bestowed on her. "Now, if you'll excuse me, I have some things to tend to."

Helen McKendrick found herself standing in the hallway, staring at the closed door with no clear idea of how she'd come to be there.

Inside the room, Meg turned and stared at the newly unmade bed. Her breathing was too rapid and her hands were clenched into tight fists at her side. Frustration and anger boiled inside her, demanding action. Without giving herself a chance to think, she grabbed hold of the sheets and stripped them from the mattress with quick angry motions, bundling them together and then throwing them into a corner of the room.

Suddenly light-headed, she sank onto the bare mattress and sat there until her head stopped spinning. *Damn this weakness!* If only she didn't feel so tired all the time, she'd be better able to cope with the constant barbs about her failure as a wife. If only she didn't already more than half believe them, they wouldn't sting quite so much.

Her hand was shaking as she lifted it to brush her hair back from her face. She forced herself to take deep, slow breaths, swallowing the sickness that rose in her throat, telling herself that it couldn't be good for the baby for her to get so angry. She might as well just face the fact that there wasn't anything she could do to change her mother-in-law's opinion of her. She could scrub the house from top to bottom, bake blue-ribbon pies, and smile till her teeth ached and Ty's mother would still find fault.

The only thing Helen McKendrick wanted was for her to get out of Ty's life. If only she could be more sure that Ty didn't wish the same thing, she thought.

Finding herself on the losing end of the only argument she'd ever managed to force Meg into did nothing to endear Meg to Helen. Having accepted that there was nothing she could do change the other woman's opinion of her, Meg stopped trying. She spent more time in her room, quilting or reading or sometimes just staring out the window, watching for the first signs of spring.

A few days after Meg's confrontation with her mother-in-law, the weather suddenly turned warm. It was as if winter had given way to spring overnight. Not that winter would really give in so easily, of course. March is a month marked by the tug-of-war between two seasons, with old man winter winning most of the early battles. But spring's youthful vigor must always win out eventually. This year the first signs of that triumph gave Meg's flagging spirits a sorely needed lift.

She'd planned to visit her mother, but looking at the clear blue arc of sky overhead, she hesitated for a moment, thinking that she'd much rather go into Regret and find a bench in the park to sit on and let the sun's warmth sink into her bones. An immediate wave of guilt followed hard on the heels of that thought.

She'd had no contact with her mother since that terrible night when she'd run out into the rain, her only thought to reach Ty. Meg had written twice from California, short impersonal letters that said little beyond the fact that she was well. She hadn't even told her mother that she was going to have a baby. It was time, and past, that she went to see her.

Ty had bought a battered truck for use on the farm. Since they'd sold her little Ford before leaving California, he'd left the keys to the roadster with her. Meg timed her visit carefully to minimize the possibility of running into her stepfather. She even slowed as she neared the hotel, looking to make sure that his car was there. It was and she drew a relieved breath as she passed.

As she turned into the drive, Meg was shocked to see how different her old home looked. She stopped the car but made no move to get out, staring instead at the white frame building, trying to place the changes. It crept over her slowly that it wasn't the house that had changed—it was her.

She wasn't the same frightened girl who'd run from this place all those weeks ago. She was a woman now, with a husband and a baby on the way. In her memory, the house had been bigger, more threatening. It had been darker, looming over everything around it. But she saw now that it was nothing more than a small wooden building, the paint starting to fade a little, the narrow flower beds that flanked the porch empty now, showing nothing of the color that would brighten them later in the year.

Meg got out of the car and walked slowly up to the house, her reluctance oddly reinforced by the changes she sensed in herself. She had the urge to turn and leave, but she could see the front door already opening and then her mother was pushing open the screen door and stepping out onto the porch. Meg stopped at the top of the steps, looking at her mother, seeing the changes in her. Or was it simply more evidence of how much she herself had changed?

"Hello, Mama."

"Meg." Ruth's thin fingers pulled her sweater tighter around her narrow frame, her faded blue eyes sweeping over her youngest daughter. Meg wondered if there was any outward evidence of the changes she felt inside. And if there was, would her mother see it? "It's cold out. Come inside" was all she offered by way of greeting.

Meg hesitated a moment before following her mother inside. She didn't want to set foot in that house again, but that was absurd. She'd come to see her mother, and they could hardly stand on the porch and talk. Shivering a little, though not from the cold, Meg followed her mother inside, flinching as the door shut behind her.

Nothing had changed. Ruth led the way into the parlor. A fitful fire burned on the hearth, supplementing the stingy load of coal Harlan would have ordered last fall. There was a quilt stretched in the frame, a Trip Around the World done in rich pastels.

"Mrs. Stuart?" Meg asked, touching her fingertips to the quilt.

"I don't think that woman knows another pattern," Ruth said, by way of confirmation. She sank into her chair and picked up her needle to continue the line of quilting she'd begun.

Moving as if in a dream, Meg went to other side of the frame. Her thimble sat on top of the quilt, along with a packet of needles and a spool of thread. After sliding the needle into the fabric, she popped the knot at the end of the thread through the top, burying it in the cotton batt as she began stitching. Mrs. Stuart bought at least three quilts every year, always the same pattern, a series of arcs that covered the quilt top like rainbows.

The two women quilted in silence for a few minutes. Meg couldn't even begin to guess how many hours they'd spent like this, rarely speaking, the stillness of the room broken only by the steady ticking of the clock on the mantel, their needles rocking in and out of the fabric in kind of harmony they'd never achieved anywhere else.

It was as if nothing had changed, Meg thought, almost hypnotized by the rhythmic movement of her needle. As if everything were just as it had been, as if it would continue in the same way all the days of her life.

Only everything had changed. Nothing was the way it had been. Her old life was gone forever. And it was a sad realization that there'd been so little in it to regret losing. Not even these quiet moments. She'd liked to think that she and her mother were close at times like this, that the quilting brought them together.

But she realized now that the closeness had been an illusion. All the hours they'd spent sitting across a quilting frame from each other and she couldn't have said, with honesty, that she knew her mother as well as she knew Millie Marquez. She didn't know if Ruth had hopes or dreams; whether she ever longed to escape the life she'd built; whether she thought of anything beyond getting through each day as it came.

Trembling, Meg put her needle down and slipped the familiar thimble from her finger.

"I'm going to have a baby, Mama." She lifted her head as she spoke, looking across the frame at her mother. Ruth's hand faltered for a moment and then picked up the rhythm of the quilting again.

"Are you happy?" she asked without looking up.

Happy? Meg didn't know how to answer that question. She was married to a man she loved more than life itself. She carried his child. Yet how could she be happy knowing Ty didn't love her the way she loved him?

"Yes," she answered at last, knowing it was only a partial truth.

"I knew the McKendrick boy would take care of you," Ruth said, sounding satisfied.

But wasn't there more to a marriage than just being taken care of? Meg longed to ask. *What about building a future together? What about love?*

But she didn't ask any of those questions. She realized suddenly that her mother's whole life had been built around choices made in the hopes that she could find someone to take care of her. It struck Meg as indescribably sad that her mother should want something so simple and have failed so miserably to grasp even an edge of that dream.

"How are you, Mama?" she asked softly.

Ruth's fingers trembled and she let her hands rest on the quilt top. "The hotel's failing," she said slowly, not lifting her eyes to Meg's face. "Harlan isn't taking it well."

The mention of her stepfather's name sent a shiver up Meg's spine. As far as she was concerned, if the hotel were to collapse around him, it would be no more than he deserved, but there was worry in her mother's voice. Still, it was more than Meg could do to express sympathy for Harlan Davis's troubles. She was silent, tracing her fingertip along a row of pink squares, noticing how neatly the seam matched.

"He blames your husband for what's happened," Ruth said abruptly.

"Why?" Meg's eyes shot across the quilt, and this time Ruth was looking at her, her face creased with anxious lines. "We haven't even been in the same state."

"Harlan thinks the McKendricks are telling people to stay away, that they're discouraging business."

"Maybe it's the fact that people have no money that's discouraging business," Meg said sharply. "Or hasn't he heard that there's a depression going on?"

"I know that, but when a man sees everything he's worked for suddenly slipping away from him, he needs somewhere to lay the blame."

"Well, he can just find somewhere else to lay it," Meg snapped. "Maybe he should look to himself for a change. If he wasn't such a skinflint and spent a little of his precious money on repairs for that old place, maybe people would want to go there."

"You shouldn't speak so harshly of him," Ruth said automatically. "He's not—" She caught her daughter's look and broke off abruptly, perhaps realizing the irony of telling Meg that Harlan Davis was not a bad man.

They sat in silence for a few minutes, but the earlier sense of familiarity was gone. Meg stirred restlessly, thinking it was time she left. She didn't know what she'd hoped for from this visit. Maybe what she'd always hoped for when it came to her mother, a feeling of closeness, a feeling of connection. That feeling had eluded her all her life, and it seemed as if nothing had changed.

"I should be going," she said, pushing back her chair and standing up.

"Wait. I have something I wanted to give you." Ruth rose and walked from the room, leaving Meg alone. She waited impatiently, suddenly anxious to be gone. She didn't like being here.

"I'd planned to give this to you when you got married," Ruth said as she came back into the room.

Meg had been looking out the window, but at her mother's words she turned, her eyes dropping to the quilt Ruth carried draped across her arms.

"That's Grandma's wedding quilt," she said, startled. She had never met her maternal grandmother, but she knew the quilt well. Stylized red and green tulips were appliquéd in the center while a green vine with red flowers and perfectly round red berries twined around the border. The white background had been heavily quilted with feathered wreaths and diagonal cross-hatching so that there was not an inch left unstitched.

The quilt was, as far as Meg knew, the only thing her mother had brought to her first marriage other than the clothes on her back. It had always been kept well wrapped in a sheet, brought out on rare occasions when she and Patsy had been allowed to touch the stuffed berries and marvel at the perfection of the work. It was her mother's most prized possession, the one treasure she'd held on to no matter what.

"You can't give me Grandma's quilt," Meg protested, putting her hands behind her back like a child resisting temptation in a candy store.

"I'd always planned to give it to you," Ruth repeated. Her worn fingers stroked bright tulip. "Your great-grandmother gave this to my mother on her wedding day, and she passed it on to me when I married your father. She told me I was making a mistake," she said, half to herself. "But she said the quilt was mine, mistake or no. I'd've given it to Patsy but she doesn't care much for such things. I never could teach her to quilt properly, and she'd just as soon have something store bought."

She stopped and sighed, her hand trembling a little as she cradled the quilt. "Things didn't work out quite the way either of us might have wished, but I'd still like you to have this."

"I can't, Mama. It's your best quilt."

"I want you to have it," Ruth repeated. She looked at Meg, her eyes pleading. "You take it and give it to your daughter someday and you tell her where it came from, how it's been passed down through the family.''

Seeing the determination in her mother's face, Meg reached out reluctantly. The quilt was heavy and she drew it close, cradling it in her arms. Ruth's eyes lingered on the quilt.

''Don't you ever forget, Meg, building a marriage is like making a quilt. Some people have nothing but scraps, and they turn them into something fine and solid. Some folks can go out and buy fabric brand-new and they can't put together so much as a single block. It's all in what you do with what the Lord gives you.''

''What about you, Mama? What kind of a quilt have you made?'' Meg hadn't intended to ask the question, but the words were out and couldn't be recalled. For a moment she thought her mother was going to ignore the question, but then her mouth twisted in a half smile.

''Some people just choose a poor piece of fabric, that's all. And then you do the best you can with what you've got.'' She looked at Meg and, for a moment, Meg saw a deep sadness in her eyes. Then Ruth blinked and it was gone. ''But you've got good, solid fabric,'' she said briskly. ''You just be careful what pattern you choose.''

Meg wanted to ask what her mother meant. Hadn't the pattern already been chosen when they'd married? A marriage wasn't like a quilt. You didn't just pick out the colors you liked and stitch them into a pleasing pattern. Did you? But before she could say anything, she heard the sound of a car coming up the drive.

Both women stiffened, their eyes meeting as they realized whose car it must be. Without a word, Meg started for the door. She couldn't be in the same house with him. If she had to crawl out a window, she'd do it, but she wouldn't be in this house at the same time as her stepfather.

She reached the front door just as he was stepping onto the porch. Fumbling in her haste to be outside, Meg shoved open the screen, aware of her mother hanging back in the hall as the screen door banged shut.

''I heard you were back in town,'' Harlan said, his thin

mouth twisting in a sneer. "Mrs. McKendrick now, isn't it? Mrs. High-and-Mighty McKendrick."

He'd been drinking. The realization came as a shock. She couldn't remember ever seeing her stepfather drink to excess. Not that he had to be drunk to be dangerous, she thought. She swallowed down the fear that rose in her throat and edged to the side.

"Come back to gloat, have you?" he demanded, his speech slurred. "Come back to see what a good job that husband of yours has done in ruining my life?"

"Ty hasn't tried to ruin anyone's life," she said, though her better judgment suggested that it was futile to argue with him. He was too drunk to hear anything she said. Even sober, it wasn't likely he'd listen.

"Well, you've come back too soon," he said, ignoring her denial. He leaned toward her and she could smell the whiskey on his breath. "The McKendricks haven't succeeded in destroying me. Not yet, they haven't."

"Let me by," she ordered, feeling her stomach start to roll at his nearness.

"Getting mighty high in the instep, aren't you? Think you're somebody now that you've married McKendrick. Well, you're nobody," he snarled, pushing his face close to hers.

Meg felt blackness hovering at the edge of her vision, but she fought it off. She couldn't faint. If she fainted, she'd be helpless.

"Get away from me." She wanted the words to sound like a command, but they came out as a terrified whisper.

"Come inside, Harlan." Ruth's prosaic suggestion didn't get so much as a flicker of attention.

"You're always going to be a nobody," Harlan told Meg.

"Let me go," she said, beyond caring if it sounded like she was begging. She turned her face away from his, her stomach heaving at the smell of his breath.

"Look at me when I talk to you," he snapped. Meg whimpered with fright when he caught her face in his hand, his fingers digging into her jaw as he turned her toward him. "I know what you are. You're trash. Just like your sister. You're nothing but trash. You may be able to pretend for a while, but sooner or later McKendrick will find out what he's married. Just like I found out after I married your mother.''

''Let her go now, Harlan.'' Ruth had come out on the porch and was tugging pleadingly on her husband's arm. Meg couldn't take her terrified eyes from her stepfather's twisted face.

''Ty will kill you,'' she whispered. ''If you touch me, he'll kill you.''

''Please, Harlan. Let her go now. Don't make trouble for yourself,'' Ruth was saying.

Whether it was his wife's pleading or her own threat, Meg didn't know, but her stepfather's hand dropped from her face and he stepped back, clearing a path to the steps. She didn't wait to give him a chance to change his mind. She lunged away from him, almost falling down the steps in her haste to escape.

''You tell them they're not going to win,'' Harlan shouted after her. ''I'm not going to let them ruin me.''

Meg scrambled into the car and slammed the door shut. Her fingers were shaking so hard, it took her two tries to turn the key in the ignition. The engine roared to life, drowning out anything else he might have said. Meg backed out of the drive so fast that the wheels spit gravel.

By the time she reached the McKendrick house a few minutes later, she was shaking as if she had a fever. After leaving the roadster parked at a crooked angle and leaving the precious quilt lying in the passenger seat, she hurried up the walkway and let herself inside. She leaned against the front door for a moment, her breathing ragged, her skin flushed and damp.

She was safe. He couldn't hurt her now. But the knowledge did nothing to slow the pounding of her heart. If she closed her eyes, she could see his face thrust close to hers, his hate-filled eyes glittering at her, smell the sour bite of whiskey on his breath. Her stomach rolled. Meg clapped her hand over her mouth and pushed away from the door. She heard her mother-in-law call to her when she was partway up the stairs, but she didn't dare pause. As it was, she made it to the bath-room just in time.

Meg continued to kneel on the hard linoleum for a long time after her stomach had emptied itself. Too weak to stand, she crouched there, trembling with reaction, her body aching as if she'd been beaten. She'd spent months trying to forget that terrible night, to forget the feel of her stepfather's hands on her, the cruel anger in his touch. In a few short minutes, Harlan Davis had brought all the memories rushing back, all the feelings of helplessness, the fear. He'd made her feel as if the safety she'd found were nothing more than an illusion. Even here, where she was surely beyond his reach, she didn't feel safe anymore. Of course, he'd have to confront her mother-in-law to get to her.

The image of Helen McKendrick's reaction to a drunken Harlan Davis demanding to see the daughter-in-law she de-spised drew a spurt of choked laughter from Meg. Hearing the edge of hysteria in the sound, she drew a deep, sobbing breath and tried to stifle the fear that clawed at her.

She wanted Ty. She needed to see him. Needed to feel his arms around her, to hear him tell her he wouldn't let anything happen to her. Then she could feel safe again. When he held her, nothing could hurt her, not even Harlan Davis.

Meg was in their room when she heard the front door open and the sound of Ty's voice. She didn't go down to greet him, knowing that his mother would already be there and not feeling up to dealing with the other woman. The incident with her stepfather and the bout of sickness afterward had left her feeling a little fragile, and she didn't feel much like coping with her mother-in-law's subtle contempt.

So Meg stayed where she was and continued to knit on the baby blanket she was making out of soft buttery yellow wool. She'd been knitting for the past couple of hours, letting the steady rhythm of the needles soothe her ragged nerves.

Ty's footsteps on the stairs were slow and heavy, tired sounding. She frowned, her hands slowing. He was working so hard, trying to get the farmhouse in shape for them to move in, trying to prepare for spring planting. Most nights he came home chilled to the bone and exhausted. She was guiltily aware that he was doing all this for her, because he was convinced this was what was best for her and the baby. He pushed open the door and Meg let her knitting drop to her lap as she looked at him.

"Hi."

"Mother said you came in earlier and rushed right by her without a word," he said by way of greeting. "Are you all right?"

It didn't take a psychic to guess that Helen hadn't given him this piece of information out of any concern for Meg. More likely she'd been pointing out how rude Meg had been in not speaking to her.

"I wasn't feeling well," she said. "I—"

She broke off as Ty came closer and she saw the lines of exhaustion that bracketed his mouth. His shoulders were slumped with fatigue, and he was covered in dirt from head to toe. Flecks of pale sawdust powdered his black hair, and mud smeared across the front of his shirt and pants. There was a rip in the knee of his jeans and a tear that ran the length of one sleeve.

With a concerned cry, Meg rose, stepping over her knitting as it tumbled to the floor.

"What did you do to your arm?"

"It's just a scratch," Ty said, giving the injury an indifferent glance. "Tell me about you. What was wrong this afternoon?"

A quick glance confirmed his assessment of the wound. Her hands resting on his arm, Meg looked up at him and opened her mouth to tell him about the confrontation with her stepfather and found herself noticing the tired lines around his eyes.

"It was just your son acting up," she said lightly. "I rested for a little while and I'm practically good as new."

"Are you sure?" The relief in his eyes warmed her heart even as it made her wonder at her acting ability. Millie would be proud of her, she thought wryly.

"I'm sure," she said without hesitation. She felt guilty for even thinking of telling him about the ugly scene with her stepfather. He had so much to worry about already. "Now, why don't you go get cleaned up. You look exhausted."

She met his searching look steadily, smiling a little to show that there was no reason for concern. After a moment he nodded, apparently satisfied that she really was all right.

"I'm beat," he admitted, rolling his shoulders as if they ached.

"Sit down."

"I'm dirty," he protested as she urged him toward the chair she'd been sitting in.

"It's nothing that won't brush off." Meg bent to pick up her knitting and set it on the table as Ty sank into the wing chair with a sigh that said more than words about how tired he was.

"What did you do today?" Meg knelt at his feet and began unlacing the heavy work boots he wore.

"Thanks. I'm so stiff, I'm not sure I could get down there," he admitted with a rueful grin.

"Just doing my job," she said, smiling up at him as she tugged off first one boot and then the other.

"Your job is to take care of yourself and the baby," he contradicted.

"I think I can do that and still manage to help you off with your boots."

"Are you sure you're feeling okay? You look pale." Ty's fingertips stroked across her cheek. Meg leaned into his touch, closing her eyes against the quick sting of tears. She cried so easily these days.

"I'm fine." She hoped he wouldn't notice the huskiness in her voice.

"Mother says you spend a lot of time in here." He was still frowning. "You'd tell me if anything was wrong, wouldn't you?"

"Nothing's wrong." She hoped he was too tired to notice that she'd sidestepped his exact question. "I spend time up here because it keeps me out of your mother's way." She realized her mistake when Ty stiffened, his brows lowering in a frown.

"Has she said anything to you?"

Briefly, Meg wondered if "anything" encompassed Helen McKendrick's subtle stream of criticism. "No, she hasn't said 'anything.' " Laughing, she shook her head. "Stop worrying about me. I'm not a helpless child, Ty."

"I know. But my mother can be hard to get along with. God knows, I haven't managed to learn the knack and I've known her all my life."

"Well, I'm doing just fine," she said briskly. It wasn't exactly a lie. She hadn't come to blows with the woman yet. Stilling kneeling in front of him, she reached for the buttons on his shirt.

"It's nice to know you missed me," Ty said. Despite his fatigue, his smile had a wicked edge that made Meg's face warm.

"I'm just trying to get you out of these dirty clothes," she said primly.

"Oh." He let her slip another button loose and then reached out and began unbuttoning the top of her dress.

"What are you doing?" Her hands flew to stop his.

"I'm just helping you out of your dirty clothes," he said, widening his eyes innocently.

"This dress is perfectly clean."

He shook his head, pulling his mouth into a regretful line. "There's a smudge right there." Meg turned her head to see where he was pointing, and he leaned forward to kiss the vulnerable skin just behind her ear.

"I—I don't see a smudge," she whispered. A shiver ran up her spine as he nibbled on her earlobe.

"You just aren't looking hard enough." His fingers were quickly finishing the task of opening her bodice.

"Ty, we haven't even had supper yet." It was a weak protest but the best she could manage with his hand cupping her breast through the soft cotton of her slip.

"I'm not hungry."

"You said you were tired."

"I'm not that tired." His thumb brushed across her nipple, his touch so exquisitely gentle that Meg felt tears come to her eyes. She turned her head so that their lips met, giving in to the need he'd sparked. With a groan, Ty scooped her off the floor and settled her across his lap, deepening the kiss.

She wound her arms around his neck, pressing close, letting the hard strength of his body chase away the last of the afternoon's fears. As long as Ty held her like this, as long as he wanted her, nothing else in the world mattered.

Chapter 19

Ty gave the nail one last whack with the hammer and then stood up. Bracing his hands on his hips, the hammer dangling from between his fingers, he looked down at his handiwork and allowed himself a pleased smile. The old porch floor had been rotted through in more places than it had been solid. Luckily the joists underneath had still been sound so replacing the floor had been a relatively simple job, requiring little more than some new boards and a sunny day. The weather had obliged with an unseasonably warm spell, he'd provided the boards, and the porch was no longer a hazard for unwary feet.

One job done and probably only about a thousand left to do, Ty thought ruefully, turning to look out at the property. When he'd made the decision to give up wings for a plow, he'd known he was in for some hard work. What he hadn't realized was how much would have to be done before he could even consider putting in a crop.

The house wasn't the only thing that had suffered from neglect. The chicken house, which had been his grandmother's domain, had been so rickety that a good, hard push had collapsed it. He and Jack had spent two days patching the holes in the barn roof, a job Ty hoped never to have to do again. He'd been thousands of feet in the air in a plane and never given a thought to how far down the ground was. Braced on the steep-sided roof, he'd been vividly aware of just how hard he'd bounce if he fell.

Once the barn roof was as solid as they could make it, Jack had begun the task of dismantling the old tractor that had sat rusting in the barn these past six years. When the tractor was working again, Ty thought it might be possible to believe he was really a farmer. Though the calluses on his hands ought to be evidence enough, he thought ruefully.

"Admiring your empire?" Jack's question preceded him as he walked up from the barn.

"Thinking about how much is left to do." Ty shook his head. "I had no idea."

"You can still change your mind."

"No." He didn't add anything more to the flat refusal.

Jack stepped up on the newly repaired porch and fixed Ty with a curious look. "You're enjoying this, aren't you?"

The question surprised Ty. Enjoying it? Well, there was certainly satisfaction to be found in seeing the work they'd done.

"I like seeing things look the way they did when my grandfather was alive," he said, giving an oblique answer to the question.

"I suppose there's something to be said for good old physical labor. Nothing printable."

"You were getting too soft," Ty told him, grinning at Jack's sarcasm.

"I like soft," Jack complained. "Soft doesn't hurt as much." He rolled his shoulders and winced.

"At least the weather's warmed up," Ty offered as consolation. A week ago they'd been bundled in coats and gloves. Today it was warm enough for shirtsleeves.

"It's warmer in California." Jack wasn't in the mood to be consoled. "If you don't need me for anything, I'm going to quit for today."

"Sure. You've put in as many hours as I have. I appreciate the help."

"What are friends for?" Jack had draped his jacket over

the porch rail earlier, and now he picked it up and slipped it on. "I've got . . . somebody to see."

"Somebody like Patsy Baker?" Ty asked shrewdly. He'd been wondering how long it would take his friend to get around to seeing her.

"Maybe." Jack reached in his coat pocket and pulled out a pack of Chesterfields.

"Are you sure you know what you're doing?" The hammer slipped back and forth in Ty's fingers as he looked at his friend.

"Hell, no." Jack lit the cigarette and looked at Ty through a thin veil of smoke.

"Might be smarter to keep your distance," Ty suggested mildly.

"Nobody's ever accused me of being smart," Jack said, his grin only a little forced. "I've got to stop in town and get a new pan gasket, anyway. I tore the one I had."

"I'll see you tomorrow, then," Ty said.

"Bright and early," Jack said, the words drifting back over his shoulder as he walked to his car.

Ty watched him leave, his dark brows lowered in a frown. He had the feeling somebody was going to get hurt in this situation. He just hoped it wasn't Jack.

Jack was aware of Ty's concerned gaze following him as the car bumped its way down the rutted lane to the road. He would have offered some reassurance if there'd been any to give. But the fact was, Ty was right—he'd be a hell of a lot smarter if he just kept his distance from Patsy Harper—Baker. Damn, but it was hard to remember her married name. But he could no more stay away from her than he could flap his arms and take off flying.

Funny, for almost five years he'd managed to put her out of his mind, thought she was gone from his heart. Yet all it had taken was seeing her at Ty and Meg's wedding, and five years suddenly seemed like the blink of an eye. All the time he'd been in California he'd thought about her, remembered her.

He'd be smarter to keep his distance, but he wouldn't be human.

The house looked just as he remembered it. Neat and tidy and nothing like the Patsy he'd known. What had happened to her determination to shake the Iowa dust from her shoes and find her fortune elsewhere? He parked the car and got out, his footsteps slowing as he walked up onto the porch. He had no right to be there. What was he going to say if her husband answered the door? *Excuse me, but I used to be your wife's lover and I just dropped by to say hello?* But she'd said that her husband traveled a lot, and since there was no car in sight, it seemed safe to assume that he was away from home.

Jack knocked on the door and waited, counting every beat of his heart as it slammed against his breastbone. Damn. He was as nervous as a sixteen-year-old boy on his first date. He heard the sound of footsteps inside the house and then the door was opening and Patsy was standing there, only the thin barrier of the screen door between them.

"Jack." His name was a flat statement, and he had the odd impression that she wasn't really surprised to see him.

"Patsy." He slid his hands into the pockets of his jacket, aware that the subtle tremor in his fingers could spoil his casual image. "I was in the neighborhood and thought I'd drop by and see how you were."

"I'm fine." She made no move to open the screen door.

"Can I come in?"

She hesitated, her fingers wrapped around the edge of the door as if ready to slam it shut. Jack waited, watching the expressions flicker through her eyes, knowing she was torn between what she *should* do and what she wanted to do. At least, he hoped she wanted to let him in. After a moment she reached out and flicked up the hook on the screen door. He didn't give her time to change her mind but pulled the door open and stepped inside.

The house still smelled of beeswax and lavender, but overlaying both of those scents was the warm fragrance of fresh baking.

"Something smells good," he said, sniffing appreciatively. He gave Patsy his most winning smile. "Smells like chocolate cake."

"It is." She hesitated and then gestured to the right. "Would you like a piece?"

"When have you ever known me to turn down a piece of cake?" he asked, deliberately putting their relationship in the present tense.

"You always did have a sweet tooth," she said. She put it in the past, but her smile was a little less wary.

Jack followed her into the kitchen and sat at the table while she dusted the warm cake with powdered sugar before cutting two squares. She set a plate in front of him and, without asking, poured him a glass of milk.

"Chocolate cake and milk," he said reverently as she returned the glass bottle to the ice box. "I feel like I've died and gone to heaven."

"My neighbor gave me the recipe," she said as she sat down. "I like to bake. If fills in the time when Eldin's gone."

At the mention of her husband's name, Jack felt the moist cake turn to ashes in his mouth.

"You mentioned that he travels a lot?" he asked, amazed at the casual tone of his own voice.

"Yes. It's harder for him to make a sale these days, what with people not having much money. Have you seen Meg lately?" she asked.

"A few days ago." Jack accepted her change of topic. He didn't particularly want to discuss her husband.

"How is she?"

"She seems well enough. A little pale, maybe. But living with Helen McKendrick would be enough to turn just about anyone pale."

"Is she a difficult woman?" Patsy sounded anxious for her sister.

"Not as long as she gets her way."

"I hope she and Meg are getting along all right." Patsy dabbed her fork against the top of her untouched cake. "Meggy shouldn't be upset in her condition."

"Ty will look out for her," Jack said easily. Seeing that

she was still frowning, he sought to distract her. "I suppose asking for another piece of cake would be rude." His tone was wistful as he eyed the remaining cake.

"I swear, I've never met anyone over the age of five with a sweet tooth to match yours, Jack." Despite her gently scolding tone, there was a flush of pleasure on her cheeks as she got up to cut another piece of the cake and set it on his plate.

Looking at her, Jack was struck by how beautiful she was. She leaned over the table and he was unable to resist the urge to touch her. His fingertips brushed against her cheek. She froze, her eyes jerking to his face. Jack kept his gaze steady on hers as his fingers traced the curve of her cheekbone.

"I thought I'd imagined how soft your skin was," he said slowly.

As if his voice broke a spell, Patsy straightened and moved back to her chair, her movements jerky, like a marionette controlled by an amateur puppeteer.

"I'll have to tell my neighbor how much you enjoyed the cake," she said, her voice a shade too high.

"What's he like?"

"My neighbor is a woman. Mrs. Leary. She's elderly and—"

"Your husband," Jack said abruptly. "What's your husband like?"

"I don't think I should discuss Eldin with you," she said. She dropped her hands into her lap, but not before he'd seen that they were trembling.

"I've always been curious about him," he said in a conversational tone at odds with the tension in his gut. "You can't blame me for being curious about the guy you married a few weeks after telling me you'd always love me. I kind of think I've got a right to know something about him," he said, giving her a rueful smile.

Patsy felt at war with herself. She stared across the table at Jack, reading nothing but mild curiosity in his look. He could have been a casual acquaintance making polite conversation. But their acquaintance was far from casual, and her instincts said that discussing Eldin with Jack was a mistake. On the other hand, perhaps he *did* have a right to ask about her husband. Maybe she'd granted him that right when she married someone else without a word of explanation.

"He's a good man," she said slowly.

"How old is he?"

"He's forty-six." She saw Jack's eyebrows go up and lifted her chin. She knew what some people thought of her marrying a man more than twice her age, but she'd make no apologies to anyone, not even to Jack.

"No children?" he asked, his eyes questioning.

"Not . . . not yet." The words were difficult to get out past the ache in her throat. She dropped her eyes to the table, not wanting him to see what a nerve he'd touched with that question. "I keep hoping."

Jack stirred restlessly as if finding the topic uncomfortable. "I'm glad you're happy," he said abruptly.

Happy? That wasn't the word she'd have used, Patsy thought. Content, perhaps. Comfortable. But happy? Seeing that Jack was staring out the window, she let her eyes linger on his profile, hungry to see every small change in the face she'd once known almost as well as her own, updating the image she carried in her heart.

As if sensing her gaze on him, he turned his head, and for a moment, their eyes met. She looked away immediately, but not before she'd seen the hunger in his eyes. A hunger that made her heart beat a little faster even as guilt brought color to her cheeks.

"I've missed you," he said quietly.

For an instant Patsy stopped breathing. She stared at the oak surface of the table, noticing every tiny nick and scratch, cataloguing them as if her life depended on it. *Jack had missed her!* The knowledge sang through her veins.

She was a married woman, she reminded herself sternly. She summoned up an image of Eldin, his gentle eyes smiling at her in forgiveness. But there'd already been enough in her life for which she needed to ask forgiveness. She wasn't going to add another sin to the list already in place.

"I think you should go," she whispered, keeping her eyes on the table.

There was a moment's silence when she thought Jack might ignore her request. His chair scraped across the floor as he pushed back from the table, and the sound seemed to leave a scratch across her heart. He was leaving. Again.

Hearing his footsteps as he walked away, she couldn't stop herself from looking up, her eyes hungry for the sight of him. He stopped in the doorway, one hand on the door jamb, and spoke without turning.

"I'd like to see you again."

"I'm married, Jack." Patsy twisted the wedding ring on her finger as if needing to remind herself of that fact.

"I just want to see you again."

"We shouldn't." With the use of the word "we" she'd linked herself to him, admitted that she wanted to see him again.

"Do you want me to stay away, Patsy?" Jack turned to look at her, his eyes gray-green and demanding total honesty.

She stared at him, feeling her heart pounding against her breastbone. If she told him to stay away, he would. He'd walk out of her life and she'd never see him again. Five years ago she'd thought him gone forever and learned to live with his absence.

But now her sister's marriage had brought him back into her life. She'd seen him, touched him, been close enough to smell the familiar scent of his aftershave, felt herself come alive in ways she'd all but forgotten. And now he stood there, asking her to decide whether or not she could give all that up again.

"Do you want me to stay away?" he asked again.

God help her, she couldn't say yes. She shook her head, knowing she was a fool, knowing she was only asking to be hurt. Something hard and fierce flared in Jack's eyes and for a moment she thought he might come back and catch her up in his arms. Caught between alarm and hope, she pressed her hand to the base of her throat, her half-frightened eyes staring into his.

But he didn't move toward her. Instead he nodded, as if satisfied with her response. He gave her a quick grin that increased her heart rate to double what it should have been and then spun on one heel and left. Patsy sat just where she was long after the sound of his car's engine had faded into the distance.

What had she done?

The second week in March brought icy rain and cold winds that made it clear winter wasn't quite ready to call it quits. The false spring vanished without a whimper, and with it went Meg's brief spurt of energy.

She woke tired and stayed that way. Her stomach rebelled at the thought of food, refusing to retain more than a few bites of whatever she managed to force down. Meg did her best to hide her illness, not wanting to worry Ty. But it was impossible to hide it completely from her mother-in-law, not when the two of them were alone in the house a good part of each day.

Ty's mother made it known that she thought Meg was coddling herself, lying in bed most of the day. *She'd* managed to give birth to three children with hardly a day's sickness during any of her pregnancies. And *she* had a delicate constitution.

Meg let the veiled criticism wash over her, her concern more for the baby she carried than for Helen McKendrick's opinion of her. But she did wonder if something might be wrong. To hear her mother-in-law tell it, she should be filled with energy, not barely managing to drag herself out of bed. When Meg noticed that she was spotting a little, she felt a tiny spurt of panic. But she'd overheard talk and she knew that it wasn't necessarily something to worry about. She worried anyway.

There was no one she could ask. It didn't even occur to her to go to the doctor. The only time she could remember anyone in her family seeing a doctor was when Patsy had broken her arm falling off a fence. Doctors cost money and they'd never had any money to spare for something that wasn't an absolute necessity. Remembering what the doctor in California had said, Meg stayed in bed as much as possible and tried to rest.

And prayed that nothing was wrong.

Ty shrugged out of his coat and hung it on the coat rack near the door. The rich smell of pot roast followed his mother from the kitchen as she came to greet him.

"You're late."

"There's a lot to be done." He dropped an obedient kiss on her forehead, wishing, not for the first time, that the farmhouse had been habitable. Living under his mother's thumb was even more difficult now than it had been when he was a boy. If he'd had only himself to consider, he'd have camped out in the farmhouse. But then, if he'd had been only himself to consider, he wouldn't have been back in Iowa at all.

He walked into the living room and exchanged greetings with his father, who was reading the newspaper.

"How'd it go today, son?" Elliot asked, putting the paper down.

"Not bad. Jack's got the tractor running."

"That's good."

"Yes." Ty sank down on the sofa, aware of a bone-deep tiredness. He'd never have believed he could work so hard for so long and still have so much left to do. "Where's Meg?"

"Upstairs," his mother said with a snap. "She hasn't been downstairs all day. I know she's your wife, Tyler." Clearly, it galled her to have to admit as much. "But this isn't a hotel and the least she could do is have the courtesy to get out of bed."

"Did you make sure she's all right?" Ty asked, on his feet again, his tiredness forgotten. "This pregnancy hasn't been easy on her."

Helen sniffed. "She's making a fuss over nothing. Her kind pops out babies like shelling peas."

"Her kind?" Ty had been in the doorway but he turned, his face tight with anger. "Just what kind is that?"

"People of that class," Helen said, oblivious to the warning in her son's eyes.

"Meg's a McKendrick now, Mother. So when you refer to her class, you might remember that it's the same as yours."

"I—" Helen's mouth opened, her eyes flashing her indignity at the thought of Meg and herself sharing the same class or anything else, for that matter.

"Helen." Elliot's quiet voice held a warning. "I think you've said enough."

Ty didn't wait to find out if his mother was going to heed his father's advice. He was already on his way up the stairs. Meg was lying in bed and she was so still that Ty thought she was sleeping. But at the quiet click of the door closing, she rolled her head toward him.

"Ty." She started to sit up but Ty was beside her in an instant, his hands on her shoulders, urging her back against the pillows as he sank onto the edge of the bed beside her.

"I must have fallen asleep," she said self-consciously, as if she'd just lain down a short while ago. But since she was still wearing her nightgown, Ty doubted she'd been out of bed for more than a few minutes all day.

"How are you feeling?" He reached out to brush her hair back from her forehead, frowning at the dampness of her skin. The room was comfortably warm but not warm enough to cause a sweat.

"I'm fine," she said, making an effort to smile up at him.

The lie might have been more believable if her skin hadn't been the color of buttermilk, the pallor broken by the dark circles under her eyes.

"How long have you been sick?" Concern made his voice sharper than he'd intended, and quick tears sprang to Meg's eyes.

"I'm not sick," she protested, but he saw the fear behind the denial.

"It's not a crime to be sick, Meg." He tamped down the worry clawing at his throat and made his voice gentle. "Tell me what's wrong."

"I don't know." Her hand came up to catch his, her fingers clinging as if to a lifeline. "I don't know if anything's wrong. I—I've been spotting a little," she admitted. "I thought that might be normal. But today I've had pains."

"What kind of pains?" Ty asked, with a calm he was far from feeling.

"Sort of cramps in my stomach," she whispered, pressing one hand against low on her belly. "I'm scared, Ty."

"I'm sure there's nothing wrong," he lied automatically, wanting only to ease the fear that darkened her eyes. "I'll call Doc Corey and ask him to come over and take a look at you."

But when he called the doctor on the phone in the living room, Mrs. Corey informed him that the doctor was out delivering a baby. If Ty wanted to call in the morning? Ty didn't want to call in the morning. He wanted the doctor to look at Meg immediately, but since that wasn't possible, he reluctantly agreed to call first thing in the morning. He set down the phone, telling himself that he was probably overreacting but unable to shake the feeling of urgency.

Ty had forgotten that he wasn't alone until he turned and met the sympathy in his father's eyes. Obviously Elliot McKendrick had heard his conversation with the doctor's wife.

"I imagine she'll be just fine," Elliot said, offering the same thin comfort Ty had given Meg.

"Sure." Ty rubbed his hands down the sides of his pant legs. "She's pale."

"That doesn't mean she's going to lose the baby," his father said, putting words to the fear Ty hadn't yet dared to name.

"Of course not." The knowledge that it was out of his hands made the denial all the more emphatic.

"Your mother was sick for nine months when she carried Dickey," Elliot said, smiling a little at the memory. "And everything worked out just fine. I'm sure it will with Meg, too."

"Sure it will." Ty thrust his fingers through his hair. "I think I'll stay with Meg. Would you tell Mother I'm not hungry?"

"Of course," Elliot said placidly, as if he didn't know as

well as Ty that his wife was likely to throw a conniption fit at the news that Ty wasn't going to eat her dinner.

When Ty told Meg that the doctor was unavailable, he saw fear flicker through her eyes, though she quickly tried to hide it. "I'm sure there's nothing to worry about," she said, forcing a smile.

"Probably not, but it won't hurt to have Doc Corey look at you." Sitting on the edge of the bed, holding her slender hand in his, he hoped that he was doing a better job of concealing his concern than she was.

It was going to be all right, he told himself firmly but he'd be relieved when the doctor came tomorrow.

But "tomorrow" was too late.

At three o'clock in the morning, Meg woke from a restless sleep, crying out in pain. Ty sat bolt upright in bed, one hand reaching for the light switch while the other sought out Meg. The lamp came on just as her fingers clamped around his with bruising strength, a groan of pain wrenching its way from between her clenched teeth.

He saw the terror in her eyes, the denial, the sure knowledge of what was happening in the instant before his gaze swept down the bed. He didn't need a doctor to tell him what the bloodstained covers meant.

She was losing the baby.

"There'll be other babies, Ty. I know that's not much consolation now, but there's no reason to think Meg won't carry the next one to term." Doc Corey's deep voice was both sympathetic and bracing.

Ty said nothing but only continued to sit in the straight-back chair his father had brought upstairs for him, his gaze focused on the runner that covered the hall floor. The runner had been there for as long as he could remember, one of many things he grown up with in this house. He'd never paid any attention to it before, but in the past few hours, he'd become intimately acquainted with every bloated blossom woven into it. He knew just how many faded red roses it took to march across its width and the exact position of the vines twining in and out among them. And he hated every miserable inch of it, he thought with sudden savagery. He'd never realized it was possible to hate an inanimate object the way he hated that runner. He wanted to rip it up off the floor and burn it, to see it reduced to ash.

"This is nature's way of telling us that there was something wrong," Doc Corey was saying. "You're both young and healthy. You'll have plenty of babies. I know it's hard but you have to believe that the Lord has a good reason for everything He does."

"Is Meg all right?" Ty wasn't particularly interested in the Lord's reasons right now. What possible reason could there be for Meg to suffer as she had?

"She'll be fine," Doc Corey said, no hint of impatience in his voice, though it was the fourth time he'd answered the question.

"There was a lot of blood," Ty said, half to himself.

"That's natural," Doc Corey said. "She's sleeping now and that's the best thing for her. When she wakes up, you let her cry all she needs to. There's no quota on the number of tears it takes to ease a hurt like this. So you let her cry all she wants."

Ty nodded, his own eyes burning. Meg could cry an ocean if it would make her feel better. He only wished he could do the same.

But when Meg woke in the late afternoon, she showed no inclination to weep. After the doctor left, Ty had dragged the wing chair over next to the bed so that he'd be close. He spent some time just watching her, worrying over her pallor. She looked so small and fragile lying there. There were new hollows beneath her cheekbones and a bruised look around her eyes.

She was so young, he thought, the ever-present guilt tugging at his conscience. Too young to have known so much pain. And this time her suffering was his fault. If he'd been thinking, if he hadn't let his hunger for Meg drown out his common sense, he wouldn't have gotten her pregnant in the first place. But he had and now she was paying the price for his lack of forethought.

Now she'd lost the baby, and he couldn't shake the thought that it was his fault. If he'd brought her home sooner. Or maybe they should have stayed in California. Maybe the trip had been too much for her. If he hadn't made love to her. Or if that wasn't it, maybe he should have made sure she ate more.

He sat there, watching Meg sleep, his mind churning with possibilities—things he should have done, things he shouldn't have. Somewhere, Ty heard Doc Corey's slow voice saying that there was nothing anyone could have done, that what had happened was what was meant to be, but he couldn't stop thinking that *he* could have—should have—done something.

His thoughts twisted and turned, looking for reasons where there weren't any, handing out blame where there was none to be given. At some point, his mother came and tapped on the door, telling him to come and eat something. Ty told her that he wasn't hungry. He expected her to insist and perhaps she would have, but he heard the low rumble of his father's voice. Ty couldn't hear what he was saying but, after a moment they both went away.

It was long after dark before Meg woke. Ty had been half dozing, his head propped on the side of the chair, but he came awake abruptly. He'd turned on the lamp beside the bed, tilting the shade so that the light wouldn't shine directly on Meg's face. He ran his hand over his face, blinking the tired fog from his eyes as she stirred.

"How are you feeling?" he asked softly.

She looked at him blankly for a moment, obviously not quite awake, not yet remembering. He'd have given anything if she didn't have to remember, ever. He knew the exact instant that memory returned, saw the impact of it in her eyes, the quick flare of pain and loss.

"I'm so sorry, Meg," he whispered, feeling her pain as if it were his own, which in a way it was. He'd lost a child, too.

She closed her eyes and turned her head away, and Ty

knew that she blamed him just as he blamed himself. He deserved nothing more, but the knowledge didn't lessen the impact of her rejection. He felt the pain of it like a stiletto in his heart.

"Are you in any pain?" he asked, his tone flat, offering her the distance she so clearly wanted.

"No. I'm fine." The words were polite, emotionless. When she turned to look at him again, all the emotion had been washed from her eyes. They were dull blue, revealing nothing of what she was thinking, what she was feeling.

"Doc Corey left some pills, if you need them."

"No. Thank you. I'm all right."

If she'd screamed at him, railed against her loss, blamed him for what had happened, Ty would have known what to do. He could have offered her comfort, begged her forgiveness, promised her that they'd have other children or sworn that they'd never take the risk again. But she lay there, so self-possessed and still, looking at him with those eyes that revealed not even a whisper of her thoughts.

"Would you like something to eat?" he said finally, at a loss.

"No, thank you."

Ty reached for her hand, taking it in his own. She allowed it to lie there and he looked down at her delicate fingers, so fragile compared to his. She had to be feeling something. She'd wanted that baby. He knew she had. It couldn't be good for her to be bottling everything up inside the way she was.

"Would you like to . . . talk about things?" He lifted his eyes to her face, watching her.

"What is there to say? I lost the baby. I know you wanted it and I'm very sorry."

"You don't owe me any apologies, Meg." He was appalled that she should think she did. "I just thought you might want to talk about . . . the baby."

"There is no baby," she said flatly. Ty thought he felt her fingers tremble against his, but then she withdrew her hand, as if even that small contact was unbearable.

Ty sat there, wondering how to reach her, wondering if

she even *wanted* him to reach her. Was she hiding her pain because she thought it would upset him?

"It's all right to cry, Meg," he said quietly. He started to take her hand again, but she drew back before he touched her, rejecting the contact with quiet finality.

"I don't feel like crying," she said. Closing her eyes, she turned her head away. "I've very tired."

The only way she could have made it more clear that she wanted to be left alone was if she'd come right out and asked him to leave. Ty felt himself flush and then the heat receded, leaving him drained. He was suddenly conscious of being exhausted in a way he'd never known before, tired all the way to his soul.

"Would you . . . would you rather I slept in my sister's old room tonight?" he asked, and then waited, praying that she'd say no. If she'd just turn to him, let him hold her, let him tell her that it tore him apart to know they'd loss their baby, maybe they could heal each other.

"That might be best," Meg said without looking at him. She was staring at the wall on the other side of the bed, and Ty wondered if she hated him so much, she couldn't even bear to look at him.

"If you need me, I'm just next door," he said finally, his flat tone concealing the pain in his gut.

She nodded, still without looking at him. He hesitated, feeling as if there were something more he should say or do. Something to breach the chasm that had opened between them. The seconds ticked by so slowly that Ty could count their passing. Maybe she just needed time, he thought finally. The loss was so recent.

Reluctantly he turned and went to the door. He paused there and looked back at Meg, hoping she'd give him some sign that she didn't want him to go, that she'd allow him in to share her pain. But she kept her face turned away and, after a moment, Ty left, hoping that perhaps, once she was alone, she'd let herself cry, let herself start to heal.

* * *

But Meg didn't cry. Not that night, nor the following day, nor any of the days after that. She listened to the doctor's reassurances that she could have other children, that there was no reason not to try again as soon as she'd had time to heal. She nodded, thanked him for his time, and gave him a polite little smile that made him frown. He left, shaking his graying head.

She accepted her father-in-law's genuine sympathy politely, no more moved by it than she was by his wife's perfunctory words of regret. Meg knew her mother-in-law was just as glad that she'd lost the baby, that she saw it as one less tie binding her son to his unsuitable wife. But the knowledge didn't mean anything.

For once Meg couldn't find it in her to disagree with Ty's mother. He should never have married her. She'd disrupted his life, caused him to give up his dreams of flying, and now she couldn't even manage to keep his baby safe.

Oh, she believed Doc Corey when he said that there was nothing she could have done to prevent the miscarriage. When she thought about it, she knew she'd done everything she could have to keep the baby. Even if she'd gone to him sooner, all he'd have been able to tell her was to stay in bed, to rest as much as possible. And to pray. She'd done all those things and it hadn't been enough. Her baby was gone.

Meg mourned the child she'd never hold, but she might have been able to drag herself past that loss if she hadn't been nearly suffocated by the weight of her own failure. Ty had wanted this child, wanted it enough to give up flying, to come back here and start a new life, one he believed would be better for his son or daughter. Only now there wasn't going to be a child.

The fact that he was worried about her only made Meg feel her failure even more acutely. From the first, all she'd done was take from him. From buying her ice cream sundaes at Barnett's to marrying her to keep her safe, even to moving back to Iowa, Ty had given to her at every turn. And she'd had little enough to offer in return. Only her love, and there was no reason to think he wanted that.

But the baby—that had been different. He'd wanted the baby. And it had seemed as if this was something she could give him—a child, the start of a new family. But she hadn't been able to do even that much. Though he tried to hide it from her, Meg knew Ty was angry with her. How could he not be? He must see now what a terrible mistake he'd made in marrying her.

Chapter 20

Three days after the miscarriage, Meg was still lying in bed at almost noon. She thought vaguely that she should get up, brush her hair, perhaps go downstairs. Physically, she was certainly well enough to be up and about. But she didn't move and she didn't bother to open her eyes, not because she was tired but because there just didn't seem to be any reason to do either one. She didn't feel like reading or quilting or even looking out the window at the gray square of sky that was all she could see from the bed.

She didn't bother to open her eyes when she heard the door open. It was probably Ty, coming to check on her. Though she'd assured him that there was no need for him to stay at home on her account, he hadn't gone back to the farm since she'd lost the baby. Perhaps tomorrow, he'd said, his dark eyes worried as he looked at her. Meg found herself vaguely resenting his worry. It seemed like one more gift from him, one more debt she owed with no hope of repayment.

So now she kept her eyes closed, hoping he'd think she was asleep so that he'd go away and leave her alone.

"Meggy? Are you awake?" Patsy's voice was a whisper, too soft to disturb even a light sleeper.

For a moment, Meg considered pretending to be asleep. She didn't want to hear another word of sympathy, didn't want to hear one more person tell her that there'd be other babies, as if the child she'd lost was a broken knickknack that could be replaced. But since Patsy didn't have a car, she must have been worried to have made the effort to get someone to drive her here from Herndale. Reluctantly Meg opened her eyes.

"Patsy." Her voice came out flat and emotionless, as dead as she felt inside.

"Ty called yesterday and told me what had happened. Eldin's in Kansas this week so Jack came and got me." She crossed the room and sat down on the edge of the bed beside Meg, reaching out to take her hands. Patsy's eyes filled with quick tears. "Oh, honey, I'm so sorry about the baby."

"Thank you." Meg let her hands lie in Patsy's, not because she needed the comfort but because it wasn't worth the effort to move them. "I'm young. There'll be other babies," she said, repeating what she'd been told, offering it to her sister as if Patsy were the one who needed comforting.

"That doesn't make this one hurt any less," Patsy said fiercely. "Don't you let anyone tell you not to grieve, Meg."

"No one's told me not to grieve." Restless under her sister's questioning look, Meg drew her hands away from Patsy's and pulled herself a little higher against the pillows.

"I saw Ty downstairs," Patsy said after a moment. "He's worried about you."

"Well, he shouldn't be." Meg had herself under control again, all her emotions neatly tucked away where she didn't have to look at them. "I'm fine." She smiled to show just how fine she was.

"Oh, Meggy. No woman's fine three days after losing a baby she wanted. And saying it doesn't make it so." Patsy's voice was soft with understanding, and Meg felt a twinge of pain in her chest, so sharp it took her breath away. But she shoved it aside, determined to ignore it.

"I really am fine," she insisted in a brittle tone. "A little tired, but Doc Corey says that's normal. I'm just a little tired, that's all."

There was a short silence. Meg avoided her sister's eyes, concentrating instead on the restless movements of her fingers as they plucked at a tuft of thread in the candlewick bedspread. She wished Patsy would go away. Obviously Patsy had come prepared to offer her shoulder for crying. But Meg didn't have any tears, not for herself, not for Ty. Not even for the baby she'd lost.

Patsy would probably think she was heartless, and maybe she was. Certainly it felt as if there was an empty place where her heart had been.

"I had a baby. She died."

If Patsy had been hoping that her abrupt announcement would get her sister's attention, she succeeded. Meg's eyes jerked upward, and she was jolted out of her self-absorption by the stark pain in Patsy's face.

"I didn't know," she whispered.

"No, you wouldn't have. It was the first year Eldin and I were married."

"What happened?" This time it was Meg who reached out to take Patsy's hand.

"I don't know. I put her to bed one night and when I went to get her in the morning, she was dead." Patsy's voice was even, but her fingers gripped Meg's painfully tight. "The doctor said it was a crib death and that it just . . . happens sometimes."

"I'm sorry." There was nothing Meg could offer beyond the same hopelessly inadequate words she'd been given.

"I've learned to live with it," Patsy said with a painful smile. "I don't forget, but I learned that life goes on. No matter how sure you are that it won't, it always does. I know how much you must be hurting inside, Meggy. I don't want you to think you're alone."

Meg nodded, her eyes dropping to their linked hands. She wished she could call up a few tears, just to make Patsy feel better. But her eyes remained dry.

"When we were growing up," Patsy said, "I sometimes thought that Mama had made a mistake and that you were really the older." Meg smiled, as she was meant to. "I know I haven't always been there for you, Meggy," Patsy continued. "But I'm here now."

"I know." Meg looked at her helplessly. What was she supposed to say now?

When the silence stretched, Patsy sighed a little and patted Meg's hand. "You must be tired."

"Yes, I am." More than that, she wanted to be alone. She smiled to soften her quick agreement. "I'm glad you came."

"If you need me, you just have to call," Patsy said as she rose.

"Thank you," Meg responded politely. Patsy sighed again, her eyes reflecting a trace of hurt that Meg was helpless to erase.

"Jack said he'd like to see you, if you're up to it."

"I'm really very tired," Meg lied, unable to face the thought of more sympathy, more questioning looks. "Maybe tomorrow."

"I'll tell him." Patsy lingered a moment more, looking as if there were more she wanted to say. But she seemed to change her mind and, with another assurance that Meg had only to call, she took her leave.

Meg felt nothing but relief as the door shut behind her sister. It was nice of Patsy to be so concerned, but there was really nothing to worry about. She was fine. The blank emptiness that filled her soul was much easier to deal with than the anguish they all seemed to think she should feel. As far as she was concerned, if she never felt anything again, that would be just fine.

Jack glanced at Patsy as they left Regret. Her expression was pensive, a little sad. He found himself wanting to reach out and take her hand, to tell her that, whatever it was that made her look that way, he'd take care of it. His hand had actually started to lift from the wheel when he happened to glance down and see her wedding ring, the plain gold band seeming to glow in the weak sunlight.

He clamped his fingers around the steering wheel, his grip so tight that his knuckles whitened. She was married. Funny, how easy that was to forget. But then, wasn't it always easy to forget something you didn't want to remember?

"How is Meg, really?" he asked, needing to break the silence as much as he wanted an answer. When Patsy had come downstairs after seeing her sister, she'd told Ty that Meg was fine, that she just needed rest. But Jack had seen the worry in her eyes.

"She'll be all right," Patsy said, her tone forceful, as if she could will Meg's recovery.

"Ty says she hasn't cried. Seems odd, considering how much she wanted that baby."

"Some hurts go too deep for tears," Patsy said quietly.

Just what was it that had hurt her too deep for tears? Jack wondered, looking at her profile. Five years ago he would have asked, but things had changed.

"It's tough, her losing the baby like that," he said. "I know she and Ty were both looking forward to being parents."

"I don't think there's anything quite like the pain of losing a child," she said softly, speaking more to herself than to him.

"You sound like you're speaking from experience," he said slowly.

Patsy blinked and glanced at him as if just now realizing whom she was talking to. Color ran up under her skin and she lifted one shoulder in a half shrug.

"I'm just speaking as a woman," she said, sounding casual.

Too casual? The most incredible idea had begun to form in his head. It was based on nothing more than intuition and perhaps on the need, even after five years, to have some explanation for the woman he'd loved choosing to marry another man. Hardly aware of what he was doing, Jack pulled the Packard to the side of the road, shutting off the engine, half turning in his seat so that he faced her.

"I really need to get home," Patsy said, looking uneasy.

"Five years ago we were sleeping together," he said slowly, working out the possibilities in his head even as he spoke.

At his blunt statement, Patsy flushed and then paled. Her mouth compressed into a thin line. "I don't think there's anything to be gained by discussing the past, Jack. I'm married now and . . ."

"I took my mother and sister to Europe to give them a chance to get over my father's death," he said, barely aware that he'd interrupted her. "You said you'd wait for me."

"Jack, I don't . . ."

"You said you'd wait forever, if necessary. But I'd been gone only a few weeks when Beryl's friend wrote and mentioned that you'd married someone else. Beryl read me the letter so I could hear what was happening at home. She didn't even know that I knew you."

His first reaction had been disbelief. It couldn't be Patsy Harper she was talking about. Not *his* Patsy. For a few crazy minutes he'd almost managed to convince himself that there was another Patsy Harper who lived in Regret, Iowa. The Patsy he knew had said she loved him more than life itself. That girl wouldn't have married someone he'd never even heard of.

"Jack, I'm sorry." Patsy reached out, her fingertips brushing his hand where it lay along the back of the seat, her eyes full of regret. "I never meant to hurt you."

"Didn't you?" The question was sharp with remembered pain.

"Of course not. I loved you. The last thing in the world I wanted was to hurt you."

"I was barely out of sight when you married someone else," he said, the words less an accusation than an observation.

"I . . ." Patsy's fingers knotted together in her lap. She looked away from him, staring out the windshield. "I don't see any point in discussing this now. It all happened a long time ago."

"I never could figure out why you'd marry someone else," Jack said, as if she hadn't spoken. "It just didn't make any sense."

"Jack . . ."

"Unless there was a reason you needed to get married in a hurry," he continued slowly.

"Jack, please."

"A reason like finding out you were pregnant and the baby's father was half a world away."

Jack stopped and waited for her denial, waited to hear her tell him he was making something out of nothing. Even if he didn't believe it, he wanted to hear her say he was wrong. But the seconds ticked by and she said nothing, only continued to stare out the windshield, her body rigid, her skin nearly as white as the collar on her dress.

"My God." The words were a breath, as much prayer as profanity. What had been wild speculation was slowly sinking in as the truth. "My God. You *were* pregnant, weren't you?"

He saw her throat work as she swallowed, but that small movement was the only evidence that she'd heard him; that she wasn't a statue but a living, breathing woman. A woman who'd betrayed him in a way he'd never have believed possible.

"What happened?" he asked hoarsely. "Where's the baby?"

When she didn't respond, he reached out and grabbed her shoulders, jerking her around to face him, uncaring that his grip was bruisingly hard.

"Tell me, damn you!"

"She died." The words were stark, flat, without emotion. Yet they carried the impact of a knife thrust. Jack released her as if her skin had suddenly become red hot.

"What happened?"

"It was a crib death," she said, still in that unemotional tone. "The doctor said it just happens sometimes. No one knows why."

"How . . . how old was she?"

"Three months."

"What was her name?"

"Sara. She looked like you." The words seemed almost involuntary, as if she was surprised to hear herself saying them.

Sara. Jack stared past Patsy at the field that edged up against the road. He couldn't absorb what she'd told him. He'd had a daughter. Her name had been Sara and she'd lived for three months and then died without him ever knowing of her existence.

"Why didn't you tell me?" he asked, bringing his eyes back to her face. The anger was gone now, leaving bewilderment in its place. "Why did you marry someone else?"

"Because he was a good man and he cared for me."

"I *loved* you," he said.

She flinched as if the words were tiny darts. "You were gone and Eldin was here. I'd met him when I was working at Rosie's. He was . . . kind."

"Did he know when he married you? About the baby? About . . . about Sara?" The name sounded odd on his tongue.

"He knew. He said it didn't matter." Patsy lifted her chin. "He loved her as if she were his own."

"But she wasn't, was she? She was mine. And I never even knew she existed. My God, Patsy, how could you keep something like that from me? Did you think I wouldn't marry you?"

"No. I knew you'd marry me."

"Then why?" he asked, struggling to understand.

"Oh, Jack, it wouldn't have worked. *We* wouldn't have worked. We were from two different worlds. There were so many things . . ." She shook her head and Jack saw the sheen of tears in her eyes. "You'd have ended up hating me."

"You didn't even give us a chance to try," he said, half hurt, half angry. "You simply decided it wouldn't work and married someone else. Didn't you think I had a right to know I was going to be a father? Dammit, Patsy, how do you think I feel, knowing she died without me ever even seeing her?"

"I never intended for you to know."

"And what I didn't know wouldn't hurt me? Is that it?" he asked bitterly.

"The last thing I wanted to do was hurt you," she said.

"Well, you did a hell of a job of it for someone who wasn't even trying."

He saw her wince at the savagery of his tone, but he didn't try to soften his anger. She'd had no right to make the choices she had. No right to shut him out, to keep him from his child. Unable to bear to look at her a moment longer, Jack started the car again and pulled out onto the road.

The drive to Patsy's house was completed in silence. Jack could think of nothing to say to her, nothing that could express his anger, his hurt, his grief over the child he'd never had a chance to know. It was a betrayal even deeper than her marriage, one he didn't know if he could get past.

He pulled the car up in front of her house and pushed open his door before the sound of the engine had died. He strode around the front of the car and opened her door for her, but he didn't offer his hand. Right now he couldn't bear to touch her. She stepped out of the car but didn't move toward the house. Instead she stood looking up at him.

The pale sunlight found gold highlights in the soft brown cap of her hair and illuminated the porcelain clarity of her skin. Despite his anger, Jack couldn't stop himself from noticing how beautiful she was. No other woman had ever affected him the way this one did. In five years, he hadn't been able to forget her. There was more than a touch of despair in the thought.

"I did what I thought was right, Jack," she said quietly.

"You made choices you had no right to make—choices for me." But the anger was gone.

"I'm sorry I hurt you."

"Five years too late," he said with a kind of weary acceptance.

He saw tears start to her eyes, but it was beyond him to offer her comfort. His own pain was too raw, too new.

"I'm sorry," she said again.

"So am I."

Patsy waited a moment longer, as if hoping he'd say something more, but he just continued to look at her, his eyes bleak. She turned away and started toward her house. But she'd only gone a short distance when she stopped. Her back still to him, she spoke.

"Will I . . . will I see you again?"

Jack could hear what the question cost her. He wanted to

tell her no. He wanted to walk away and never see her again. To put her from his life once and for all.

He wanted to go to her and take her in his arms, to beg her to tell him how she could have kept his child from him, how she could have married someone else, how she could have broken his heart in so many pieces that he doubted it could ever be repaired.

"I don't know," he said finally.

She hesitated a moment longer and then nodded, accepting his answer. He watched her with a hunger he resented but couldn't deny as she continued up the short walk and into the house. She closed the door without looking back. Only then did he go back around the car and slide behind the wheel.

She'd lied to him. She'd kept him from his child. She was married to another man. But he knew he'd be back. God help him, he couldn't stay away.

Meg attended church, as usual, the second week after her miscarriage. Since returning to Iowa, she and Ty had gone to church with his parents every Sunday. Her own family hadn't been much for churchgoing—her father having been violently opposed to hearing sermons about the evils of liquor. After her mother married Harlan Davis, they'd begun to attend church on a more regular basis, and Meg had always been secretly amused by the pained look on her stepfather's face whenever the collection plate had been passed around.

But since her marriage, Meg actually enjoyed the time spent in the little church. She could snuggle her arm against Ty's and count her many blessings while the pastor preached hopefully of better times being just ahead.

This week she'd just as soon have stayed home. Though she knew there were those who'd say such thinking was a sin, Meg didn't feel as if she had very much to thank the Lord for. She'd lost her baby and, with it, her last hope that Ty would come to love her. How could he love her when she couldn't even be trusted to keep his child safe?

No, she wasn't much in the mood for church. But staying home would have created a fuss. Her mother-in-law would have muttered about her poor upbringing and what other people would say about her son marrying a girl who couldn't even be bothered to attend church, like a decent, God-fearing citizen.

Meg could have turned a deaf ear to the other woman's complaints. But she couldn't ignore the concern in Ty's gaze. If she said she didn't feel like going, he'd probably want her to see Doc Corey again. And Doc Corey would come out and look at her and tell her it was time to get on with her life. And she'd nod, even as she wondered how she was supposed to go about getting on with her life when she felt so completely dead inside, when she couldn't even bear to look at Ty without nearly drowning in guilt.

So, when Ty asked if she felt up to leaving the house, Meg lied and said it sounded like a fine idea. She knew she'd made the right decision when she saw the relief in his eyes.

He was solicitous of her, holding her arm as they walked up the few steps to the church, as if he thought she might slip on the perfectly dry ground. Meg found herself resenting his concern, resenting his kindness. She knew he must be angry with her, must blame her for the miscarriage, yet he treated her as if she were one of his mother's precious figurines—fragile, helpless. Useless.

Meg paid little attention to the sermon. She sat stiffly upright in the pew, her hands neatly folded together in her lap, her eyes on the pastor, and wished for nothing more than to be somewhere else

If the future of Ty's immortal soul had depended on his attentiveness to the sermon that day, he would have been in trouble. His attention was more for his wife than for the pastor's talk of the Lord's goodness. To tell the truth, at the moment he wasn't in the best of charities with the Lord. Not when Meg was sitting next to him like a statue and holding just about as much life.

In the almost two weeks since the miscarriage, he hadn't seen more than a flicker of emotion from her. He knew that she mourned the loss of the baby, knew she'd wanted it as much as he had. But she hadn't cried, not in front of him, anyway. And he was willing to bet that she hadn't shed any tears when she was alone, either.

Ty glanced at her, wondering what was going on behind the still mask of her face. She must have sensed him looking at her, because she turned her head. Their eyes met for an instant before she glanced away, leaving Ty with the impression of empty blue pools that revealed nothing of what she was thinking, feeling. As if the Meg he knew had gone away, leaving a hollow shell behind.

After the sermon, the worshipers slowly filed out, pausing to talk with the pastor before drifting out into the sunshine that bathed the grassy area in front of the church. Once outside, Ty drew a deep breath and reached up to loosen his tie. It seemed as if spring had finally managed to elbow aside winter's chill.

He glanced at Meg to see if she felt the warm promise in the air, the soft renewal of life to come. But she gave no sign of noticing a difference. She walked beside him, her gloved hands neatly clasped in front of her, her face half shadowed by the brim of her hat. He doubted she'd have noticed anything less than a marching band stopped directly in their path.

He started to make some comment about the weather but he felt Meg stiffen. Her hand came up to take hold of his arm, her fingers tense against his sleeve. It was the first time she'd voluntarily touched him since the miscarriage, and Ty might have taken it as a positive sign if he hadn't followed the direction of her gaze.

Harlan Davis stood just ahead of them. It was the first time Ty had seen him since their return to Iowa, and he was half surprised by the rage that swept through him just at the sight of the other man. Looking at that round face, with its small, pale eyes, Ty had a sudden flash of memory—Meg, shivering with cold and fear, the marks of her stepfather's brutality starkly visible on her pale skin, her eyes dazed with shock. Now, as then, Ty felt an overwhelming urge to feel the other man's bones crunch beneath the impact of his fists.

So focused was he on Harlan that it was a moment before Ty noticed Ruth Davis standing next to her husband. Her eyes, a washed-out version of her daughter's, were fixed anxiously on Meg. It was obvious she longed to speak to Meg, equally obvious that she would not make the first move, whether out of concern for Meg's feelings or out of fear of her husband, Ty neither knew nor cared. His only concern was for Meg.

To get to the car, which was where they'd been going, they'd have to walk right past the Davises. He slowed his pace, aware that half the town of Regret was within view. No one appeared to be paying them any attention, but one of the inexorable facts of small-town life was that someone was always paying attention. If he and Meg walked past her family without speaking, there'd be gossip burning up the party lines by nightfall. And as his mother was so fond of pointing out, his marriage to Meg had already caused more than enough speculation. For himself, he couldn't have cared less what people said, but he didn't want Meg to be the subject of any more gossip.

Trying to look casual, he glanced over his shoulder to where his parents stood talking to Edwina Vanderbilt and several other of their friends. He put his hand over Meg's and started to turn her in that direction. They were still far enough from the Davises that it would look as if their paths just hadn't crossed.

But it was too late. Apparently Harlan did not share Ty's reluctance for a meeting. He may have thought that his all-important good name would suffer at even a hint that his step-daughter and her new husband were avoiding him. He hurried forward, pulling Ruth with him as he stepped directly into Ty and Meg's path.

Ty felt Meg's fingers tremble under his. To hell with gossip. He wasn't going to subject Meg to exchanging polite greeting with the man who'd tried to rape her. He started to walk around them, but Meg tugged on his sleeve, stopping him.

"It's all right," she said quietly.

"You don't have to talk to him," Ty said in a low voice that failed to hide his anger.

"It doesn't matter."

The hell it didn't. But they were now standing directly in front of the other couple, and short of making a scene, there was no way to avoid exchanging greetings.

"Hello, Mama." Meg's voice was steady, but Ty could feel the tension in her fingers. He'd wanted her to come out of her shell, but this was hardly what he'd had in mind.

"Meg," Ruth whispered. Her eyes darted to her son-in-law. "Tyler."

"Mrs. Davis." Ty's greeting was terse but not hostile. No one spoke to Harlan. Out the corner of his eye, Ty saw the other man flush at being so pointedly ignored.

"How are you, Mama?" Meg asked quietly.

"I'm fine." Ruth was gripping her handbag so tightly that her knuckles showed white beneath the skin. "I—I heard that you'd lost the baby. I'm sorry, Meg."

"I'm young. There'll be other babies," Meg said, parroting what she'd been told, in a flat, emotionless little voice.

Ruth frowned and started to say something, but Harlan spoke first.

"The sins of the parents are often visited on the child," he said in a sharp, carrying voice. "Even on the unborn child," he added self-righteously.

Perhaps he was counting on Ty's natural, civilized desire to avoid a scene. Or that, with so many people around, he could say what he pleased without fear of repercussions. He may even have believed what he said and thought that the truth would protect him. Whatever his thinking, Ty proved him wrong on all counts.

As if watching from outside himself, Ty saw his left hand come out, his fingers closing on the front of Harlan's neatly pressed white shirt. He saw the shock in the smaller man's face, heard Meg say his name, whether in protest or encouragement he couldn't have said. And then his right fist connected with Davis's nose, feeling the satisfactory crunch of breaking cartilage.

The impact of the punch was like a stone falling into a pond. Silence rippled around them in little waves as the churchyard became dead silent, and all eyes turned to the tableau of the four of them. Everyone seemed frozen in place. Then Harlan cried out, one hand coming up to cup his nose, staggering a little as Ty released his hold on his shirt and the spell was broken. Suddenly there was a babble of voices, exclamations, cries of shock.

"You broke my nose!" Harlan wailed, groping for a handkerchief to stem the flow of blood that dripped onto his pristine shirtfront.

Ty leaned close, taking a savage pleasure in the way the other man's eyes widened over the handkerchief, his cheeks blanching.

"Next time I'll break your miserable neck. I told you once to stay away from Meg. I won't tell you again." His tone was quiet but left no doubt as to his sincerity.

"What have you done?" That was his mother's voice, a quiet wail of horror from behind him.

Assured that Harlan had taken his warning to heart, Ty deliberately turned his back to the older man, dismissing him with unmistakable contempt. He reached out, taking Meg's hand and setting it on his arm, feeling the trembling of her fingers. But there was no time to reassure her, not with his mother standing before them like the wrath of God personified.

"Have you gone mad?" she demanded, careful to keep her voice low. Aware of watching eyes, she arranged her face in a tight little smile, though Ty couldn't imagine how she could think that a smile would help to smooth over the scene he'd just caused. "You just hit your father-in-law."

"Yes, I know." *And it had felt damned good.* But he could hardly say as much. He put his hand over Meg's where it rested on his arm. She was taut as a bowstring and he could sense that she was near the breaking point. "I think it might be best if we went home now."

"Now? Now?" If a whisper could be a shriek, then Helen McKendrick managed it. "Why couldn't you have decided that five minutes ago? Before you hit someone right here in the churchyard." She caught a movement out the corner of her eyes and moaned softly. "And Edwina Vanderbilt watching."

Ty wasn't sure which upset her more, the possibility that

God might be watching or the fact that Edwina Vanderbilt definitely had been.

"I think it's time we left." That was Elliot McKendrick, as always the voice of calm reason. "We've provided enough entertainment for one day, don't you think?"

Helen nodded weakly and took her husband's arm. "I don't know how I'm going to explain this to my friends," she said, moaning softly as the four of them made their way to the car, the ripples of speculation and gossip already cresting behind them.

Ty knew he should feel regretful about having caused a scene. But all he could think of was that slamming his fist into Harlan Davis's pale face was the most satisfying thing he'd done in a long time.

Chapter 21

Though she'd disapproved of Meg's pregnancy, the miscarriage, in some perverse way, served to confirm Helen McKendrick's opinion of Meg's unworthiness. Her sympathy was perfunctory, at best, offered because it would have been ill-mannered to do otherwise. As far as she was concerned, the blame for the miscarriage could be laid firmly at Meg's door. Meg had failed in the most basic of feminine duties, and that failure deserved neither sympathy nor compassion.

Now, surely, Ty must see what a terrible mistake he'd made and could be persuaded to rectify the situation. Ordinarily she didn't approve of divorce, but there were exceptions to every rule. She had no desire to see her son waste his life digging in the dirt just because he'd had the poor judgment to marry Meg Harper.

But she knew that Ty's sense of honor and responsibility would never allow him to suggest a divorce, no matter how unhappy he was. So the suggestion would have to come from Meg. Helen considered it her maternal duty to help her along in making that choice. The scene in the churchyard only served to strengthen her determination.

* * *

"I don't know what I'm supposed to tell people," Helen said plaintively.

Meg looked up from where she knelt on the floor, partway through rolling up the living room rug, preparatory to dragging it outside to be thrown over the clothesline so that the dust could be beaten from it. Her mother-in-law had decreed that spring cleaning was to begin immediately, and, faced with the daunting amount of physical labor that went into the job, she'd deigned to allow Meg to help.

"Tell people about what?" Meg asked.

"About what?" Her mother-in-law's voice rose on an incredulous note and she turned to stare at Meg. "About that terrible scene at church yesterday. That's about what!"

"Oh." Of course that's what she was talking about. Meg brushed back a loose strand of hair and bent down to push the rug another half turn.

"Oh? Is that all you have to say?" Helen demanded. "The most humiliating moment of my life and all you can say is 'Oh'?"

Meg didn't really see why the other woman should feel humiliated over a scene in which she hadn't even participated, but there was no reason to point that out.

"I'm sorry," she offered, hoping that was the desired response. It wasn't.

"Sorry?" Helen sniffed. "I suppose I should have expected no better. Someone from your background could hardly be expected to understand how mortifying a scene like that is to people raised in a more refined atmosphere."

There didn't seem to be any appropriate response so Meg said nothing, concentrating instead on rolling the rug a little farther. It was starting to get heavy and took considerable effort to turn it. It would have been a lot easier with two people, but though her mother-in-law wore a floral-patterned smock donned to protect her neat housedress, she showed no inclination to get the garment dirty.

"You're probably accustomed to scenes of that sort." Helen picked up a china figurine and stroked a dust rag over it, her expression pensive. "I've always thought it a terrible mistake for a person to marry out of his or her class," she said thoughtfully, seeming to be speaking to the china shepherdess in her hand. "It's so difficult for both parties. The woman struggling to live up to standards she simply cannot understand. And it does seem as if it's always a woman who marries above herself, doesn't it?"

She didn't seem to expect a response, which was just as well, because Meg couldn't think of one.

"And the husband trying to make the best of things, although he soon realizes what a mistake he's made. And, of course, it's even worse when he's married her out of pity. A man is so much at the mercy of his sense of honor, don't you think?"

"I don't know," Meg said, when the pause lengthened and it became obvious that the other woman was waiting for a reply. She shoved the rug away from her, her nose itching from the dust that rose from it.

"No, perhaps you wouldn't, coming from the kind of background you do," Helen said with a sigh.

Meg had never really never thought of a sense of honor as being confined to any particular class, but apparently her mother-in-law disagreed.

"Tyler's always had a very strong sense of honor." Helen's tone indicated that she thought it might be a bit *too* strong. "After his older brother died, he tried so hard to take his place. Not that anyone could take the place of my beloved Dickey, of course. But he's always tried so hard to please me."

Meg wondered where Ty leaving college to become a flyer fit in with always pleasing his mother, but she didn't say anything.

"And compassion. He's always had a great deal of compassion. I can't tell you how many stray animals I had to get rid of after he'd brought them home." She paused and then heaved another sigh. "I thought maybe he'd outgrow that habit once he got older."

Meg felt her mother-in-law's eyes on her, but she didn't look up. With a final heave, she finished rolling the rug. She stood up and dusted off her hands.

"I'll go wash my hands and then get started on taking down the curtains," she said. She saw frustration flash across her mother-in-law's face. Obviously Helen had been hoping for some response to her not-so-subtle barbs. *If only she'd known that she was preaching to the converted,* Meg thought as she turned and left the room.

There wasn't anything Ty's mother could say that Meg hadn't already said to herself. That she'd ruined Ty's life, that she should never have married him, that he regretted their marriage. She'd thought all those things and was more than half convinced they were all true. The final one, at least, she knew was accurate: Ty did regret marrying her.

He hadn't said anything to her, but then, he wouldn't. His mother was right about that—he did have a strong sense of honor and of responsibility. Hadn't he proved it again and again? He'd married her out of a sense of responsibility. No matter how much of a failure as a wife she'd proved to be, he still felt responsible for her.

Instead of washing her hands in the kitchen, Meg climbed the stairs to the bathroom she shared with Ty, wanting at least the illusion of privacy. After turning on the faucets, she thrust her hands under the tepid flow and stared at her reflection in the small mirror above the sink. It was not an appealing picture. A young woman whose eyes seemed too large for her pale face. Her hair was dragged back and pinned into a bun at the back of her head. Looking at it in the light that filtered through the cotton curtain, Meg thought that it seemed as if all the gold had faded from her hair, leaving it a dull brown, as drained of life as she felt.

She sighed. No wonder Ty chose to sleep in his sister's old room rather than share a bed with his wife. Even if he was able to forgive her for losing the baby, there was nothing about her to make him want to touch her, to hold her.

Maybe if she wore her hair down, perhaps put on a little rouge to add color to her face, and a pretty dress . . . Meg's shoulders, which had begun to straighten, slumped again. There was no sense in lying to herself. Ty didn't want her and the reasons went deeper than rouge and a pretty dress. He didn't want her because, deep down, he couldn't forgive her for losing his baby. She understood that because she couldn't even begin to forgive herself.

Meg turned off the taps and shook her hands to dry them a little before reaching for a towel. She supposed that, before too long, she would have to find a way to release Ty. She couldn't just ask him for a divorce, because he wouldn't give it to her unless he was sure she had something else to go to—a job perhaps. She should start trying to find something, try to make some kind of arrangements . . .

She sank down on the edge of the tub, struggling against an almost suffocating wave of depression. It was too soon, she thought shakily. She couldn't think about leaving Ty—not so soon after losing the baby. Even if he was already lost to her, she needed to hold on just a little while longer, just until she found some way to fill the terrible emptiness inside. She just needed a little time.

"Why don't you come out to the farm with me today?" Ty was standing in front of the dresser, and he watched Meg's reflection in the mirror. "The weather's nice. You could take a look at the place, see what work we've done so far. Maybe we could take a picnic. The apple tree's starting to bloom."

He wondered if she'd think of their last picnic out at the farm. That had been the first time he'd kissed her, the first time he'd realized just how much he wanted her. He wanted her now, he thought, watching her reflection as she made the bed. The bed where she slept alone each night.

They hadn't shared a bed in over a month—not since the miscarriage. His offer to sleep in his sister's room had drifted on long past the one or two nights he'd originally envisioned. He kept thinking that all he had to do was move back into their bedroom. And then he'd look at Meg, see the careful emptiness in her eyes, and he'd be overwhelmed with guilt, remembering the pain she'd suffered.

So he'd continued to sleep in Louise's narrow bed, not sure if he was a fool or simply doing the decent thing. But he'd kept his clothes in the room they'd shared. It was inconvenient as hell, but at least it kept a link between the two of them, even if it was tenuous.

"How about it? You feel like driving out to the farm?"

"I don't know." Meg straightened away from the bed and lifted her hands to pull her hair back from her face. The movement thrust her breasts against the front of her cotton robe, and Ty felt his body tighten in response. He swallowed hard and looked away, feeling guilty.

"It would do you good to get out," he said, reaching for his wallet and thrusting it into his pocket.

"I don't think so," she said slowly. She let her hands drop to her sides as he turned to look at her.

"Why not?" He thought she looked started at the question. They'd already exchanged more conversation than they had in weeks. It wasn't the first time he'd suggested that she come out to the farm. Each time she'd refused, and he'd accepted that refusal without question.

"I don't really feel up to it," she said, her eyes sliding away from his.

"Doc Corey gave you a clean bill of health, didn't he?" Ty couldn't have said just what it was that was making him persist this time. Maybe it was the feeling that she was slipping farther and farther away from him.

"Yes, but I really have other things to do today."

"Like what?"

"I . . . Well, I should help your mother . . ."

"I'm sure she could manage for a day without you." Anger was starting to throb in his temples, but Ty couldn't have said just whom the anger was directed toward—Meg, for her stubborn refusal to get on with life; himself, for being the cause of her withdrawal; or fate, for creating the situation they were now in.

"I'd just be in the way," she said with a quick smile that didn't even come close to her eyes.

Ty looked at her a moment longer and then lifted his shoulders in a quick shrug. "I won't drag you."

He picked up the car keys and walked to the door but he stopped before opening it. Dammit, they couldn't go on like this forever. He spun back toward her, struggling to control the unreasoning anger that made him want to put his fist through a wall.

"Life keeps moving, Meg. It doesn't stop just because you wish it would."

"I—I don't wish it would," she stammered.

"You have to keep going," he said, ignoring her protest. "Hiding in this room isn't going to change what happened."

Without waiting for her response, he turned and left, the door closing behind him with a distinct snap. Frustration carried him down the stairs and out the front door, dismissing his mother's question about breakfast with a curt "I'm not hungry."

The frustrated anger lingered throughout the day, leading him to attack the jobs at hand with a ferocity that raised Jack's eyebrows, though he didn't comment but only matched Ty's pace, perhaps working out some frustrations of his own.

By the end of the day, Ty was physically tired, but he hadn't managed to do more than soften the edge on his mood. The sun was starting to set and the light was nearly gone, but he didn't feel like going home. He didn't want to see Meg look at him with all the light gone from her eyes. He wanted her to shout at him, to tell him she hated him. If she'd just give him something solid to fight . . .

"Ouch!" He'd been hammering a nail into the side of the barn, repairing a loose board. In the poor light, he'd misjudged and the hammer caught his thumb a glancing blow.

"A very wise man once told me that you should never use a hammer in the dark," Jack said from behind him.

Scowling, Ty turned to see his friend leaning against a fence post. "It's not dark," he snapped, nursing his aching thumb. "I thought you went home."

"I came back." Jack straightened away from the fence and walked over to where Ty was standing. Throwing one arm around his shoulders, he pulled him away from the barn. "It occurred to me that we've put in a ridiculous amount of work on this place without once stopping to celebrate our progress."

"I don't feel much like celebrating tonight, Jack," Ty protested wearily.

"All the more reason to do so."

The logic in that reasoning escaped Ty, but before he could say as much, they'd reached the newly repaired front porch. Sitting there, the amber liquid catching the last of the light, was a bottle of whiskey and two glasses. And Ty suddenly realized that what he wanted, more than anything in the world, was to get roaring drunk.

"Jack, you are a true friend." Ty sank onto the top step, feeling an ache that went deeper than sore muscles. Jack sank down next to him, watching as Ty twisted open the bottle and poured a generous serving into each glass.

"To true friends," Ty said, grinning as he lifted the glass.

He waited to see Jack lift his glass in return and then took a hefty swallow, feeling the liquor burn its way down his throat.

"Damn!" He looked at Jack through watering eyes. "What did you do, piss in a bottle of kerosene? This stuff is godawful."

"Best I could find on short notice." Jack shrugged and then lifted his glass again, his grin taking on a bitter twist. "To women. Who the hell needs them?"

Without waiting for a response, Jack downed the remaining contents of his glass, barely wincing at taste of the whiskey. Ty swirled his own drink in his hand. *Who needed women?* He wasn't sure he *needed* Meg exactly. But he couldn't just dismiss her, either.

At the sound of a bottle clinking against glass, he turned to watch Jack pour himself a second drink. In the last gray light of dusk, Jack's face was grim. It was an expression Ty had seen a lot these past few weeks. Since Meg's miscarriage when Jack had brought her sister to see her. Ever since then, there'd been something riding Jack. Ty had been too occupied with his ownproblems to pay much attention and he felt a sudden twinge of guilt.

"You want to talk about it?"

"No." Jack didn't look up from the glass he was nursing between his hands. "I want to get drunk."

"Sounds like a fine idea." Ty lifted his glass and took another drink. Perhaps the first swallow had served to numb his throat, because the second one didn't burn nearly as much going down. And the third tasted almost good. He smiled as he drained his glass, feeling the whiskey settle in a pleasantly warm pool in the pit of his stomach, driving out the chill that he'd lived with for so long.

Meg glanced at the clock for the third time in as many minutes. It seemed as if the hands were crawling around the face. Past ten o'clock and still no sign of Ty. He sometimes worked after dark, but he'd never worked this late before.

When he hadn't shown up in time for dinner, his mother had put his meal on a plate and left it in the oven. Her comment that it was hardly any wonder that he didn't want to come home had been accompanied by a pointed look in Meg's direction that made Meg wonder if her mother-in-law had overheard any of their quarrel this morning.

If it had *been* a quarrel. She wasn't sure that was the right word for it. Ty's anger seemed to have been directed at himself as much at her. He'd looked almost . . . hurt. As if she might have hurt him. That thought had been in her mind all day, unsettling her, nibbling at the wall she'd so carefully built around her emotions, weakening it.

Meg didn't want that wall weakened. She'd spent the past few weeks trying hard not to feel anything, starting with the pain of losing her baby. The realization that she'd also lost her husband had sent her scurrying to build the wall higher, making it easier for her to cower behind it, eyes closed, her hands clamped over her ears.

But the scene with Ty this morning had shown her that she couldn't hide forever. It wasn't fair to him. Life went on, he'd said. She couldn't imagine what kind of a life she'd have without him, but she'd been selfish long enough. It was time to let him go, even if it tore her heart out to do it.

Meg looked at the clock again, feeling her heart bump

with worry. Where was he? What if something had happened to him? What if there'd been an accident? Jack had been working with him, she reminded herself. He'd have gotten Ty to Doc Corey's. Then it occurred to her that Jack might not have been at the farm today. Or maybe they'd *both* been hurt in the same accident.

Before Meg's imagination could run completely wild and present her with ever more terrible possibilities, she heard the distinctive sound of the roadster's engine as it pulled up in front of the house and stopped. He was home! She was out of her chair in an instant, the book she'd been trying to read thumping unnoticed to the floor.

After yanking open the bedroom door, she hurried down the stairs. The front door opened as Meg reached the bottom of the stairs and she stopped, one hand pressed to her heart, holding her breath, half afraid of seeing some terrible injury, too caught up in her fear to realize that Ty would hardly be driving himself home if he was terribly injured.

But there was not a bandage in sight. From what she could see in the dimly lit entryway, he looked perfectly healthy. Unaware of her presence, he shut the door behind him and shrugged out of his jacket, hanging it on the coat rack in the corner. It wasn't until he turned toward the stairs that he saw Meg standing there, her white nightgown very visible in the darkness.

"Hello." He stopped abruptly, swaying just a little.

"Where have you been?" she demanded, all her worry turning into quick anger.

"At the farm." He spoke slowly, as if the words took some concentration. "With Jack," he added, in case that was important.

Meg stepped off the last stair and moved toward him, her nose wrinkling when she got close enough to smell the whiskey.

"You're drunk!" She was horrified.

"Not nearly as much as I'd like to be." There was an edge to his voice that might have given her pause at another time. But she was too busy absorbing the shock of seeing him drunk to register anything beyond that.

"You don't drink," she protested foolishly.

"Not often."

And not enough, he thought, looking down at her. If he'd had enough to drink, then maybe he wouldn't notice how softly appealing she looked in that plain white nightgown. He thought of telling her as much, but from the way she was starting to frown, he didn't think she'd appreciate the compliment.

"Good night, Meg." With a sigh, he stepped around her and started up the stairs. But he'd only reached the third step when his head started to spin. He grabbed for the railing as the world tilted. That would teach him to drink on an empty stomach, he thought. Then Meg was beside him, taking his arm and putting it over her shoulder.

"Hang on to me," she said sharply.

"If you insist." Though the dizziness was gone, Ty had no objection to keeping his arm around his wife. His very pretty wife. She was even pretty when she was scowling, the way she was now. "I could have made it on my own," he felt obliged to point out as they neared the top of the stairs.

"You'd most likely have fallen and broken your fool neck," she snapped, sounding angry.

Ty couldn't ever remember seeing Meg angry. Lately, of course, he hadn't seen any real emotion from her at all. But even before the miscarriage, he didn't think he'd ever seen her angry. He might have given some thought to the significance of this piece of information if they hadn't reached the top of the stairs and come face-to-face with his mother.

"Where have you been?" she demanded furiously, her attention all for Ty.

"I've been at the farm. With Jack." Hadn't he answered this question once already?

"Tyler Douglas McKendrick, you've been drinking!" She sounded, if possible, even more offended than Meg had.

"Yes." He smiled at her. "Rather a lot. But not as much

as Jack. Jack's sleeping in the barn tonight. I thought about sleeping in the barn, too, but the hay was scratchy so I came home.''

"You should get to bed at once. I'll take care of this," Helen said, acknowledging Meg's presence for the first time. She gave Meg a regal nod and reached for Ty's arm, but Meg shook her head.

"I'll get him to bed."

"I'm his mother," Helen began, her cheeks flushing with annoyance.

"I'm his wife."

Ty thought of pointing out that he was more than capable of putting himself to bed. Despite his early determination to get roaring drunk, he'd soon discovered that he had little taste for actually doing so. He'd stopped after a few drinks, and then watched while Jack systematically drank himself into a stupor. He'd put his best friend to bed in the barn, almost envious of the oblivion he'd managed to achieve. Other than a mild buzzing in his ears and a pleasant who-gives-a-damn feeling, he was quite sober.

"Considering the state of affairs between the two of you," his mother was saying, "I think Tyler would prefer—"

"We are still married," Meg said firmly.

"We'll see how long that lasts," Helen snapped.

Ty frowned but before he could say anything, his father's quiet voice came from his parents' bedroom. "Come back to bed, Helen."

She hesitated a moment, her mouth pulled tight with anger. She looked at her daughter-in-law, but there was no give in Meg's steady gaze. With an annoyed huff, Helen spun away and stalked down the hall. The door closed behind her with a quiet *click* that spoke volumes.

Ty's arm still rested on Meg's shoulder and he felt a slight tremor go through her, as if she'd just narrowly escaped some danger. His frown deepened. Just what had been going on between her and his mother? She'd said they were getting along, but the scene he'd just witnessed didn't look like "getting along."

"Let's get you to bed."

All speculation about her relationship with his mother vanished from Ty's thoughts as she turned not toward his sister's old room but toward their bedroom, where she'd been sleeping alone these past few weeks.

He allowed her to guide him into the room and sit him on the edge of the bed. She knelt at his feet and began unlacing the heavy work boots, tugging at the laces with quick, angry movements. Ty watched her, noticing the way her hair spilled onto her shoulders and swung forward to conceal her face. It was like a fall of golden silk in the lamplight, and he reached out to touch it.

"Don't!" She jerked away from his fingers as if scalded.

The rejection was so immediate, so complete that it felt as if he'd just been kicked in the gut. His hand dropped against his thigh, the fingers curling into a fist.

"I'm sorry," he said dully. God, he should have had more to drink.

"Sorry." She snorted her contempt of the word as she yanked off first one boot and then the other, tossing them toward the foot of the bed. She stood up but she didn't move away from him as he'd expected. Instead she planted her hands on her hips and looked down at him.

"Do you know what time it is? I thought you'd been hurt. Killed, even. And then you come home, drunker than a waltzing pissant and not hurt at all."

Her tone made it difficult to determine whether she was most angry because he was drunk or because he wasn't hurt. And what the devil did she care, anyway? Ty thought, feeling his own anger stir to life. She'd made it abundantly clear that she didn't want anything to do with him.

"Next time I'm late, I'll try to make sure it's because I've broken a major bone," he said with heavy sarcasm.

"Better that than drunk," she shot back.

He stood up, deliberately using his height as an advantage, but Meg didn't back up even an inch. She tilted her head to stare up at him. There was color in her cheeks and her blue eyes flashed fire. She looked more alive than he'd seen her in weeks. But he noticed that only peripherally.

"I don't see what difference it makes to you whether I'm drunk or not."

"I won't have you drinking. I won't tolerate it the way my mother did with my father. If you're that unhappy, why don't you just come out and tell me you want a divorce?"

Divorce. The word hung in the air between them, shocking them both to silence. Ty felt his head spin. A divorce? Was that what she wanted? Did she hate him so much? Blame him so much for the miscarriage?

"God." He sank back down on the bed, shoving his fingers through his hair, cursing the lingering fuzziness from the whiskey that made thinking difficult. Or was it fear that made it hard to think? Had he really lost her so completely?

"I—I know I should have said something before." All the anger was gone from her voice, leaving it soft and sad.

"A divorce." He rolled the word on his tongue, finding the taste of it sour and ugly.

"It was selfish of me to let it go so long," she was saying. He saw her link her hands in front of her but it wasn't enough to conceal their trembling. "I knew how you felt."

"Did you?"

"Yes." Her voice quavered on the word and then steadied. "I don't want you to feel bad about . . . about how you feel."

"How I feel about what?" *Damn the whiskey anyway.* Ty rubbed his fingers over the ache starting between his eyes.

"About me. About . . . the baby." Her voice nearly broke on that one, the closest he'd seen her come to crying since the miscarriage.

"I'm sorry about the baby, Meg," he said slowly. There was something here, something not right in what she was saying.

"I'm sorry, too." She drew a shaky breath. "I know it was my fault and I don't expect you to forgive me, but I—"

"Forgive you?" Ty's voice was so harsh that she jumped. Her eyes jerked to his face and for the first time in weeks, he could see what she was feeling, see the pain she'd been living with. "Forgive you?" he said again, more quietly. "Meg, there was nothing to forgive."

"I lost the baby."

"You had a miscarriage," he corrected her. "The baby wasn't a—a trinket that you set down and forgot, Meg. It wasn't your fault."

"I should have seen a doctor sooner."

"Doc Corey told you that wouldn't have made any difference." He reached out and caught her hands in his, drawing her closer despite her automatic resistance. "There was something wrong, honey. Nothing could have changed what happened."

"I should have—"

"No." His fingers tightened over hers. "There's nothing you 'should have' done. You did everything you could have. It just wasn't meant to be. I never, for even a second, thought it was your fault. If it was anyone's fault, it was mine."

"Yours!" She'd been staring at their linked hands but now her head jerked up, her eyes startled. "How could it be your fault?"

"I shouldn't have gotten you pregnant in the first place." He looked away. "You were too young."

"Oh, Ty, there's women a lot younger than me having babies all the time."

"I still should have done something to prevent it," he said stubbornly. "And I should have brought you home sooner. I *knew* you were worried about me flying. If you hadn't worried so much, maybe the baby would have been all right."

"That's not so. And even if it were, it would be my fault for being so foolish. Max told me that you were the best pilot he'd ever seen. I should have believed him." Meg leaned toward him, her body tense with the need to convince him. It had never occurred to her that *he* might be feeling guilty.

"Maybe I shouldn't have made love to you after we found out you were pregnant," he said slowly. "Maybe that's what happened. Maybe, if I'd—"

"There wasn't anything you could have done, Ty," she

said fiercely. "There wasn't anything anyone could have done. It wasn't anyone's fault."

The words seemed to echo in her head. Meg stared at Ty, stunned by the sound of them. She lifted her hands to her face, pressing her fingers over her mouth, feeling something hard and tight start to dissolve inside her.

"It wasn't my fault," she whispered.

"No one ever thought it was, sweetheart." He stood up and reached out to put his arms around her, his touch tentative, as if he expected her to pull away. "It just wasn't meant to be."

"Oh, Ty." All the pain she'd tried so hard to deny rose in her throat, nearly choking her. She came into his embrace, her fingers clutching his shirtfront as the first sob broke from her.

Meg had no idea how long she cried. It seemed as if there were an ocean of tears inside her and she'd been near to drowning in the pain of holding them back. Ty didn't try to stop the flood. He simply held her and let her cry it out, his arms strong around her, his cheek pressed against the top of her head.

When the tears finally slowed, Meg became aware of Ty holding her cradled across his lap in the wing chair. Her head rested on his shoulder and she could feel his heartbeat beneath her palm, strong and steady.

"I'm sorry," she whispered, her breath catching on a half sob.

"You should have cried like that weeks ago." His voice was a low rumble in her ear.

"I didn't want to upset you." Her words were slurred by the wave of exhaustion washing over her.

"It upset me more to see you so unhappy."

He was so good to her, she thought tiredly. So good. If only he loved her. If only . . . The emotional storm had taken its toll, and she fell asleep without finishing the thought.

Meg woke suddenly, startled and disoriented. The first pale-gray shadows of dawn had crept into the room, more an easing of the dark than true daylight. Her body felt oddly heavy, almost weighted down. She blinked groggily at the window, her mind foggy with sleep. She didn't remember coming to bed. She'd been sitting up, worrying about Ty and then—Ty.

She turned her head and saw his face on the pillow beside hers. He slept on his side, his leg thrown across her hips, his arm across her body, one hand nearly cupping her breast. No wonder she'd felt weighted down. Meg felt something unfurl inside her, a warmth, a need—love. Things she hadn't let herself feel in a long time. As she watched, his eyelids quivered and then lifted and he stared directly into her eyes.

"Good morning." His voice was husky with sleep.

"Good morning." Meg felt herself blushing like a child. It seemed so long since they'd awakened like this. She looked away from him to hide her foolish embarrassment.

"I slept here last night," he said, stating the obvious.

"I noticed."

There was a short silence and then: "Do you mind?" he asked.

The question brought her eyes back to his face. He looked . . . uncertain, she thought. As if he weren't sure of his welcome. How could he not know how she'd ached to have him beside her at night? But he was looking at her with a vulnerability she'd never associated with him. The thought of Ty being vulnerable was a novel one.

"I thought you didn't want to be here," she said quietly.

"I thought you didn't want me here." His mouth twisted at the irony of each of them thinking they knew what the other was feeling.

"I've missed you," she admitted, opening a window for him to see into her heart. She lifted her hand to his face, her fingers brushing against the early-morning stubble that shadowed his jaw.

She saw his eyes change, a new awareness entering them, a hunger that sparked an answering need deep inside her. He brought his hand up to catch hers, bringing her palm to his mouth. Meg felt her breath catch and the spark became a fire.

"Meg?"

So many questions in just that soft word. For a moment,

she felt a spurt of panic. It was as if she were standing just
outside the safe wall she'd so carefully built to shield her
emotions. She could turn now and run back behind it. She'd be
safe from hurt. And so lonely. Or she could give him the
answer that beat in every bit of bone and blood. And risk being
hurt again.

"Yes." The answer was a sigh of surrender, to her own
needs, to the hunger that filled her. "Yes."

"Yes." He echoed the word with a purely masculine emphasis that made her shiver. And then his mouth was on hers
and Meg was melting against him.

He made love to her with fierce gentleness, holding her as
if she were fragile as porcelain, yet still demanding—and getting—a deep, womanly response. He wasn't content until she
was shuddering against him, her soft cry of pleasure swallowed
by his mouth, her trembling climax spinning him into his own
fulfillment.

Meg fell asleep almost immediately afterward, a deep,
dreamless sleep from which she woke three hours later feeling
relaxed and rested in a way she hadn't known in a long time.
Ty was gone but on the pillow beside her was a tiny bouquet of
crocuses. With a whisper of pleasure, Meg lifted them, savoring the softness of the petals in her hand. She knew just where
he'd picked them and wondered if Edwina Vanderbilt would
notice that her flower bed had been vandalized.

Beneath the flowers was a note: *Back at noon. Dress for a
picnic. Ty*

It was hardly a love note, but Meg folded it carefully and
tucked it away in the old cigar box she kept at the bottom of
her underwear drawer. It didn't hold much—a few childish
trinkets, a postcard from Paris, sent to her by an aunt who'd
died when she was eight. Folded neatly to one side was the
handkerchief Ty had left behind at the stream all those years
ago, and tucked in its fold was a pressed yellow rose from the
bouquet he'd given her for her birthday. Not the most exten-
sive collection of mementos, she thought as she added the note
to the box and closed the lid. But there'd be others.

She lifted her head and looked at her reflection in the

mirror, startled by the changes she saw. This wasn't the same girl who'd looked back at her recently. This girl had color in her cheeks and a sparkle in her eyes. Even her hair seemed to have regained its bounce. This girl was alive, happy.

Meg smiled at her reflection, liking what she saw. It had been a long time since she'd felt hopeful, since she'd dared to think that all her dreams just might come true. But last night had proved that miracles were still possible. Ty cared for her. And she clung to the belief that caring could become love.

Meg shook off the somber mood that threatened to take hold of her. She had to let the future take care of itself. At the moment, her most pressing concern was what to wear to a picnic.

"There's still a lot of work but we're chipping away at it. I thought we'd paint this summer." Ty leaned back on his elbows and looked at the house, imagining what it would look like with a fresh coat of white paint.

"I saw a house once that was painted white with dark-green trim," Meg said, a touch of dreaminess in the comment.

"Green it is," Ty said, mentally painting over the blue shutters he'd envisioned.

"Really?" she said, sounding surprised and pleased.

"Sure." He turned his head to look at her. "It's your home, Meg."

"I know." The look she turned on the house was hopeful but held a trace of doubt, as if she couldn't quite believe in the reality of it.

And why should she? Ty thought. There'd been little enough in her life to encourage her to have much belief in the future. Just as there'd been nothing in her past to make her think he *wouldn't* blame her for the miscarriage. He'd been such a fool. So wrapped up in his own pain and guilt that he hadn't stopped to think that she'd naturally blame herself.

Meg's eyes were still on the house and Ty let his gaze linger on her. She was so beautiful. Sometimes he almost forgot how beautiful she was, and then he saw her like this and she almost took his breath away. Sunlight filtered through the branches of the apple tree, bare but for the delicate tracery of soft white blooms. It caught in her hair, turning it to a pure gold that made his fingers itch to feel its warmth. They'd spent some time walking around the farm while he showed her the work that had been done. The sun had left a dusting of color across her nose and cheeks, a pretty flush on her pale skin. Her eyes were a pure deep sapphire, and even after all these months, Ty still felt as if it might be possible to drown in their clarity.

He chuckled to himself and Meg turned an inquiring look his direction. "I was just thinking that today has been quite a contrast to yesterday," he said, surprised to find that he could smile at the memory.

Meg flushed and looked down at the blanket on which they'd spread their picnic. "I'm sorry I wouldn't come out here, Ty. I just— Oh!" Her apology broke off on a startled gasp as he reached up and grabbed hold of her shoulders, dragging her down on top of him as he lay back against the blanket.

"No more apologies," he said in a mock-stern voice.

"But I—" Meg flattened her palms against his chest and pushed herself up until she could see his face.

"I'll have to charge a penalty for every apology," he warned her.

"A penalty?" She gave him a wary look.

"It'll cost you a kiss for every apology," he told her firmly.

She blinked in surprise. There hadn't been much teasing in her life, and he could see a trace of uncertainty in her eyes as she looked at him. But what she saw must have reassured her because her mouth curved in a slow smile that made his pulse race. He doubted she had any idea of how she affected him. Though she was an eager participant in their lovemaking, she retained a certain innocence that was somehow sexier than the most experienced courtesan could have been.

"I have to kiss you every time I say I'm sorry?" she asked, wanting to clarify the rules of the game.

"That's right."

She glanced at him from under her lashes, her teeth tugging on her lower lip while she considered the possibilities. Ty watched her, wondering if she'd take up the challenge or back away.

"I'm sorry," she whispered. The pink in her cheeks was caused by more than the sun, but the look in her eyes was pure invitation.

"That's one kiss." Ty made an effort to sound stern, but it was difficult when he could feel his blood heating in his veins.

She dropped a quick kiss on his mouth, jerking her head back before he had a chance to respond.

"That was hardly a kiss," he complained.

"I'm sorry. Oops. Now I owe you another one."

He made sure this kiss was slower. Ty's fingers found their way beneath her hair, cupping the back of her head and holding her mouth against his. When he finally let her lift her head, they were both breathing a little raggedly. Ty stared up at her, seeing the sensuous daze in her eyes. God, he'd missed this, missed her.

"I'm sorry," he muttered.

"What for?"

"I'm sorry that I didn't do this sooner. And that's two I owe you." He rose up, his mouth closing off any response she might have made. He heard her gasp as he turned so that she lay beneath him on the blanket. But her fingers were already burrowing into the thick dark hair at the base of his skull, pulling him closer, her slender body arching into his.

There, beneath the worn branches of the old apple tree, their bed lightly dusted with apple-white flower petals, Ty and Meg completed the healing process they'd begun the night before, reaffirming life and their marriage in the most fundamental way possible.

Chapter 22

The afternoon passed in drowsy contentment, and Ty found himself somewhat guiltily glad that Jack's excesses of the night before had made it easy to persuade him to go home this morning. He couldn't remember the last time he'd enjoyed a day as much as he had this one. Watching Meg walk through the house, seeing her tentative pleasure as she absorbed the idea that this was her home, to do with as she pleased, was more than enough reward for the hours of hard work that had gone into the place.

She seemed highly impressed with every nail he'd hammered, every shingle he'd replaced. Ty found himself trying to think of still more things to show her just for the pleasure of hearing her tell him how clever he was. It would be easy to get addicted to that kind of praise, he thought ruefully.

He'd been keeping half an eye on the storm clouds building to the west, hoping the rain would hold off. He didn't want to have to cut the day short. The weather obliged until almost dark, when the breeze veered abruptly into a gusting wind. The rain began just as they finished loading the picnic things into the roadster. Ty quickly put the roof up, securing the windshield latches and sliding into the car just as it began to rain in earnest.

They didn't talk much during the drive home, but it was a

peaceful silence, not like the silence that had lain between them for the past few weeks. Ty parked the car next to the curb, but neither of them moved to get out. The day had been too perfect to want to see it end. But a crack of thunder overhead broke the quiet moment.

"Go ahead. There's no sense in both of us getting wet," Ty said, nodding to the steady fall of rain. "I'll get the picnic basket and be right in."

Meg nodded and reached for the door handle. But before she touched it, she turned back. "I had a wonderful day, Ty. Thank you."

She brushed a quick kiss on his mouth and then was gone, ducking out into the rain. Ty watched her hurry up the walk, his mouth curved in a smile whose contentment might have startled him if he'd seen it. He waited until he'd seen Meg reach the door before he pushed open his own door. Despite the rain, he didn't hurry to reach the shelter of the porch. He hated to see the day end, even if prolonging it involved getting a little damp.

Another week or two and maybe they could move out to the farmhouse, he thought, frowning at his childhood home. He appreciated his parents letting them stay here for the past few weeks and the money they'd saved would come in handy, but, remembering the exchange between his mother and his wife the night before, Ty wondered if it wouldn't have been better to have tightened their belts a bit and rented a place to stay. Too late to worry about it now, he decided as he reached the porch.

Meg had left the door open a crack for him. Smiling a little, Ty pushed it open and stepped into the entryway. The sound of his mother at her most cutting wiped the smile from his mouth.

". . . out all day without a word," she was saying.

"I'm sorry if you were worried," Meg said in a subdued voice.

"The only thing I was worried about is what you might be doing," Helen cut in, her voice laced with an icy indifference that made Ty remember the times she'd used that same tone

with him when he was growing up. "After all, you are a Mc-
Kendrick now. I'm not sure someone of your background
could possibly understand what that means. As Tyler's wife,
you have a certain standing in the community. You could do
his reputation irreparable harm."

Ty nearly laughed aloud. Trust his mother to make it
sound like the McKendricks of Regret, Iowa, were on the same
social level as the Astors of New York. But the strain in Meg's
voice when she spoke wiped out any black humor he might
have found in his mother's remarks.

"I would never do anything to hurt Ty," Meg said, all the
animation drained from her voice.

Feeling anger lick through him, Ty started forward, intending to put a stop to the unpleasant little scene. His
mother's next words froze him in his tracks.

"You hurt him a great deal when you lost his baby," she
said almost gently. Ty heard Meg gasp as the knife slid in just
where it would hurt the most. "Of course, I know you didn't
mean to lose the baby," she added. "Coming from the background you do, it's no wonder that you don't understand
proper—"

She broke off as Ty appeared in the doorway behind Meg.
His expression must have made it clear that he'd heard at least
part of what she'd been saying, and she flushed, her eyes shifting guiltily away from his.

"Meg, would you mind going upstairs while I talk to my
mother?" He set his hand on her shoulder, aware that he was
actually trembling with rage.

She twisted her face to look up at him and he saw her eyes
widen when she saw his face. "It's okay, Ty," she said
quickly. "I don't mind."

"I do. I'll be up in a few minutes." He didn't want her to
hear what he had to say.

"But—"

"Please." He forced a smile to reassure her. "It's all
right."

She looked as if she wanted to argue but then changed her
mind. She walked past him, leaving a thick silence behind her.

Ty waited until he heard the bedroom door close upstairs before looking at his mother. True to character, Helen chose to go on the attack.

"I didn't say anything that wasn't the truth, Tyler, so there's no sense in you giving me that look." She picked up the apron that lay across the back of a chair and tied it around her waist, only the slight jerkiness of her movements revealing any sign of nervousness.

"How long have you been browbeating Meg, Mother?" He was surprised by how even his tone was, how calm he sounded.

"Browbeating her? Don't be melodramatic, Tyler! I was only speaking the truth."

"Have you told her before that you think the miscarriage was her fault?"

"Well, if it wasn't her fault, I don't know whose it was. *I* managed to carry three children, despite a delicate constitution. If I could do it, I don't see why someone of her class couldn't do the same. Pure carelessness, if you ask me."

"I didn't," Ty said. "And quite frankly, Mother, I don't give a damn about your constitution. All I care about is what you've been saying to my wife."

"How dare you speak to me like that!" Helen's face flushed a mottled red.

Ty ignored her indignation. "Are you completely without compassion? Couldn't you see what losing the baby did to her? To me? Or didn't you care?"

"Of course I cared. I knew you were upset but I thought perhaps you'd come to see that it was for the best."

For a moment, Ty thought she was going to trot out the same speech he'd heard from Doc Corey—about how this was nature's way of saying that there'd been something wrong. But she continued and he realized he'd been wrong.

"Once there was no baby to tie you to that girl, I knew you'd see what a terrible mistake you'd made," his mother explained in a tone of sweet reason.

"Are you saying you were *glad* Meg lost the baby?" He

hadn't believed that there was anything his mother could do to surprise him, but she'd just proved him wrong.

Perhaps she realized that she'd gone too far, because she quickly softened her tone. "Of course not. I'm just saying that, though it was a tragedy, it's given you a second chance. God never closes a door without opening a window," she quoted piously.

Ty stared at her as if seeing her for the first time. He'd believed that he had no illusions about his mother, that he saw her clearly, with all her strengths and weaknesses. But he saw now that he didn't know her at all. He could never have believed that she—that anyone—could be so utterly without compassion.

Perhaps she read the contempt in his eyes because she flushed and then paled. "I only want what's best for you, Tyler." Her fingers twisted uneasily in the crisp, embroidered muslin of her apron.

"You only want what you want," he corrected her. "You don't really care about anything except getting your way."

"That's not true. And I don't appreciate your using that tone of voice with me," she added, trying to sound stern.

"I don't care what you appreciate," he said bluntly. "All I care about is that you don't upset Meg."

"Meg." She spat the name out as if it tasted foul. "Her kind can take care of themselves. I don't know how she managed to trick you into marrying her, but you must see by now that she's totally unsuited to be a McKendrick. Why, I wouldn't be surprised if she deliberately lost the baby just to gain some sympathy. Someone like her—"

"That's enough, Mother." Ty took a quick step toward her, his hands clenched into fists, his control on his temper stretched almost to the breaking point. In that moment, he came perilously close to hating his mother. "I don't want you to ever say another thing against Meg. Not one. Do you understand me?"

She must have read something of what he was feeling in his eyes, because the color drained from her face and she backed up a quick step, pressing one hand to the base of her throat, her eyes almost frightened.

"What's going on here?" Elliot McKendrick's quiet voice seemed to boom in the stillness of the kitchen, shattering the tense moment. "Are you two fighting again?" he asked, shaking his head as he dropped his briefcase on the table.

"Oh, Elliot." His wife's face crumpled as she pressed one trembling hand to her mouth. "Tyler practically threatened me."

"Threatened you?" Elliot's dark brows shot up in surprise, and he glanced at his son.

"I told her I didn't want to hear any more criticism of Meg," Ty said shortly, offering no apology for his harshness.

"That doesn't exactly sound like a threat, Helen." Elliot looked at his wife questioningly.

"I was just trying to make him see that, since she's not going to have a baby anymore, there's no reason he should still be trapped in this awful marriage," she defended herself, her voice hovering on the edge of tears.

"I've told you before not to meddle in things that don't concern you," her husband told her without sympathy.

"Mother seems to think it's a good thing that Meg lost the baby," Ty said, the words bitter in his mouth.

"Helen!"

She jumped at the unaccustomed sharpness in her husband's voice. Her eyes filled with tears but there was no softening of his stern look. Denied the sympathy she felt she deserved, she took refuge in her favorite reproach.

"Dickey would never have treated me this way. *He* would have realized that I had only his best interests at heart."

Despite his anger, Ty felt the old pain twist inside him. For eighteen years he'd been listening to comparisons between himself and his dead older brother, and he'd come up with the short end of the stick every time. No matter what he did, he'd never be able to compare to the son she'd lost. He'd realized that so long ago, he was surprised to find the knowledge still had the power to hurt.

"The Dickey I remember would have been horrified by what you've done," he said.

It was the first time he'd ever questioned his mother's portrayal of her older son's perfections. Helen had been dabbing at her eyes with the hem of her apron, but, at his words, her head jerked up, her expression shocked.

"The brother I remember wasn't the plaster saint you've made him out to be, but he *was* kind. I think he'd have been ashamed of you if he knew what you'd done," he said bluntly.

"That's enough, Ty." His father's quiet voice stopped him from saying more.

It was probably more than enough, Ty thought. He hadn't intended to say as much as he had. His mother was staring at him in shock, her face pale as the muslin of her apron. It struck him suddenly that she was no longer a young woman. Odd, how she'd always seemed ageless. Now she suddenly looked older than her years.

Ty ran his fingers through his hair, aware that his hand was shaking. There was a tangled knot of emotion in his gut, so thick and hard, he was almost sick with it. It was time and past—eighteen years past—that she let Dickey lie in his grave. But she looked so shocked, as if he'd struck her, which he supposed in a way, he had.

"I don't want to hurt you, Mother," he said slowly. He looked at her, feeling the anger drain away, leaving behind a deep weariness. "Meg and I are married. And we're going to stay that way. God willing, we're going to have children someday. If you want to be part of your grandchildren's lives, maybe you should give some thought as to how you treat their mother from now on."

He looked at her a moment longer, wanting to impress his seriousness on her, and then he turned and left the room.

He left behind him a silence so thick, it was almost a third presence in the kitchen. After a moment, Helen drew a shaken breath and straightened her slumped shoulders, almost visibly drawing a protective mantle about herself.

"It's that girl," she said finally. "She's the one who's turned him against me."

"No, she hasn't." Elliot shook his head. "It's your end-less need to be in charge that's put the walls between the two of you. You've been trying to bend him to your will since he was a boy."

"I thought I could count on support from my own hus-band," she said, her eyes filling with quick tears.

"You've always had my support and my love. You know that." The look he gave her was compassionate but unbending. "But if you aren't careful, you're going to lose another son. *We're* going to lose another son. Is that what you want?"

"Of course not! I just want what's best for him."

"He's a grown man, Helen. You can't force him to do what you think he should. You've got to accept that or we're going to lose him." Seeing her genuine distress, he came around the table and put his arms around her, drawing her close. "Dickey's gone. Louise is living her own life in New York and doesn't show much interest in starting a family. Ty is all we have left."

"But—"

"No 'buts.' He means what he says about not letting you see your grandchildren. You know how stubborn he is." He drew back, his smile gentle as he looked down at her. "You ought to know, since he inherited it from you."

She looked as if she wanted to argue but then changed her mind. With a sigh, she laid her head on his shoulder as if in surrender.

When Ty pushed open the bedroom door, he found Meg sitting in the wing chair, her feet neatly placed together on the floor, her hands clasped in her lap, as stiff as a tardy pupil waiting to be called into the principal's office. The moment the door opened her head jerked up, her eyes searching his face for some clue as to what had happened downstairs.

"I don't think she'll say anything about the baby again," Ty said as he shut the door behind him.

"I don't want to cause any trouble between you and your mother," she said, distressed.

"The trouble between the two of us goes back a long way.

Even before Dickey was killed, we were butting heads,'' Ty told her wearily.

"Well, I'm sorry I was the cause of more trouble.'' She rose and came toward him, a concerned frown creasing her forehead. "Your shirt's damp,'' she said. "You should get out of it before you catch a chill.''

"I'm surprised getting so angry didn't dry it instantly,'' he said wryly.

"It wasn't worth causing a fuss,'' she said as she began unbuttoning his shirt.

"It was worth it to me.'' He looked down at her. Her head was lowered as she concentrated on her task, and all he could see was the soft golden curtain of hair that fell around her face, concealing her expression from him.

"Why didn't you say something?''

"About what?'' As the last button slid free, she tilted her head back to look at him. She looked genuinely puzzled.

"About the way my mother's been treating you. Why didn't you tell me?'' He brought his hand up to brush her hair back from her face.

"Why should I have told you?'' she asked, frowning.

She really didn't know. It had never occurred to her that he wouldn't have let his mother treat her the way she had. And why should it have? As near as he could tell, there'd never been anyone in her life to defend her. Why should she believe it would be any different this time?

"I should have realized,'' he muttered, angry with himself for not having seen what was happening sooner.

"It's okay,'' she said, smiling up at him. "I don't pay much attention to what she says.''

Ty wondered how his mother liked that. The thought made his mouth twist in a half smile as he imagined her frustration at not being able to get a visible response from Meg. Without even knowing it, Meg had probably extracted a certain amount of revenge.

But that wasn't good enough. Looking down at Meg, he saw color in her face and a sparkle in her eyes and thought of how long it had been since he'd seen either of those things. He couldn't take a chance on seeing the life drained out of her again. Meg might say that his mother's words didn't matter, but Ty had had enough experience with her ability to cause the maximum amount of pain with the minimum number of words to know that he couldn't leave Meg at her mercy any longer.

"What would you think of moving into the farmhouse immediately?" he asked slowly.

The sudden flare of excitement in her eyes gave him an answer even before she spoke. She caught hold of the edges of his opened shirt. "Could we?"

"There's still a lot of work to be done," he cautioned her.

"That's okay. I don't mind work." Her smile grew a little wistful. "I'm not as helpless as you think I am, Ty."

"I don't think you're helpless." He brought his hand up and let his fingers sift through the soft gold of her hair. It wasn't that he thought she was helpless. But she'd never in her life had someone to really take care of her, and he was determined to change that.

"I got a letter from Millie today," Meg said as Ty and Jack cut into the buttermilk pie she'd made for dessert.

"She can write?" Jack widened his eyes in mock surprise.

"I bet she had help," Ty commented, reaching for his coffee cup.

"Of course Millie can write," Meg told them, trying to look stern—not an easy task when she was as happy as she had been the past couple of weeks. "Do the two of you want to make nasty remarks about her or do you want to hear the letter?"

"I didn't think we made any nasty remarks, did you?" Ty gave Jack a questioning look.

"Some people just don't like hearing the truth about their friends, Ty," Jack said, looking thoughtful. "Like the time Becky Loudermilk told me you had big ears. I didn't like hearing it, even if it was the truth."

"I know what you mean." Ty shook his head as he cut off

another bite of pie and lifted it on his fork. "I felt the same way when Mary Kate Davidson told me that she'd like to go out with you if you were just a little less cross-eyed. It hurt me to hear it but it was the truth."

"I'll tell you another truth," Meg said in a friendly tone. "I think the chickens would probably enjoy the rest of that pie."

The implicit threat brought a shocked silence. Meg held her breath, wondering if she'd gone too far. This kind of teasing was still new to her. The two men exchanged horrified glances. Jack shook his head sadly. "Marriage'll do that to a woman, I guess. Turn a sweet girl into a cruel harpy. We'd better listen to the letter, Ty. No telling what she'll do if we don't."

Ty nodded, drawing his face into downtrodden lines that were at odds with the laughter in his dark eyes. "I guess my life just isn't my own anymore."

Meg relaxed. "I take it that means you'd like to hear Millie's letter?"

Ty looked at the pie in the center of the kitchen table. "I'd love to hear Millie's letter."

"I thought so." Meg's prim look dissolved in a smile. She pushed the pie forward so that it rested between the two men before pulling the letter from her apron pocket.

Dear Meg,

I'm glad to hear that you've moved to your own place. Living with your mother-in-law is a mistake. Take it from me. If it hadn't been for Larry's mother, we might still be married today. Of course, then I wouldn't have asked for the bungalow when we got divorced and that means I wouldn't have met you and if I hadn't met you, I probably wouldn't have met Joe so I guess things worked out for the best, after all, even if it didn't seem that way at the time.

I met this lady who can see into the future and she says that Larry's mother being so mean to me and thinking I wasn't good enough to be a Smith and everything was probably a result of divine intervention because it's obvious that I was meant to meet Joe and that I'm real lucky because not everyone finds their true soulmate but I did and I should be thankful. Which I am, of course, because who wouldn't be thankful to have found a swell guy like Joe?

Jack snorted with laughter. Meg looked up from the letter long enough to give him a quelling look and then continued.

We all miss you. Joe and Billy and all the other guys. They sometimes come over to my place but it's not the same as it was when you were here and it's not just that I can't cook, either. Though really, I'm not such a bad cook, no matter what Joe says. I mean, how was I supposed to know that you weren't supposed to beat biscuit dough real good and it's not really my fault that there wasn't enough water in the pan when I made a pot roast. I put the water in and how was I to know that it would go and boil away? And anyway, I don't see why he made such a fuss because the roast wasn't really ruined, it was just a little black on the bottom and if you chewed it real good, it wasn't all that bad.

Meg ignored the open laughter from her companions, though her own lips were twitching.

But I guess it's okay that Joe thinks I can't cook, even if I can, because it means he takes me out to dinner a lot. We've gone to some swank places. Last week we went to the Brown Derby and we saw Clark Gable and I wanted to go talk to him and ask him if he knew I hadn't been cast in his movie, because it was obviously such a mistake. I mean, I was perfect for the part and everybody could see it, only then I didn't get the part. Joe didn't think it was such a good idea and he said I probably hadn't been cast because of jealousy. And I guess maybe he was right, because what other reason could there be?

"How about they thought that red hair would blind the cameraman?" Jack suggested.

"I wouldn't have thought it possible but she writes just like she talks," Ty said, shaking his head.

"There's only a bit more," Meg told them.

Anyway, to get back to the point—Joe says I have trouble sticking to the point sometimes but I know he's wrong—we all miss you and Ty and Jack. And Max.

Meg's voice faltered.

Things just weren't the same after poor Max was killed. With all of you gone, it just isn't the same here. Joe wants to know if you guys are thinking about coming back. He says flying isn't the same without Jack and Ty. And he says to tell Ty that he's taking real good care of his plane and if Ty ever wants to buy it back, it's his for the asking.

I've rambled on long enough so I'll sign off for now.
                              Write soon. Your friend, Millie

Meg folded the letter carefully and tucked it back in the envelope. The soft rustle of paper sounded unnaturally loud in the quiet kitchen. She was afraid of what she might see if she looked at Ty, so when she looked up, it was Jack she focused on. But Jack was looking at Ty, and in his eyes she could see her own questions. Questions she was afraid to ask. How did Ty feel about being reminded of the way things had been? Did hearing that Joe would happily sell his plane back to him make him want to go back to California?

He'd never really talked about how he felt about giving up flying, but Meg knew it couldn't have been easy. She remembered the way he'd talked about flying, about what it meant to him. The fact that he'd given it up because he thought it was best for her and the baby was one just one of the regrets she carried inside. When she'd lost the baby, that knowledge added to the guilt she felt, as if Ty's sacrifice had been in vain after all. But he hadn't suggested giving up the farm and leaving Iowa again, and she hadn't had the heart to bring it up herself, to be the one to suggest that he go back to risking his life every day.

Now she waited to see if Millie's letter had opened old wounds, had reminded him of all he'd given up. Afraid of what she might see, Meg forced herself to look at Ty. But if he was overwhelmed with longing for what he'd given up, there was nothing in his expression that revealed it.

"I'm surprised Joe hasn't strangled Millie by now." Ty pushed away his pie plate and leaned back in his chair. "Just to shut her up," he added with a grin.

"Well, since Joe never talks, maybe he likes having some noise to fill up the silence," Jack said. He tapped a cigarette out of the pack, his eyes meeting Meg's as he lit it. She knew that he'd wondered what Ty's reaction would be, but she couldn't be sure he was relieved by the choice Ty had made. Though she liked him tremendously, Jack had remained something of an enigma to her. She had the feeling that he concealed much more of himself than he revealed.

"If you don't need me, I've got some things to do this afternoon," Jack said, drawing in a lungful of smoke and then releasing it slowly.

"Sure. Considering the wages I'm paying, I can't complain if the hired hand takes some time off," Ty said with a grin.

"Meals like this are more than enough pay," Jack said.

Despite the smile he threw in her direction, Meg thought she detected a sadness behind his eyes, a sense of loss. Before she could grab hold of the impression, he pushed back his chair and stood up.

"Thanks for lunch, Meg. It was terrific, as always. I'll see you first thing tomorrow morning, Ty." With another smile, Jack pushed open the screen door and walked out, leaving the acrid tang of smoke behind him.

Meg stood up and reached for the plates, frowning a little. "I don't think he's happy," she said as she carried the plates to the sink. When she turned back, Ty was looking after his friend, his expression worried.

"Jack has his own reasons for coming back to Iowa," he said, when he caught her eye.

"A girl?" Meg was immediately intrigued.

"More or less." He caught her interested look and shrugged uneasily. "She's married."

"Oh."

"Yeah. Oh."

"Couldn't you talk to him?"

"And say what?" Ty arched one brow in question. "He's old enough to make his own mistakes, Meg."

"I guess." She brushed a damp cloth over the table. "It's just that— Oh!"

Ty grabbed her around the waist and toppled her onto his lap. "It's just that nothing. Jack can take care of himself. We're his friends, not his parents."

"I know." Meg toyed with the button at the top of his shirt. She liked the sound of that "we." It sounded natural, right. "Don't you think—"

"The only thing I think is that it's been a long time since you've kissed me," Ty said.

He pulled her more snugly against his chest, giving her a look that made Meg forget all about Jack and his affairs.

Jack knocked on the neat white door and then waited for a response. He was a fool to be here, he thought, angry with himself. He had no business standing on Patsy Baker's doorstep. He'd managed to stay away from her this long, holding on to the knowledge that she'd kept him from his child, nursing the anger and hurt. But here he was, back like a bad penny, no more able to stay away than he was to stop breathing.

He heard footsteps inside and his palms were suddenly damp. The reaction made him frown, and that was the expression Patsy saw when she opened the door.

"Jack." Her voice was husky with surprise, and he was unreasonably glad to note that the fingers she pressed to the base of her throat were far from steady. A little nervousness was the least of what she owed him. Still, he couldn't deny the hunger he felt as he stared at her through the screen.

"Can I come in?"

"I don't think that's a good idea." Her voice trembled as much as her hand.

"I can just stand here on the porch but I think the neighbors might notice. And you never know what they might say to your husband." The last word was bitten off, as if it had an unpleasant taste in his mouth.

"They'll be able to see your car, anyway," she pointed out, but she unlatched the screen and pushed it open.

Jack followed her into the house, drawing in the now-familiar scent of furniture polish and lavender. She led him into the living room, which was neither large nor elaborately furnished. A solid, plain room, in a solid plain house, the very essence of midwestern America. He still couldn't place the girl he'd known in these surroundings yet there she stood, wearing a pale-blue dress that reflected the color of her eyes, her hair a little mussed and her cheeks flushed.

"I didn't expect to see you again," she said when the silence had stretched uncomfortably.

"I don't know why I came." *Liar. You came because you couldn't do anything else.* He squashed the mocking mental voice. He wanted to hold on to the anger, the hurt. He wanted to make her tell him—again—why she'd felt she had the right to keep his child from him. He wanted to hear her admit she'd been wrong. He wanted to take her in his arms and kiss her until she admitted that she loved him, that she'd never stopped loving him.

Jack turned away from her and jammed his fingers through his hair, aware that now it was *his* hand that was not quite steady. Damn, but how did she do this to him? It had been five years and he had every reason to hate her. Why didn't he?

"It's a nice house," he said, filling the awkward silence.

"Thank you." There was a pause and then: "Why are you here, Jack?"

"Damned if I know," he admitted with a half laugh. He

turned back to her with a shaky laugh. "If I had any sense, I'd have stayed away. I'd have never come within a mile of you." The bitter humor in his voice made Patsy flush. She dropped her eyes to her hands, which were linked together in front of her, the knuckles showing white with the force of her grip.

"I know you have every right to hate me," she said quietly. "I couldn't blame you, if you did."

"Couldn't you?"

A beam of sunlight had found its way through the filmy curtains and then gotten itself tangled in her hair, picking out the gold highlights in the soft brown curls. Hardly aware of his actions, Jack reached up to touch his fingertips to that sunlit area.

"Jack." It was a warning but he ignored it, responding instead to the ache in her voice, an ache that matched the one in his gut.

His fingers threaded through her hair, finding her sensitive nape, feeling her shiver at the touch.

"Jack, please."

He didn't know whether Patsy was pleading with him to let her go or to continue what he'd begun. He doubted she knew. His eyes holding hers, he drew her closer. Her hands came up against his chest but she didn't push him away. Jack lowered his head until his mouth hovered a whisper away from hers.

This was crazy. It was wrong. But it had been five years since anything had felt so right.

He felt the shudder that ran through her as his mouth touched hers. Five years, he thought. Five years and she still tasted of sunshine and mint. And then he stopped thinking at all but only felt. Felt the half-forgotten fire race through his veins, felt the familiar pressure of her body against his as she melted into his embrace.

It was so right. Nothing had ever been like this.

His mouth slanted over hers, deepening the kiss. Patsy's fingers curled into the fabric of his shirt, clinging to him as if he were the only solid thing in the world at that moment, just as she was the only thing in his. He kissed her with the hunger of a man long denied, with a need only she had ever been able to fulfill.

It was heaven. It was homecoming. It was completion after all these long years. And then Patsy tore her mouth from his, her hands suddenly pushing frantically against his chest.

"No. No. No." She repeated the single word in a breathless rush as she jerked away from him.

Their eyes met and Jack saw a wild tangle of emotion in hers. She looked as if she were being torn apart inside. She looked just the way he felt. Jack reached out in automatic response to her pain but, with a moan of denial, Patsy turned and ran from the room. From him.

He stood in the middle of the tidy little living room, listening to the sound of a door slam somewhere in the back of the house. The room still smelled of wax and lavender, but it seemed as if the sun must have gone behind a cloud, because it was suddenly dark and gloomy.

Moving slowly, like a man recovering from an illness, Jack left the house, stepping out into bright spring sunshine, with not a cloud in sight. He shouldn't have come here, he thought as he started the car. He'd known better, known that nothing but trouble could come of him seeing Patsy. Looking over his shoulder, Jack backed the car out onto the road. It had been a mistake to open old wounds. But as he looked at the plain white house, he knew he'd be back.

Chapter 23

Ty and Meg had been living on the farm for three weeks when his parents came for Sunday dinner after church. It had been Meg's suggestion. Though she could have gone to her grave without ever seeing Helen McKendrick again, she had developed an affection for her father-in-law. And even if she hadn't, she didn't want Ty to lose touch with his family because of her.

The visit was a modest success. Ty had never told her what he'd said to his mother the night he'd made the decision to move out to the farm immediately, but whatever it was, it must have made an impression on her. While Helen was far from warm, she did seem to be striving for something approaching cordiality. She didn't go so far as to compliment Meg on the meal, but she did mention that the fried chicken was quite pleasant—this was said with a thin smile that made Meg think the words caused a physical pain.

But she'd made the effort and that was more than Meg had expected her to do. All in all, the afternoon was not *un*-pleasant, and that was all Meg could have hoped for. She thought perhaps her feelings were shared by the others, because there seemed to be a general feeling of relief when the older couple prepared to leave.

Ty and his father had already gone outside and were

standing on the porch talking. The women had been delayed by the necessity of Meg fetching her mother-in-law's sweater from the bedroom. But when Meg returned to the entryway, Helen was in the living room. Reluctantly, Meg followed her.

The living room, like the rest of the house, was sparsely furnished. So far, the one permanent item was a sofa, upholstered in an undistinguished blue fabric. It had been given to them by Ty's mother, with the admonition that it had belonged to his maternal great-aunt Eulalie, who'd died quite young, and that they were to take care of this family heirloom. It was Meg's theory that the discomfort of sitting on the sofa might have contributed to Aunt Eulalie's early demise, but she hadn't said as much.

She draped Helen's sweater over her arm and waited to hear some complaint about the positioning of the sofa or that the bare surroundings hardly did it justice. But the older woman walked past the sofa and stopped at the quilting frame that sat near one of the windows where it caught plenty of light. The quilt was stretched between narrow boards that were laid across the backs of four chairs, and Meg had covered it with a sheet to protect it from sun and dust.

Meg winced when Ty's mother flipped back the sheet. She'd finished the top only last week, an overall pattern of blue and white pieced baskets filled with appliquéd flowers in a variety of warm pastels. She'd been happy with her efforts, but she had no doubt that her mother-in-law would soon point out the error of her ways.

"I've just started the quilting," Meg said, hating the apologetic sound of the words and yet unable to hold them back.

"*You* made this?" Helen turned to look at her, making the question sound accusing.

"Yes."

Helen turned to look at the quilt again, bending close as if searching for a flaw. She was frowning when she straightened up. "The workmanship is . . . quite fine," she said. She sounded so disgruntled that Meg bit the inside of her lip to hold back a smile.

"Thank you." She hesitated a moment, debating her next

words. But if they were ever to achieve any kind of decent relationship, it was going to be up to her to find a middle ground. "I could make you a quilt, if you'd like," she offered.

Helen's face tightened and her mouth pursed as if she'd just tasted something unpleasant. Meg held her breath, waiting for the curt rejection she'd laid herself open to. Helen's eyes flickered to the exquisitely worked quilt and she frowned.

"That would be kind of you," she said slowly. "Perhaps we could discuss patterns and colors at a later date."

Meg was so stunned by her acquiescence that it took her a moment to find her voice. "I—I'd be happy to," she stammered uncertainly.

"Of course, quilting is such a *useful* kind of hobby," Helen said. She flicked the sheet back over the quilt before turning to take her coat from Meg. "I never learned. My mother thought most needlework better left to the lower classes, except for perhaps a little tatting or embroidery."

Having carefully reestablished their relative positions in society, she swept past, leaving Meg to follow, as befitted her lowly background.

A few minutes later, Ty and Meg stood on the porch, watching as his parents' sturdy Ford bumped down the lane to the gravel road that would take them back to Regret.

"That wasn't too bad," Ty said. He dropped his arm around Meg's shoulders and hugged her against his side. "I think she'll come around."

"I hope so." Meg stared at the dust that hung in the air, even after the car was out of sight.

"She didn't say anything to you, did she?" Ty asked, frowning down at her.

"No." Meg was warmed, as always, by his concern. "She was very pleasant." She decided to ignore her mother-in-law's parting remarks about needlework.

"Good. Maybe she's figured out that if she says anything to upset you, she won't be welcome here again."

"Ty! She's your mother!"

"And you're my wife," he said calmly. "She's got to learn to accept that."

Meg leaned her head against his shoulder, feeling the impact of his words echo inside her. *You're my wife,* he'd said, as if that were a given, something that would always be. After all these months, it still surprised her to hear him refer to her as his wife, to realize that she wasn't going to wake up tomorrow and find this was all a dream. She closed her eyes against the quick sting of tears and wondered if it was possible to be too happy.

A few days after Ty's parents came to visit, Meg ran out of thread in the midst of a row of quilting. It was midafternoon and she had plenty of time before she needed to start dinner for Ty and Jack, so she slipped on a clean dress, dabbed a bit of powder on her nose, and drove into Regret.

Meg parked the car down the street from Lewison's General Store and walked along the sidewalk, enjoying the sunshine on her face, the feeling of well-being that was still new to her. She saw one or two people she knew and exchanged greetings with them, wondering if she looked any different to them now that she was Meg McKendrick and not just drunken George Harper's younger girl.

She certainly felt different, though it had nothing to do with bearing the McKendrick name, despite her mother-in-law's insistence on the importance of that. It had to do with being married to Ty, knowing she could make him a good wife, having a place in the world worth holding on to.

After the bright sunlight outside, it took Meg's eyes a few seconds to adjust to the pleasantly dim interior of Lewison's. She'd come here so many times for her mother—to buy thread or a packet of needles or perhaps a bolt of muslin for backing quilts.

"Afternoon, Meg." Bill Fenton's thin face creased in a smile when he saw her. "What can I help you with?"

"I just need a spool of thread, Mr. Fenton. I think I can find that myself." Meg returned his smile and moved toward the side of the store where the fabric and sewing notions were kept. Behind her, she heard him return to the task he'd been doing when she entered the store.

She couldn't help but think of how things had changed. A year ago, when she'd come in the store, she'd been invisible until it came time to pay for whatever she purchased. The few bits and pieces she bought for her mother were not enough to make her a valuable customer. Now, as Mrs. Tyler McKendrick, she was worthy of a smile and an offer of assistance.

Of course, maybe Mr. Fenton had more reason than most to appreciate the power of a name. He'd bought the store from old man Lewison before the Great War and changed the name to Fenton's Emporium. But the only place the name change registered was on the sign out front. Lewison's it had been for nearly forty years; Lewison's it stayed in the townspeople's minds. After a year or two, he'd taken the sign down and restored the old name to the front of the wooden building. The Fenton's Emporium sign had been nailed to the side of Bill Fenton's barn and was carefully repainted whenever it showed signs of wear. It had been there so long that most folks hardly realized it was there. But occasionally someone would take notice of it and shake their head over the peculiarities of others.

The old story was running through Meg's mind as she stepped past a neatly stacked pyramid of canned peas and nearly bumped into another customer.

"Excuse me," the other woman muttered. Without lifting her head, she moved to walk around Meg.

"Mama?"

At the sound of her voice, Ruth's head jerked up, her faced blue eyes startled. "Meg? I didn't realize it was you."

"Well, it is," Meg said, smiling. "How are you, Mama?" She could already see the answer. Meg wouldn't have thought it possible, but her mother was even thinner than she had been. There were new hollows in her cheeks and under her eyes.

"I'm fine," Ruth said, smiling. "How are you?"

"Just fine."

"Haven't seen you in a while," Ruth said.

"No. It's been a few weeks."

There was an awkward silence while both considered the circumstances of their last meeting, when Ty had punched

Ruth's husband. As if remembering what Harlan had said to incite Ty's violent reaction, Ruth flushed a little, her eyes dropping away from Meg's.

"I wanted to tell you how sorry I was about what Harlan said—about you losing the baby and all. He didn't mean anything by it. He was just—"

"He meant every word of it, Mama. And you and I both know it."

Ruth's flush deepened, dark color flooding her thin face. "He'd just got word that the bank was foreclosing on the hotel and he was upset."

"Please don't defend him to me, Mama." Meg's tone was soft but held a firmness that surprised her.

"He's my husband," Ruth said painfully, as if that fact explained everything.

"Did he do this to you?" Meg reached out to touch gentle fingers to the bruises that marked her mother's arm.

"He'd been drinking." Ruth pulled her sleeve down with a quick nervous movement. "It's been real hard on him to lose the hotel. He's not a bad—" Catching Meg's look, she broke off, her eyes dropping to the wooden floor between them.

Meg stared at her mother's downbent head. In the past year, the last traces of gold had faded from Ruth's hair, leaving it a dull gray. The sweater she wore was one she'd had as long as Meg could remember, and the dress it topped was almost as old. There was a patch near the hem where Ruth had caught the garment on the edge of the chicken house. Meg could remember watching her mother patch the hole with fabric she'd taken from the hem, carefully matching the print so that the patch was all but invisible. That had been—six? seven?—years ago.

It occurred to Meg that she couldn't remember the last time she'd seen her mother wear something new. There'd never been much money to buy things, but what little there had been, Ruth had spent on her children—always on necessities because there hadn't been any money to spend on anything else. Most times there hadn't been enough even to cover the bare essentials for the two of them, but Ruth had done the best she could with what she had.

Looking at her now, Meg felt a soft rush of love tinged by sadness. Her mother had made mistakes, some for which she and her sister had paid dearly. But she'd tried. No one could do more than that.

"Come and stay with us, Mama." The offer was made on impulse, without taking time to consider the consequences.

Ruth's eyes jerked to her daughter's face, wide and shocked. "What do you mean?"

"I mean you should come and live with Ty and me." Meg winced inwardly at the thought of what Ty would say, but she couldn't back out now. "There's plenty of room at the farmhouse."

"Oh, Meg." The color faded from Ruth's face, leaving her so pale Meg worried that she might faint. "I couldn't."

"Why not?" Meg demanded, praying that Ty would forgive her.

"I couldn't leave Harlan," Ruth said, shaking her head slowly.

"I don't see why not. What's he ever done to deserve you staying?"

"He's my husband," Ruth said, as if that explained everything.

And Meg saw that, as far as her mother was concerned, it did. It didn't matter what he'd done to her children or what he did to her, they were married, and that was all that need be said. Though Meg couldn't deny a certain feeling of relief that she wouldn't have to try to explain to Ty how Ruth had come to be living with them without him being consulted, she also felt frustration at her mother's choosing to stay in an untenable situation. Meg appreciated the sanctity of the wedding vows, but surely, the lines about no man setting asunder what the Lord had joined had never been meant to apply to a man like Harlan Davis.

"You told me once, Mama, that a marriage was like a quilt and that it was up to me to build something good and solid with what the Lord had given me. Remember?"

Meg waited until Ruth nodded before continuing. "Well, you can't make a quilt with fabric that's rotten. No matter how small you cut the pieces or how careful you are, it'll tear every time you slip a needle into it. When you've got fabric like that, maybe you just have to throw it away."

In the silence that followed her words, Meg could hear Bill Fenton shifting things near the front of the store. She could hear a car drive by outside, the sound of someone hailing a friend across the street. She listened to the steady thump of her own heartbeat as she waited for her mother to respond.

"You always did have too big a heart, Meg." Ruth's smile was soft and her fingers trembled as she reached out to touch her daughter's smooth young cheek.

"I didn't know it was possible to have too big a heart, Mama. Only one too small."

"You never did see why the world couldn't be what it ought."

"I still don't," Meg whispered, feeling suddenly very young.

"Because things are the way they are," Ruth said, as if stating an immutable law of nature. "Some things just can't be changed."

"They could be if you tried," Meg said stubbornly.

But Ruth was already shaking her head. "Things are what they are, Meg. But I thank you for asking me to stay with you."

Meg might have argued further, but just then the big grandfather clock that stood on the floor at one end of the counter in the front of the store began to bong the hour. Ruth jumped as if a lash had been laid across her shoulders, the brief moment of animation wiped from her features, leaving them worn and gray.

"I've got to go. Harlan will be wanting his supper."

With a quick, uncertain smile, Ruth walked around Meg and hurried to the counter to pay for the packet of needles she'd selected. Meg stayed where she was, turning only when she heard the sound of the bell over the door. Through the big front window, she watched her mother walk down the sidewalk, her shoulders hunched, her thin fingers clutching the front of her sweater over her faded dress. Meg watched until she'd gone out of sight beyond the window and then blinked back the tears that burned in her eyes.

"I saw my mother today." Meg spoke abruptly as Ty came into the bedroom, a towel wrapped around his waist, his torso still damp from the bath.

"You didn't go to that house, did you?" The thought that she might have risked going to Harlan Davis's house put an edge to his voice.

"No." Meg shook her head. "I went to Lewison's to get some thread and she was there, too."

Ty studied her reflection in the mirror that hung over the squat oak dresser they'd found in an outbuilding and cleaned up enough to bring in the house. Her mood had seemed pensive all evening, and he saw that same expression now. It bothered him to see her upset.

"How is she?"

Meg shrugged. She held the silver-backed brush that he'd given her for Christmas, but instead of lifting it to her hair, she was stroking her thumb back and forth over the soft bristles, her eyes on the aimless movement. "The bank foreclosed on the hotel," she said, by way of answer.

"I'd heard." And felt nothing but satisfaction at the news. As far as he was concerned, the loss of his business didn't even begin to compensate for Harlan Davis's crimes. Tarring and feathering might have partially satisfied Ty's desire to see the other man punished, but only partially.

"I—I asked her to come stay with us." The admission came out in a rush, because Meg needed to get it out quickly or not at all.

Ty had just lifted a towel to dry the last droplets of moisture from his shoulders, but his hand froze as he stared at her in shocked silence. Sensing his gaze, Meg lifted her eyes to meet his in the mirror.

"I konw I shouldn't have without talking to you first," she said miserably. "I'm sorry."

"No, that's all right." Ty struggled to keep the dismay from his voice. The last thing he wanted was another person moving in with them. "If you want your mother to live here, of course it's all right with me."

"It wasn't so much that I wanted her to live with us. I just hate to think of her with him."

Ty couldn't argue with that. He wouldn't have left a dog in Harlan Davis's care. "Well, that's fine, then," he said, hoping his enthusiasm didn't ring as false in her ears as it did in his. "There's plenty of room."

"She won't leave him," Meg said bleakly.

Ty was ashamed of the instant relief he felt. Meg was obviously upset. Tossing the second towel over his shoulder, he crossed the room to her, his bare feet silent on the wooden floors. He took the brush from her and set it on the dresser before putting his hands on her shoulders and turning her to face him.

"Your mother has to make her own choices, Meg," he said gently.

"But how can she stay with him? How could she stay with him, knowing what he did to Patsy, what he tried to do to me?"

The mention of Patsy only confirmed something Ty had suspected for a long time. If Davis had attacked Meg, why not his older stepdaughter, too? Ty spared a brief thought for Jack, wondering if he knew, wondering if he had any idea what he was dealing with.

"I don't know how she can stay with him," he answered Meg honestly. "Maybe she feels she has no choice."

"But I offered her a choice," she said, tilting her head back to look up at him. "I asked her to come stay with us. And all she said was that he was her husband and she couldn't leave."

"Well, that's her decision, then." Ty brushed his fingertips over Meg's cheek. "You can't force her to do what you think she should."

"I know." She brought her hands up to rest on his chest.

"I just wish—" She broke off with a sigh, unable to put into words what it was she wanted.

Ty kissed her forehead, wishing that he could take away the hurt she was feeling, wishing that he had an explanation for why things were the way they were. Unable to find the words he wanted, he settled for feathering soft kisses down the side of her face, seeking to distract her from thinking about things she couldn't change.

Meg's response was hesitant at first but Ty persisted, his hands sliding under the soft white cotton of her nightgown to find the warm curves of her, his kisses stealing her breath until she was clinging to him, her mouth opening under his, her body leaning into his strength.

Ty picked her up and carried her to the bed, the idea of distracting her completely forgotten, only the hunger and need left behind. Their lovemaking was fiercely tender, an emotional and physical coming together that left Ty exhausted yet more alive than he'd ever felt in his life.

Holding Meg afterward, listening to her breathing slow and steady as she fell asleep, it occurred to Ty that his life seemed more complete than it had ever been before. He still missed flying, would probably always miss it. Yet the aching emptiness he'd felt when he first realized he was going to have to give it up was gone. The work on the farm had helped fill that emptiness, but it was Meg who'd made everything whole again, who'd made him whole again.

The thought made him frown but he was asleep before he could give the idea any more consideration.

"You've made it a real home, Meggy." From her seat at the kitchen table, Patsy smiled at her sister.

"It was already a home. I've just put in a little elbow grease." Meg gave the bread dough a few quick strokes with the heels of her hands to drive the air from it, then patted it gently to flatten it for cutting into rolls.

"You always wanted a home like this, didn't you? You're happy here." There was a trace of wistfulness in Patsy's eyes as she watched Meg cut the dough with the top of a water glass.

Meg paused a moment, looking out the kitchen window to the fields, already showing the crisp green of newly sprouted corn. She could just make out Ty and Jack at the far end of the field, their figures attenuated by distance.

"I'd be happy anywhere with Ty," she said finally. She transferred the rounds of dough to a baking sheet, giving each one a quick brush of butter before folding it over on itself.

"You love him a lot." The words were a statement rather than a question, but Meg answered anyway.

"More than life," she said simply. She flipped a clean tea towel over the rolls and dusted her hands on her apron as she turned to join her sister at the table.

Patsy's visit had been unexpected but welcome. She'd called that morning to say that her neighbor was going to be heading that way and, if Ty wouldn't mind driving her home, she'd like to come and spend a few hours with Meg. The neighbor had dropped Patsy off an hour ago, and Meg had enjoyed the chance to show off the farmhouse, which was still sparsely furnished but beginning to look as if someone actually lived in it.

With the preparations for lunch well in hand, Meg studied her older sister across the table. Something was wrong. There were dark circles under Patsy's eyes and lines of strain bracketing her mouth. When they were children, Meg wouldn't have hesitated to come right out and ask what was wrong, but she didn't feel as if she could do that now.

"How is Eldin?"

"He's fine." Patsy stirred one finger through a small spill of sugar on the tabletop. "He travels a lot, you know."

"You must miss him."

"Yes." But there was no emotion behind the agreement.

Meg groped for something else to say, but Patsy suddenly lifted her head and looked directly at her, so much pain in her eyes that Meg almost cried out with it.

"I envy you, you know," she said slowly. "It must be wonderful. Being married to the man you love."

She'd inadvertently touched a nerve; the one dark cloud on Meg's horizon. Meg flinched, thinking that "wonderful" was not exactly the word she'd have used—not when Ty didn't love her in return. But that was her problem and not one she was willing to share with her sister.

"You love Eldin, don't you?"

"Yes." Patsy shrugged. "He's a sweet man. And so good to me. Yes, I love him. But not the way you love Ty."

"If you felt that way, why did you marry him?"

"For the same reason you married Ty." Patsy's mouth twisted bitterly. "To get away from home. The only difference is that your white knight happened to be the man you loved. Mine was a dear, sweet friend." She sighed abruptly and forced a brighter smile. "But he loves me. And I do love him."

Meg didn't even hear the last of what her sister said. She was busy absorbing the idea that Patsy had married a man she didn't love to escape the terror of their stepfather's abuse. Would she have done the same? If Ty had been nothing more than a friend, would she have married him? She didn't know.

"There was someone else, wasn't there?" Meg asked, looking at her sister. "Someone you loved?"

She saw the truth flicker in Patsy's eyes in the instant before she shook her head. "No. Nothing so dramatic." Her smile shook around the edges. "I just wonder, sometimes, what it would be like to be married to someone you loved the way you love Ty."

"I can't imagine being married to anyone else," Meg said simply. She considered pressing Patsy for the truth but decided it would be cruel to do so. Whoever she might have loved before she married Eldin, it was much too late to do anything about it. Talking about it would surely be like rubbing salt into an old wound.

"I saw Mama day before yesterday," Meg said, changing the subject.

"How was she?" There was more duty than interest in Patsy's question.

"Not good. The bank foreclosed on the hotel and he's taking it out on her. I think maybe he's drinking."

"Just like Pa used to do," Patsy said, shaking her head. "Funny, how people repeat the same mistakes over and over again."

"I asked her to come stay with Ty and me."

That announcement jerked Paty's eyes to her face. "Oh, Meggy, you didn't! You don't want somebody else living here, not when the two of you are just getting started."

"You don't have to worry. She turned me down, said she couldn't leave her husband." Meg got up to fetch the pitcher of tea from the icebox. After bringing it to the table, she topped off Patsy's drink. There was ice left in the glass so she didn't bother to chip any more from the block that had been delivered the day before. "But I couldn't see her like that and not offer to help her," she said stubbornly.

"Let her help herself for a change," Patsy said, her words hard with old anger.

"You don't mean that!" Meg protested.

"Yes, I do." Patsy's fingers clenched into a fist on the table. "Where was she when we needed her? Where was she when Pa took his belt to one of us? Or when *he*—"

Her voice broke and she stopped abruptly, drawing in a shuddering breath. Meg was momentarily speechless in the face of her sister's pain. When she spoke, she chose her words with care.

"I can't say that she was right to make the choices she did," she said slowly. "But I know she did the best she could for us."

"Well, it wasn't good enough!" Patsy snapped.

"Maybe not but it was still the best she could do and you can't ask anyone for more than that."

"She should have left him," Patsy muttered.

"I imagine she was scared. How would she have taken care of the two of us?"

"She still should have left him," Patsy insisted, but the anger was gone from her voice.

"Yes. I think she knows that," Meg said, remembering

the haunted look in her mother's eyes. "She'll have to live with that guilt for the rest of her life."

From the look in Patsy's eyes, she thought that perhaps it was the first time she'd considered that possibility. Meg glanced at the clock on the wall and stood up with an exclamation about getting lunch started.

After a moment, Patsy offered to help. Meg put her to work peeling potatoes to be boiled and mashed. She thought Patsy was probably as relieved as she was to have an excuse to drop the subject of their mother and the choices she'd made.

Despite the emotional intensity of the conversation that had gone before—or perhaps because of it—the two women worked in companionable silence, preparing fried chicken, mashed potatoes and gravy, and a salad of lettuce thinnings mixed with the first sweet green scallions and topped by a hot vinegar dressing.

Meg fried the chicken while Patsy set the table. Glancing over her shoulder, she noticed that there were only three plates on the table.

"We'll need another plate," she said, turning back to the chicken sizzling in a skillet of melted lard. "Jack always has lunch with us."

"Jack?" Patsy's voice was sharp but Meg was too busy turning the browned chicken to notice.

"He works with Ty just about every day. I don't know what we'd have done if he hadn't come back from California to help us."

Before Meg had a chance to do more than register the silence from her sister's direction, the back door was pushed open and Ty and Jack entered. Jack was in the lead and, when he saw Patsy, he stopped so abruptly that Ty ran into his back.

"What the—" Ty broke off when he saw his sister-in-law. "Hello, Patsy." He stepped around Jack's frozen form and continued into the kitchen.

"Hello, Ty."

Meg had watched the byplay from her place in front of the stove, but she wasn't quite sure what it was she'd just witnessed.

"I could smell that chicken frying halfway across the field," Ty said as he walked to the sink to wash his hands. "I'm so hungry I think I could eat a bear. How about you, Jack?"

The question seemed to break the spell that had held Jack in one place. With a sound that could have been either a yes or a no, he dragged his eyes from Patsy and joined Ty at the sink. Patsy turned to get another plate from the cupboard, and Meg was left to wonder if she'd imagined the entire scene.

But the finely drawn tension at the lunch table was definitely not her imagination. It was nothing she could put her finger on, unless she counted the way Jack and Patsy avoided looking at each other or the fact that neither addressed so much as a single word to the other.

At one point, Meg glanced up to find Patsy's head bent, her attention apparently absorbed by the contents of her plate. Jack was looking at her and the pain in his eyes was so raw that Meg felt it as if it were her own. Her glance skidded from his face to Ty's, their eyes meeting for a moment. She thought she read something in his gaze—sympathy? And then he glanced away and said something to Jack.

Meg picked up a forkful of mashed potatoes. They tasted like paste in her mouth, but she chewed, paying no attention to the conversation going on between the two men. The most incredible idea was turning around in her head. Ty had said that the cause of Jack's unhappiness was a married woman. And hadn't Jack spent time in Regret not long before Patsy suddenly married Eldin Baker? It was impossible, of course. Not Jack and Patsy. And yet . . .

Meg was sure she wasn't the only one who was glad to see the meal end. And she wasn't surprised when, the moment the last dish had been cleared from the table, Patsy announced that she really should be getting home.

"Just let me put the dishes in to soak and I'll take you," Meg said.

"I can take you home, Patsy." Jack's offer fell into a pool of silence, like a stone into water, the ripples from it spreading outward.

Meg spun away from the sink, feeling her heart beating much too fast when she saw the look that passed between her sister and her husband's best friend.

"That's okay, Jack. I don't mind taking Patsy home. There's no sense in you making a special trip." She hoped her words didn't sound as rushed to everyone else as they did to her.

"I was quitting after lunch, anyway," Jack said, giving Meg an easy smile that did nothing to reassure her. From the way Ty's brows rose, Meg guessed it was the first he'd heard of Jack's plans to quit early. "How about it, Patsy?" Jack asked.

Meg held her breath, willing Patsy to tell him no, to say that she'd been looking forward to Meg taking her home. Patsy hesitated and then nodded slowly. "If you're sure it's no trouble, Jack."

Meg opened her mouth—to say what, she couldn't have said. But she caught Ty's warning look and closed it again without speaking. She was probably making something out of nothing at all. And even if it was something, she could hardly forbid her sister to let Jack drive her home.

But she couldn't prevent a worried frown as she and Ty stood on the front porch and watched Jack help Patsy into his car. Ty slid his arm around Meg's waist as Jack circled the hood and pulled open the driver's door. With a wave of his hand, Jack slid behind the wheel.

Meg nibbled on her lower lip as he backed the car around and then sent it bumping down the lane. What if her suspicions, crazy as they were, were right? What if Jack was the man Patsy had loved when she married Eldin, the man Patsy had said didn't exist?

She was so lucky, Meg thought, suddenly fiercely grateful for the weight of Ty's arm against her waist. Ty might not love her the way she loved him, but she could still hope for that to change. What if she'd married someone else? What would there be to hope for then?

* * *

Patsy watched the fields drift by beyond the window of the car. Though neither of them had spoken a word since leaving Ty and Meg's, she was vividly aware of Jack's presence just across the seat. If she stretched out her arm, she could touch his shoulder, she thought. She didn't do anything of the sort, of course, but that didn't prevent her from feeling a tingle of awareness at the possibility.

Oddly enough, the silence was not thick with the tensions that had lain between them the last two times they'd seen each other. It had more of a waiting edge to it, a feeling of expectation. Patsy was reminded of a tornado that had touched down near Regret when she was a girl. She'd seen the funnel cloud from a distance and had watched it approach, fascinated by the power it represented, the terrible beauty of it.

She'd felt this same kind of expectation then, the breathless feeling of teetering on the brink of a huge new discovery. Her mother had come and snatched her up and carried her into the cellar to wait out the tornado, keeping her safe. This time there was no one to shield her from danger but herself. The question was: Did she want to be shielded?

They still had not spoken when Jack pulled the car to a stop in front of her home. Patsy stared at the little white house, paint gleaming in the midafternoon sun. For almost six years her life had revolved around that house, cleaning it, tending the garden, keeping it neat and tidy, inside and out. When she looked into the future, she saw the rest of her life being lived out within its simple walls, her horizons never expanding beyond what could be seen from its windows.

"Would you like to come in?" She didn't look at Jack as she proffered the invitation. She felt, rather than heard, his indrawn breath.

"Yes."

Such a simple response to a such a simple question, she thought as he got out of the car and came around to open her door. Only there was nothing simple about it and they both knew it.

As she opened the front door and stepped into the dim interior of the house, Patsy was very conscious of what she was about to do. There was nothing impulsive about her decision, and there'd be no pretending that it had been out of her control.

She heard Jack close the door behind them as she dropped her handbag on the small table in the entry. She stepped out of her shoes as she walked past the living room doorway. The house was warm with the accumulation of a day's heat. If she'd been home, she would have opened windows to let the heat escape. But even if she'd opened every window in the house, it wouldn't have cooled the heat she felt.

Still without speaking, she reached the hallway that led to the bedrooms. Patsy didn't have to look back to know that Jack hesitated a moment before following her. She'd known he'd hesitate and known just as surely that he'd follow her. After all these years, she still knew him so well.

Patsy walked past the bedroom she shared with her husband when he was home. It was foolish, considering what she was about to do, but it would have seemed like a betrayal to take Jack in there. Instead, she pushed open the door to the seldom-used guest room. As if the location could soften the sin she was committing, she thought, amused by her own foolishness.

She stopped in the middle of the room and turned to face Jack. He stood in the doorway, as if he could still turn and walk away. But he wouldn't, she thought, almost dreamily. They'd both lost this battle a long time ago. They'd just been too stubborn to admit it.

Patsy reached behind her and began unbuttoning her dress, hearing the sudden catch in Jack's breathing as his eyes dropped to her breasts, which were thrust forward by the awkward angle of her arms. He didn't offer to help but only stood there, not moving, not speaking, hardly breathing as she stripped to her skin. She saw his throat work as he swallowed, his eyes moving down her body, trailing fire wherever they touched.

"Patsy . . ."

"Don't." She moved toward him, reaching out to take his hand and draw him into the room. "Don't talk. Not now."

She saw the protest in his eyes, the knowledge that what they were about to do was wrong. And she saw a reflection of her own hunger, of the need that burned inside her.

Loving him, she took the decision from his hands and rose on her toes, balancing herself with one hand on his shoulder, and brought her mouth to his. There was a moment, but a moment only, when she felt him resisting the pull of what lay between them. But it was too strong for both of them. It always had been.

With a sound halfway between a sob and a groan, his arms were suddenly around her and his mouth crushed hers with an avid hunger. Patsy melted against him, feeling herself complete for the first time in more than five years. There'd be hell to pay later, but she'd gladly pay the price for these few minutes of heaven.

Chapter 24

Jack didn't show up at the farm the day after Patsy's visit. Meg debated about calling her sister but decided, reluctantly, that Patsy would probably be justifiably annoyed to have her younger sister check up on her. But that didn't prevent Meg from worrying.

She and Ty had carefully *not* discussed what had happened between Jack and Patsy, if anything had happened outside her own imagination. Whatever he knew was something private between him and Jack and Meg wouldn't have asked him to betray a confidence. Still, she couldn't help but wonder . . .

Perhaps Ty sensed that she needed a distraction, because instead of going back out to the fields after lunch, he suggested a trip into Regret. He'd said he had some things to pick up at the hardware store, but he seemed in no particular hurry to get them once they'd parked the car.

Linking her arm through his, Ty strolled down the sidewalk as if he had all the time in the world. Meg found herself relaxing. Whatever Patsy had done in the past or chose to do in the future, sitting around worrying about it wasn't going to change anything. The sun was shining, it was a beautiful late-spring day, and Ty was with her. It just wasn't possible to worry about anything.

When Ty turned into Barnett's Drugstore and headed for the gleaming soda fountain, it seemed exactly the right touch to the afternoon.

"Well, look who's here." Eddie Dunsmore leaned against the tall marble counter and grinned at them as they sat down. "Haven't seen you two in a while. Not since you got married and left for sunny California. Heard you were back but wasn't sure I believed it. Who'd leave Hollywood for Iowa in the middle of winter?" Meg smiled at his exaggerated shiver.

"Hello, Eddie. It's good to see you."

"It's good to see you, too, Meg." He grinned at her and Meg felt Ty shift abruptly on the stool next to her. She glanced at him questioningly, wondering if something was wrong, but he was looking at Eddie, frowning.

Eddie must have noticed his disapproving gaze because he straightened and swiped a damp rag across the already spotless counter. "What'll you have? No, wait. Don't tell me." He held up his hand, narrowing his eyes in concentration. "Let me guess. "Cherry Chopped Suey Sundae for the lady, right?"

"You read my mind," Meg said.

"And a coffee soda for the gentleman," Eddie finished, glancing at Ty.

"Exactly."

"Coming up." Eddie sent Ty a pitying glance as he turned away. Ty mumbled something under his breath but when Meg asked him to repeat it, he shook his head.

"I'm so glad you thought of this," she said, smiling up at him happily.

Ty threw a doubtful glance in Eddie's direction before agreeing. "It is nice."

"It reminds me of last summer," she said, her voice warm with memories.

"A lot's changed since then." Ty reached out and smoothed a loose strand of hair back behind her ear. It was a simple, husbandly gesture and served to point up just how much things had changed in the last year.

Meg smiled her thanks at Eddie when he set her sundae in

front of her. He looked as if he might linger but then a customer sat down at the far end of the counter and he departed, sped on his way by a less than friendly look from Ty.

"Don't you like Eddie?" Meg asked, having caught this last look.

"Sure I do." Ty pulled his soda close and took hold of the straw.

"Then why did you scowl at him just now?" Meg picked up her spoon and waited expectantly for his response.

"He's a nice kid but he's a little too friendly sometimes," Ty muttered into his drink.

Too friendly? Meg dipped her spoon into her sundae and pondered the thought. Odd that Ty should think Eddie was too friendly. She'd never noticed it herself. Perhaps Eddie sensed that Ty didn't appreciate his company, because he kept himself occupied while they were enjoying their treats.

"You're awfully quiet," Ty said as he paid for their ice cream.

"Just thinking." Meg smiled and waved at Eddie as she slid off her stool. No matter what Ty thought, she liked him.

"Thinking about what?" Ty slid his hand under her elbow as they left Barnett's, pausing on the steps for a moment to allow their eyes to adjust to the sunlight.

"About last summer. About all the times we went to the movie and then you took me to Barnett's for a soda afterward. It was fun, wasn't it?" She looked up at him, suddenly anxious for reassurance.

"Yes. And who'd have thought we'd end up a stodgy old married couple just a year later?" He grinned down at her and Meg could see no shadows, no regrets in his eyes.

She smiled and then lowered her head before he could see the gleam of tears in her eyes. One thing that hadn't changed was how much she loved him. Nor her longing for him to love her in return. Meg wondered if there was something wrong with her, that she couldn't be satisfied with what she had. But no matter how many times she told herself that it was so much more than she'd ever expected, than she had any right to expect, she still couldn't stop herself from wanting the one thing that might remain forever out of reach.

While she'd been thinking of what might never be, Ty had led her across the street. To get to the hardware store, they had to walk past her stepfather's hotel. Its doors were closed and the windows stared blindly out into the street. Looking at it, Meg had the odd feeling that the building was surprised to find itself empty and abandoned.

She was so busy staring up at the brick facade that she didn't notice when someone stepped into their path. But she felt the quick tension in Ty's arm the instant before she heard a familiar whine.

"Come to gloat over the remains?" Harlan Davis stood in front of them, his small eyes narrowed, his mouth twisted in bitter anger.

Despite what her mother had said about how hard he'd taken the hotel's closing, Meg was shocked by the changes in her stepfather. He'd always prided himself on his neatness. From the perfect crease in his hat to the shine on his shoes, Harlan Davis was a neat man. Or he had been. The man standing before them was carelessly shaved and even more carelessly dressed. He looked as if he'd slept in his suit and combed his thin hair with his fingers, leaving the pink skin of his scalp to show through the poorly arranged strands.

"Get out of the way, Davis," Ty said in a low voice.

"Don't think I don't know that you're to blame for this," Harlan said, waving one hand toward the empty hotel. "I should have known that you'd find a way to destroy me."

"You're a lunatic." Ty started to lead Meg around him, but Harlan stepped into their path again.

"You told your friends at the bank to foreclose, didn't you?" he hissed angrily.

"Maybe you haven't heard, but there's a depression. Banks don't need anyone to tell them to foreclose."

"I know what you did." Harlan lifted his arm to point an accusing finger at Ty's chest, swaying slightly.

Meg could smell the liquor on his breath even from where she stood, and she felt her stomach turn in automatic response to the sour smell. She was aware of the discreet and not-so-discreet glances coming their way. After the scene in the churchyard a few weeks before, there probably wasn't a soul in Regret who didn't know that there was no love lost between Ty and his father-in-law. From the iron tension in the muscles under her hand, Meg knew Ty was fighting the urge to punch the other man again.

"I don't give a damn what you think you know, Davis," he said, his voice low and hard. "If you've got the sense God gave a tree stump, you'll stay out of my way and stay away from my wife. As long as you do that, you're welcome to go to hell any way you damned well please."

Without waiting for a response, Ty led Meg around the other man. But Harlan was determined to have the last word, even if he had to shout it at their backs.

"I know what you did, McKendrick. Don't think you're going to get away with it."

Ty made a sound low in his throat and slowed but Meg's hand tightened around his arm.

"Please," she whispered, vividly aware that they were the cynosure of every eye. To her relief, Ty continued down the sidewalk. Meg had never been so happy in her life to step into the cool darkness of the hardware store.

"You go ahead. I think I'll just wait here." She was proud of the steadiness of her voice but Ty wasn't fooled for a minute.

"Are you all right?"

"I'm fine." Seeing the concern in his eyes, she summoned up a smile. "I'm not going to say I wouldn't rather have avoided that scene, but I'm fine."

He looked doubtful but when she made a shooing gesture with one hand, he reluctantly went to get the parts he needed. Meg waited until he'd disappeared toward the back of the store before allowing the smile to fade and her shoulders to sag a little.

Why was it that, just when everything was going so well, her past reared up to haunt them? Blinking back tears caused by anger as much as anything else, Meg turned to look out the front window, thinking that the sunshine didn't look as bright as it had before the encounter with her stepfather. Why couldn't he just leave them alone?

Jack was gone for two days. When he did show up at the farm, he looked like he'd been dragged through a knothole backward and so Ty bluntly informed him.

"Thanks." Jack's grin lacked its usual devilish edge. He cupped both hands around the mug of coffee Ty had poured him from the vacuum bottle Meg filled for him every morning. He'd found Ty in the barn, milking the cow he'd bought from a neighboring farmer the week after he and Meg moved to the farm, because, as Jack had pointed out, what was a farm without a milk cow?

The minute Meg had seen the Jersey's soft brown eyes, she'd named her Molly, and she was well on her way to becoming a pet. Ty shuddered to think what would happen when Molly calved. He couldn't imagine Meg being willing to sell a sweet-faced calf to be butchered and had visions of himself becoming a cattle rancher as well as a farmer.

Once he saw his friend's hands securely wrapped around the sturdy mug, Ty reseated himself on the milking stool to finish the task Jack's arrival had interrupted. For a little while, the barn was silent except for the rhythmic splash of milk into the bucket between his feet.

"I never thought I'd live long enough to see you become a farmer," Jack commented.

"Not exactly where I thought I'd end up," Ty agreed, thinking of his plans for starting some kind of flying service with Jack. But the old dreams caused only a brief pang of regret.

"Heard you had some trouble with Davis," Jack said.

"Some. He thinks I had something to do with the bank foreclosing on his hotel. Made me wish I'd thought of it," Ty said regretfully.

"Man's crazy." Jack shook his head. "How'd Meg take it?"

"She was upset."

"Yeah, I guess she would be." Jack's voice was absent. When Ty glanced at him, he saw that Jack was staring at the wall, his thoughts obviously elsewhere.

Ty gave one last tug on the cow's udder and stood up, pushing the stool out of his way. He bent to pick up the milk bucket and set it out of harm's way before he loosened the knot that had held Molly's head close to a post to keep her from moving while he milked her. Molly gave him an enigmatic look out of long-lashed eyes before turning and ambling off down the barn.

"You're asking for trouble, you know," Ty said, almost conversationally.

"I know." Jack didn't pretend not to know what he was talking about. "When I first saw her again, I just wanted to know what had happened five years ago, why she'd married someone else."

Ty thought of what he knew about Patsy, of what her stepfather had done. Should he tell Jack why she might have been so desperate that she'd married another man rather than wait for Jack to come back from Europe?

"And then she told me," Jack said, speaking more to himself than to Ty. "At least she told me part of it. But there are things I don't understand about her."

"I don't think anyone ever completely understands another person," Ty said. He'd never seen Jack like this. Never seen that bleak look on his face, the emptiness in his eyes. What good would it do to tell him everything? "Does it really matter what happened five years ago?" he asked quietly. "It doesn't change the fact that she's married. Are you willing to break up her marriage?"

"In a minute, if she'd have me." Jack's mouth twisted in a bitter smile as he met his friend's gaze. "I suppose that sounds pretty terrible."

"No. But it sounds like a way for a couple of good people to get pretty badly hurt."

"Yeah. The question is: Who gets hurt the worst? Me, Patsy, or her husband? Damn. I've never even met the guy. Why do I feel as if I've just kicked a puppy?"

There wasn't anything Ty could say. He had his answer, if he'd needed one, as to what had happened between his friend and Meg's sister. It wasn't his place to judge. What if it had been Meg who'd married another man? He was surprised by the almost savage wave of denial caused by that thought.

"Maybe it's time I went back to California," Jack said slowly, distracting Ty from considering his own reaction.

"Could be. Might do you good to be gainfully employed again instead of loafing around here getting in my way."

Jack's grin was a little thin around the edges, but Ty was pleased to see a subtle lessening of the shadows in his eyes. "Hope I haven't slowed you up too much," he drawled.

"Nothing I can't recover from," Ty reassured him. "Come on up to the house. Meg baked cinnamon rolls yesterday and I think there may be one or two left."

He picked up the milk bucket as Jack followed him from the barn.

About a week after the unpleasant incident with Harlan Davis, Ty ran out of nails halfway through rebuilding the chicken house. Since Meg was already nurturing a batch of chicks in a box in the kitchen and since they showed a remarkable ability to escape the confines of their small home and scatter to all corners of the room, a chicken house had become a necessity.

Considering the way Meg had reacted to Molly's arrival and the fact that she was already starting to name the indistinguishable balls of yellow fluff, Ty had already resigned himself to having a flock of pampered pets. He could just imagine how she'd react to the idea of one of her feathered friends ending up in a stewpot a few months from now.

A smile tugged at the corners of his mouth as he set the hammer down. He didn't mind, as long as she was happy. Funny how, over the past few months, her happiness had come to mean more to him than his own. He frowned as he considered that idea. But before it could take hold, he saw Meg working in the garden.

She was wearing a faded dress, so old that the red and

white print had blended into an indistinct pink blur. On her head was a straw hat to shield her face from the sun. She looked practical, slightly silly, and utterly desirable. For a moment, Ty debated the possibility of forgetting about the chicken house and persuading his wife to come to bed, but then he remembered that Jack had said he'd be out around midafternoon. Besides, from the look of the clouds building up to the west, they were in for some rain, and he really did want to get the roof on before then.

By the time he'd told Meg where he was going, confirmed that she didn't want to go with him, and taken time for a kiss or two—she really did look irresistible in that silly hat—a breeze had kicked up and the clouds wre visibly closer. Ty doubted that he was going to get the roof done before the storm hit, but he'd still need the nails to finish it tomorrow.

With the nails in a paper bag on the floor of the roadster, he drove out of Regret. The breeze now carried the smell of rain and he could see small clouds scudding across the sky, like messengers running before the dark bank of thunderheads behind. He turned his head automatically as he drove past Meg's old home. Maybe it was the threat of rain in the air, but he had a sudden flash of her running from the little house, out into the storm, coming to him for protection.

Thank God she had, Ty thought as he accelerated past the house. Otherwise, he'd have gone to California and left her behind. And he'd probably have been too stupid even to realize that he was only half alive without her.

Only half alive. The roadster slowed to a crawl as Ty realized where his aimless thought had brought him. My God. He was in love with his wife. He'd been in love with her for months and just hadn't been bright enough to recognize it. He'd thought he was marrying her to protect her, when he'd been in love with her all along.

It was, perhaps, not the most romantic moment to realize that he was in love with Meg. But if the shock of it hadn't lifted his foot off the accelerator, he might not have recognized the woman walking along the verge of the road. Ruth Davis. As he stopped the car next to her, she turned to look at him and Ty bit off an exclamation when he saw her battered face. Before he could turn off the engine, she was tugging open the passenger door and falling into the seat.

"What happened?" Ty demanded, as if he didn't know what had happened. Obviously, her husband had taken out his frustrations on her.

"Hurry." She was out of breath, as if she'd been running. And from the scratches on her arms and legs, Ty guessed that she'd fallen.

"It's okay, Mrs. Davis," he said soothingly, reaching for her hand. "You're safe."

"Noooo." The word was a moan as she struggled to catch her breath. Her thin fingers grabbed his arm, digging in with surprising strength. "He's crazy mad. I tried to stop him but I wasn't strong enough."

"It's all right." Beneath the bruises, her face was so alarmingly flushed that Ty was afraid her heart was going to give out. "Calm down. We'll report him to the sheriff. He won't hurt you again."

"Not me." She gasped. "Meg. He's gone to your place. Said he was going to kill the both of you."

Ty stared at her for a second, his mind's eye filled the picture of Meg working in the garden, smiling at him as he left, her face flushed from sun and kisses. Meg alone on the farm.

Gravel spun beneath the rear wheels as he pulled out onto the road. Ruth subsided into the passenger seat. Her breathing was still ragged, but she offered not a word of protest as he took a corner fast enough to send the car skidding halfway across the road.

There was no need to panic, Ty told himself. Jack was probably already there. He'd keep Meg safe. If not, then Meg might have heard Davis's car. She'd hide somewhere. There were a thousand places to hide. She'd be all right.

She had to be all right. He couldn't lose her, not when he'd just realized how much she meant to him. God couldn't be so cruel.

Ty coaxed a little more speed out of the engine and prayed like he'd never prayed in his life.

Meg crawled along the length of the row, carefully setting tomato seedlings into the ground and patting soil around them as carefully as if she were tucking a baby into its crib. She wanted to get them all in before the rain started. The rains would settle them into place and keep them so happy that they wouldn't even know they'd been transplanted. Or so she hoped.

She'd always loved to garden. When Patsy had complained about the heat and the bugs and the dirt, Meg had been enjoying the rich, earthy smells of soil and growing things. There was nothing quite like the smell of a tomato plant, she thought happily as she sat back on her heels at the end of the row and brought her hand up to her nose to sniff the warm, pungent scent.

Ty had suggested that she was making the garden too big, that she didn't have to try to grow all their food this first year, but she'd dreamed all her life of a garden big enough to get lost in. Of course, it wasn't possible to get very lost when none of the plants was more than a few inches tall, but come August, it would be a different story. It didn't take any effort to imagine the wild tangle of greenery she'd have then.

Hearing a car in front of the house, Meg climbed to her feet and bent down to brush the dirt off the hem of her old dress. Either Ty was home sooner than she'd expected or Jack was here. She was almost halfway to the house when she saw someone come around the side of the house. Since the straw hat dangled from her fingers, she lifted her free hand to shade her eyes, her mouth curved in a welcoming smile.

But it was neither Jack nor Ty walking toward her. It was Harlan Davis. Her smile vanished and she felt a frisson of fear run up her spine. She stood her ground, setting her chin. This was her home and she wasn't going to let him frighten her. Not here. But the closer he came, the more she doubted the wisdom of taking a stand. She remembered the way he'd looked when he'd accosted her and Ty in town, disheveled, unkempt, the sanity a thin veneer in his pale eyes. He was still walking toward her, and there was something eerie about that steady, silent approach.

Making an abrupt decision, Meg turned and ran. Immediately she heard the thud of his footsteps pounding after her, lending wings to her feet. He was between her and the house, but if she could circle it, get to the road, there might be someone passing by. She was young and healthy, surely she could outrun him. She couldn't let him catch her. The thought of him putting his hands on her again was too horrible to contemplate.

Meg might have made it if her foot hadn't caught on an exposed tree root just as she reached the front of the house. She stumbled, fighting to stay on her feet as her momentum carried her forward to sprawl in the scrubby grass near the side of the porch. She was scrambling to her feet the minute she hit the ground, but it was too late. The few seconds had been all he needed to reach her.

A scream tore from her throat as she felt his hands close over the back of her dress, heard the sound of tearing fabric. It was like the last time, she thought, momentarily dazed by the horror of it. He was ripping her clothes. She could feel the terrible lust in him, the anger, the need to hurt and humiliate.

She jerked her elbow back and had a moment's satisfaction at his grunt of pain. But then he'd grabbed her shoulder and flipped her onto her back, his hand cracking across her cheek with stunning force. Meg saw stars, felt a black mist creep over her. She blinked, forcing it back, refusing to give in to the urge to simply sink into the welcoming arms of oblivion.

This wasn't going to happen. Denial roared in her head. She wasn't going to let this happen. She brought up her hands, her fingernails gouging for his eyes as she bucked beneath his weight.

"Ty will kill you," she spit breathlessly. "He'll kill you!"

"Not if I kill him first." Harlan cackled, the last traces of sanity gone.

Meg froze for a moment and then began to fight with

redoubled strength, this time fighting not just for herself but for Ty.

He was tearing at her bodice now and her hand flew out, groping for something she could use to stop him. His hand found her breast, squeezing painfully, but Meg's fingers closed over a fist-size rock. Using all her strength, she slammed it against his temple. It was an awkward blow, the angle preventing her from getting any significant force behind it. But it served to stun Harlan momentarily. He grunted with pain, his hands slackening on her.

The effect didn't last long, but it was long enough for Meg to scramble away.

"Bitch!" She felt his hand swipe at the hem of her dress as she gained her feet. She didn't hesitate but took off running.

If she could just get to the road, she thought. He wouldn't dare attack her there, where someone might see. If she could just get that far. Ty would be home soon. She heard the heavy rush of his footsteps behind her as she rounded the front of the house, and she cast a terrified look over her shoulder.

And then she slammed into a hard male body.

The scream that tore from her had its origins in the depths of her soul. Her only thought was that Harlan had somehow managed to get in front of her. Never mind that she'd just heard him behind her. She screamed again as strong arms closed around her, her head whipping back, her frightened eyes fastening on her captor's face.

And saw Ty's dark eyes staring down at her.

"Oh, God." She collapsed against him, her breath coming in deep, racking sobs.

"It's all right," he said, his arms hard around her. For a moment she believed him. But then she remembered her stepfather's threat, the madness in his eyes.

"We have to run," she said frantically. "He's crazy. He's going to kill you."

She felt Ty looking over her shoulder and knew he was staring at her stepfather. She began to push at his chest, trying physically to move him away from danger. "Oh, God, please, Ty. We have to run. He'll kill you."

* * *

Ty allowed her to edge him backward, thinking more in terms of getting Harlan Davis out into the open than of protecting himself. He was going to kill the bastard, he thought, almost dispassionately. For what he'd done to Meg—and he didn't know the full extent of that yet—Harlan Davis was going to die.

"Thought you could get the best of me," Harlan said, foolish enough to follow them to the front of the house. Ty said nothing, carefully judging when he should make his move. He wanted to be sure Davis was far from cover. He didn't want to have to drag him out from under the toolshed, for example.

He'd heard Meg scream as he brought the car to a skidding stop. And he knew the sound of that scream would be etched on his soul forever. Death was not nearly punishment enough for the man who'd forced that scream from her, but it would do for a start. He'd leave it to the afterlife to deliver the rest of Harlan Davis's sentence.

"You stop right there, Harlan."

Ty's head jerked toward the sound of Ruth's voice. He'd forgotten she was there, forgotten everything but the need to make sure Meg was safe and the equally strong need to kill her attacker.

"This has gone far enough," she said, her voice quavering uncertainly. She stood next to the car, one hand in the pocket of the same gray sweater she'd worn just about every time Ty had seen her.

"Shut up," Harlan snarled. "This is all your doing. You and those whoring daughters of yours."

Ty would have gone for his throat then and there, but Meg's fingers were clinging to his arms, refusing to release him.

"This ain't their doing, Harlan." Ruth stood straight, oblivious to the wind that blew the skirt of her dress back against her thin body. "What you've done is wrong. And I was wrong to turn a blind eye. Lord knows I've regretted not stopping you every day of my life. But I'm stopping you now."

"You stay out of this. I'll deal with you later." Harlan

started toward Ty and Meg, and Ty tensed, ready to thrust Meg away from him, adrenaline pumping through his veins.

"You'll deal with me now," Ruth said.

Something in her tone made Ty's glance flick to her. What he saw nearly shocked the breath from him. Ruth had taken her hand from her pocket and in it, steady as could be, was a pistol, pointed directly at her husband. Ty heard Meg gasp as she turned her head toward her mother.

Harlan stopped in his tracks, shock flickering over his pale features, followed an instant later by disbelief and then contempt. "You won't pull that trigger. You don't have the courage." He bent to pick up a good-size branch that had fallen from one of the trees that shaded the farmhouse.

"Harlan. I'm warning you." Ruth's voice was as steady as her hand, but he didn't seem to hear her. Lifting the branch, he started toward the young couple.

Ty didn't know whether he believed Ruth would pull the trigger or not, but he thrust Meg behind him and braced for Harlan's attack.

"I'll teach you." Harlan lifted the branch, planning to bring it down like a club. But the movement was never completed.

The sound of the shot was nearly lost in a faraway roll of thunder. A neat round hole appeared in Harlan's forehead and his pale eyes looked startled. For an instant he was frozen, the branch still poised to strike. Then the weight of it toppled him over onto his back.

In the silence that followed, Ruth's voice seemed loud.

"He never would listen to me," she said plaintively.

The hours that followed were chaotic. Jack arrived within minutes of the shooting and was understandably surprised to find a body lying in the front yard. Ruth was huddled on the front porch, the gray sweater pulled tight around her thin body as she rocked herself softly back and forth. Meg sat beside her, a robe dragged on over her ruined dress, her face white and shocked. Ty had called Ben Marlon and then found a tarp to throw over the body.

By the time the sheriff got there, it had begun to rain, a slow steady patter just right for settling in new seedlings and watering the thirsty soil. There were questions to be asked, answers to be given. Ty had called Patsy and she arrived in a taxi—damn the cost.

She hesitated a moment when she saw Jack, but then her eyes flickered past him to her mother and sister. She went to them, putting her arm around her mother, rocking her as if she were a child.

Everyone knew Harlan Davis had been getting crazy as a peach orchard boar, and Ben saw no reason to doubt the story that Ty and Meg gave. Ruth said almost nothing, answering only when spoken to, seeming to stare inward at some picture only she could see. There'd be a formal hearing, of course, but Ben didn't doubt that the verdict would come back as self-defense.

The body was loaded into the back of the neighbor's pickup and hauled off to town, and Jack discreetly kicked plenty of dirt over the bloody stain on the ground. The rain would soon wash away any remaining traces of the violence that had occurred there.

Hunching his shoulders against the dampness, Jack went inside. Patsy and her mother were sitting at the kitchen table. Patsy glanced up as he entered and then looked away again. Ty leaned on the edge of the sink, his arms around Meg's waist, pulling her back against him. Jack didn't think he'd let her get more than a foot away from him in the past two hours. From the look on Ty's face, Jack suspected his friend had finally figured out what had been obvious for months—that he was in love with his wife.

"I should be getting home." Ruth said, stirring herself out of the stupor that had gripped her.

"You can't go back to that house," Meg protested immediately. "You can stay here with us."

"I don't want to be a bother," Ruth said, shaking her head.

"You wouldn't be a bother, would she, Ty?"

"You're welcome to stay with us, Mrs. Davis." There was

no doubting the sincerity in Ty's invitation, and Ruth wavered for a moment.

"Come stay with me, Mama." Patsy's offer was quiet. "Eldin's away from home so much of the time. I'd welcome the company."

Ruth looked at her elder daughter, her eyes searching. "You don't have to offer me a place to stay, Patsy," she whispered.

"I know that. I want you to stay with me. Please, Mama."

Jack didn't know exactly what had happened between the two of them, but he knew he was witnessing the start of healing of an old wound.

"I—I'd like that," Ruth said softly. Her hand trembled slightly as she reached out to touch her daughter's arm. "I'd like that very much."

"I can drive you home, if you'd like," Jack said, not giving himself time to think.

He felt Ty watching him, but his attention was on Patsy. Her eyes came up to meet his. In them, he saw the memory of what had happened the last time he'd driven her home. Then she blinked and looked away, nodding slowly.

"Thank you. That would be very kind of you." The formal tone pinched something in Jack's chest, like a forerunner of greater pain yet to come.

The farewells were subdued, though the three women hugged with a fervor that said more than words could have. Ruth and Patsy climbed into the back of the Packard, and Jack shut the door on them before sliding behind the wheel. No one had much to say during the drive. Jack glanced in the rearview mirror from time to time, half hoping to catch Patsy's eye, but she seemed engrossed in the view out the side window, leaving him with only a glimpse of her profile.

When they arrived at the Baker home, Jack followed the two women inside. This might not be the best time, but he had to talk to Patsy, even if only for a moment. Since she didn't try to persuade him to leave, he assumed she felt the same.

He waited in the living room while Patsy settled her mother in bed and tried not to wonder if it was the bed they'd shared a few days ago. Listening to the rain outside, it hit him that he hated the smell of lavender and furniture wax. Restrained, confining smells.

Though his back was to the door, he knew the minute she walked in. He spoke without turning.

"How is she?"

"Tired. I'm not sure she really knows what's happened."

She sounded tired and he turned to look at her, his eyes hungry as he took in every detail of her, from the soft cap of curls that framed her face to the soft flare of her hips beneath the print dress.

"I drove by a time or two this past week, but there was a car parked in front of the house."

"Eldin was home for a few days. He's gone off to Illinois now." She didn't look at him as she spoke but stared at the polished top of an end table instead.

"I'm going back to California next week."

The words fell into a pool of silence. He waited for her to say something, though he couldn't have said just what. He wanted her to beg him not to go or to ask to go with him. To tell him that she couldn't live without him. The silence stretched.

"You're not going to leave him, are you?" he said softly, the words like knives in his gut.

She shook he head slowly and her eyes finally lifted to meet his. "I can't. He's a good man. A kind man. And he loves me."

"I love you, dammit!"

"I know. But you don't need me." Her mouth twisted in a rueful smile. "You'll do fine without me, just the way you have these past few years. One of these days, you may even fall in love again. I hope you will." Her voice caught, as if the words hurt. "But Eldin won't," she continued more strongly. "I love you, Jack. But I love him, too. And he's my husband."

Jack wanted to argue with her. He wanted to tell her how wrong she was. He wanted to take her in his arms and kiss her until she admitted she couldn't go on without him. But he saw the look in her eyes and knew that she was hurting every bit as much as he was.

"Well, I guess that's it, then," he said, looking away from her.

"Yes."

The pain in her voice was almost his undoing. Every instinct screamed at him to take her with him, by force if necessary. But he knew he'd only destroy what was left of their love. She'd go with him if he insisted. But she'd hate him in the end.

"Take care of yourself," he muttered. His shoulder brushed against hers as he walked past her and he hesitated for a moment, not sure he had the strength to walk out. His head turned and he saw the plea in her eyes, begging him to be strong because she had no more strength to give.

Without another word, he walked out onto the porch, closing the neat white door quietly behind him, closing in the smells of lavender and furniture polish. He stood there for a moment and then slowly walked down the porch steps and out into the rain.

"Are you sure you're all right?" Ty asked for at least the twentieth time.

"I'm fine," Meg assured him, just as she had ever other time. Her jaw ached where her stepfather had slapped her. And she knew there'd be other bruises, but none of them mattered. Nothing mattered except that the most incredible miracle had come out of the day's tragedy. Ty loved her.

"Tell me again," she asked, snuggling beneath his arm.

"I love you," he obliged.

"I love you, too." The words had been locked inside her heart for so long. It felt wonderful to be able to say them out loud.

Meg sighed and looked out at the garden. The rain had stopped and she'd already gone out to check on her tomato seedlings, patted the bare earth around them. It might have been silly, but she'd felt better being out among the growing things, as if the new life around her could block out the terror she'd experienced.

"I don't know why it took me so long to figure it out," Ty said, rubbing his cheek against the top of her head.

"I've heard that men can be a little slow-witted about those things," she said, amazed that she felt secure enough to tease him.

"Well, I certainly was." Ty turned her in his arms so that she stood facing him. The look he gave her was so full of love that Meg felt tears burn in her eyes. "It was just so much a part of me that I didn't even realize what it was. *You* are so much a part of me. I don't know what I'd do if something happened to you."

"Nothing's going to happen," she said, smiling through her tears.

"I'm going to make sure it doesn't," he said fiercely, wrapping his arms around her and catching her close.

Meg held on to him, feeling as if she'd just been given her heart's desire, which she had. All these months she'd dreamed of hearing him say he loved her. For a moment it didn't seem possible that she could be so happy, that so many of her dreams had come true.

"Look." Ty's voice was hushed and Meg turned in his arms to look in the direction he'd pointed. There, arching over the far end of the field of young corn, was a perfect rainbow, sparkling like a band of jewels in the late-afternoon sunshine.

"Do you suppose there's a pot of gold at the end of it?" Ty asked softly.

"Could be." But it didn't really matter. She had everything she could ever want right there.